Portals of Albion

~The Nameless Chronicles~

Book 1

Joshua Kern

Contents

Other Books by Joshua Kern

Refton & Thomas

Forgotten Spies

Forgotten Child

The Game of Gods

Arc 1 – Human

The Beginning

The Death of Champions

Arc 2 – Demi-God

Prologue

A portal gleamed in the middle of a large room, the surface undulating gently.

Zack glared at the man holding his little sister tightly by the neck, her small sock-clad feet barely scraping the ground. His own small hands were trembling in a mix of fury and fear. Anger like he had never felt before warred helplessly against the fear he felt at doing as they requested. Fear for his sister and himself.

There was no guarantee he would come back if he went through the portal, and then who would protect her? Even more worrying, though, was the thought of whether or not they would even do as they said they would? They had already experimented on her as well, even though they had said they wouldn't. It was the entire reason he hadn't fought them as they ran their experiments on him. He hadn't known. Then he found the scars on her neck.

Zack was all she had left in the world. Their parents had died years before when she was little more than a baby. Her safety was his responsibility. It was a heavy weight for a ten-year-old's shoulders to bear. Still, she was only barely seven, and he would do anything for her.

Even if it meant believing them for now.

The experiments that were supposed to only be run on him had found their way to her whenever he could no longer handle the pain. He could still see the bruises from the straps they had used to hold her against the chair, and the tiny track of needle marks at the base of her skull.

They were the same marks he had, though his were far more numerous.

The hand holding her slim, pale neck tightened enough for the skin to turn red and her feet to come completely off the floor. Zack knew in that moment he would go through the portal, and he would come back, even if he had to do it all alone.

His eyes burned with shame and the prick of hot tears as he forced himself to look away and step closer to the portal. There wasn't supposed to be one here wherever here was. The locations of all the portals in the world were supposed to have been recorded since they appeared over a hundred years ago. No new ones had been reported since, and none had disappeared.

It made no sense that one wouldn't be under the control of the government or larger corporations. They were intensely valuable commodities. Even as a child, he understood that. Not that the knowledge was doing them any good at the moment.

"Are you ready?" One of the scientists standing off to the side asked.

Equipment lined the walls, each piece connected to a different sensor they had strapped to his body.

"This isn't going to work anyway, so we might as well hurry!" Zack snapped at them irritably, desperately wanting to scratch at the fresh line of stitches lining the back of his neck. The portal stood silently at his back as he turned one last time to look at his little sister.

Instead, he was just in time to catch her, as she was thrown at him like a rag-doll. Her ever present teddy-bear Zelda gripped tight in one tiny little hand. Their parents had named the bear after a long-eared princess in a story. The impact pushed them both through the portal and through to the other side.

Zack held his sister tight as the portal fought against their entrance. They were both too young, not to mention that neither had even awakened their status pages or the ability to go through the portal yet. That only happened when someone was halfway through maturity, around fifteen years old for most people.

The experiments the scientists had been doing on them were all designed to overcome that limitation. Despite the pain they were both feeling, it was clear that whatever had been done to them had worked as they fell to the ground on the other side. Now they only had to survive for twelve hours, and they would be automatically ejected back into their world.

Leaving before then was not an option. This side was dangerous. But the other was hell.

Chapter 1

The shining spires of the Albion Travelers Academy rose high into the sky. It was majestic with pure white fluffy clouds ringing the marble structures. Rather, it would have been majestic or at least awe-inspiring in person. Unfortunately, Zack was looking at nothing more than a mere glossy pamphlet picture.

Zack's younger sister, Zariah, leaned over his knee and poked at the shiny page. "Is that where we're going?" One of her favorite stuffed animals was clutched tightly in her hands, looking out-of-place given her current age of twelve.

"No, we won't be!" He threw the pamphlet roughly across the tattered and worn coffee table to the man sitting across from them and stood. "The invitation was apparently only for me. They made no mention of you, despite knowing our circumstances. I will not be attending any school that ignores you or tries to separate us." His voice held a hint of steel that had the older man pushing back into the frayed cushions of the couch.

With an embarrassed shake of his head, the plump man jumped up and pointed his finger at them, sputtering. "You should be grateful for this opportunity. Who has ever heard of an orphan getting a full-ride scholarship to the academy in the first place?" He ended with a snarl, his face turning red.

Zack held his sister close as she tugged at his shirt. "Well, apparently, the people in charge saw something they liked. Now get out." It didn't matter to him if they knew his potential, not if it meant leaving his only family behind.

A moment later, the old front door slammed shut. The strips of metal reinforcing it, rattling in annoyance as the numerous locks jiggled against them.

"Are you sure that was alright?" Zariah, or Zara as she preferred to be called, asked him softly. She was holding her stuffed bear tight and hiding her face behind its large, fluffy head. Given her usual avoidance of people they didn't know, he was surprised that she had even dared to enter the room, let alone stay the entire time.

"Would you rather I had accepted and left you behind?" He asked with a shrug.

"Nooo," She drew out the word sadly. "Not that. I mean kicking him out. Won't that come back to bite us in some way?"

"I don't see how it would. This is protected government housing, so they can't kick us out. The most they can do to us is make our regular school lives harder, but let's be honest here. You don't even go to class and I'm usually working side jobs so we can afford to eat, so I almost never go." He locked the door and took an objective step back to look at their apartment. It was a rundown mess. The ceiling sagged in the corner by the couch from water damage and the paint was peeling on all the walls. Despite that, it was clean, it was cozy, and it was their home.

It was where they had been dumped after being rescued by the military and being shuffled through the system. They had promised to stay in touch and to provide help for the young, emotionally scarred, and experimented upon orphans. That had been a lie. None of those people had so much as reached out to them since.

That was fine with Zack, it just meant he didn't owe them anything. Especially now that he had reawakened the ability to go through the portals, naturally this time.

"Status," He muttered aloud, the familiar screen appearing before his eyes.

Only those who could go through the portals could see them. His original had disappeared when they sealed his traveler abilities after being rescued. Now it was back, and he wasn't going to let anyone take it from him again. It guaranteed any who had it a comfortable life and enough money that they would never have to work multiple dead-end jobs to feed their family. They never had to see the ribs of their younger sisters poking out painfully from threadbare clothes.

Zackary ??		Level: 0	Exp to next Level: 0/1
Class: ???		Race: Dimensional Child	
Titles: Child of the Portals			
Strength: ?? | ??		Intelligence: ?? | ??	
Dexterity: ?? | ??		Magic: ?? | ??	
Constitution: ?? | ??		Agility: ?? | ??	
Abilities: Life Burner Lv. 4		SP: ??	

Zack held back the grin he got every time he opened his status. Most of the information was a bunch of question marks and would remain that way until he entered a portal for the first time.

What was important was that four things remained the same from before. He still had no last name. Something he shared with his sister, along with their peculiar Race, and Title. Two things he made sure no one besides them ever discovered. The other was the ability listed.

Before, it had allowed him to burn his life force and turn it into magic at a one-to-one exchange rate when the ability was level one. For every one part of health he burned, it turned into one parts magic. The ability had only grown stronger with use as it leveled. It was the one ability that had allowed them to survive on the other side of the portals. He had become a magic user that concentrated on Constitution instead of Intelligence, which directly increased the size of his magic pool.

He got access to a greater-sized magic pool by increasing his constitution and burning his health than he did the normal way. Especially with the ability already at level four, it would be a struggle to run out of mana with low-level spells. At least that was the case with normal magic classes. The one he'd had in the past hadn't been quite so normal.

With his current status attributes not visible until he went through the portal again, it was impossible to say for certain. Besides, it wasn't like they did anything for him normally, magic could only be used on the other side of the portals. Then there was the other thing.

Every person who could cross through the portals had two sets of attributes linked to them. One for when they went through a portal, and the other for normal, everyday life. You could be a veritable god of destruction over there, but the second you came back through, you were nothing more than a slightly strong human. If you increased your fighting or portal-based attributes by one, then it increased your normal attributes by point one.

You could become extremely healthy, or a superstar athlete that way, but little more.

He had learned his lesson from before. You couldn't depend on anyone but yourself and your family. Those people from the military had lied and told him they would be in touch; he certainly couldn't depend on them. Out of sight, out of mind, was a popular saying for a reason.

After he and his sister had been cleared to live on their own, they were out of sight and then forgotten. It was a lesson he was not going to forget.

Zack glanced down as his sister tugged on his arm and pointed to the clock hanging on the wall.

With a muttered curse, he ran to his room to change. He was minutes away from being late for work, and it would take him at least ten to get there. Thick pants made for working outdoors were tugged on alongside a thin t-shirt and reflective jacket. The construction crew building the new hospital nearby had taken him on for certain labor-intensive jobs.

He didn't mind; it was all he was good for, anyway. He had no training, and they couldn't afford for him to take the time off work to go to school full time. Some things were simply more important than getting a decent education, like making sure his sister never went hungry again.

Zara was clutching her bear tight when he came back a minute later.

"Lock the door and don't let anyone inside." He reminded her gently, while tying his work boots. Not that she needed the reminder. She was terrified of leaving the apartment and would only open the door for him. The researchers had almost broken her mentally years before, and she was still recovering.

That was another thing he was never going to allow to happen again, and one of the many reasons they needed to keep their status pages secret.

He gave her a quick hug and then was out the door, smiling, when he heard the deadbolt sliding home behind him. It was a warm day, near the end of a mild summer. He had been glad for the cool weather, as it kept him from overheating while working, and also kept the apartment livable. Magitech engineered cooling boxes were getting cheaper every year, but that didn't mean they were affordable.

It was only when he reached the work site, panting and out of breath, that he began to get some tingles at the back of his mind. They weren't anything special, just a long-forgotten part of his mind telling him that something wasn't right. If there was anything that set his mental tingles apart from everyone else's, it was that he knew to listen to them.

They had warned him of approaching trouble more than a few times in the past.

Zack slowed and looked around, noticing that none of the other workers would meet his eyes. It was a distinct departure from their normal boisterous interactions and over-the-top greetings. The subdued atmosphere felt out of place, and an apprehensive weight settled into place in his stomach.

He had told his sister that they had nothing to fear from the man. Now his gut was telling him those words had been a lie.

A shiny black Vortex carriage sat silently beside the temporary building set up to house those in charge of the construction crews. It was too nice a vehicle to belong to anyone actively working on the job site. Even the owner drove an older model Hilden carriage with a flatbed on the back.

Pausing outside the closed door of the office, he gulped in a fresh breath of air and sighed before opening it. Jane was sitting behind her desk, a severe frown spread across her kind, grandmotherly features.

"You don't want to be here right now," She told him in a strained whisper, slipping a hastily scrawled note towards him and then pointing back to the door. "Hurry and go," She mouthed silently.

The voices in the closed office to the side of her grew louder as he turned and fled, clutching the paper tightly. Hot tears ran down his cheeks as he fled, ignoring the people who called out to him.

Zack let his feet carry him away from the construction, and more importantly, away from the apartment. He didn't want to see the look in his little sister's eyes as he was forced to tell her she had not only been right, but that he had also let her down. He never wanted to see that.

His boots felt unusually heavy as they carried him towards the edge of the city. Deeper into the slums that their government-subsidized apartment building bordered. Without the promise of respectable work to support his sister and himself. He was going to have to find other ways to provide for them.

It was doubtful that any of the other legitimate companies in the area would hire him after that day. Word of this nature had a way of spreading that defied the speed of logic.

He stopped just before reaching the invisible line that separated the two zones and sighed. Zara had made him promise to never go back to working over there. The kind of work he could get over there was always morally questionable, straddling a grey line that he had become numb to. It was also the only reason they had been able to afford food or school supplies. Those jobs were the reason they were still alive, but he had promised her.

Turning around, he walked back the way he had come. The soles of his boots scraped across the pavement as his feet dragged with each unwilling step. He needed to talk with his sister before doing anything else. They were in this together, and he wouldn't cut her out of the decision, no matter what it was.

Zack stopped outside of their apartment building with a final resigned grimace. His booted foot kicked at a stray rock as he entered the stairwell, sending it skittering out into a distant wall. The climb to their floor hadn't felt that long since the early days in their apartment. The days when he was struggling to find enough work to make sure they were fed.

It was a painful reminder that he had screwed up.

He hadn't believed they could be touched, and yet that man had found the one area that would hurt them the most. It was a grave miscalculation on Zack's part, and not one he could hide from his sister. Whatever their next step was, would need to be discussed between the two of them.

Who knew that the school, or that man at least, possessed enough influence to waste on a pair of orphans that nearly everyone had forgotten about?

His arm felt like lead as he raised it to knock on the door. Zara would not be expecting him to return after being away for a mere hour or so. His knuckles rapped out a sequence on the door and he waited for her to return the knock. It was part of the system they had established during their early days in the neighborhood. It had kept her safe more than a few times, and the heavy reinforced door and entryway made sure no one could get in other ways.

The door opened a minute later, after they had finished the process, and Zara looked up at him with sad eyes. "What happened?" She asked, already having guessed.

"You were right. Kicking that pompous windbag out was not the best move I could have made." Zack poked at the worn bear in her arms, gently pushing her back into the apartment. The various locks clicked shut automatically as the door closed behind them. She had left them in a half-unlocked state, instead of fully unlocked.

"Your job?" She asked, keeping one arm on the teddy bear and wrapping the other around him.

He nodded dejectedly. "Someone was already there when I arrived. Jane warned me away as soon as she saw me." Zack had mentioned the nice old secretary to his sister in the past.

"What are we going to do?"

"That's why I came back, so we could figure that out together. I could have easily gone back to my old work, but you made me promise not to do that anymore." He collapsed onto the couch. "So, here I am."

"Is it something that we really need to worry about? We have a little money set aside in case something like this happened." She clutched her bear tight. "Besides, I'm sure we'll hear from other Traveler Academies soon enough."

***

Zack lay in bed that night, his mind reliving the last time he had seen the people from the military and the promises they had made. It had been just outside of a drab intake facility, one meant for orphans rescued by the military.

The commander of the unit had taken an interest in him and his sister. Partly because he had already gone through a portal, and partly because of what they had gone through. They didn't know that Zara had gone through the portal as well. With the death of the researchers, no one but the two of them knew that. It was a secret they meant to keep. The other part was just plain sympathy for the emotional, mental, and physical scars the duo now bore.

That commander had been the one who promised him they would keep in touch, that they would be there to help as needed. He had lied, not that Zack had ever believed in him, anyway. He only had one priority, and that was making sure the intake facility didn't separate Zara and him. Something that they luckily did not even think to try after seeing how much the young girl depended on him.

Turning over, he dismissed those melancholy thoughts and focused more on the present.

Days ago, he had scored high on the psych and portal compatibility assessment at the local testing facility. After going in to report about being able to see his status sheet, he was forced into the test. There had been two outcomes he had hoped to happen from that visit. One was that they might find a decent place for him to work, and they could move into a better apartment. The other option, and the one he believed was more likely, was they would report his scores to the interested academies.

He knew his assessment would be high, possibly even off the charts. It made sense that multiple academies would want him. Not everyone who could see their status was mentally able to deal with what they would need to do after going through a portal. There were some people who were uncomfortable or just unable to cope with what happened on the other side. That was where the psych portion of the test came in.

After that was their compatibility with the portals themselves. It was a test that Zack had never learned the meaning of, only that it had shocked the researchers when he was younger.

It was an expanding majority that were beginning to view the tests as essential information. They held an especially large amount of weight with the academies and the corporations.

Survival was enough for now; he didn't mind taking it slow. Someday, he would have the money and power to go after the people behind that research institute. Maybe then he would also learn why they had been shuffled through the system and forgotten. He could only assume that their situation hadn't been any more abnormal than the other kids they had seen at the facility.

It was an assumption that felt wrong, no matter how many times he came back to it. None of those other kids had been forced through a portal or had their status page sealed away and their levels stripped. He wasn't even sure how they had managed that, or how they had known to seal Zara's as well. No one knew she had gone through the portal but them. It didn't matter because no one else there had experienced those things.

He and Zara were unique, but they had still been forgotten.

At last, he closed his eyes and drifted off to a fitful sleep. Nightmares of their time in captivity came, intruding and unbidden. The same as they did every time he entered the realm of dreams.

Until when late at night Zara crawled into bed next to him. She had her own nightmares to deal with, and most nights her oldest teddy bear Zelda was up to the task of watching over her. Other nights, only the presence of the one person who had protected her back then was enough.

Chapter 2

An incessant knocking from their front door woke them early the next morning.

Zack was pressed against the wall beside the bed, a teddy bear in-between him and his curled-up sister. It was the same position as always. She wanted that closeness, but hated it when anyone touched her while she was sleeping.

Grumbling softly to himself, he extricated himself from the bed and hurriedly pulled on a fresh shirt. The knocking at the front door continued.

"Who is it?" Zara asked incoherently, sitting up with drooping eyes as he left the room.

"Go back to sleep. I'll take care of this." He closed the bedroom door and approached the entrance to the apartment. The small looking glass set at eye level revealed a group of people in business suits arguing with each other. Each would take turns to rap their knuckles on the hard metal surface while maintaining the heated exchange of words.

Flipping the myriad of locks to the unlocked, resting position, he swung open the door and glared at the men.

"What do you all want? Do you have any idea how early it is?" He growled at them.

Zack had no idea what time it was, but he knew it was early enough that they had woken him before his alarm had gone off. Then he remembered that he had turned off the alarm the night before, since he no longer had to wake up for work.

The man closest to the door shook the sleeve on his arm, revealing a high-end crystal pocket watch. A tiny sliver of processed magi-crystal was enough to keep the device running for decades, all while keeping perfect time. It was an extravagant display of wealth that had the other men frowning and tugging at their own sleeves to keep their cheaper versions hidden.

"It is half-past nine in the morning, or a couple hours into the normal workday," The man said, dropping his wrist and taking the opportunity to hand over his business card.

"If it is a couple of hours into the workday, then why are you banging on my door?" Zack restrained the urge to snarl. "If this had been any other day of the week, then I already would have been gone!" He wasn't about to let the matter go just because he was the one who had slept in late. It was the first time he had been able to do that in forever and they had ruined it. A quick glance at the card revealed what he had already suspected. These were people from the other traveler academies that had been sent his test results.

They blinked in unison and shared a look. It clearly hadn't occurred to them that he would be working. Why would it? The vast majority of the kids they recruited weren't struggling orphans.

"But you're not?" One of them at the back protested.

He scowled and stepped back, preparing to shut the door in their faces.

"WAIT!" They each shouted, hands reaching out to block the closing of the door.

He glared at them and decided to lay out the single condition he would not budge on. "I have a younger sister who I take care of, and who needs to go with me. If your schools or academy's are unable to accommodate that, then please leave. I'm going to get changed and then come back. Any of you that are still here at that point had better be able to take us both."

Zara had managed to crawl out of bed by that point and was waiting for him when he walked into the kitchen. "I told you more of them were going to show up."

He grunted at her and went into his room to get dressed. A minute later, he came back out, this time fully dressed. "I'll make breakfast for us once I talk with any of the academy reps that are left."

She shook her head. "I can do it. There are only a couple of options left in the cupboard, in any case."

Zack nodded and focused on the small looking glass in the front door once more. All the men from earlier had left, leaving the hallway outside empty. He rested his head against the metal door and began flipping the locks closed. A small part of him had been hoping at least one of them would have stayed.

It was a long shot, and they had always known that. Despite what the compatibility test would have you believe, as far as he knew, after a certain point on the scale, having a better score just didn't matter too much. So, while the score had been good enough to get him a full-ride scholarship to the academies. It wasn't enough to let him dictate demands.

That was life for them, and he had more or less expected it to be the case. Constant disappointment of all adults with power, and most people in general, was something both the siblings had plenty of experience in.

Zara was reconstituting the last of their bland, flavorless oatmeal when he went back to the kitchen. The cupboards were open, highlighting their bare status. She'd had to hunt for enough oatmeal to make it worth eating for them both. They would need to go shopping for more food later that day.

"They didn't stick around?" She asked softly. Her free hand moved unconsciously to where her one of her teddy bears, Zelda or George, would have normally been.

"Nope. Do you want to go out shopping with me after breakfast?" She seldom went with him, but he still made it a habit to ask, just in case. Occasionally, he made her go with him, just so she didn't go too long without leaving the apartment.

It was rare for her to leave of her on her own. School had been the sole exception for a while, and then some of the kids had begun to make fun of and bully her. She was poor and always had a teddy bear for comfort and emotional support in her arms. The other kids hadn't liked that, or more accurately, they had simply decided that she was the easiest target at the school. None of their families could be considered well-off, but few of them were struggling as much as Zack and Zara.

"Can I bring George?" She asked softly. George was the teddy bear that left the house most often with her lately.

"Sure." He had never had an issue with the ways she coped with what had been done to them. He was simply glad that she continued to try, even when people made fun of her. Besides, he understood better than anyone that there was more to it than simply coping. "Where is the list of everything we need?"

"I'll get it." She scampered away from the table, her dirty bowl empty and forgotten.

Zack smiled in relief and grabbed her bowl along with his, sticking them in the sink for later washing. His little sister came back a minute later, fully dressed for leaving the house, with George already clutched tightly in her arms. His fur was worn in places, and the underlying cloth had begun to fray.

"I'm ready," She declared.

The unfortunate thing about them both leaving the apartment was that they were limited to only using the locks that could be accessed from both sides of the door. Not that they truly had anything to steal. Those extra locks were there to keep Zara safe when he wasn't there. Locking the door from the corridor outside their apartment took a matter of moments, and then they were on their way.

A man in a cheap suit approached them as they walked out the front door of the building. "Are you Zack and Zara?" His words were clipped and precise. There was something slightly familiar about the man that they couldn't place.

Zara hid behind her brother as he nodded.

"Finally," They heard him mutter softly to himself. "We've been looking for you for the last couple of years. There was a mistake made during your processing at the facility after your rescue."

Zack blinked and leaned closer to the man, suddenly understanding why he looked familiar. "You were there! You were part of the group that rescued us that day."

Zara tilted her head out from behind him and looked closer at him.

"I was. Back then, the Major or rather at the time Captain, our company's leader, told you we'd look out for you and we failed at that. It was only when the results of your test came out that we managed to find you again. The two of you were never supposed to be thrust into the system and forgotten. Though, honestly, it may have been for the best."He moved them to the side, away from the entrance to the building. "If that processing mistake hadn't occurred back then, it's possible you might have both undergone more experiments, except by the government this time. I remember the higher-ups were curious about how they had managed to force your awakening, Zack. There is no telling what they might have done to learn more about how that was done."

It was a possibility that the siblings had considered in the past. Without knowing that their entrance into the system meant for orphans was a mistake of epic proportions. They had simply assumed the government didn't care. Now they learned otherwise. Maybe they had gotten lucky that day.

"What are you doing here now?" Zara asked, growing slightly bolder now that they knew who he was.

"I came to offer our help with whatever you might need, to do what we had promised we would back then."

"What did you have in mind?" Zack himself was slightly less weary of the man once he found out who he was.

Before he could reply, a shiny black Vortex Carriage, stopped beside them. It was the same one Zack had seen the day before at the construction site. Sure enough, the rear door opened a moment later and the smug face of the recruiter for Albion Travelers Academy stepped out to join them.

Zara scuttled firmly behind Zack once more, using his back as a barrier from the plump man.

The recruiter glanced disdainfully at the cheap suit the other man was wearing and smirked at the kids. "I heard you had trouble at work yesterday after you threw me out."

Zack raised his brow and looked pointedly at the vehicle. "You know, I saw a carriage that looks remarkably like yours sitting outside the office yesterday."

The man they had been talking to coughed and pointedly addressed the recruiter. "I'm sorry, I was here first. What school did you say you were representing?"

The recruiter's lip curled in a sneer. "I didn't, but I can guarantee it is better than whatever backwoods institute you represent!"

"He's from the Albion Travelers Academy. They offered me a full ride scholarship. I refused when they wouldn't accept Zara as well." Zack informed the military man after seeing they had a mutual disdain for the recruiter.

"Did they now?" It was his turn to smirk. "Well, I think I just found my answer." He nodded to Zack and Zara with a wink. "I'll be in touch within the next day or two. Better start packing your bags. The semester begins soon."

He spun on his heel and walked away, leaving them alone with the confused school representative. The pudgy man scowled, upset that the wind had been taken from his sails. "I've made sure no business, legitimate or otherwise, in this city will hire you, boy. You had better pray that whatever school he was from accepts you both!" With those parting words, he climbed back into the carriage and left.

"Do you think that man from the military will be able to help us?" Zara asked quietly, still clinging to her brother's back.

"I'm not sure, but he certainly seemed to think they could." He wasn't ready to trust the man just yet. The excuse that they had been lost in the cracks of the crappy government system seemed a little thin to him. The government knew where they were to pay for their housing. So, there was some record related to them somewhere. Right?

"Should we keep going?"

Zack glanced down at his sister, momentarily lost in thought. "Yeah, we still need to get some food for later either way." It hurt him to see her like this. She had been such a bright child before they were taken. Her mind had been incredible. Now she was so scared of everything that it had dulled. They both were.

Together, hand in hand, they headed towards the small, nearby shopping area. The food there was always close to its official expiration date, but was also the cheapest they could find as a result. The variety of food changed from day to day, and someone almost never knew what they would find there.

Meat was uncommon and went quickly when it did appear. Vegetables and canned goods, however, were always there in some fashion. It was the dried and dehydrated items that the siblings went for most often. The bland taste and odd consistency meant fewer people bought them, which drove the price down even more.

A lower price meant they would have more to eat for less. They could put up with the bland food if it meant filling their bellies. Besides, things had been better recently. Zack's job with the construction company had been stable work with a small but steady income. That had allowed them to splurge a little on meat and vegetables.

Now it looked like they were back to the cheapest possible foods they could find.

Zara crowded closer to her brother as they pressed through the crowds surrounding each of the item packed stalls. She would tremble and cling tightly to him anytime someone so much as accidentally brushed against her.

They were both known by the owners of the various stalls, Zara less so, since she rarely left the house. The sight of her always clutching the teddy bear George, however, was a sight that few could readily forget. There was something about the image of a scared girl following her older brother shopping that stirred up their protective instincts and cemented her in their minds.

"How much were you able to save?" Zack asked her softly, as they stopped in front of a stall containing some semi-rotten fruit. He had a little bit leftover in his wallet from the last time he had gone shopping for food, and that was it.

She passed George to him and indicated he should open the small zipper on the worn bear's back. It was an addition he had made to the plushie years before, during their time as test subjects.

He pulled down the small, concealed zipper and reached inside the hidden space. A roll of money hit the tips of his fingers and he pulled it out to count, shoving it back in before others could see the amount. His little sister had managed to save a fair bit of money. If they were careful in how they spent it, the amount would last them several weeks. It would be for cheap and possibly spoiled food, but it would be edible.

Their bodies were long past the point of getting sick over such trifles like spoiled meat and vegetables. They needed the protein and vitamins more.

Passing the bear back to Zara, he reached into his pocket for his wallet. He wanted to count the money he had left from before. Instead of feeling the leather money holder, he found the note the secretary had given him the day before.

He had forgotten about it in his rush to leave the construction site behind. Neat handwriting filled the note with everything the kind older woman had heard through the thin walls of the office.

With a sigh, he crumpled it up and tossed it into a nearby trashcan. What the recruiter had told him that morning was true. He really had been blacklisted. It would be next to impossible for him to get any respectable work.

He could only hope that what the man from the military had said was true, and that he would get them into a school.

Switching pockets, he found his wallet and quickly counted the money. It was enough to buy some food for lunch, dinner, and breakfast the next morning, if they were careful.

Zara suddenly stiffened, her hand gripping his shirt tight. "We're about to have company!" She whispered in annoyance.

He saw why a moment later. Walking towards them, ignoring the crowd of people, was a messenger from one of the local gangs. It wasn't someone he knew personally, but the patches lining the arm of his jacket identified the group he was with. It was a group Zack had worked with in the past. Back in the beginning, when they were first released from the group home after that supposed processing error.

"The boss heard you might be looking for work again," The man just out of his teen years said without preamble, stopping in front of them.

Zack felt his sister tremble slightly at the close proximity of the unfamiliar person. "Jace knows better than to send someone to approach me like this while I am with my sister!" He growled, his fists clenched tightly at his side.

"Jace isn't leading the group anymore," The messenger shrugged, "He was... displaced, by Cooper a couple of months ago."

Zack spit to the side at the revelation, splattering the dirty road. He had never liked Cooper, and the man knew that. This reeked of some kind of power-play against him, one that was designed to keep him off-balance or worse. "Tell Cooper then that this is not the way to approach me, and I don't know who has been feeding him information, but they're wrong.

I'm not looking for work. The two of us are leaving to go to one of the traveler's academies within the next few days."

He carefully looked the brother and sister duo over before shrugging again. "Doesn't matter to me. I was just told to deliver the message and now I have. I'll tell Cooper what you said." His voice dropped to a whisper as he leaned in close. "I'd make sure my doors were locked tight if I were you. Cooper has been trying to expand the operation. After I tell him where you are headed... Well, I can guarantee he isn't going to just let you go without trying something."

Zack sucked in a breath and quickly looked at the people around them. "Is he stupid? All of the portals are controlled by the government or large corporations!" The one the research institute had been in possession of had been an oddity in that regard. "Without a portal of his own, it won't matter how many travelers he has under his control."

"I wouldn't know anything about that. In any case, I've said more than I should." He nodded to them and left as abruptly as he had come.

"What are we going to do?" Zara asked from her spot glued to his back.

"We're going to finish shopping, and then we are going to make sure all the locks back home are as secure and tight as we can make them."

Chapter 3

Z ack carried the small bag of nearly rotten and expired food, along with some cheap packets of oatmeal they had managed to find. The duo hurried back to their apartment, constantly looking over their shoulders. The longer they had remained in the shopping area, the more gang members they had seen hanging around the fringes. Ducking through the throng of crowded people, they quickly made their way unseen back to the main road.

Neither wanted to stick around and see what would happen if they were caught.

Their disappearance was quickly noticed, and yells of "Find them!" echoed through the shopping area as they ran. The back alleys kept them safe long enough to reach the apartment building, and then up the stairs to their home. Down below, they could see the angry, flushed faces of the people that had been chasing them.

"Are the locks going to be enough to keep them out tonight?" Zara asked, scared, and holding tightly to her brother and the worn bear.

"The door will hold. It's reinforced with extra metal strips. It has to. The locks, on the other hand, might not, if they try long enough and with enough force." Zack frowned and ushered her inside, beginning to flip the myriad of locks closed. "We'll move the couch and anything else heavy in front of the door tonight before going to bed."

The rest of the day was spent in subdued silence, with both of the siblings repeatedly checking the locks on the door. It was a good thing their apartment didn't come with any windows that looked out over the corridor. It was one less thing that they would need to worry about securing that night.

Dinner that evening consisted of oatmeal and washed overripe berries. The water took care of the parts too far gone to eat. The peppers would keep until morning and would be used to spice and flavor the can of meat they had gotten with the rest of his money. That would be their breakfast. If the soldier didn't come back, then they would simply have to risk going shopping again.

They assumed that the issue with the gang would be resolved that night. If it wasn't, then that would severely restrict their options in the future.

After dinner, Zara wordlessly carried her two stuffed animals along with some papers into his room, and then took her bath.

Meanwhile, he began moving the old heavy couch into position. Jamming it in-between the door and the lip of the floor. Just inside the front door was a small, tiled area for them to leave their shoes before continuing farther inside the apartment. The siblings rarely bothered with it, but the small step up from the tiles to the fake paneling of the hallway was useful in this instance.

Zara was dressed in a snug onesie when she came out of the bath a while later. The outfit had rabbit ears on top of a hood he had sewn to it for her years before. As adorable as it was on her, it was an outfit he hated seeing.

She only wore it when things were really bad, and clutching her bears tight wasn't enough.

Zack sighed and shut off all the lights in the apartment. Moments later, he followed her into his room, where she was busy drying her hair. A hand-drawn picture of a bear had been placed in each corner of the room, with two more on each side of the doorway. He didn't know when she had drawn them, but they were good.

Her two actual bears, Zelda and George, were splayed across the bed already, waiting for them.

"You know that doesn't work here." Zack whispered, giving her a warm, tight hug.

Zara nodded and dropped the damp towel into his laundry bag when he let go. "I know, and it wouldn't work with the drawings anyway. But the reminder will help me to feel more secure tonight."

Zack grimaced as he closed the door to his room. Cooper had better pray he never got his hands on him, otherwise he would make him pay. Zara had been forced to pull out all the stops tonight, all because some low-rent thug had put them in their sights. He shut off the light and climbed into bed, fully dressed. If something did go wrong and they managed to get inside the apartment, he wanted to be ready.

It took a while, but Zara drifted off to sleep first. She had curled into a ball around Zelda, with George and her brother at her front and back, respectively. The soft, even breaths of his sister lulled him to sleep a few minutes later.

Muffled swearing and the repeated impacts against the front door of the apartment woke him sometime later. The gangsters had finally begun their efforts to break into the apartment. They would find the heavy door sturdier than they were expecting, no doubt. The modifications he had made to it, along with all the locks he had added when they first moved in, would keep them at bay. The strips of heavy metal meant to reinforce it, and the couch in the entryway wouldn't break easily.

These weren't the first people who had attempted to break into the run-down apartment. They were simply the latest, and possibly the most determined. It wouldn't matter. In the end, they still weren't going to make it inside the apartment.

The couch would ensure they never made it inside.

There was no chance of it magically making its way over the lip of the floor, no matter what they tried. The piece of furniture may have been old and worn, but it was solidly built and wouldn't break. Not with the door in the way, blunting any impact that made it through.

The chances of them sufficiently breaking enough of it to make it inside were slim to none. There wasn't enough room in the hallway outside the apartment to get that kind of leverage and power.

Zack put a hand on Zara's back, making sure she was still asleep, and looked blankly up at the darkness above. He would stay awake, listening, just in case that one-in-a-million chance of them breaking through happened. He wasn't going to play around with either of their lives.

He strained his ears for the next hour, picking up each muffled noise he could before they stopped entirely. As far as the people outside were concerned, they could come back the next night or the one after that with better equipment and force their way inside. Only he and Zara knew there was a possibility they would be gone by then.

A slim one admittedly, but there was a chance the military man would actually do what he said he would.

Either way, they would be packing up everything in the apartment that day. There was no way they could stick around after this. He had been blacklisted, which meant he had no way of making legitimate money. If he went the other way, against his sister's wishes, then it would have been for Jace, someone he somewhat respected. There was no way he would work under Cooper.

All of which pointed to them needing to move on somewhere else. Hopefully, it would be to a school, but either way, they were leaving.

Exhausted, he slipped into a light, troubled sleep sometime after the people outside left.

A knocking on the front door hours later woke him a second time. The room had begun to lighten with the early morning sun as he carefully extricated himself from the bed. Stumbling blearily towards the front door, he stopped abruptly, noticing where the metal had deformed near the top.

"Who is it?" He called out, carefully inspecting the damage before moving onto the couch.

"It is Sergeant Grieves. We met in the parking lot yesterday." He paused and tapped lightly on the door. "Is everything alright in there? The door is looking rather... broken on this side."

"Give me a moment," Zack replied, recognizing the voice. "There is a couch in the way. Let me move it and then I'll open the door."

"Did he just say there is a couch in the way?" Grieves asked someone outside.

"I believe that is what he said," Someone else answered in a less military-stiff tone.

Zack grunted and strained to move the heavy piece of furniture. He hadn't realized just how jammed into place it would get during the night. It did not want to move in the slightest.

Taking a step back, he eyed the spot closest to the floor, where it was jammed tightly against the lip of the floor. Grabbing his boots, he quickly pulled them on and tied them tight. Kicking the couch near the floor repeatedly, he was able to break it free. It was only after that he was able to pull it fully away from the door and out of the entryway.

Clear of the furniture obstructing his view, he was able to see the condition of the door for the first time. The metal was bent and pulling against the frame and the locks. It had held strong throughout the night; however, it had taken some damage doing so.

Metal screeched as he forced open the locks after peeking through the spyhole. Content with the knowledge that it was the same person they had met before, he tugged on the door. It opened about a foot before squealing to a stop on bent hinges.

He poked his head around it and into the corridor beyond. "Can I get a little help here? It's stuck."

A heavy foot slammed into the door. The warped joints screamed and buckled into useless pieces of metal as they were forced past their respective breaking points. With a crash, the door swung open and rebounded off the wall. It came to a stop, tilting uselessly to the side as a single screw held a broken hinge mostly in place.

Grieves nudged the man who had forced the door open to the side and looked at Zack. "Do you want to talk about whatever happened here now or on the way to the school?"

"Let's do it on the way, but you know we haven't packed anything yet. We were going to do that later today," Zack informed them, awkwardly running a hand through his hair.

"That's fine. I brought some of my unit along, just in case." He stepped inside first, followed closely by three fit men and a lean, wiry woman who looked like she could take them all on at the same time and win. "Pack up everything but the furniture! The Major expects us at the academy this evening. I want to be headed back there within two hours."

Zack blinked, processing what the man had just said. "The school is fine with Zara coming with me?"

Grieves nodded and pushed him to the side as one of his men ran back out the door to fetch some boxes.

Zara poked a sleepy head around the door to his room and looked out at them. "What's going on? Did they get in?"

"No, it's just the man from the military that we met yesterday. They are here to pack up the apartment and take us to the school, so go get dressed." Zack reassured her while looking sideways at the sergeant to make sure what he was saying was correct.

There was a returning nod. "We'll be traveling for several hours; I would suggest that you both get changed into something comfortable. Also, you may wish to pack a bag with anything that you will need in case you are unable to unpack in time tonight." He looked Zack in the eye and spoke in a firm voice. "We will discuss what happened here last night once we are underway."

***

Zara had changed out of her security pajamas for the trip. Predictably, however, Zelda and George had come with them and were sitting on either side of her inside the large mana-driven carriage. It was different from the shiny Vortex carriage that Zack had spotted outside the construction office before. This one was made to carry more than the four or five people that could fit in those machines.

It was smaller than the one they had ridden in when they were first rescued years before. That one had been referred to as a troop transport carriage. The soldier sitting up front beside the woman who was driving it had referred to it as a caravan carriage. In the back were the few boxes of clothes and other items that the brother and sister duo wanted to bring with them to the school.

Grieves waited until they were underway before bringing the matter from earlier up again. "Now, explain to me what happened last night that had you blocking the door in case whatever happened, happened."

Zack was unsure of the best way to answer that question. Did he tell the man everything about how he used to work for the local gang? Or was it better to just mention them meeting the messenger in the marketplace? If he did that, though, it might make them wonder why the gang knew of him in the first place.

He took a breath, and after turning away from the window, decided to go with a modified version of the truth. "It was one of the local gangs that did it. Yesterday, Zara and I were approached by a messenger while we were out shopping. From what he was saying, there had been a recent change in their leadership, and the new leader had heard about my test results.

"He didn't say how, but I gathered it was the recruiter from Albion Travelers Academy doing. As I'm sure you gathered from what he was saying yesterday, he went around, letting everyone know I had been blacklisted. It wouldn't be hard to put the two together."

The sergeant's gaze sharpened, as though he didn't quite believe the young man. He nodded after a few seconds, "And they what, came to forcefully take you away after I'm assuming you refused?"

He nodded. "We saw them tailing us after we left the market with our groceries. When I saw them hanging around the apartment building last night, I figured the odds were good that they would try something." Zack looked back to where Zara was sleeping, pressed against George. "You're sure that whichever school you are taking us to is fine with her being there as well?"

"The Major personally took care of it. I wasn't told if she will be allowed to attend classes, but her living there with you is not a problem. Her food has been taken care of as well, though from what I understand, the two of you will be working part time each night for extra money."

The teen let out a relieved breath and smiled. "I'm fine with working. As long as they don't try to separate us, I'm fine with anything."

The look in the man's eye softened as he continued. "On a different note, you are aware that this is not going to be easy for you, right? The faculty has been mostly taken care of, but the other students will look down on you and your sister for whatever menial reason they can conjure up. The children of nobles will be the worst I imagine, while the normal ones will be content to avoid you and any trouble that would have come from the association."

"I am," Zack answered softly, glancing back at Zara, who was talking with Zelda and George. "They'll learn soon enough not to mess with us. Words are fine. I won't retaliate for those. Actions are a different story; I won't risk us being taken advantage of by refusing to react to their provocations."

The sergeant frowned and then nodded. "If that is what you are determined to do, then make sure that any actions you do take close the issue for good. Just don't go too far overboard."

"I know, I won't do anything that will risk us being separated."

***

The sun was high overhead and beginning to dip towards the horizon when the gates and fence that surrounded the academy came into view. It was only then that the siblings learned which school they would be attending. The group of military personnel seemed to have gotten a kick out of refusing to tell them.

It was Albion Travelers Academy, the same one the recruiter that had caused them so many problems, worked for.

"What about the man from yesterday?" Zara asked from behind them, looking concerned.

"He was already let go," The woman driving them spoke up for the first time the entire trip. "Apparently, you were not the first prospective student he had caused troubles for, though you may be the most serious. None of the others had a local gang trying to come after them."

The gates were pulled open by a guard stationed in a small building to the side, who waved them through without delay.

Zack was growing increasingly confused by everything, and them being waved through was just the icing on the proverbial cake. Albion Travelers Academy was a well-known school with strict entry requirements. It was one of the top training academies in the country, if not the top one. Yet their carriage and all its occupants had just been waved through without even a check of identification. It didn't make sense to him.

There had to be something more going on than they had been told.

He thought about it for a moment and then mentally shrugged. It wasn't a bad thing for them if the military or this mysterious Major and his squad were associated with the school. It might even be useful for when he inevitably got in trouble.

The sergeant had been right in that regard. They were going to be teased and bullied by those who incorrectly thought they were better than Zara and him. It would be a rough beginning for them, without a doubt. His schooling undoubtedly lagged behind what the people here had been taught, so his grades would be abysmal. To those teasing them, it would be further proof that they were better.

It wouldn't be until they were allowed to go through the portals again that he would be able to truly prove them wrong. Until then, they would have to endure and push back as much as they could.

"How closely related to the academy is the military?" Zack asked them as the carriage came to a stop in front of a large dormitory building. The stone exterior gleamed white in the areas not covered by the green and red creeping vines that were prevalent on all the older school buildings.

Grieves snapped his head around to look at him before slowly smiling. "If you had asked me that question yesterday, I would have said not at all. Now, I don't know." He winked and threw open his door. "Welcome to the Albion Travelers Academy, our country's premier training ground for future travelers."

The doors to the dorm building opened and a matronly woman with a severe scowl pasted across her face appeared.

Chapter 4

"**A**re these the two late additions?" The woman asked, her eyes flicking over Zack and then to where Zara was hidden inside the carriage.

"They are indeed. Have the preparations and their room been sorted?" Grieves inquired, walking over to her. Behind him, everyone else began unloading the few boxes stored in the back of the metal machine.

The scowl transformed into a concerned frown as Zara stepped into view, fearfully clutching Zelda and George tight.

"They have. Luckily, no one has moved in yet, otherwise this might have been a problem. The largest dorm on the main floor has been set aside for their use. It contains two bedrooms, a bathroom, and a common area with a small kitchen. It is usually reserved for the highest-ranking noble attending that year. We shall keep that information to ourselves, lest this... situation causes problems in the future."

Zack stayed back as the soldiers he had never gotten the names of hurried past, their arms laden with boxes. Only the sergeant remained behind to talk to them.

"Well, this is as far as we go, for now at least. I'm sure I'll be seeing you again at some point. Try to stay out of trouble, and keep from getting in any duels. Make sure to keep your sister safe. I remember her state when we first rescued you both back then. The progress she has made since is remarkable, but you need to always remember that it is easier to backslide mentally than it is to move forward and grow past a traumatic experience.

"It will be even harder for someone as young as she was, who suffered for as long as the two of you did." He looked them over one last time and nodded as the rest of his group came back empty-handed. The one trip had been all that was needed to transfer the few belongings they possessed.

It was advice that Zack wished someone had given him when they were first rescued and then shuffled off into the broken system for orphans. He had done the best he could with the information he had on hand. It had been barely enough, and it could have been so much more effective with the proper knowledge.

"Wait, what do you mean duels?" He cried out as they climbed into the metal carriage.

"Nobles attend this academy. They consider themselves above getting into mere fights and common brawls. Most will settle their differences through official duels with more on the line than the risk of a bloody lip or broken bone." With those parting words, the doors snapped shut, and they sped away with a gentle whir of the mana-tech engine.

The siblings shared a worried glance and then turned to face the building they would be calling home from now on.

"Are we going to be okay here?" Zara asked, coming up to his side.

"Once I make it through the portal, no one will dare to bother us again. We just have to survive until then. After they realize just how much our abilities are worth, we'll never have to worry about money or people with an inflated sense of self-worth coming after us."

She nodded once and took a single step up the stairs. "Just be careful. We can't fight the corporations. Not yet, anyway. Maybe not for a longtime to come."

Zack gave her a light nudge and together, they entered the building. Immediately, their eyes grew wide at how nice and opulent everything was. As one, they looked down at the gleaming wooden floors, clean carpet runners, and then at the shabby, slightly dirty state of their clothes and footwear.

"I have a feeling that we are going to stick out like sore thumbs here," Zack muttered as they spotted the dorm matron from earlier waiting for them to the side near a hallway.

"My name is Edith Rammore. You may either refer to me as Edith or Matron," She began as they drew close. "Behind me, you will find the door to your dorm. No one but the two of you are allowed inside it. That is to prevent rumors from arising regarding your peculiar treatment. I repeat, do not let any of the other students inside your dorm unless you wish to make your lives more difficult."

She handed them each a key to the door. "Feel free to take some time to freshen up and then come find me when you are done. There is much that I need to show you regarding the academy grounds, as well as getting you registered for classes and other such nonsense." She pointed to a nondescript door to the side of the hallway. "That is where I live, and where I will be when you are ready."

She abruptly opened her door and left them alone.

"I don't think she likes us," Zara said as they walked through the door of their dorm apartment.

"No, I don't think she does either."

They stopped in shock at how nice the furniture was in the main room. At the back was a small kitchen with gleaming appliances. They scattered at the same time to look at the two bedrooms off to the side and the bathroom that was nestled between them.

"This is like a million times nicer than our apartment could have been when it was new!" Zara was pale and rubbing her chin on the top of George's head. "What if we break something?"

It was a good question and not one they had an answer to yet. It was on the growing list of things they needed to discuss with Edith later.

Zack peeked in at the large room that would be his, with a complicated expression. That one-bedroom was larger than his and Zara's old rooms combined. There was so much space that even if he ignored the spots taken up by the wardrobe, dresser, and desk, it was still too large. It all felt like it was too much. What was he supposed to do with all of it?

"Look at the size of this tub!" Zara screeched in awe at what looked like a small swimming pool to her.

"We shouldn't waste too much time in here. Let's get back to Edith and finish doing everything with her before unpacking." Zack dropped the bag he had packed for the short trip on the couch and motioned for her to do the same.

Somewhat hesitantly, she placed Zelda beside the bag and held onto George. "Fine, let's go back and get this over with."

Outside their new home, Zack raised his hand and knocked on the matron's door. What he had hoped would be a confident knock changed into something hesitant and unsure of itself by the time his hand descended awkwardly on the wooden surface. He shrugged mentally and knocked again, his hand steadier the second time.

They waited for a minute, shuffling their feet, and wondering if they should knock again when the door opened.

A slightly less severe frown than before decorated Edith's face as she stared at them. "Are you already ready to continue?"

"We're ready. There is no sense in delaying this. We'll finish unpacking tonight after we have finished everything that the academy needs us to do."

"Very well then. Let's get the two of you registered and semi-fitted for your uniforms, as those will take the longest. I imagine you will want them a little loose, for when you get a little meat on your bones. After those are done or underway, I will give you a tour of the grounds and buildings as well as show you where you will need to go each night for your jobs." She ushered them out of the dorm building.

"It's the building from the picture, the one with the spires!" Zara exclaimed as they walked down the stairs. It was the first time the siblings had gotten to look around the area. They hadn't been near enough to the windows inside the carriage earlier to spot anything besides the ever-present trees.

The building in question had been on the front of the pamphlet they had looked at with the obnoxious recruiter before.

"That is the central building. It has the administrative offices inside, along with the admissions and registration offices on the first floor." Edith explained, leading them towards it along a path that cut through the grove of trees.

"Where is everyone?" Zack asked as they neared the towering structure made almost entirely of marble.

"Not here yet. The new semester doesn't begin for another week and a half. The earliest, most students will begin arriving is still a couple of days away. Only those of us who live on the academy grounds full-time are here currently."

"What about the headmaster? Do we need to meet with him?" Zack stuttered to a stop, craning his neck to look at the sole office near the top of the spire.

"The headmaster has indeed expressed some interest in the two of you, but not the kind I believe you will like. You will not be meeting him today, however. He was forced to fire his brother-in-law due to the two of you and then accept you both regardless of his feelings on the matter. I'm sure you can understand how that has colored his opinion on you." She sighed and turned to face them. "I'm not going to lie to you. Despite your test results being reported as frankly off the charts, your time here will be tough. Few of the teachers will be willing to get on the headmaster's bad side to show you any type of favor."

Zack nodded weakly and began the mental process of revising their plans. If the teachers and those in authority at the academy would be acting against them, then their time here was indeed not going to be pleasant. It would have been hard if they were dealing with just the students. Now it was looking close to impossible.

It was becoming increasingly likely that the mysterious Major would have to step in on their behalf once more. He could only hope that the man had his subordinates watching them closely.

"That is worse than what we were expecting honestly, but I don't see as to how we have any other choice. The only thing we can do is push back when they are being unreasonable. Besides, I have a feeling that the academy will find it hard to expel us for such a weak reason."

The older woman tilted her head in thought and nodded once. "As long as you are aware. Come along. We have other places to visit and things to do." Her disposition was noticeably warmer than in the beginning as they climbed the polished steps.

The process of getting Zack registered for his classes was a short one, as all first years had to take the same classes. Getting them both measured for uniforms, however, took longer. They had come with few clothes and the academy-provided uniform was going to need to take up the slack.

It had already been decided that even though Zara was not an official student, she would still get a supply of uniforms, since she would be working there.

After that, they went to a different section of the building and were given cards with tiny processed magi-crystals embedded in the upper corner. The cards acted as a form of identification and would also allow them to buy things on and off campus. They were even connected to a newly created official bank account in their names. Since they didn't have one before, the school had been forced to create one for them so they could be paid for their part-time jobs.

Edith waited patiently as their measurements were taken in separate rooms and a set of clothes were quickly modified for them. They would start wearing them the next day.

"Where to now?" Zack asked, his arms full of clothes. He was carrying his sister's uniform along with his own.

"Why is there no ivy or other plants crawling up the outside of the building?" Zara wondered before the older woman could say anything.

"It was decided that certain buildings were more imposing without them. In the case of the dormitory, it was believed the plants softened the feeling it gave off, which helped the students relax easier at night." Edith pointed back at the central building and its looming spire. "Not that some of the buildings need the help to be imposing." She shook her head and led them away. "Now, first I am going to show you the grounds, and where your classes will be held. Then I will introduce you to the people you will be reporting to each night for work."

Zara walked a half-step behind her brother as they toured the grounds. There was an arena, several training grounds with workout equipment and padded blades, and, of course, a multitude of buildings with classrooms hidden within. That was discounting the other dorms and the large cafeteria with restaurants nestled in-between them all. Then there were also the gardens, and groves of trees growing fruit that were for more practical purposes.

At last, she led them to a lone single-story brick building sitting off to the side of one of the lesser-used sidewalks.

"This is where you will report to each night. The staff will then decide if you are needed for the night or are free to do other things. I would plan on being busy each night, simply because of what we discussed earlier about the headmaster. That said, you are only allowed to work for two hours a night, no matter what they might say. You can leave after those two hours are up. Plus, look on the bright side. It will mean more spending money coming your way."

They could always use more money. It was impossible to say what would happen in the future and being able to save up for the unexpected would be a nice change of pace.

"What do we do now?" Zack asked her, as they stopped outside their dorm building.

She looked up at the position of the sun before answering. "There is still some time left before dinner will be served. Why don't you finish unpacking and then just relax? I'll knock on your door when it is time."

Edith had continued to warm up to them as the day wore on. By the end, the frowning, scowling woman they had initially met was nothing more than a memory.

Inside their dorm, Zara collapsed onto the comfortable-looking couch, exchanging George for Zelda at the same time. She lay there, nestled between their bags, and looked blankly up at the ceiling. "Are we going to be safe here?" She asked at last.

Zack was sitting on the floor with his head resting against the couch near her. "What do you mean?" He returned. Hers had been a loaded question.

"Wellll…" She drew out the word. "I guess we're probably safe from the gang. No way are those idiots going to follow us here. We have a steady supply of I'm guessing of good and healthy-ish food." She stopped and gulped at the thought of non-rotting food, with flavors besides the cloying taste of mold or cardboard. "The students may bully us, but as you said earlier, we can just fight back without worrying about the major repercussions. I guess what I'm worried about is interacting so closely with the nobles, military, and then there is still the research institute."

"They caught everyone there." He said weakly.

She snorted. "You know as well as I do that there were other facilities, and considering that they supposedly lost us in a system of their own making. I have no faith that they managed to catch everyone involved. Before we were hidden, no one knew where we were. That isn't the case anymore. People can find us now, both the good and the bad ones."

Zack reached behind his head and grabbed her arm, and then her hand. "I'll do whatever I need to keep us safe."

"That's what I'm worried about. Neither the military nor the institute know all our secrets. If word of them ever gets out-" He could feel her curling into a ball on the couch. "I'm not going to become a test subject for anyone ever again, and I won't let them do that to you either!"

The pure venom and hate in her voice should have been shocking to the teen, except he felt the exact same way. That lack of ability to save her, let alone himself, and then to be forced to watch as they were experimented upon. Never again, would he let them go through that. He had no problems understanding her feelings on the matter and matching them with his own.

"What do you think I should do, then? Just roll over and let it get worse. Never standing up for myself or us?" Depending on the situation, he had nothing against turning the other cheek. In a school environment, with a bunch of spoiled rich kids if he did that, it would only make things worse. It would encourage the bullies and convince them that the siblings were an easy target.

"No." The words were muffled as they were spoken into the side of a stuffed animal.

"It doesn't matter in any case. I'm no different from any of them until I go through a portal again. Even then, it is only when I'm over there that they would be able to tell the difference."

"Oh, that's right, for a moment there I forgot." Zara joked. She uncurled and rolled over to speak into his ear, her hot breath tickling the fine hairs within. "That means you are limited to your fists if anyone does track us down or tries to take us."

He shrugged and stood, swiping at the phantom tickle in his ear. "Come on, let's stop worrying about things that likely won't happen. We need to get our stuff put away, and then I don't know about you, but I am going to give that tub a try until dinnertime."

"Not fair, I called dibs on it first!" George soared through the air and hit him in the face as Zara jumped up with Zelda in hand and sped into the bathroom, locking the door shut behind her.

"You betrayed me for a tiny swimming pool?" He yelled at her in mock anger, placing the stuffed plushie back on the couch.

She dared to open the door wide enough to poke her head through and stick out her tongue.

It was moments like this that allowed Zack to honestly believe that they had begun to heal.

Chapter 5

The rest of the teachers were the first to arrive a few days later, with the richer, upper-crust commoner students appearing a day after that. The noble born students, the few that lived on campus, were the last to arrive. Zack and Zara avoided them all as much as possible, only leaving their dorm when it was time to eat or work. They had long since finished exploring the grounds and buildings and knew all the back ways to get around.

During their meals in the cafeteria, they would select a table in the corner, away from everyone else. Both were content to avoid interacting with people they had little in common with. The life they had lived was vastly different from the nobles and other rich students.

Each night, they went to work for two hours and then left, after making sure that their hours had been properly recorded. True to Edith's word, the few teachers they had met up to that point and the rest of the general staff had given them the cold shoulder.

That was fine with them. As long as it was just a cold shoulder, then it meant little to them. It was the inevitable progression that came after that would determine the sibling's response.

The time they had spent alone on the academy grounds had familiarized them with the teacher's housing area as well. Most of the teachers lived on the grounds during the year and then left during the breaks. A few of the more senior professors lived close by and commuted each day.

If they wanted, they could get inside the educators' living area and make their lives uncomfortable. It was not an action they wanted to pursue as that would set them on a slippery slope, but they were prepared just in case.

***

"I heard we have someone who tested off the charts this year!"

Zack slowed his running pace and stuck himself to the side of the building. It was early in the morning, and he had thought he could get in some exercise before the pampered rich kids began waking up. Unfortunately, it appeared that at least some of them got up earlier than he had been expecting. He wasn't interested in mingling with any of them just yet.

"That's nothing. I heard that the school accepted a couple of orphan charity cases."

There was a sniff of disdain as the voices walked closer to the corner where Zack was jogging in place beside the wall. "I heard that as well, but I didn't believe it."

"Just wait until our parents learn of it, the academy will be made a laughingstock. The prestige of attending what was once considered to be the premier traveler's academy in the country will entirely vanish!"

"Oh, don't exaggerate. The academy always lets a few of the less fortunate in each year."

"Yes, but they still come from the upper crest of the commoners, those who were bound to elevate their family's position. My father described it as the academy investing in their potential, in hopes of reaping future benefits."

He had been expecting the news about them to make the rounds at some point. The expectation, though, had been for it to happen at some point during the first semester. Not for it to happen before classes had even begun.

They rounded the corner and almost ran into Zack, who had stopped jogging and was now casually leaning against the wall. His sweat-soaked shirt sticking against his lean chest. The last week of good, healthy food had already added a little meat and muscle to his otherwise painfully thin frame.

They both looked at him in disdain and stepped further away from the area he was occupying. It was only then that they deigned to continue their conversation, acting as though he no longer mattered.

"I see some of those commoners I just mentioned have already arrived. Honestly, they all act as though they can suddenly get in shape after being accepted. Don't they know what our training is going to be like?"

"Of course, they don't. They're commoners!" They both looked back at him with a sneer and continued on their way. The sound of their conversation lingered, as neither bothered to whisper.

Zack paid no mind to their words and continued with the remainder of his run. He was used to hard work and was actually in pretty good shape. Well, good shape for someone who, until recently, had been getting the absolute bare minimum in protein and nutrition.

Edith was waiting for him in the entryway of their dorm building when he returned. She was frowning, and her eyebrows were pulled together in a worried fashion. "The headmaster wants to see you and your sister after breakfast."

"Why now?" He inquired, a frown of his own appearing. "He's been here ever since we arrived."

"He probably decided he couldn't keep putting it off. The semester does start in a few days," Edith offered, the worry not leaving her face.

"Maybe," Zack said doubtfully. "Fine, whatever. I'll go wake up Zara and then we'll head over to breakfast first."

She nodded and held up a hand as he walked by, her voice coming out in a near whisper. "Be careful. Don't forget the headmaster has a grudge against you and your sister."

"I know, but we still have the people who forced him to fire his brother-in-law at our backs." He smiled reassuringly and continued into the dorm, thinking over what he had said.

It was supposedly the truth, but once again, the people from the military had seemingly disappeared. He hadn't heard a word from them since they were dropped off at the academy. Maybe they believed they had done enough, or possibly they were simply busy. It was annoying to not understand or know what was going on, but he was used to it.

The inside of Zara's room was busy with drawings of the stuffed animals that helped to comfort her. As always, Zelda and George had been placed on her bed.

The first few nights they had spent in the dorm had seen her coming to sleep with him. The unfamiliar location had initially unnerved her. She hadn't felt the need to join him after that, as she came to understand that they were safe. For the moment, at least.

Gently, he shook her awake and then headed into the bathroom for a quick shower. She was ready to go eat when he came out a few minutes later, wisps of steam still coming off his freshly scrubbed skin. He was wearing most of the academy uniform, with the long sleeves rolled up to his elbows.

The assigned uniform was always the same regardless of the classes they would be attending that day. Where one was made to be comfortable and stylish while inside a classroom or meeting area. The same would be less effective if they were training or going through the portal. Training uniforms and armor would be assigned to them at those locations.

While on academy grounds, the normal academy uniform was to be worn during all learning hours.

Zack had purposely left off the tie and suit jacket when he dressed. It gave him a certain devil-may-care image that fit well with his current general attitude. He had already decided on what he thought of the headmaster and wasn't going to give him any more respect than he gave them.

He ran a hand through his damp hair and after seeing that she was ready and holding George; they left to get some food.

Breakfast at the cafeteria was one of the few times the richer students actively ate there. It seemed that they were content to mostly eat their other meals at the expensive restaurants around it. The siblings appreciated the quiet time, but knew it would soon come to an end. Regardless of whether the wealthier students decided to continue eating at the restaurants, the sheer number of students ensured the cafeteria would always be packed.

The Albion Travelers Academy had dorms to support well over the typical five hundred students that attended it. The single large cafeteria and restaurants remained open almost all day just to support them all.

"Where are we going?" Zara asked, as they left the cafeteria behind. Their bellies were pleasantly full of good food.

"Oh, that's right. I didn't tell you earlier. The headmaster finally wants to meet with us." A look of disdain flickered across his face as he spoke, his lip curling upwards unpleasantly.

Her arms tightened around the worn bear. "I had hoped he'd forgotten about us."

"Not likely. Don't forget, we're the reason he had to fire his stupid brother-in-law."

She turned her head away with a humph. "It was the idiot's own fault! He shouldn't have treated you that way, to begin with, and especially not in front of another person he didn't know."

"Well, you're not wrong." Together, they climbed the gleaming stairs into the central building, both falling silent as they entered. The walk up the staircase that led to the spire was a long and difficult climb.

Zara was sweating when they arrived at the top, and even Zack was slightly out of breath. A set of doors designed to be large and imposing stood beside a desk with a fit older woman sitting behind it.

"Do you have to climb those every day?" Zack asked after a moment to catch his breath.

"Oh, heavens no, I only do that climb about once a week to stay in shape. The rest of the time, I take the elevator." She pointed to a second set of doors across from her that they hadn't noticed before. This revelation prompted Zara to kick him in the shin.

"Hey! What was that for? You didn't know they had an elevator here either!" He hopped away from her, clutching at his freshly bruised leg.

The woman laughed lightly at their antics, shaking her head. "I assume the two of you are here to meet with the headmaster?"

The doors opened as they were about to answer. A young woman around Zack's age stepped out, still talking to someone hidden inside the room beyond. "I'll let you know what I decide before classes start."

She turned to face them and stopped. She had deep red hair and clear hazel eyes that shifted between the green of her blouse and the red of her hair. Her gaze wandered over them, taking in their uniforms and the aged state of the bear in Zara's arms. It was clear that she was confused as to their identities when she nodded politely and then walked over to the elevator.

"You two, get in here!" The headmaster shouted, seeing them through the slowly closing doors to his office.

They waved to the nice secretary lady and entered the room; the doors closing behind them with an ominous thud. A gigantic window took up most of the wall behind the headmaster, giving any who dared to look a view out across the academy grounds.

"I expected you here some time ago!" The headmaster grouched as they drew close enough to see him. He was a slightly pudgy man of indeterminate age, with a severe 'V' shaped widow's peak extending to above his ears.

Zack shrugged and sat on a couch close to the window while Zara walked straight up to the glass, ignoring them both. "We had to eat breakfast first, and I didn't get the message until I was done with my morning run, anyway."

There was a slam as a meaty fist descended on the solid wood desk. "Don't give me any of that lip, boy! I can have you kicked out here in a second-"

"Can you though?" Zack returned calmly, understanding that the pissing contest had already begun. "I was under the impression that the military, specifically Sergeant Grieves and his Major, were keeping an eye on me here. Imagine what they would say if you kicked me out, or better yet, imagine what they would do?"

A strangled cry burbled out of the impotent headmaster as his face flushed in anger. The man had no idea that the teen knew what he had been forced to do.

"You should know that your brother-in-law brought this upon himself. If he had just treated us with respect, or at the very least not reacted the way that he did in front of others. None of this would have ever happened. He is the one who blacklisted me in the community, and he is the one who stupidly let the local gangs know I had the potential to be a traveler. Honestly, I wouldn't be surprised if the military brought him up on charges. You should know better than most how seriously they take anything related to the portals."

It was a thinly veiled threat that Zack had no way of following through on. Not that the headmaster would know that.

The reminder worked as the man paled and leaned back in his chair with a barely audible gulp. "Yes, that is true." There was a hint of defeat coloring the words.

"Anyway," Zack prompted, hoping to keep the conversation moving forward. "What did you want to talk to us about? I doubt that was all."

The headmaster blinked as life came back into his eyes. "Right, yes, I did actually call you both here for a reason. Miss Rammore made a request the other day in regard to your sister." They both glanced to where she was still looking out the window, ignoring them.

"I wasn't aware she had requested anything related to Zara?"

"She wondered if it would be possible for the girl to either attend some of the regular classes or if that was impossible, be taught by herself?"

"And what have you decided?" Zack didn't believe for a second the man would let her attend classes.

"She is not a student of this academy, and as such, is not allowed to attend any of the official classes. I cannot, however, stop Miss Rammore from spending her free time on frivolous activities."

"So, this was all just a thin excuse to get us up here so you could flex your imagined authority?" Zack objected, standing from his place on the couch. "We didn't need to come up here just to be told something obvious."

The headmaster didn't answer, instead clicking his tongue at the boy in annoyance.

Shaking his head, Zack didn't believe that he could be any more disappointed in the people running the academy than at that moment. "You know, for a school with so much history and pride on the line. You and the students are awfully quick to drag its touted name through the mud. Come on Zara, we're heading back. Apparently, we need to have a conversation with Edith about your schooling."

The woman he assumed was the headmaster's secretary looked at them curiously as they left his office and walked over to the elevator. Pushing in the button, they waited for the lift to arrive, listening as the large doors finally closed with a thud.

Zack nodded politely to the woman as they stepped into the small elevator and began their rapid descent.

"You did the exact same thing again. You antagonized him the same way you did the recruiter." Zara said softly once they were alone.

He leaned against the back of the lift and ran a hand through his hair. "I know. I took it way too far, farther than I intended when we first went in. I was going to play it cool, and calmly remind him that we supposedly have the military on our side."

She sighed and tucked her head into George's back. "You realize that he is going to do everything he can to make sure our lives are difficult now, right? Before, he probably would have done something because of his brother-in-law, and now he'll go all out."

"I know," He repeated, again. He had no good excuse to give her. It wasn't as though he had gotten mad or overly emotional. He simply hadn't stopped when he should have.

The rest of the ride down was filled with silence.

Edith was waiting for them when they stepped out of the elevator. "How did the meeting go?" Her worry from earlier had not dissipated in the slightest, and if anything had grown worse.

During the last week, she had gotten to know the two and was gradually coming to care for them in a way that was unsuited for a dorm matron. The siblings were slow to trust anyone, including her. It had taken some time, but she had discovered enough to learn how hard their life had been up to that point.

Zara pulled her face from the stuffed bear's back and tilted her head to the side. It was a cute mannerism that fit with a young girl holding a stuffed animal, if not one her exact age. "It could have gone better, or worse."

Edith quirked an eyebrow and turned to Zack, looking for a better explanation.

"I... may have antagonized him a little bit," He coughed and looked away. "A-anyway," He stuttered. "The headmaster said that you are allowed to teach Zara if you want."

Her lips pulled up at the corners, even while her eyes grew colder. "That is good news and just what I expected. However, let us go back to you and what you just said though. What do you mean, you antagonized the headmaster?"

"Um," He tried to think of a way out of the mess he had partially created, and then found himself in. "When we were up there, I just kept talking and pushing. It got a little out of hand, is all."

"Not. Good. Enough!" Each word was clipped and spoken with precision. Edith leaned closer to him, crossing her arms in disappointment. "I know there are things, many things, I don't understand or know about the two of you. What I do know is that people from the military were involved with you being accepted and enrolled here with your sister.

"Maybe they have your back on something like this. I hope they do. But you need to remember that creating enemies needlessly or causing friction between you and the other staff is not a smart idea! You may have people backing you up, but so does almost every other person here. Teachers and the student nobles alike, they are all acquainted with someone who has power of their own."

It was a message that Zack sorely needed to hear. He was not untouchable at the academy. The small amount of protection he had couldn't protect him from everyone. He still needed to be careful.

Chapter 6

Zack sat alone and to the side, watching the new students trickle into the auditorium for the commencement ceremony. He had been one of the first ones inside that morning, specifically for that reason. He wanted the freedom to choose the spot he was going to sit in. Preferably one that allowed him to watch as everyone entered.

The first few to walk in after him had stared at where he was sitting, and then proceeded to sit closer to the front. Gradually, the rest of the new student body trickled in. He would recognize a person occasionally from among them, someone he had seen while eating, or when he was out running.

The one who drew his eye the most was the girl he had met coming out of the headmaster's office. She was surrounded by a swarm of people trying to get close to her, while also keeping others from approaching.

Finally, the teachers and rest of the staff filed onto the raised platform at the front of the crowd. Everyone immediately grew quiet and sat up straight as the ceremony was about to begin.

The headmaster approached the podium and began to speak. "I would like to welcome everyone to the academy as we begin a new semester with a fresh class. I would like to take this opportunity to remind everyone that even though this academy is a training ground for 'Travelers', that is not all we do here. The other classes you will be taking are to prepare you for life once you have graduated, regardless of your status."

"What that means to you is that if you don't keep your grades up in all your classes, you may become ineligible to go through the portal for further training. I will leave it up to your teachers to relay the more salient details, however." He looked out across the gathered students, his eyes pausing on Zack before he continued speaking. "Now, without further ado or interruptions, please welcome a special guest speaker who has prepared a thought-provoking message for you all. I present to you George Trask, the current CEO, founder, and lead designer at the prestigious Albion Mana Tech Research Firm!"

From the side of the platform, a man barely taller than the headmaster climbed the short set of stairs and stopped in front of the podium. He was dressed in a sharp suit, with glasses thicker than they should have been perched on the bridge of his nose. From his position off to the side, Zack could see the soft glow of a small magi-crystal plugged into the tip of the temple shafts behind his ear.

"Hello everyone, as your headmaster said, I'm George Trask. And not many people know this, but I am a traveler. In fact, this academy is my alma-mater. I came here not for the traveler training however, but for the mana tech research facilities. Few other academies had those twenty years ago."

A cultured voice, filled with a passion for the chosen subject, filled the audience with that same fervor and hope.

**

Zack once more sat at the back as the rest of the class followed him in. They had come directly to the room after the ceremony and the names for each class had been called out. The teacher was the last one in and made sure the door was closed before walking to the front.

"My name is Rose Carter, and I will be the one in charge of your training and portal-based activities." Her voice was rough, and there was a light scar that extended from the bottom of her chin to her throat. "As you can see, I do not enjoy talking for long periods of time, so do not make me repeat myself ever! Your homeroom teacher will be in a moment, be respectful to him."

"He is my husband, and he enjoys telling me all about the problem students that need extra exercise." She coughed and rubbed a hand across her throat. "I used to be a traveler for many years. That is how I got this lovely decoration. I will train you to the best of my abilities, regardless of what some may wish." Her eyes lingered on Zack as she announced that. "It will be up to you all to make the best use of what you are taught from there." Her voice had grown noticeably rougher during the short time she had been speaking.

There was a soft knock on the closed door just then, which she accepted with a relieved grin.

A man with his head shaved on the sides and the dark hair on top cut short stepped into the room. It was apparent from the first glance that he was someone who could handle a class of rowdy, self-obsessed teens. His arms were thick with muscle and aged scars. There was the slightest hint of a limp affecting his walk that showed through as he hurried up to the front of the room.

"Sorry I'm late, it took me longer to get this than I thought it would," He spoke in a rich but soft voice as he handed a mint-leaf wrapped lozenge to his wife.

He turned to face the class, his eyes growing cloudy and his voice deepening. "I am Quinn Carter, and this is my wife, as I'm sure she already told you. If any of you give her any problems during your training periods, then I will make sure you fail every single class I possibly can! Nod if you understand!"

The class swallowed in unison and nodded their heads in understanding.

Rose rolled her eyes and smiled as she sucked on the medicine for her throat. "I'll see you all tomorrow for our first training session. Make sure you all are ready to impress me. Our first portal dive will happen next week, and only those who impress me will be going." She patted her husband on his arm and quickly left the classroom.

Quinn glared at them for a moment longer before relaxing against the edge of his desk in the corner. "Today is a short day, meant for each of you to get acquainted with your homeroom teacher. That would be me, your classmates, classes, and the facilities. Tomorrow is when your lessons will begin for real, so as my wife said, be ready. Now, before we get into everything, do any of you have any pertinent questions?"

A snooty-looking brat with slicked-back hair and a smarmy smile raised his hand at the front of the class. "I have one. My father told me that the academy accepted an orphan charity case this year. Is that true?"

"What? Not even one of the better off commoners, but an actual orphan?" Whispers erupted as another student exclaimed in shock.

A thick, meaty hand swung down and slapped the top of his desk as Quinn stood. "I asked for pertinent questions. Not something related to the petty squabbles of the weak-willed nobles you were apparently raised by. I will say this here and now. I have little love for most of the nobles. During the course of my previous career, I worked with many of your parents or other family members at some point. There were only a few I considered worth working with a second time."

A student stood abruptly, his chair clattering as it fell over. "Just wait until-"

"SIT DOWN!" Quinn thundered. "Your parents have little power while you are inside the walls of this academy. If you want to continue playing your little games, that is fine, but do not bring them inside my classroom."

The student picked up his chair and meekly sat down on trembling legs.

"I do not care if you like me, but you will respect my rules while in this room. You will no doubt quickly learn that my wife and I are a small subset of teachers that weren't originally nobles. Our views were shaped by our past experiences. If you don't want to be despised by those, you will be working with inside the portals in the future, then be better than your forefathers. Be the respectable nobles that you were supposedly raised to be."

A female sitting in front of Zack timidly raised her hand, only speaking when the teacher nodded at her. "What are the classes that you keep mentioning? I've heard that they change from year to year."

Quinn nodded and stood, walking over to the large whiteboard on the wall. He picked up a marker and twisted the top to select the desired color. "You are right, the classes do change from year to year, but I think you might have heard incorrectly. It would be more appropriate to say the classes are only different between years."

He began to write on the board in a bright red, easy-to-read color. "First years always have the same classes. Ones that will give them a good foundation for hunting inside the portals. Second years are allowed to choose some of their own classes based on individual interests, but again they also have certain classes that are always the same and build on what was taught the previous year. The same goes for the rest of the years."

He gave them a moment to read what he had written. "Does that make sense?"

The girl nodded and then shook her head. "Yes, and no. Your explanation makes sense, and I can see why I might have heard it wrong. But what is the actual difference between the classes 'Portal Hunting 1' and 'Portal Hunting 2'?"

The teacher put the cap back on the marker before answering. "As a loose example, you can think of it this way. This year, we will be going through all the different beasts and monsters that have been discovered inside the portals. Part of that will be how to effectively hunt them, so your mana crystal miners are never in danger.

"Next year, you would be introduced to their specific weak points. Shortcuts, if any, to finding, trapping, and then killing them. As well as spending time training with mock-ups on the training fields. As I said, they build off each other and progress."

"Thank you," She said politely, ducking down into her seat. Her ears were burning red as she avoided the gazes of the class.

Zack had a feeling she came from one of those better-off commoner families that had been mentioned, or possibly a lower noble family. There were too many students in the academy for all of them to be from the noble families. He had a feeling there were more commoners in some of the other classes than people thought.

"Are there any other questions, or can we move on?" No one else raised their hand. "Alright then, continue it is. In addition to the portal-centric classes, you will also be taking regular, more mundane classes, as the headmaster announced earlier.

"My wife and I, along with many of your parents, are living proof that one rarely stays a traveler for their entire life. You each need to be prepared to handle life once that happens. Some only make it five years, others twenty. There is no knowing which you will be until you have gone through the portal and faced your first monster."

That was not what Zack wanted to hear, due to their circumstances, he hadn't been able to attend much of school. He knew how to read and write and even do basic arithmetic, but none of those were anywhere close to the level of what he would be expected to perform at.

The teacher glanced up at a clock set into the wall at the back of the classroom. "Alright then, I think enough time has passed that we should be fine to start touring the grounds. While we are walking, I want each of you to take this opportunity to get to know the rest of your classmates. You will be depending on them during the training exercises, so it is best to get along with each other. You never know when they might be needed to save your life or protect your back in a fight."

Zack let those words trickle through his mind before deciding to reject the advice. There had never been anyone else to guard his back or save him before. It had always just been him and Zara, and most of his time inside the portals was spent alone, without even her. He could see the wisdom in the man's words, but he wouldn't rely on them.

Besides, he didn't even remember how to make friends anymore. The last one he had was back when they were still in the orphanage a lifetime ago.

Slowly, everyone in the class stood and looked around. Most of the nobles already knew each other and felt no need to introduce themselves to those of a lower station. None of them had taken the teacher's words to heart, at least not yet.

Shaking his head, Quinn stood and ushered them all out of the room after noticing what they were doing.

"To our left, you can see one of the training fields. That will be the one everyone in your year will be using." The muscular teacher droned on as they walked in a loose group. "Coming up, we have the 'Mana Tech and Applications' building. I know it has a grand name, but honestly, all they really do there is process the crystals you will be bringing back. You will be shown how that is done, and not much more for now.

"All the more extensive research is done below and is off-limits to first years. I would suggest you stay on the good side of any scientists or alchemists you might meet. More than one student has been forced into an experiment they were conducting." He paused, as though considering whether he should tell them more.

"Were they alright afterward?" A student asked from the middle of the group.

"Most of them survived, if that is what you mean," Quinn grinned sadistically. He pushed them through the sprawling campus, labeling each building and site as they passed it. "We have one last stop and that is to the top of the hill behind the academy. From up there, you will be able to see the complex that has been built around the portal we use for training purposes. When we aren't using it, portions of the military and certain corporations will rent it out for their own training programs."

The path up the hill was one Zack used most mornings during his runs. It wasn't a large hill, but the back of the short incline was actually an artificially created cliff. It had been cleared out years before when the school was first built. Back then, people were still unsure if the monsters could come through the portal and attack everyone. As a result, a military bunker had originally been built around the portals as a precaution.

Then the existing nearby private school was converted into the first Travelers Academy in the country. A few years later, they were given exclusive rights to the portal, and as the years went by, the regulations relaxed. Now the bunker that once obscured it had been partially torn down, though the portal itself was still hidden by the walls.

He had seen the various buildings surrounding the portal each morning since they arrived, and was anxious to go through it once more.

***

Zack was standing in front of the Edith's door after school had let out for the day. He hadn't talked to a single one of his classmates the entire day. Really none of them had talked to anyone they didn't already know. It was an oddity he didn't think the teacher had been expecting.

He certainly hadn't.

What kind of teens got together, and then only talked to people they knew?

Granted, he hadn't actually been around that many kids his own age, especially recently. He had, however, heard the various fathers talking about their kids at the construction job sites. What he had experienced earlier was nothing like what they had described.

Were the social lines just too clearly drawn still? Maybe in another day or two everyone would relax and start talking to each other. Either that or something else would get them talking regardless of the boundaries.

Shaking his head to dispel the thoughts of people he didn't understand, he raised his hand and knocked. Zara should be inside, having started her lessons with the kind older woman that day as well. That, however, was not his reason for knocking on the door at that moment.

He needed help with one of his own problems. The more traditional classes were going to cause him issues if he couldn't find a tutor for them fast.

Edith opened the door a moment later, the harsh frown she had prepared leaving her face as she saw who it was. "Did the first-day orientation already end?" She asked, stepping to the side and inviting him in.

He nodded, "I actually need to ask you for some help related to that." He glanced past her to where he could see Zara hunched over a short table working on something. Her teddy bear George was sitting beside her, leaning against a leg of the table. "You know how much I struggled to keep food on the table before we came here?"

"I do," She nodded.

"Well, being busy always working didn't leave me with a lot of time to go to school. I was only able to go maybe once every other week. The teacher for my class mentioned that we would need to take regular subjects alongside our more specialized ones." His hands fisted together as he built up the nerve to ask her for help. "Would you be willing to tutor me in those subjects, so I don't fail?"

She thought for a moment and then shook her head. "No. If I tutor you, it will be for more than the bare minimum of not failing!"

Zack, who had felt his heart fall at her presumed refusal, felt some whiplash form alongside the hope her words gave him. "I'm fine with putting in that kind of work and effort, if you mean it?"

She smiled and tilted her chin towards Zara and the small table, "If you are anything like her, then it won't be a chore in the slightest. The other students must have been terrible to force her to stop going to classes. She is slightly behind what I would expect someone her age to be at, but the sheer desire she has to learn is a delight for me. Not to mention that she is by no means a slow learner."

He smiled as they came up behind the young girl absorbed in whatever she was working on. "I'm afraid you will be disappointed in that case. She has always been the smarter one. Don't get me wrong, I don't think I'm a slow learner either, but I'm not anywhere close to her level."

"Few are," She tapped Zara on the shoulder. "Come on, your brother is here."

Chapter 7

"It was so nice!" Zara continued to gush about her time with the dorm matron.

The common area inside the dorm building was quiet as the two walked through it to their apartment dorm. They ignored the shocked looks of the three people sitting around a small table littered with papers. The secret that Zara was living there as well would get out eventually either way. It was better to deal with any problems it might cause sooner, rather than have it hanging over their heads, causing stress and other issues.

"Is she a good teacher?" Zack asked, unlocking their door.

Zara made a noise of approval. "She's been a dorm matron for a long time now, so she has naturally had to learn all of these things."

Zack abruptly pulled her behind him as he smelled something in the air. No one should have been in their dorm after they left that morning, and yet he was smelling a scent that didn't belong there.

"Finally, you're back!" Sergeant Grieves stepped into view from the small kitchen at the back. A steaming mug of something dark in his hand. "We didn't realize your classes would run so long on the first day."

"We?" Zack questioned, relaxing his grip on Zara.

The female soldier who had been driving the carriage came out of the bathroom and picked up her own steaming mug from the small table in front of their couch. They had never gotten her name or the names of any of the other squad members that had come with the sergeant to move them. They hadn't been wearing the tops of their uniforms that day, which meant he hadn't been able to just read their name patches. The military wasn't big on introducing their people when there wasn't a reason.

"He means me." She took a sip and cocked her head at the two. "I have been asked to liaise between you, the sergeant and the Major. I'll be taking up a position as one of the sub-trainers so I can live on the grounds and have easy access to you."

Zack felt his heart clench at her announcement. "Why is the military going out of their way like this? The two of us are just a couple of orphans who were tortured by madmen and deranged researchers. I doubt that normally warrants a soldier being stationed close-by."

Sergeant Grieves frowned and placed his mug on the nearby counter. "I agree, however, the Major specifically asked that we do this. He doesn't need to explain his reasoning to us. We just have to follow orders, though I will admit to being curious in this case..." He looked them over and then shook his head. "Regardless, Specialist Jean McCleary here will be stationed nearby in case you need to reach out to us, or vice versa."

"I don't understand." Zack had learned to trust his gut, and it was telling him something was wrong. "I thought you said there were people already here at the school, working for your Major or the military in general?"

"I did," He agreed, without saying more.

Specialist McCleary dared to roll her eyes behind his back, an action that caused Zara to giggle. "Well, why don't we go on a short field trip to the portal and get to know each other at the same time?" She offered.

"Why do you want to go there?"

"One of the duties all the trainers have is to go through the portals with the students. I haven't seen it in person just yet, and while we can't go through it today, I would still like to at least take a look around the area." She handed her nearly empty mug to the sergeant and waved the siblings back to the door. "Don't worry about him. He'll leave after we are gone."

The common area was empty when they went through it a moment later and hurried out of the building.

"What's with the rush?" Zara was struggling to hold on to George, along with the papers Edith had given her to study later.

"No rush. I just really want to see the portal right now." She grabbed the items from Zara and pointed them towards a small older model carriage built by the Albion government's own manufacturing company. "Do you like it? I just picked it up this morning. It's used, but that is the only way I could afford one of these. It is not as good as a Vortex, but Alberitas carriages tend to sell for cheap when they are used. The consumer base for this brand is always upgrading to the latest model and then selling their old ones."

Zack climbed into the front seat, while Zara and George took the back. McCleary sat in the driver's seat and then twisted to look at them, passing the items back to Zara at the same time.

"Alright, you two listen up. Something is going on. I have no idea what it is, but the Major called sergeant Grieves last night and today I am stationed here. As far as I know, everything was done last minute and under the table through unofficial lines. I can't say what that means for sure, but something has the Major on edge. And that man does not get spooked easily." She reached into the inner pocket of her jacket and pulled out a key with a small dark stone in the center of the metal.

Zack swiped the key from her hand before she could insert it into the middle of the steering wheel. "Hold on, why tell us now instead of in there? What aren't you saying?"

"The sergeant didn't want certain information said inside your dorm-"

"Are people listening to what is said in there?" Zara asked, clutching George tight enough that stuffing bulged from his seams.

"I don't know," She growled in exasperation at their constant questions. "I have no idea what they are worried about, remember? I can't say whether anybody even knows who you are. For all I know, it could be our own government or one of the nobles who are interested in you. All I can say for certain is that we are being careful. Okay?"

Zack and Zara shared a look, and then nodded. "Alright. What's the stone in the middle of the key for? It doesn't look like a normal mana crystal." He wondered while handing it back to her.

McCleary let her head fall against the hard material of the steering wheel and closed her eyes. "It's called a Dark Stone or more usually a Control Stone. They're super cheap and are found naturally here in our world. For whatever reason, they work as a near-perfect conduit for mana. So, these stones are engraved with patterns that steer the energy from the crystals to where it needs to go. Alberitas creates each key specifically for a singular vehicle so they can't be easily copied and stolen. Does that answer your question?"

"Yeah, I've just never seen a stone like that before, is all." None of the construction equipment he had used in the past had anything that fancy.

"They're only used on premium goods, like this carriage and certain high-end powerful mana-tech devices." She pulled up her head and slid the key into place. With a thrum of quiet power, the motor, using mana crystals as a power source, started up. "Now let's hurry up. I want to see the portal without any of the larger groups around."

It was something that was only possible when a travelers group had already crossed over and still had hours left before their return. The groups were closely monitored, so there was only an hour or so of overlap between them.

"Why are you so interested in seeing this portal? I thought they all looked the same? That it was only the insides that are different." Zara was listening closely from the back seat without saying anything.

The specialist removed a hand from the steering wheel and let it waver from side to side. "That is what we tell the masses, but it isn't actually the truth." They surged forward, leaving the dorm behind. The expensive machine making the ride comfortable and smooth. "Most of the portal that people see is indeed indistinguishable from any other. If you look at the edges, however, you begin to notice some thin lines. Those lines are what we have come to call power markers. The thicker and more numerous the lines, the more powerful the monsters inside the portal will be. Those also tend to have denser mana crystals as well."

"And you are curious about the lines on the school's portal?" Zara questioned from the back, holding George in her lap. The stuffing had receded from the seams, though Zack would undoubtedly need to sew him back together soon.

"Yup, there have been some whispers from the companies that rent it from the school that the monsters inside have been growing stronger. The sergeant asked me to look it over while I was here. I could wait until our first training session inside, but that could end badly if they truly are getting stronger."

"Do portals grow stronger? I thought they never changed." Zack was quick to ask as the complex surrounding the object in question came into view.

"That is only something we let the civilian masses believe. It is an open secret among travelers that they do change occasionally. It doesn't happen often, but it does happen."

The rest of the short trip was filled with silence as the siblings processed what was to them a bombshell. Zack was trying to remember everything he could about the portal at the research facility. He had seen it every day for years and nearly everything was crystal clear in his mind. The problem was, he had never examined the edges closely. There had been no reason to.

Zara, on the other hand, had remained with the researchers when he went through. They had only tossed her in with him a small handful of times. She had examined the shining unstable surface of the portal so many times it was ingrained on the back of her eyelids. The thickness and number of bands or lines around the edges were clear in her mind's eyes.

She was determined to keep that information to herself until after they had seen the school's portal.

They stopped in front of the partially torn-down bunker that had once hidden the portal. People were walking to and from the surrounding buildings, each busy with their own activities and work. No one paid attention to the two teens and the woman escorting them.

The inside of the bunker had been entirely dismantled and emptied out, leaving only the walls as a reminder of what had once been there. Even the ceiling had been removed. There was a single guard at the entrance to the building, ensuring that they kept track of who went inside the portal. That was it.

The level of caution and awe that had once surrounded the mystical doorways to another place had long since faded with time.

Zack felt his feet stutter and stop as the shining, rippling surface of the portal came into the view. It had a thick syrup-like consistency that grabbed onto anything going through it. Strands of it would sometimes cling to a person for a second or two after they went through it.

It was a feeling he had become intimately familiar with as a child. He hated the memories it brought back, and the familiar yearning that came with the portals.

Behind him, Zara was shaking as repressed memories from their time as research subjects came to the forefront of her mind.

This was a complication that neither of them had thought they would face. They were scared of the portal, or more accurately, they were scared of the memories it was causing to resurface.

Steeling his nerves, Zack took a step forward, followed by another, until he had reached the undulating doorway to another world. The memories inside his mind, of the many times he had been thrown through that same surface, began to retreat. They weren't forgotten, but a wave of intense anger at the thought that the researchers had any influence over him still began to take its place.

The thought that he might be controlled by anything related to those people was anathema to the core of his person.

Zara squeezed George as tight as she could. Suddenly falling into a crouch, as a similar, if not more pronounced, reaction than Zack had gone through occurred with her. Unlike her brother, who had often been gone through the portal, she remembered everything inside the research facility. The lies they had told her brother about how they wouldn't experiment on her, and then when they did exactly that. She remembered the constant prick of the needles and cold scalpels as they went about their sadistic research.

It had gotten to the point that she relished the times she was allowed to go with him and experience the other side. Something that never happened enough.

Even Zack didn't know how bad it had truly been for her. She had never let him know. Even then, at her young age, she was concerned about what he would do if he learned the truth. Seeing the portal brought all those memories back to the surface, followed by a pained scream as she collapsed unconscious to the floor.

Zack rushed back to his sister's side. Back at the entrance, the guard was watching them closely, not understanding what was going on.

The specialist quickly took several pictures of the lines on the edge of the portal and ran back to them.

"I think seeing the portal just caused some bad memories to resurface," Zack told her softly, while he cradled his younger sister. "It did the same to me, but unlike her, I wasn't stuck with the researchers all the time."

He had seen the scars that covered Zara's body when they were first rescued. It was too late for him to do anything by that point. Despite what she believed, he knew they had been experimenting on her far more than they said they would. Thankfully, most of the skin-deep scars had faded over the last couple of years. The mental and emotional trauma was something they were both working on still.

McCleary sucked in a breath. "I'm sorry. I didn't even think of how seeing one again would affect the two of you."

He waved away her apology and stood with Zara's light body in his arms. "It's alright, I don't think either of us thought of how we would react to seeing it either. Besides, it is better for me to get it done now than with my classmates."

"I... suppose that is true," She replied awkwardly. "Well, I have what I need. We should leave before anyone starts asking questions about what just happened."

He nodded and walked after her. His arms were trembling by the time they reached her Alberitas carriage. Years of malnutrition had long since taken their toll on his muscles and stamina. The last week of good food and exercise had begun the process of fixing the damage and enhancing what he lacked. It would take several weeks before he would begin to see any noticeable gains. It would be even longer before he was fully recovered.

Going through the portal, for him at least, would likely shorten that time period. It would really depend on if everything remained the same with his abilities as the first time or if awakening a second time changed them.

It was a question he wouldn't know the answer to until they crossed over for one of the classes.

Carefully, he shifted his sister from his arms to the back seat. He was tempted to sigh when he saw the condition of George's seams, but held back since he had been expecting it. The old bear had been fixed before, not as many times as Zelda, but the number wasn't too far off either. It was a good thing they still had some thread from the last time he had needed to sew it together.

"You know, the higher-ups never told the squad what the facilities scientists were doing to you two. Once we were there and found the undocumented portal, everything got swept under the rug. I'm guessing that is at least partly to blame for you being lost in the system and forced out on your own." McCleary was talking as she drove them back to the dorm. "At your age, you should have gone back to an orphanage, or a special facility equipped to help you both heal. Instead, you were cast aside and forced to almost scavenge to keep yourselves fed... ... ... Sorry."

Zack looked out the window as they paused at the academy gates. "I always wondered what had happened. The commander from back then, I'm guessing, your Major. He promised to keep in touch, that the squad would be there if we ever needed the help." His teeth ground together as he forced the words out through a haze of growing anger. "He lied. None of you were there when we needed you.

"I'm grateful that he managed to get us into the academy and away from the gangs before anything else happened. But don't think for an instant that I trust any of you! The entire situation reeks of politics and back-room-dealings. Who has ever heard of two kids who just rescued getting lost in the system, but still having their housing covered? None of it makes sense."

The leather wrapping on the steering wheel groaned and flexed under the specialist's grip. Her knuckles turned white from the pressure, and the veins in the back of her hands bulged out.

"You're doing it again!" Zara snapped, her hand whacking the back of his head weakly. She had woken up a few minutes earlier.

"I admit mistakes were made," McCleary said in a strangled voice. "But that does not mean the Major lied! You have no idea what both he and sergeant Grieves have gone through to find you! The number of favors they were forced to call in, and all of it was for NOTHING!" She yelled, barely stopping herself from hitting the steering wheel. "There was nothing about where you had gone after the rescue. There was a single record of you being admitted to the facility right afterward and then nothing."

"Why did they try so hard to find us? Anyone else would have simply pretended we didn't exist and moved on." Zack asked in a quiet voice, his anger having left as abruptly as it appeared.

"I don't know, maybe the Major felt bad for you, or maybe he thought the research facility had done more to you both than you said. Something different, and possibly game-changing, was obviously going on there. That was plain for all of us to see." She slowed the carriage to a stop in front of the dorm. "He had his reasons for wanting to find and help you. Never call him a liar again. Especially not in front of a squad member. You'll be lucky to come out alive if that ever happens."

It was a promise of the untold brutality that would rain down on him if he wasn't careful.

"I understand, and sorry. I seem to have developed a bad habit recently of not watching my words as closely as I should." Zack opened his door while speaking and then turned to bow to her.

She smiled and nodded. "I understand. I was that age once as well." Her eyes flicked to the back where Zara was climbing out as well. "I'll see you tomorrow in class. Zara, make sure to keep your brother in line."

Chapter 8

"Do you want to talk about it?" Zack asked Zara, as the door to their dorm closed. "About what happened at the portal?"

She glared at him and shook her head. "No, not right now, at least." She thrust George into his arms. "Fix him, and then we'll go eat!"

Shaking his head, Zack took the bear into his room to find the sewing kit. The methodical nature of sewing the seams on the bear back together gave him a chance to think over the things he had said in the carriage. The inability to control his mouth was something that had happened in the past, mainly during their time at the institute. It was a habit that only came out when he didn't feel in control of his life.

Something that was definitely the case every time the military personnel appeared. They had their own agenda and power that he was unable to guess or deny.

Unfortunately, it was also a habit that was beginning to cause problems for them. It didn't matter when they were younger. There was little else the researchers could do to them that they weren't already doing.

In a school environment, where they were also partly depending on those same people. That was not the case. He couldn't risk antagonizing every-one who held power over them any more than he already had.

The needle glided through the worn and balding fabric as he stitched the bear back together at the seams. Most of them were still holding together. It was only in a few spots that they had burst.

"Woah," He muttered as he caught a particularly pungent whiff of the unwashed plushie. "When was the last time Zara bathed either of you?" Finishing up, he tossed the stuffed animal into the tub to begin soaking and went to get his sister.

She looked up as he knocked on the open door. Zelda was in her lap, and she was currently drawing a small sparkling bear with long bloody claws on its paws.

"George is soaking in the tub right now. He needed a bath." She looked away at that, as though it wasn't her fault. "I'm ready to go eat if you are?"

"It's going to be crowded in there by now. You know that, right?"

He shrugged. "It's not like we're hiding. Everyone is bound to find out that we're poor, or working part-time for the school, or that you are here, eventually. I've told you before, it doesn't matter. We'll handle whatever comes, if and when it does. Now come on, I'm hungry even if you aren't."

She nodded and picked up Zelda, setting the drawing and her pencil on the desk by her bed. She was going to need the extra comfort that only her oldest and favorite stuffed animal could provide. "Let's go get some food then."

True to their mutual expectations and worries, the cafeteria and the restaurants nearby were all packed with students. Zara drew a constant stream of stares as they entered the building. Not only was she younger than them all by several years, but she was also a fairly cute little girl holding tight to a stuffed animal.

Zack held her close as they got into line, ignoring everyone else around them.

"Would you like your food to go?" The old man who took their dinner order asked, glancing past them to all the people staring at the siblings.

"I didn't even know that was an option."

"It's not, usually. The staff sometimes make exceptions for people we like. The two of you have been here longer than the rest and have always treated us with respect." He pointed their attention to a student further down that was berating the staff for improperly plating his food. The vegetables were touching the sauce on top of some thinly sliced strips of meat.

"Ah, then if it isn't too much trouble, I believe that would be a good idea for tonight. It's better to get everyone used to her being here slowly, I think."

During the short exchange, Zara had pressed harder and harder against his side, as the constant stares started to affect her. It would take her some time to get comfortable around people that constantly stared at her. She had never been comfortable being the center of attention. Having people focus on you had always meant something bad was about to happen. It was a lesson they had learned in the institute, and one of the reasons Zack had always tried to keep the focus on himself instead of her.

Soon enough, a bag containing their food was handed to them, and they scurried out of the building with a quick word of gratitude.

"Are you ready to talk about what happened at the portal yet?" Zack asked as they sat around the small dining table in their dorm. The food was spread between them on dishes they would need to bring back in the morning. He would make sure to clean them that night before going to sleep. It would be bad manners to return them dirty when they had been done a favor like this.

Zara paused, her fork stopping above a small green vegetable that looked like a tree. "You know? I once heard a rumor that these things were actually the homes of really small creatures called Elf's. They supposedly make some incredible sweets during the day in the deep forests, and then come back at night to their homes. Except we humans keep cutting them down to eat as a vegetable."

Zack speared the object in question and brought it to his mouth with an amused expression. "There is no such thing as Elf's on Aperra. They probably exist inside one of the portals somewhere, but certainly not here. Where did you hear that anyway?"

She shrugged and switched to a different food. "I don't remember anymore. Maybe it was from one of the caretakers in the orphanage." She chewed and then placed the utensil on the table. "Seeing the portal just brought everything from the past back all at once. The experiments, the names they used to call us, the things they did to me when you were forced to go through the portals. Everything I've been trying to forget since we were rescued, it all came back in crystal clear detail. It was like we had never left."

Zack twirled his fork around a noodle, shame keeping him from looking at her. "You know, we never talked about the full extent of the experiments they did on you. They were supposed to only be doing them to me. Unless they were punishing me for something and then they made me watch as they cut into you.

"For a long time, I thought they were actually holding to that promise. It was the only reason I cooperated as much as I did, after all. Then I began to notice the little details you tried to hide. The needle marks on the back of your neck, the bruises on your arms and legs from the leather straps. Then again, when we were finally rescued, I saw the full extent of the scars they had given you."

Tears trailed down his cheeks as he spoke, unafraid of showing weakness and emotion to his sister. "I thought I had been doing my best to protect you the entire time. When, in reality, you had been suffering more than I ever knew."

Zara stiffened as she listened to him. She had no idea he had seen all that in the end. "It's not your fault. We were kids. There was never a reason for them to hold on to a promise they had given you. The most I could do is keep it a secret from you. If you had ever found out while we were still under their control, you would have gone berserk."

The fork fell to his plate and bounced off the edge, all desire to eat fleeing alongside his hunger. This was a topic that they rarely approached, with both thinking that it was better to forget those days than dwell on them. Leaning back, Zack looked at his sister and ran a hand over his face.

"Ugh," He groaned. "I would have. I really would have. Everything I was doing was supposed to keep you safe, and in the end, none of it mattered. We never had a choice in anything we did or that was done to us."

He stood and pulled Zara into a hug. He would clean the table and everything on it later.

"Should we have talked about what happened back then, before now?" Zara asked softly, pressing her head against his sternum.

"It's probably a good thing we didn't," He said with a dry, mirthless laugh. "I can imagine how I would have reacted if we had talked about it before coming here. It would have been the straw that broke me. Let's face it Z, we were stuck in that apartment, barely making ends meet and making little if any progress with our lives. If we had talked about this, then I would have likely gone straight to the gangs just to fight someone. It would have been a disaster."

She sniffled and laughed a single time sadly. "Yeah, I can see you doing that."

Zack let his chin drop and rest on her head. Then he said something that he had never said before. "I wish mom and dad were still here. They would have known what to do and say."

Zara stilled in his arms while he began mentally cursing himself for his stupidity. Their parents were another subject they never talked about. She blamed them for everything that had happened to them, and in a way, she was right to. If they hadn't died, or gone missing, they never would have ended up in that orphanage. They never would have been turned into human lab rats for years on end.

"Are we having that conversation today as well?" Her voice was completely devoid of emotion. It was a scary side of his sister that only came out when their parents were mentioned.

"No, no, forget I said anything! It was just a slip of the tongue and nothing more, I swear!" He tightened his arms around her until he felt her relax. His inability to control his tongue was really becoming an issue.

It was a stupid thing to say in the first place; it wasn't like he really remembered them anyway. He didn't even remember their names or what they looked like. They had died when he was five and Zara had been just over two years old and beginning to walk. It was only due to Albion's policy that existing family members stay together inside the welfare system that they weren't separated.

Of course, once someone showed interest in taking them both, little was done in checking to make sure they were fit parents. That was how they had ended up inside the research institute, or as was more likely the case, he believed they had simply been sold by someone inside the orphanage.

Zara had no memories of them, period, and she was fine with that. In truth, neither sibling even knew if their parents had died or simply vanished. Zack remembered taking care of his sister alone for a few days, and then government officials had come to take them away. The official word was they had died; however, they had never been told anything more or allowed to see the bodies.

They didn't even know where or if they had been buried, and unfortunately, it was too late to discover anything now. They had been entered into the government system with no last name, and Zack certainly couldn't remember what it had been.

There was no way for them to learn anything more than they already knew.

"I don't think I'm hungry anymore," She muttered softly into his chest after they had been standing in silence for a few minutes.

"I'm not either. It was a bad topic to discuss during dinner. I'll put the food in the coldbox and clean the dishes. Why don't you go and clean George? I'm sure he has been soaking for long enough at this point." She nodded, the top of her head banging lightly against his chin.

They separated after another moment and went about their individual tasks. Each lost in their own thoughts on topics it was best to avoid.

Zack transferred the food over to one of the few containers that had made the move with them. With that done, he began cleaning the table and the dishes that they had gotten from the cafeteria. The small kitchen hadn't seen much use since they moved into the dorm. It was simply easier and cheaper to go to the academy-funded dining facility.

"Thanks for fixing George," Zara said gratefully, as she came out of the bathroom a while later. Her arms were wet, and there were some soap suds clinging to the front of her shirt.

"Of course. Where is he?"

"I put him in the sink. That way, the rest of the water can drain out of him while he dries, without causing a mess." She sat on the couch and stared at him. "What did you think of your first day of classes?"

He shrugged and dropped the small hand towel onto the front of the sink. "That's tomorrow. Today was really just introductions to the facilities and some of the teachers. I think I'll struggle in the regular classes until I have worked with Edith enough to catch up. As for the more Portal-oriented classes, I'll probably be fine, especially once we go through it."

They sat and talked until Zara couldn't contain her yawns any longer.

Zack lay in bed that night and mentally reviewed everything that had happened that day. The people he had seen and met in his classes, and more importantly, everything that had occurred after talking to Edith.

His memories of the man they kept referring to as the Major had faded since the rescue. He remembered the promise the man had made and little else. Zack had been more worried about Zara's condition at the time than anything else.

He wanted to trust that the man and his squad of subordinates had their best interest at heart. Their time living alone had drilled home a different lesson, time and time again. People looked out for their own interests first and foremost.

He could only believe that while the Major and his people may actually be interested in helping them, they had some other goal in mind as well. Thinking of it that way made everything easier for him to process and understand. He was fine with being used in that manner; it was a part of the natural order of things. As long as whatever they were being used for didn't harm them in any way, why should he care about those plans?

His mind settled at last, Zack rolled over and fell asleep.

***

There was a large group of nobles talking quietly outside the classroom when Zack arrived the next morning. They stopped talking as he drew close and separated without a word so he could enter the empty room.

Choosing the same spot as the day before, he sat in the back and waited. It was the ideal spot to watch the other students, while also remaining out of the way.

The group of nobles and rich kids, including the snooty brat with slicked-back hair, traipsed into the room. It was impossible for him to hear their whispered words, but from the way they kept looking towards him, it wasn't hard to determine who they were talking about.

"It's you, isn't it?" The brat asked suddenly. He stepped to the front of the group, his eyes zeroing in on the sole person in the room, not part of their conversation.

"What's me?" Zack asked in a bored tone. He knew where this was going. It was undoubtedly related to the question the smarmy idiot had asked the day before. Undoubtedly, word had already made the rounds after he and Zara had both shown up at the cafeteria the night before, and then again that morning.

"The orphan," The rich teen said the word as though it was a filthy curse. "The charity case we've all heard about. The reason behind this academy's prestige is currently being dragged through the sewer!"

From the corner of his eye, Zack saw the wide-muscled frame of their teacher pause outside the room. He had stopped to listen to the conversation, waiting to see how it developed, he thought.

"Maybe I am, maybe I'm not," Zack looked each of them in the eye as he answered. "What does it matter to you all either way?"

A few of them snorted and scoffed in shocked disbelief.

"I believe that answers the question right there," The same teen said, lifting his head some to look down at Zack. "Only an uncultured and uneducated orphan would dare to say something like that to us."

Zack was quickly growing tired of the way the boy kept saying, orphan. It wasn't as though he had any control over what had happened to his parents.

Quinn coughed as he stepped into the room, his gaze pinning down the group of overly privileged youngsters. "I believe we had part of this conversation yesterday." He glanced down at a loose sheet of paper in his hands. "Spencer VanCamp? Any relation to Peter VanCamp?"

"Uh, yeah, I mean yes. He's my father," The boy perked up, believing the teacher might be swayed by the connection.

"I thought so. You both like that ridiculous hairstyle, and if you are anything like him, then I pity whichever group gets stuck with you." Quinn limped farther into the room and sat on the edge of his desk, where he could see all of the kids. Both the ones that were there before him and the ones that had followed him in.

"And how would a washed-up retired Traveler know my esteemed father?" Spencer questioned, momentarily diverting his attention away from Zack.

Quinn broke into laughter at the query. "Esteemed huh, sure kid, keep telling yourself that. I told you yesterday, I have worked with most of your parents or other relatives at one point or another. The only reason

I remember dear old esteemed," Derision coated the term as he repeated it a second time. "Peter is that he is the single-most incompetent waste of space I ever had the displeasure of working with. And-" He stood before Spencer could say anything. "He is the reason I walk with a limp to this day."

Chapter 9

Quinn pulled the red-faced Spencer close to him and spoke in a deliberately loud whisper that everyone heard. "I think I'm going to enjoy having you in my class. It'll give me the chance to renew certain... relationships." He thrust the boy away and smiled at everyone.

Spencer tumbled into the group and fell to the ground, his face changing colors as he impotently raged inside his mind.

"Now, if I remember correctly, we were originally discussing how our resident orphan Zack," Unlike the rest of the people in the room, he didn't put any extra emphasis on the word. "Is supposedly bringing down the academy's reputation. Is that right?"

The group of students in question nodded silently.

"That's a real riot. It's laughable, really. I could see that even being true if we were talking about certain other students." His eyes flickered to the boy still sitting on the classroom floor. "In Zack's case, however, that is patently inaccurate. Would any of you shining examples of nobility and other rich upper-crust members of society care to guess why that might be?"

A student standing amongst the nobles raised their hand. "Is it because he has no background and is considered more neutral than anything else?"

The response was a concealed jab at all of them, whose reputation was less than stellar.

"A good guess, and one that can be considered partially true even. However, it is, in this case, not the correct answer." Quinn nodded along as he answered. "Would anyone else like to take a guess?"

A student near the door, hidden by the still-standing teens, answered. "He has the single highest compatibility score ever recorded since the system was put in place."

The crowd parted as they all turned to look at him and the speaker. Allowing Zack the opportunity to see the person who owned that soft, feminine voice. It was the red-headed girl he had seen exiting the headmaster's office.

"I apologize for missing the first day of classes yesterday. I had a sudden family emergency."

"I'm aware. I hope the matter was resolved without any further issues." She nodded at Quinn's probe. "Alright then, everyone please take your seats, and make sure they are a good one as it will be where you are sitting from now on."

The girl, Testarosa, sat at the front of the class. Choosing a spot where it would be easy to see and hear everything that was being taught to them.

He waited for them to sit before continuing. "Now, as miss Testarosa said, the prestige he brings to this academy is because of his compatibility score. Quite frankly, his attendance is worth more to the school and its reputation than several of you combined. I would suggest playing nice with the boy. His future is far brighter than any of yours."

Zack groaned mentally as the teacher unintentionally, he hoped, painted a bullseye on his back. Besides, it was something he doubted was true. The recruiters would have acted differently if he truly did bring that much to the table.

"What does the compatibility test actually represent anyway? Why is it so important?" Someone asked.

Quinn cleared his throat and scooted back to sit more comfortably on top of his desk. "As each of you know, there are two tests everyone must take when their status page first appears. The first is the psych assessment. Wherein they make sure you will be able to mentally handle and cope with what happens on the other side of a portal.

"Since you are here, obviously, you all passed that portion. Those who don't are either relegated to becoming miners or are marked as unfit, at which point they continue with their normal lives and can forget about becoming a traveler of any kind."

The class nodded along, as this part was common knowledge.

"Now, the second test is the compatibility test, which is where they decide for a second time if you are fit to be a traveler or a miner."

"What's the difference between being a traveler and a miner?" A student interrupted. The nobles and richer students all snorted at the question.

"Don't be rude," Quinn cautioned them. "It's actually a better question than most of you realize. Fundamentally, there is no difference, as both groups go through the portal, and depending on need, can perform the same function. Consider it in similar regards to a job. The miners do exactly that. They mine for the mana crystals located in deposits inside the portals.

"The Travelers," He emphasized the word so they would know there was a difference. "Are the ones who keep them safe. Their main function is to battle any monsters or beasts that appear. Along with exploring the area and picking up any loose crystals or those dropped by the monsters."

He stood and picked up a marker, walking over to the whiteboard as he continued. "Getting back to the question at hand and how the compatibility test determines which you will be is a matter of math." He began to write on the board. "What I'm about to go over and explain is not exactly common knowledge, even if it isn't restricted, so I want all of you to pay close attention. When I am done, you will understand why those of you who have higher test results are considered as being worth more."

The students all leaned forward, paying no attention to their status or how the action looked.

"Every time you defeat a monster or beast inside the portals, you gain something called 'Experience'. Don't bother asking how this works as people who are far smarter than you or I have been working on it for years and still don't have an answer. In any case, this experience is what allows you to level and grow in strength, or speed, or whatever the class you get requires. We'll cover 'Classes' another time."

Quinn studied the board for a second and then stepped to the side so everyone could see what he had written. "Now, for the sake of simplicity, let us assume the monster that you just slew gives a flat one-hundred experience. Your compatibility score determines how much of that hundred experience you actually get. As far as we have been able to determine, there are seven tiers." He glanced at Zack. "However, I'm sure that number will soon change to eight."

"If your result was between one and nine percent compatible, then you only get point-one percent of that total. In other words, at the absolute bottom tier, you get next to no experience, and it is better for you to be used as a miner. Really, anyone who scored below sixty percent or tier four is better off as a miner." He pointed to the board where all the tiers were written out.

The Seven/Eight Tiers

8. $100 = 1?? = 100??\text{exp}$

7. $95\text{-}99 = .9 = 90\text{exp}$

6. $90\text{-}94 = .8 = 80\text{exp}$

5. $80\text{-}89 = .7 = 70\text{exp}$

4. $60\text{-}79 = .6 = 60\text{exp}$

3. $30\text{-}59 = .5 = 50\text{exp}$

2. $10\text{-}29 = .3 = 30\text{exp}$

1. $01\text{-}09 = .1 = 10\text{exp}$

"I shouldn't need to explain this, but I will, just in case. The more experience you receive, the faster you grow and level up. Which is why the cutoff exists. Those people just grow too slowly for the effort involved."

"What happens to the rest of the experience, then?" Zack asked, speaking up for the first time since class began. "If someone is only absorbing part of it, where does the rest go?"

Their teacher shrugged. "We have no idea. Maybe it goes towards birthing new monsters or maintaining the portal. It's another of those questions that we currently have no explanation for."

"Wait, if tier eight is for someone with one-hundred percent compatibility, what did he score on the test?" Spencer asked, a look of dawning understanding shining in his reluctant eyes.

The class turned to look at Zack again.

Quinn shrugged a second time. "The test stops at one-hundred. They have never had anyone score that high before, let alone above it. For all we know, Zack could be above that number. It is theoretically possible for him to get one-hundred and fifty percent. In which case even more, tiers would need to be added."

The reaction to that announcement was mixed. Some students suddenly wanted to get closer to him, while others saw him as someone that could someday jeopardize their families standing. After all, for one person to rise, another must fall.

Quinn looked up at the clock and clapped his hands. "Alright, that's all we have time for at the moment. Leave all your stuff here and make your way down to the training field I showed you all yesterday. You have ten minutes to get down there, select your outfits, and then changed into your training gear. That means GO!" He yelled when nobody moved.

***

Rose Carter, Quinn's wife, was waiting for them when they arrived at the training field. Beside her stood specialist Jean McCleary. Both were dressed in padded training gear and formfitting outfits that would keep them from overheating.

Rose nodded to Jean and then turned away.

"Due to recent complications with Rose's voice, it has been decided that I will be helping her teach this year. In practice, you will find that she will be in charge of the training exercises, while I do pretty much all the talking. You may call me Jean or instructor McCleary. Now go get your gear and get changed. Class begins in five minutes. Any who are late will be running extra laps around the academy grounds!"

Zack was the first to break away and run for the changing rooms. He had seen her angry the night before and had no intentions of being the last one on the field. Doing that would ensure her ire was directed at him more than any other.

He didn't believe he would be able to find and change into his training outfit and gear in the time she had mentioned. There was, however, some amount of safety in numbers. None of the other kids in his class would make it in time, either.

Only Testarosa was waiting on the field when he ran back out six minutes later.

The uniform was a simple, stretchy affair that was made to be easy to put on and keep the wearer cool. The safety gear, which was just glorified pads, had taken longer to put on than the outfit.

Jean was glaring at her watch as she waited by Rose's side. "You both were late. However, as the first to arrive, Tessa will run one lap around the academy grounds. Zack will also do one, followed by a lap around the training grounds. Everyone after this will do even more."

Tessa shared a look with Zack, and together they set off at an even, sustainable pace. No words were spoken as they jogged next to each other. It was better to save their breath for later. Behind them, the rest of the class stretched out into a line as they, too, were ordered to run laps of ever longer lengths.

Zack was glad he hadn't gotten up earlier to run that morning. He was still lacking in stamina, as all the nutritious food he ate went to rebuilding his damaged muscles. It wasn't until they had started eating better that he realized how far their bodies had fallen.

Tessa peeled off to the side as they circled back to the training grounds. He continued on for the rest of his run.

Jean and Rose came over to him when he returned, gasping for breath. They had a critical look in their eyes as they poked at the muscles in his legs and briefly had him lift the corner of his shirt. They politely ignored the myriad of scars on his arm when they rolled up the sleeve and studied the loosely defined muscles he had been working to regain. Unfortunately, for now his ribs were still the predominant feature.

"It looks as though you used to have some decent muscle mass, but it all faded from disuse or lack of proper nutrition," Jean said as Rose pulled at his skin, testing its elastic properties. "Stay after class has ended and we'll give you a large box of nutrient bars. They should help speed along your recovery and get some muscle back on your bones."

He sat on the dirt ground of the training ring and waited as the two teachers repeated their process with each student. It was a quick inspection that let them judge the condition of each person. Unlike with Zack, all of the other students had been properly fed. While some of them may not have been in the best shape, none were as weak as him either.

Rose trotted off to the side of the field when they finished inspecting everyone. A shed and overhang were placed out of the way, concealing the wooden weapons they would be using to train.

"Everyone, stand up!" Jean commanded to a round of groans. "Since we won't know what your class will be until next week when you go through the portal. Part of this week will be spent familiarizing each of you with the more common weapons used. Swords, bows, staffs, and more. You will be spending time with each. We don't expect you to be proficient with any of them by the end of the week. Frankly, if you can hold one and not hurt yourself, that will be enough."

Rose returned with an armload of weapons, that she carefully placed on the ground in front of the students.

"The rest of the time, when you are not playing with wooden weapons, will be spent with Rose or instructor Carter, depending on her mood. She will be covering your martial art training, ensuring that you can at least defend yourself if something happens to your weapon."

Half the class went with instructor McCleary and the weapons. While the other half went to a different part of the field with Rose. Zack, of course, went with Rose; he had no reason to learn how to use a sword or bow. Unless something changed when his status came back and he reawakened, he would be a magic-user.

Same as the first time.

It was pointless anyway. With the current malnourished state of his body, and their recent exercise sapping what little strength he had. Holding a weapon, regardless of how light they may or may not be, was asking for too much.

Not that learning martial arts was likely to be any better.

Still, he followed after the silent woman and pushed his body to keep going for as long as he could. Sweat stained his training uniform, and the other students were looking at him oddly when class ended hours later.

"You should get changed and go get some food," Rose informed him after the rest of the class had dispersed for lunch. She was sucking on a lozenge for her throat, and her voice was less raspy than it had been the day before. She dropped a box of the nutrient bars beside him and then left.

"You're going to have to work harder than everyone else to regain your lost muscle mass," Jean said, pulling him to his feet.

He gave her a slight, cryptic grin and shook his head. "No, I only have to last the week."

She tilted her head in puzzlement but didn't pursue the odd remark.

The cafeteria was packed with students from all the different years. Each class got out at different times, in an effort to stagger the rush for food. It was a measure that tended to only become effective after the first few days of the school year. Before then, the teachers were still adjusting to their classes. Some would be let out early and others late during that adjustment period.

Zack didn't need to worry about bringing food back for Zara, as Edith was nice enough to feed her lunch. Carrying a plateful of food on top of the box in his arms, he selected a spot in the corner of the large eating area. There were few students in that spot since it was far away from the food. He didn't recognize any of them.

The topic of conversation among them all was the local orphan boy and his little sister. The sides seemed to be split down the middle on how they felt. Some didn't appear to care either way, not believing that the duo mattered. The other half felt the same way his noble-born classmates had that morning.

He wondered how long it would take for the news to come out that he was also the record holder? More than that, he wondered if it would affect how they saw him and his sister. The shift in his classmate's thinking had been readily apparent. Most had become neutral and curious, willing to wait until later to form an actual opinion. The rest hadn't hesitated to form a negative opinion of him and what they believed he represented.

Zack expected the rest of the student body to form similar opinions.

Keeping his head down, he ate his food and hurried back to the classroom with the box in hand. A different teacher than Quinn was busy writing down numbers on the whiteboard when he arrived.

He muffled a groan as he saw the equations being written out. Math. It was one of the subjects Edith was going to begin tutoring him on later that day.

He knew the basics and could even multiply to a degree. Everything past that had gone over his head.

It had been a cascading loss of knowledge, one that was clearer with math than any other subject. With most of the topics they were taught, it had been fine to miss a class or two. That was not the case when it came to numbers. It was a discipline that constantly built on what had been taught before.

Once he fell behind, it was impossible to catch up.

Despite that, he was determined to learn. Even if he couldn't understand any of what was taught now, in time, with Edith's help, that would change. Until then, he would take copious notes and keep his head down if possible.

As long as none of the teachers created problems for him, then everything would be fine. It was a stupid hope; he knew.

Chapter 10

Zack had his hopeful expectations of the teacher being nice, over-turned within minutes of the class starting. Jab after jab was made at him, about how the poor orphan boy wouldn't be able to understand what he was teaching. Unfortunately, he couldn't even say anything since it was the truth.

Not because he was dumb or slow, he had just never been taught the preceding material.

"Now, for those of you who have actually been taught math in the past, this should be an easy problem to solve." The teacher droned on while continuing to make unsubtle digs at one of his students. "Now, would anyone like to show us the proper steps involved?" He didn't even bother to look around as his eye zeroed in on the student sitting quietly at the back. "How about you, orphan Zack, would you be willing to show us?"

"Nope," Zack replied with an unforced yawn. "You're the one getting paid to teach, not me."

The teacher flapped his mouth open and closed in shock, apparently never having had a student refuse or talk back before.

"Can we move on?" Tessa asked from her place at the front of the class. "He's right, you're paid to teach us this material. Nothing more." She was getting angry with the teacher at that point.

He gave them a slight mute nod, and then the teacher turned back to the board and continued with the lesson.

Dutifully, Zack kept his head down, and simply copied everything that was said or written on the board for later. Every time he was asked to solve an equation, he would lean back and stare at the teacher without responding.

Eventually, the other students in the class began to speak up and deride the teacher. He was wasting their time by drawing attention to someone who clearly didn't care! Finally, with a face flush with embarrassment, the teacher finally stopped picking on Zack and continued with the lesson.

The entire episode had shifted several of the student's opinions of him. For the ones who had been on the fence about his existence, now they had tipped over and were against him. It seemed his classmates had lost sight of the larger picture.

It didn't bother Zack overly much as he ignored them all and continued on with his day. It was no different from what he had been expecting or gone through before. If he was being honest with himself, then it stung a little that everyone was so quick to choose sides. It was a portion of student and teen life that he had never properly understood.

Why would you put so much energy into something that didn't matter? Maybe it was just to him that it didn't matter, and things were different for those who had money?

He had no idea, and no one seemed willing to explain it to him.

After math, Quinn came back into the room, a large rolled-up poster tucked under his arm. "Don't go putting away your notebooks just yet. We are going to be discussing the basics of the portals and what you can expect on the other side. This is information that, while mostly common sense to a traveler, doesn't get spoken of much by others. Taking notes is encouraged."

He pinned the poster up across the front of the whiteboard and let it unfurl. A second poster dropped into his waiting hands, which he also quickly pinned by the side of the first. Monsters and beasts of different kinds were drawn on both. Next to each image was a simple description of their characteristics and elemental, if any, affinities.

Quin stepped to the side and frowned as he looked out over the class. "I doubt those of you in the back can properly see what is written. Either move your desks closer or come sit on the floor."

After a moment of confusion, all the desks at the back moved a couple of feet forward. Which prompted everyone else to move as well.

"Now I need to give you all a quick warning about what we will be going over this week. Most of what you will be learning does not apply to the school's portal, as it is a very isolated location on the other side. That said, outside of certain special portals like ours, this information will be particularly useful. I had some students complain last year that what I was teaching them didn't apply to the portal when they went through."

He sneered and smacked the posters. "Unfortunately for them, they didn't listen, and when they were brought to a different portal for training over the break, they died." He smirked. "It was so sad, and I was very heart-broken over their extremely preventable deaths. So, don't go, making me all sad and teary-eyed by dying. Instead, just listen and learn like you are supposed to." He obviously wasn't.

"Shouldn't you actually be sad or something?" A student asked hesitantly.

"No, I've seen plenty of people die before. A lot of them were torn apart right in front of my eyes. The fact of the matter is that any traveler who attends an academy has a better chance of living longer than the ones who don't. I see no reason to get all teary-eyed and sad over someone who squanders their chance to learn. I am a teacher, and while I do it to the best of my ability. I can not force any of you to learn."

The class was silent as they digested his speech and the meaning it contained.

Quinn coughed and directed their attention to the posters. "Moving on. I will cover in detail what you will find inside the school's portal before you enter it next week. This is just a broad overview of what can be found in them as a whole. You will find over your time as travelers that portals can change in different ways over time. They often seem to specialize in a certain kind of monster type or environment. All of that can change."

He looked around the classroom and shook his head. "I was going to show you on a map, but there isn't one in here. Anyway, I know of a portal where when you went through it, you would end up on a beautiful island paradise. Soft sand, blue skies, the works. There were monsters, of course, that kept it from being an actual paradise. The fish had teeth, the crabs and lobsters had shells that could deflect a sword blade and pincers that could crush a person. Then there were the beasts inside the trees." He trailed off for a moment before refocusing on the class.

"The location of that portal changed gradually over time. During the course of about a year and a half, it went from being in the tree line to the beach, and then inside the water. No one can go through the portal now, as the other side deposits them deep inside the ocean. Our bodies can't handle the sudden change in pressure."

"It's just one of the many things we don't understand about the portals and how they work. They never seem to move location on our side, so why would they move on the other? It ranks right up there with why a lot of our tech doesn't work. Guns using chemical reactive agents don't fire, and anything that uses mana-tech stops working after just a few minutes.

"They have to be repaired when they come back through. Trust me, over the years, people smarter than anyone in this room have tried every way imaginable to make it safer for everyone inside the portals. No matter what they came up with, none of it ever worked for long. Each time we would always come back to the old standbys of weapons we had moved past. Bows, swords, martial arts, and, for the lucky, indispensable few... magic."

He scratched at the short hair on his head and gave the class a wry smile. "Sorry, I seem to be getting distracted a lot today. At least this is all useful information you would need to know in the future. One last random tidbit and then we'll get back to the topic I actually meant to cover today."

Quinn limped away from the board and back to his desk. "How many of you know about the time limit inside the portals?"

Zack and a few others raised their hands.

"Zack, why don't you explain it to everyone who doesn't know what it is?"

"The time limit is how long any person or object they bring with them is allowed to stay inside the portal. After twelve hours, no matter where they are inside, alive or dead, they and everything that came in with them is ejected from the portal. Although, from what I understand, they can pass off weapons and armor to another traveler if they want to leave them inside."

Quinn looked at him curiously. "That is exactly right, and a far better answer than I was expecting from anyone in this class. Very few people that aren't travelers or working closely with them know or even remember three of the items you mentioned. Especially that last one. All items, and the dead, regardless of location inside, get ejected after the time limit. It can make the area outside the portal very crowded and gory at times. As I'm sure you can all imagine. However, as he mentioned, weapons, armor and other items can be passed off to another traveler already inside the portal."

"Is that a time limit that affects each person or the group as a whole?" Tessa asked, looking up from her notebook.

"If I understand what you are asking correctly, then you are wondering if the time limit is the same for everyone when they enter as a group?"

She nodded.

"Then no, each person would be ejected depending on when they went in, instead of as a group. Most corporations will stagger when people are allowed to go inside, so the area outside is never suddenly filled up with a large group. And before anyone asks, yes, it is a hard limit that affects absolutely everyone and everything. All those stories you've undoubtedly heard about travelers who never came back were lies made up by the company they worked for. They tend to use that as the go-to excuse whenever a particularly gruesome body is returned."

"Okay, that's enough of that. Getting back to the posters, you will see that the first one contains the twelve different kinds or types of monsters you might encounter. They all fall under one of those twelve types in some way, and there are countless variations for each."

At the top of the first poster was a dark blurry image, and a name next to it. Nightmares.

"Now, in no particular order, since I am not the one who made this poster. We will begin with the 'Nightmare' type. As you can see, there isn't really an image, and that was done on purpose. Nightmares are exactly that, monsters that can only be described as coming out of your worst nightmare. They have no place in a natural habitat or eco-system and are extremely hard to deal with as they are also generally somewhat intelligent."

"Next we have the 'Beast' type, which is easily the most numerous of any other kind on this list. They can be found in nearly every portal to my knowledge and are exactly as the name describes. They are beasts or animals that have mutated and or, grown stronger and become more vicious than normal. As I mentioned before, with the crabs and lobsters, this can happen to any kind of animal you can imagine."

"Continuing on, we have the 'Celestials'. This is a type that is a kind of odd, and not often encountered. They can take the shape of any type on this list except for nightmares, and fiends, which I will get to in a minute. Celestials can be easily distinguished by the golden glow that surrounds them. As long as you don't attack them and are injured, they will often heal you. Attack them, however, and they kill you and only you. They don't attack indiscriminately."

"Wait, you mean there are monsters that we shouldn't attack and kill?" Spencer suddenly burst out.

"Yes, that is what I am saying. There are actually a couple of different types that you shouldn't attack. Which interestingly enough, plays into the next type on the list, 'Dragons'."

The image next to the name was of a large flying monster with powerful jaws and sharp teeth.

"Dragons can fall into several different sub-categories, and we'll cover them in a few weeks. Some are stronger or faster than others, some can use magic or breathe fire. Pretty much all you need to know is if you see one run, do not attack them. You will die if you do. High-level travelers may stand a chance of surviving the first hit if they are lucky. They wouldn't last past the second attack if they did. There generally isn't a good reason to risk your life like that. Unless you are on explorer's team, in which case I would still say run as soon as possible."

"Next we have 'Elementals'. These can be considered the spirits of the land and are rarely seen. The only way to damage them is through magic or destroying their physical body or tether point if you can find it. Generally, they are harmless to travelers and are curious by nature. They will only attack if you actively mine, or get too close to a territory they have claimed as theirs. You will notice that the image in the poster is indistinct, that is because they can come in a variety of shapes and sizes. The only constant is their ghost-like transparent properties."

"Mysticals," Quinn read the name aloud and then stopped, taking a moment to scratch at his head again. "These are an odd one on the list as there were actual legends about the race existing in our world prior to the appearance of the portals. That is true for a few of the beings on this list, but is most apparent with these. They are magical creatures straight out of our legends and folklore and tend to be on the small size." He held his fingers a couple of inches apart so they would understand the scope of the word small.

"They have only been found in a couple of portals that many believe to be linked in some way. Again, even after a hundred years, we know little about the portals, or the worlds, if that is what they are, on the other side."

"What do you mean, if that is what they are?" Zack was quick to ask.

"A lot of scientists and travelers don't believe that the other side of the portals lead to fully developed worlds. The most common theory is that they go to fragments of them, ones that somehow broke off. If you are ever inside one at night, take a look up at the night sky, and if you can, remember the position of the stars. Then take a look again the next night. The position, constellations, everything will be different. Not to mention that what we consider to be the natural laws and order of things holds little weight inside them. The mana-crystals that are mined one day have returned somewhat by the next. I don't need to remind any of you that crystals do not grow overnight."

The class broke out in noise as everyone began talking at once. Zack leaned back in his chair and thought about the name of his race, according to the status page. It was listed as 'Dimensional Child', and it was the same for Zara. The name and word meant nothing to them.

They had briefly researched all the variations on the name when they were first rescued. There had been nothing, and eventually, they had dropped the subject. It was better to be curious than risk drawing unwanted attention back to themselves. Now, he couldn't help but wonder if the name held the truth to what the portals led to?

"We only have five types left, which I'll make quick, and then you can all leave." The teacher informed the class in a loud voice, silencing them. "Good. Moving on, we have 'Fiends', which is an all-inclusive term for monsters that resemble, devils, demons, and the like."

"From there we have 'Monstrosities' who are the unholy offspring of a nightmare mixed with beast or fiend. I'm sure you can guess which is more dangerous. If there is a nightmare around, then there will also be monstrosities as they often act as their foot soldiers."

Quinn hurried onto the next monster on the poster and one that had a proper image next to it. The monster was a blue tear-drop-shaped jelly monster called a 'Slime'."Slimes are jiggly puffballs that are nice to have around as they will eat anything, trash, human waste, you get the picture. They are resistant to physical attacks and the experience they give is paltry. They are another of the monsters that will only attack if they are attacked first."

"The last two types are really self-explanatory. 'Plant' monsters are exactly that, plants that will attack anything that comes near them. They are fairly common, especially in portals that have a lot of vegetation."

"Finally, the last one is 'Undead'. You've all heard the stories I'm sure of walking skeletons, zombies, and the like. They aren't super common but do appear from time to time." Quinn smacked the second poster. "We'll go over that one tomorrow before you begin your training. During the rest of the year, we'll cover each type more in-depth. Zack if you would stay behind? The rest of you can now leave."

Zack gathered up his stuff and placed it and the box of nutrition bars on top of his desk while he waited.

"You asked some good questions in class today and surprised me with your answer about the time limit," Quinn said in opening as the last of the class fled through the door. "That's not what I wanted to talk to you about, though. I'm not sure what you did, but you managed to piss off the headmaster. Pretty much all the teachers that were never travelers are going to be giving you a hard time in order to suck up to him. I imagine some of the ex-traveler ones might as well."

"I know. I had been expecting it. My admittance resulted in his brother-in-law being fired, and I believe put under investigation." Zack informed him readily. The information would come out eventually, and it was always better to lead with your own narrative. At least, that is what he had been told by gang members in the past.

The teacher raised a brow. "What did he do to cause that?"

"He went around the area I lived blacklisting me from getting any work. Which would have prevented me from being able to feed my sister or myself. Then he also went to the local gang and made sure they knew about me and my compatibility result. The night before we left, the apartment was attacked." He stopped, not wanting to say too much. He couldn't risk saying anything that differed from what he had told the sergeant.

"That would do it for sure," Quinn sucked in a breath and shook his head. "The idiot should have known how serious it was releasing that kind of information, let alone getting you blacklisted. Wait, why did he do that in the first place?"

"I kicked him out of the apartment after he was rude to my little sister." With that, Zack picked up the box and walked calmly from the room. Behind him he could hear Quinn laughing.

Chapter 11

Z ara collapsed onto the couch when they returned to the dorm after Zack's tutoring session. "I had no idea you were so far behind on some of the subjects!"

It had been a shocking revelation to Edith and Zack as well. He had known there was a lot he had missed or didn't understand, just not to the degree reality had forced on him. With what they now knew, saying he was simply behind was disrespectful to the people a year or two behind him.

For the foreseeable future, he would have no social life. He would go to class, come back in the evening to study under Edith, and then at night, he and Zara would go out to work. His days would be packed, and that was more than alright with him. He didn't know any of the other kids, and they had little in common to form any kind of friendship on.

It was better to be busy than to spend extra time thinking about what wasn't there.

"Do you want to eat now, or just grab it and eat after work?" Zack asked as he sprawled out on the couch next to her, his legs trapping her in place.

"Will they let us do that?" She squirmed against his legs, George somehow managing to end up wedged between them.

"Yeah, I asked them this afternoon after classes. They don't mind if it's us, especially since we cleaned the dishes they gave us last night." He yawned and swung his legs off her. "I'm fairly sure that as long as we continue to be respectful and clean what we use, they'll give us more leeway than the regular students."

"I'm fine with just grabbing it for later, then. The less time I spend around everyone, the better it will be for us both."

It was a sentiment that Zack did not necessarily agree with. He wanted her to get out and make friends, to escape and break free of the shell she had surrounded herself with. At the same time, he understood that this academy was not the best place for that to happen. Not yet, at least.

Given enough time, he hoped that would change. For her sake, if not for his.

He couldn't remember the last time she had just played around with a friend, or other kids her own age. They both had been forced to grow up far quicker than they should have. As the older brother, it pained him to always see her alone, with only her bears for company.

Unfortunately, it was also not something that he could change or fix in the short term.

A little while later, after depositing the food back in their dorm, they were waiting inside the small brick building. Zack was regaling Zara with slightly modified tales of everything that had happened during the day. The person who was supposed to give them the info on the job they would be doing that night was late.

"That teacher sounds like a..." Her voice was suddenly muffled as Zack put one of George's paws into her mouth. He didn't like it when she cursed. It just seemed wrong to hear those words come out of her mouth.

He wasn't sure why that was? Especially when he considered the things she had said during their time as research subjects. There had been nights where she would graphically describe what she would do to the researchers if given the chance. He was no better in that regard. If anything, the things he had wanted to do were far worse.

Her eyes narrowed into thin slits as she carefully pulled the fluffy paw from her mouth.

The door to the building opened before she could say anything. The people they worked with and under tended to change each night as they were used to fill the gaps. Anyone that needed an extra hand, whether it was in cleaning or maintenance, had the chance to employ them for the night.

The siblings were supposed to accept any job offered if it was within reason. They weren't being forced to work; it was simply a mutual benefit to both sides. Strictly speaking, they were allowed to refuse any job they didn't want. In the first place, them working each night was for their benefit more than the academy's. A way for them to earn some much-needed money.

Up to that point, they had accepted a different job every night. During the last week or so at the academy, they had done everything from cleaning bathrooms to trimming the trees.

When that door opened, Zack had a feeling they would be refusing their first job. The math teacher who had taught his class earlier that day stepped into the room. He glared haughtily down at them, a sneer flickering across his very punch-able face.

"Ah, so the two helpers are you and your sister." He paused, as though expecting them to say something. He was visibly disappointed when they didn't. "Humph, well whatever. I have a job for the two of you. It should take a little over three hours-"

"No," Zack interrupted him. "We only work for two hours a night and don't accept jobs that take any longer than that. If we did, that would mean leaving a job only half-done which we could then be blamed for."

It was a lie. All of the jobs they had been taking would be completed by the regular staff in charge of those items. They were there to help the regular staff, not to replace them.

It was a convenient excuse, however, in this instance.

Zack didn't trust the man, nor did he believe he had good intentions. Without delaying, he pulled his sister to her feet and pushed her towards the door. "Looks like we have tonight off."

The teacher was still trying to understand what had happened when they pushed past him and left.

"Was that the teacher you mentioned in your story?" Zara asked once they were back safely in their dorm.

"Yup," He began spreading their dinner out on the table. "I don't believe for a second that he had good intentions with whatever job he wanted us to do." He sat down across from her. "I think we should avoid any jobs from teachers and staff like him."

She twirled her fork around a noodle. "Are we allowed to do that? Avoiding one or two jobs is probably fine, but what if it's a lot? Won't we get in trouble, or lose the opportunity to work altogether?"

"Would you rather we just do whatever they force on us?"

She shrugged, looking down at the plate. "I'm willing to put up with it, as long as they don't cross the line. No matter what, the job should only be hard labor, not anything else. Besides," She grinned and slurped a noodle into her mouth. "We know where they sleep and how to get into their residences. It wouldn't be hard to slip inside and find some way to make their lives miserable. A little itching powder spread over their bed and clothes, some missing notes, or misplaced items. Depending on how mean they are, we could even do worse."

Zack laughed, "If we did that, it would have to only be once, maybe twice, per person. Any more than that and we would risk getting caught and anything we decided to take couldn't be hidden in here. We would have to find someplace to store it that isn't linked to us."

The siblings had no problem with stealing from people they didn't like or that didn't treat them with basic respect. The life they had lived up to that point never allowed them the chance to develop the more traditionally respected morals. Zara's protestations to him working for the gang had been a direct result of that. Hurting people they didn't know and had no issue with was bad. Taking or hurting those they had an existing problem with was perfectly fine.

"We'll give it till next week, before deciding or making a move," Zack said as they finished the last of the food. "This could be our home for the next couple of years. Any moves we make of that nature need to be thought out and made carefully."

Zara agreed and helped him quickly wash the dishes. Afterward, they settled down to talk and relax for the night. They had nothing in the way of entertainment but each other. Homework and playing with the bears would keep them occupied until they were sleepy.

***

Quinn was waiting in the classroom the next morning when Zack arrived. As per his usual, he was among the first to show up for class. This time he had been beaten by Tessa, who was conversing with the teacher.

Sitting down at the back, he munched on a nutrition bar and listened in on the conversation.

"I understand that!" Tessa said in exasperation. "But it makes no sense. Why are we the only living things allowed through the portals, and why can't we bring back any parts of the monsters when they're already dead? I know travelers have eaten them on the other side before. Does the meat just vanish from their stomachs when they come back?"

"It depends on how digested the meat is," Quinn answered her honestly. "I have heard of people who suddenly toppled over with intestinal issues after coming back. They had eaten monster meat, and it didn't have enough time to digest. When they came back, it was indeed pulled from their stomachs."

"That's what I mean," The girl growled. "It makes no sense! All kinds of mana crystals can all be brought back. What makes plants, fruit, and the meat and other pieces of a monster so different?"

Quinn sighed and shook his head. "We don't know. As I keep telling everyone in the class, there is very little that we actually know about the portals. You would think that after a hundred years we would have made progress, and to a small degree, we have. Everyone seems to forget, though, that the portals are fundamentally different from everything we thought we knew before they showed up. All our sciences have had to be rewritten, new courses of study and thought created. The bulk of the progress that has been made in relation to them, have all come within the last few years."

The desk screeched as the teacher stood and stretched, his back popping loudly. "You should understand all of this better than me, in any case. What does your father say on the matter?"

She looked around at the question, her eyes lingering on Zack before responding. "He refuses to talk about anything regarding the portals with me until I go through for the first time. He also refused to let me go through one before the official school expedition."

"Good," Quinn pushed his desk back into position. "It would have been bad for someone in his position to break that particular law. The country has forbidden anyone from taking newly awakened teens through the portals. The only exceptions are when they go through as a class group. Like what happens at the other schools and academies, or if they are already employed by a corporation. Trust me, they monitor each group we take through for the first time rather closely. It would have been very visible and obvious if he or someone else had disregarded it."

Tessa folded her arms and sulked. "I'm aware."

Rolling his eyes at the suddenly childish action, Quinn moved over to the whiteboard and unrolled the posters. It was time to prepare for class.

Zack had his own thoughts on what they had been discussing, not that he could tell anyone about them. Only a few people knew that he had gone through the portals as a child. Without going through them in person, there was no way he could explain away what he knew.

It was easier and better to just say nothing in this case. He was sure there would be another chance to talk about the subject at some point in the future.

Quinn started speaking as soon as the last student was seated. "For those of you who can't read a calendar, today is Mittwoch. The middle of the week. That means after training and lunch, you will be going to the Mana Tech and Applications building. After the class there is done, then you will come back here for your final class of the day with me."

With that out of the way, Quinn directed their attention to the board and started right into the lesson. "Yesterday, we ended the class after talking about the twelve basic types of monsters. Today we are going to talk about affinities before you head off for training. Now, who among you knows what I mean when I say 'affinity'?"

Tessa and Zack both raised their hands at the same time.

"Interesting," The teacher nodded at them both, and motioned for them to lower their hands. "It's not that hard of a question and in recent years, the term has even made itself a part of the standard lexicon. In a fashion.

You should all be able to answer the question if you took the time to think about it."

"Some of you, I imagine, have an affinity for being cruel, stupid, lazy, etcetera. That would be the standard way the term is used by normal people. For us travelers, we use it slightly differently, especially when we are talking about monsters."

"When we mention affinities, we are talking about what element of magic the monster typically uses. This is generally fairly obvious but is also useful information. If you see a monster walking around with its back on fire, its affinity is probably fire. Either that or it pissed off a monster nearby with that affinity. What that tells you is that you need to be careful of flames possibly coming your way, or extra heat at the minimum. It also tells you that it is probably weak to water or ice-based attacks.

"Most travelers have an affinity towards a specific element as well. Generally, at the lower levels, all it will do is ever-so-slightly decrease the damage you take from that element. At higher levels, and if your affinity is high enough, you may even be able to infuse your attack with some of that essence. Your sword or arrow might become burning hot or ice cold.

"You get the picture. This does not hold true for everyone. However, some people have an extraordinarily high affinity with their element from the very beginning. Of course, the opposite is also true."

Quinn continued the lecture until it was time for them to leave for training.

***

"Those of you who have not taken the opportunity to explore the different weapons will be doing so today! The same goes for those who have not done any martial arts training!" Rose told the class as soon as they all showed up in their training gear. "The rest of you can split between the two groups as normal."

The grumbles of annoyed teens filled the air as they were forced to separate. Most of them had already made up their minds about what they wanted to use or do, despite the warnings of their teachers.

Zack shrugged and wandered over to the weapons. For most people, using and exploring the different weapons was a way to help them get a class related to the weapon they were best with. All of the nobles and even some of the regular, richer kids had clearly been trained on specific weapons since they were young. Despite not knowing if they could later become a traveler.

It had long since been proven that a traveler would typically get a class related to the weapon they were best with. At least in some fashion. The first class people generally got was a training class anyway. For most, it would be something like 'Warrior' or 'Archer', maybe even 'Monk', if they were good with the staff or their fists. Some of the luckier ones would get something better.

For the extremely lucky or possibly talented ones, they would get an odd class. Bloodline classes, also sometimes called family classes, were among those.

Then there were the aberrations, the ones who were completely outside the realm of normal. They were classes that operated by their own unique rules. Zack and Zara had once been part of this group. The way they had been forcefully pushed through the portals at a young age had changed them. The classes both received had been... different.

The first recorded case of an aberration-based class had happened twenty years after the portals first appeared. The man it happened to was reportedly a rather rotund, but otherwise extremely healthy individual. Upon entering the portal, he had been given the class 'Meatshield'.

Both he and his sister had possessed aberration classes centering around magic. To anyone who had asked, he had simply told them his class was a mage, and that Zara didn't have one at all. It was true to an extent, but also far from the whole truth. The aberration moniker was closer to reality for those classes than most would ever understand.

From his first day through the portals to his last, the only time Zack had ever used a weapon was when there were others nearby. Even at his young age, he had been smart enough to know their classes were different. That was all though, and as a result, he refused to use magic, whenever possible in a group. Using a spell, he shouldn't have known was too great of a risk.

Trailing his fingers over the wooden weapons in class that day brought back memories he had tried to suppress. He ignored anything he had used during those days. Instead, Zack found himself reaching for the weapon he had used since being saved.

It was a long pole, called a staff.

It was easy to make a rudimentary version of it. Even without training, the most ignorant person could still use it like a bat or a blunt cudgel.

Jean kept a close eye on Zack as he chose his weapon, noting how his eyes simply slid over the rest of them. It was as though using the others had never even entered his thoughts. It made her remember some of the rumors that had circulated inside the squad after the sibling's rescue.

There was one in particular that she had never paid much attention or thought to. It was so ridiculous and contrary to what they knew, that it was beyond silly to even waste time thinking about it. Yet at that moment, her mind remembered that rumor and combined it with some of the things the boy had said.

Was it possible that instead of simply being subjected to tests in conjunction with the portal, he had actually gone through it? It would explain a lot about the boy, and maybe even his sister. It could also be one of the reasons the Major had been interested in finding them again.

Zack looked back at her, feeling the inquisitive gaze, and held up the staff. "I'm going to practice with this one."

Chapter 12

Z ack groaned as he slumped over the lunch table and shoveled the food into his mouth at an angle. The teachers had informed them that basic conditioning exercises were how they were going to start ending each class. It had been a grueling workout that came after everyone had already exhausted themselves.

Tessa sat down across from him, her arms shaking slightly as she carried the plate of food.

He was sitting in the same corner and table as the day before. Once more, he had been sitting alone until she arrived. "You didn't want to sit with everyone else?" He asked, not shifting from his slumped position.

She shrugged. "What the teacher said is true. With your compatibility score, unless something untoward happens, you will come out on top. I figured it was better to get on your good side now when there are fewer people there."

Zack blinked and sat up straight. "That is kind of a cold, logical way of looking at it. Isn't it?"

She carefully brought the fork to her mouth, eating with the manners that only someone highborn would have known and bothered to practice. "Is it? It is certainly practical, and my presence will help you avoid trouble as well."

Zack looked around the cafeteria and shook his head. "Actually, I think your presence will cause me more issues than anything else. Up to this point, our classmates and others in the school have been taking their time forming opinions about me. Granted, there were a few who didn't like me from the start, then a few more who decided they didn't like me after our math class yesterday. Now, though, all the people who have been ignoring my existence have seen you sitting with me instead of them."

She tilted her head at him and then took in everyone staring at them. "Oh, I see what you mean." Tessa frowned and continued eating, her brows furrowed in thought. "Maybe this was not the best way to go about doing this. It might have served better to have this conversation at a more private location."

"Why are you talking like that?" Zack pushed his now empty plate of food to the side. "It sounds all stilted, and proper. I heard you in class before. I know how you normally talk."

She mewled softly and ducked her head, as a blush that matched her red hair spread across her face. "I talk like that whenever I am nervous."

He sat back in shock. "Why would you be nervous? I'm a nobody right now. Someday I may be someone with ability. That isn't the case right now." Zack wasn't looking down on himself, nor did he have low self-confidence. He was simply stating the facts. At that moment in time, he was still a non-entity.

"I am not familiar with many people our own age," Her voice dropped to a near whisper. "As I am sure you heard this morning, my father possesses a position where certain knowledge is easy to come by. I was taught by him and my uh, well, my mother until recently. They decided it would be better for me to socialize with people my own age before it became too late."

"Ah, I understand now. That explains why I always see people swarming around you, but you never seeming to talk to them. You're so nervous and awkward around everyone else that you chose to approach the person who was alone." Zack nodded and stood. "You could have just said that from the beginning."

Tessa blinked and shook her head. "That's not, oh whatever. I guess it doesn't matter."

He grinned at her sudden change in speech. He believed the reason she had given him about choosing to befriend him or at least become acquaintances. The reason he had given her, however, had been what calmed her down.

"Wait," She called out to him before he could leave. "My name is Testarosa Ricerca. It's a pleasure to finally make your acquaintance properly."

"I know. The teacher called you Tessa this morning." Zack looked down at the plate in his hands and then met her eyes. "My name is Zackary, no last name."

There were few things that embarrassed him as much as admitting that he had no last name. Telling people he was an orphan was simply a fact of life, it was something normal. People died and left their kids without parents.

Not having a last name was different. It set him and Zara apart, while also robbing them of part of their identity. Even orphans were given a last name if they didn't already have one when they entered their first orphanage.

For some reason, the siblings had never been given one. Another sign that someone near the top wanted them forgotten.

Tessa twirled her fork absently, "I'll meet you at the Mana Tech building as soon as I'm finished eating."

He appreciated how straightforward she had been with her intentions. It was easier for him to trust someone like that. Knowing he had been approached with an ulterior motive in mind was easier to believe than someone desiring a normal friendship.

He hurried off before she could say anything more. Zack wove his way through the crowded cafeteria, and outside after stopping to deposit the items he had dirtied. It wasn't until he had stepped through the doors and into the bright sun outside that he noticed he had been followed.

It was a group of five boys, with Spencer in the lead. Two of the bigger boys each grabbed one of his arms before he could react. Working together, they dragged him towards the nearest copse of trees, paying no mind to his struggling or raised voice.

The noble-born boy wasted no time in punching Zack as soon as they were clear of prying eyes. His weak, untrained fist twisted at the wrist and crushed the thumb he had placed inside the cocoon of his fingers. It was a perfect example of how not to form a fist, and how to then improperly punch someone.

It hurt Zack, but it hurt Spencer more. As a noble, he was used to a comfortable and soft life. He was ill-prepared for what would happen when he went through the portals. Despite his parent's words, and near-constant lectures. He had wanted to enjoy his life. Exercising or even doing more than the minimal studying and weapon training he had done went directly against that desire.

From the time they had grabbed him to that first ineffectual punch, none of them had said a word to him.

"What was that for?" Zack gasped out, the food he had just been eating threatening to come back up.

The two thugs gripping his arms pressed his back against a tree and held him there. With a look of disgust at the crying Spencer, a tall, handsome student he didn't recognize, stepped forward. The last member of the group had his back to them and was busy making sure no one approached the area.

"Do you know who I am?" The tall student asked him, with a calm, even voice. His dark brown eyes were steady as he watched the gasping boy. There wasn't a shred of sympathy or emotion in them. It was as though he was looking at something no more significant than a mere bug.

Zack shook his head, forcefully calming his roiling stomach with deep breaths. It was easy for him to ignore the pain from the weak punch and focus on the situation at hand. He'd had plenty of practice in that particular art. "Should I?"

"One should always know their betters and their place." A hint of cruelty twisted his face as he cocked his arm back and stepped into a full-force punch. Unlike Spencer, this noble knew what he was doing.

Zack gasped out as he felt a lower-rib bend and crack from the force of the blow. The thugs dropped his arms, letting him collapse as he vomited onto the dirt beneath the trees.

The teen crouched in front of Zack, outside the range of the foul-smelling puddle of chunks. "You should really chew your food more." He said disinterestedly, not caring that he had damaged the boy more than originally intended. "This is your only warning. Stay away from Tessa. She and her father will one day belong to my family. Until that day comes, I would prefer that she keep away from the disease-carrying peasants."

"She approached ME!" Zack gasped out.

"As if I care." The teen stood and straightened the sleeves of his uniform. "I am Dorn Albright, the eldest son of Duke Albright. I will be the one who someday takes over Albright Industries. Do you really think, even for a second, that the two of us are on the same level?"

Zack struggled to sit up, the fractured rib protesting against the simple movement. "I agree. You are not on my level. You never have been and never will be. I don't care if you want her. That has nothing to do with me! What you just did though, that was personal."

Dorn snorted in mock amusement and stood. "You have got to be joking. I'm not on your level? You must be even more delusional and stupid than I had heard." His foot shot out and hit Zack's jaw, knocking the already injured boy into the rough bark of the tree behind him.

He was unconscious before his body hit the ground.

***

The sky was dark when Zack finally stirred. His entire body ached and bruises he didn't recognize covered his body. Evidently, the boys hadn't left without beating on him some more.

His left eye was sealed shut with dried blood from where his temple had hit the tree. The lower teeth in his mouth felt slightly loose, and his jaw pulsed painfully with each beat of his heart. He was in rough shape, and there was nothing he could have done to prevent it.

The words he had said to the sergeant when they first arrived echoed in his mind. He couldn't help but laugh at his own ignorance.

Had he really believed, even for a second, that he could stand up to these people? They didn't play by any rules and had attacked him as a group. He had no power on this side of the portals, and fighting dirty meant nothing against a situation like he had just been in.

Zack rolled onto his back, nearly passing out from the pain, and draped his bruised arm over his eyes. Everything hurt, but the one that was damaged the worst was undoubtedly his cracked rib. Even rolling over just then had pulled at the muscles holding it place to an unbearable degree.

It took him over a minute to pull himself up to a stand position. It was more than enough time for him to mentally review his actions and everything that he had said. He couldn't help but think that his mouth might have gotten away from him again.

The things he had said, without a doubt, had made the situation worse.

He needed to go through the portal soon. It was the only way for him to regain a sense of control. Without that control, or at least the belief that he possessed it, his mouth was only getting worse.

He slowly tottered away from the small grove of trees, unsteadily making his way back towards the dorms. There was no telling how late it was, but it was late enough that the paths were empty of students. The warm night did little to dispel the growing chill he was feeling.

Zack was covered in a thick sheen of cold sweat when he pushed open the door to the dorm building a little later. Mentally, he was able to ignore the pain they had inflicted on his body. Physically, however, he was struggling to keep moving.

The constant tug on his injured rib and the general condition of his bruised body had made the brief trip unbearable.

A worried Tessa was sitting impatiently in the small waiting area near Edith's door. She sprang to her feet and knocked on the door as soon as he stumbled into view. A second later, Zara burst through the door and ran to her brother. Edith hurried through the door a moment after her.

"What happened?" Zara noticed how he was holding the area above his stomach and stopped just before she would have tackled him.

His face paled, and he collapsed in front of them.

Working together, the three of them carefully dragged him into Edith's and set about taking off his upper uniform. Zara protested the action a heartbeat too late. His shirt and upper jacket had already been removed by then.

Tessa stepped back with a gasp, while Edith's eye narrowed into thin slits. Scars that no person of his age should have littered the visible skin of his stomach and side. The pale surface was a canvas for the thin precision cuts of a professional, and the long-jagged remains of monster attacks.

Zara ignored the scars and went directly to feeling the ice-cold skin and muscles beneath the many bruises. She wanted to know why he had been holding that specific area. She was very familiar with her older brother's habits. He wouldn't have been paying extra attention to that spot if it wasn't something serious.

"Are you going to help?" She snapped at the dorm matron and teenage girl.

Tessa blinked gratefully, the girl's tone shocking her into action. She hurried to the kitchen to fetch some water and towels. Meanwhile, Edith opened a cabinet back by the door and pulled out a rather comprehensive first-aid kit.

"I watch over a bunch of rambunctious boys. Things happen. Constantly." She informed the young girl, who was looking curiously at the kit she was busy spreading out.

Carefully, Edith moved Zara's hand to the side and felt at the spot she had been concentrating on. "I can't say for sure, but the area around his lower ribs is all swollen. I think it might be broken or cracked at least." Her finger traced a specific bruise above the rib that was a different color from the rest. "I'm not sure what to do about that. I've never had to deal with an injury like this before."

"What about the academy nurse or doctor?" Tessa asked as she returned with a bowl of warm water and all the towels she could find.

"Call Jean McCleary first," Zara burst out before Edith could respond. "She will know what to do."

"The weapons training instructor?" Tessa was confused. What did their teacher have to do with the siblings?

The device Edith used to 'call' the teacher, and then the nurse, was based on a tech that had been invented shortly before the portals appeared. It was called a 'Speaking Graph' back then. The introduction of the mana crystals and then time had since changed and refined the idea.

The current iteration was called a 'CryTel' and consisted of two parts. The receiver, which was a metallic box with three sets of dials on the outside, and the transmitter which was held in the hand. Mana crystals were used to not only power them but also to form a connection between them and the device they were calling.

It was a luxurious, high-cost device that Zara and Zack hadn't seen until they arrived at the academy.

Zack was still out cold when Jean arrived a few minutes later. Her lack of reaction to the boy's many scars caused Edith and Tessa to raise their brows in shock. No matter who it was, those scars should have been a shocking sight. Her lack of visible reaction could only mean one thing.

She had seen them before.

Despite what the others believed, the scars had shocked her. She had always known they existed. Everyone in the squad knew about the scars covering both children when they were rescued. She had even seen some of them the day before with Rose, on his arms.

Despite that, they had always remained hidden from view, and now she knew why. A portion of those scars could only have come from the teeth and claws of monsters. Zack had indeed gone through the portal as a child.

Jean took over his treatment, muttering angrily the entire time. "Who did this to him?" She asked at last.

All three shrugged. They had no idea.

"Why are you here, student Ricerca? Last I checked, you live off campus!" Jean glared at her, not even hiding her suspicions that the girl had something to do with the attack.

There was a knock on the door right then that stopped her from answering. It was the nurse that Edith had also called.

The scowl on Jean's face grew worse, but she didn't stop the trained woman from approaching him. The secret of his many scars would get around eventually. If it came out now, it may even make some people hesitant to attack him. At least that was what she hoped as the woman gawped at them, her eyes filling with tears of sympathy.

"His ribs?" The nurse asked, after seeing how he had been wrapped.

"I think one of the lower ones is broken," Jean told her. "It has the typical bruising pattern, along with some swelling."

"You did a good job on the wrapping," She told them after inspecting it. "There isn't much for me to do for him at this point. I can give you some medicine for him to take, or we can bring him to the hospital for a closer examination."

"No hospital!" Zara told them firmly.

"Alright then, here are some pills for the pain, and a cream that will help the damaged skin to recover faster." She hesitated and dug through the bottom of her bag. "He can also use this if he wants, it might help the scars fade some."

"Thank you, nurse...?" Zara tilted her head; she had never gotten the nurse's name.

"You can just call me Nurse Godhand, Emily Godhand."

"Thank you, Nurse Godhand," Edith gave her a relieved smile and ushered her out the door.

Zara continued to clean the blood from his forehead while they waited for Edith to return. They had cleaned the clotted blood that was keeping his swollen eye shut earlier, but had also loosened the scab that had formed at the same time.

"I believe I asked you a question Ricerca," Jean's voice held a barely controlled fury as she glared coldly at the girl. "If I find out you had anything to do with this..." She let the threat dangle as Edith walked briskly in.

"I didn't, I swear! I approached him at lunch. We talked briefly and were supposed to meet up outside of the mana tech building for our next class. He never showed up, or to our last class of the day, with Quinn. I got worried and came over to see if he was here but was stopped by Ms. Edith and Zara. I've been here ever since."

"Do you have any idea who might have done something like this?" Edith asked her kindly, shooting a look at the teacher. "Has he made any enemies in the class that you know of?"

"Yes, and no," Tessa replied with a waver of her hand. "There are plenty of students who don't like him because of what he represents. As far as I know though, none of them hate or even dislike him enough to do this. He's quiet and keeps to himself for the most part. None of us have interacted with him enough at this point to have formed a grudge."

Chapter 13

Z ack woke slowly, his consciousness fighting to the surface of a pain-induced nightmare. His entire body was stiff and sore. To make matters worse, he was lying on an extremely uncomfortable, hard wooden floor. Standing above him, arguing, were three women of differing ages. Kneeling by his side, paying no attention to the argument above, was Zara.

"What's Tessa doing here?" He whispered to his sister. His voice pitched low enough that those above didn't hear him.

Her eyes crinkled with a hint of suspicion. "She says she was worried when you never showed up for class."

His head thumped lightly against the floor as he nodded in understanding. "Don't worry, she isn't the one who did this to me, not exactly anyway." He reached up and tugged on a strand of her hair. "Who'd you bring with you today, George or Zelda? Where are they?"

The bear, it turned out, was sitting on a chair in front of the table she had been using for schoolwork.

The other three finally noticed he was awake when Zara got up to fetch the bear so he could use it as a pillow.

"Who did this to you and why?" Jean demanded as soon as he was slightly more comfortable.

Zack took stock of his body before answering. "How bad is it?"

"Mostly superficial bruising across your entire torso and we are assuming legs, along with a cracked or broken rib," Edith told him.

He cursed and looked up at Jean. "How will this affect me going through the portal next week?"

"More than likely, Rose is not going to let you go through in your current state, and we can't hide this from her, either. The academy nurse was here a little bit ago."

Zack cursed again and leaned back in momentary defeat. He needed to go through that portal!

"It was Dorn Albright, that Spencer idiot Quinn hates, and some other kids," He recounted the entire event to them in a subdued voice, ashamed of his own inability to do anything.

"He said that my father and I will someday belong to his family?" Tessa asked, her eyes growing cold. "Just wait until my mother hears about that!" She gave a short, mirthless laugh and stood. "If you all will excuse me, it seems I need to have a chat with my..." She looked at the people in the room before finishing. "Parents. Zack, I'll see you in class tomorrow. I'm sorry this happened to you merely because I chose to sit at your table. I'll find some way to make it up to you." She tilted her head at Zara, and then the two others, before leaving in a rush.

Jean pulled a chair from the table close and sat down with a sigh. "This is going to be a problem."

"The Albrights?" Edith questioned.

"No," Jean waved away the name. "They are a concern, but not the problem." She glanced at the dorm matron with a frown, deciding how much she could say in her presence.

"Why don't I make a trip over to the cafeteria and get us all some food?" Edith proposed, catching on quickly.

"The problem," Jean began as soon as they were alone. "Is that Tessa is not an idiot, and neither are her parents. If she describes your scars, her father is going to have an idea of what caused them. He will be curious as a researcher. It's in his nature. Her mother, however, could ask questions that are better left alone. What's worse is that she has the resources and authority to get the information she wants."

Zara stepped in front of her brother, shielding him. "What kind of questions?"

"There was a rumor that went around the squad when we first rescued the two of you. It was one so ridiculous that we all just immediately laughed at the idea and forgot about it. We all knew that the researchers had used you in conjunction with experiments pertaining to their portal. The members of the squad all pictured them pushing you against the surface of the portal and doing something..."

She shook her head with a wry smile. "We had no idea how researchers worked back then. The rumor, though, was that you had actually gone through the portal and had the scars to prove it. We knew you had scars, just not the full extent of them."

Zack struggled to sit up with Zara's help. Leaning against George's now squashed body, he wiggled over to the couch. His skin had a fresh sheen of sweat by the time he finished moving the short distance. "And what do you think now?" He wanted to hear her say it before he confirmed anything.

She swallowed and looked at the jagged scars visible beneath the bandage wrap on his stomach. "Now, I think that rumor was right. They found some way to get you through the portal early."

"You should probably tell the sergeant and the Major what you have learned. Along with everything else about Tessa's family, and the nurse." Zack reached for his damp uniform shirt, cringing at the thought of putting the filthy thing back on. "They both already know the truth.

"They saw the scars firsthand back then. It was them who decided to hide the information from the rest of the squad and possibly the people above them. While you're at it, can you also ask them how they sealed my status page in the first place? I didn't even know that was possible until it happened."

"That isn't possible. We don't have any idea how they work, let alone know enough to seal them." Jean shook her head. "Wait, so does this mean that you already know what your class is going to be?"

He shrugged, regretting the movement immediately after, when it pulled at his rib. "Possibly. I was a mage-based class before. There is no telling if that will be the case this time. As far as I know, no one has ever awakened their status page and class twice."

"Hold on," Her eyes snapped to his. "What do you mean, mage-based class? Were you a mage or something else? How high was your level?"

He winced at the unintentional slip of his tongue. "I'll just say I was above level ten when we were finally rescued." Hopefully, that was enough to throw her off the trail.

Travelers got their 'Junior Classes' at level five, and 'Regular Classes' at level ten. The mage class went through several evolutions and changes during that time. It was unknown if the aberration classes would evolve at higher levels as the records pertaining to them had never gone above level twenty-four. It was hard to raise one's level to that point. Only a few travelers had ever gotten their 'Specialist Classes' at level twenty-five.

There was little reason for most to even try pushing their levels higher after a certain point. With the time limit and their need to guard the miners, few travelers ever even traveled into the depths of the portal where the stronger monsters were. More than that, unless their compatibility was high enough, the amount of work involved just became too high.

There were, of course, portals with stronger monsters near the entry-point, however, few corporations actively mined them. It made little sense to spend the money paying for higher-level travelers when the payout wasn't worth it. Those portals did contain mana crystals that were more valuable, true. That didn't mean anything when people died on each trip. There weren't enough travelers for anyone to be so cavalier about their lives.

It was left to the individual governments and their military to guard any portal deemed excessively dangerous.

She squinted at him and shook her head with a sigh. "Fine, keep your secrets. I don't actually care what your specific class and levels were back then. Still, they were able to discover a way to forcefully activate your status as a child. Why haven't we heard anything about it since? I know we took all the research materials we found at the location."

"What are you going to do now?" Zack asked, wincing as he shifted uncomfortably.

"I'm going to talk to the sergeant and the Major as you suggested," She said after a moment's thought. A conflicted look crossed her face as she continued. "This attack, while it may have been a small student's spat, is going to have lasting effects. Both on you and them. You understand what that means, right?"

"I know, and after I go through the portal next week, I'll know how much I need to worry." His voice was confident.

"I already said Rose may not let you go through in your condition," Jean paced around the room, her eyes flicking back to the siblings after every step. "This is why you were so confident and cavalier on the carriage ride over that first day. After you go through the portal, either you regain your class and level, or you reawaken as a different class. In both cases, you still have all the personal, hard-earned experience you gained hunting monsters and beasts before. You would quickly be able to raise your level and prove your worth."

"That was the basic plan, yeah," He agreed readily, impressed with her deduction skills. It wasn't the whole plan, or anything even close to that. He was holding too much information back for her to get a better picture than that. Still, she had gotten the general idea.

She stopped and looked up at the ceiling with a groan. "I'll do what I can to get Rose to let you through the portal next week with everyone else. You can't get into any more fights, or rather, I should say you can't get any more injured than you already are. Is that understood?"

He nodded, and she stomped her way to the door. "I'll see you in class tomorrow. Zara, make sure he doesn't do anything stupid." It was a command, not a request.

"How much did they see?" Zack asked his sister once they were alone.

"Just your chest and sides, but it was enough."

"Yeah," He agreed. "What do you think the odds are, Tessa, or the Nurse leak info about the scars?"

"I only spoke a few words with Tessa, so I can't say with her. For the nurse lady, however, I'd say one-hundred percent chance that she has already told at least one other person."

He chuckled dryly, and using the couch and her arm as support, struggled to stand. It was nearly impossible to complete the simple maneuver without his injured rib protesting.

Edith returned with her arms full of food to find him trembling in pain and his damp uniform shirt hanging from his shoulders. Zara was standing by his side, George held tightly in her arms and a worried look on her face.

"Eat first, and then I'll help you back to your dorm." She placed the covered bowls on the table and helped him into a chair. "Honestly, the two of you should learn to rely on people more." She shook her head as soon as the words left her mouth, already regretting them. "Sorry, I know you have never had anyone in your lives that you could rely on. That has changed. There is me, and Jean," She looked sideways at Zack. "And maybe even a certain striking red-head?"

"Let's not get ahead of ourselves here, Edith. The only thing she has going for her at the moment is how frank she was with her intentions when she approached me over lunch."

"What about her staying here waiting for you?" Zara asked, handing out the utensils. Even the worry she felt for her brother did little to dampen her excitement over good food.

"I... admit that does count for something." He pushed some more food towards his sister's plate, her eyes lighting up at the sudden extra. "I just can't say for how much at the moment."

"She seemed nice enough," Edith quickly joined them in eating before it was all gone. "All I will say on the matter is to be careful. The nobles all view things differently than us common folk. The best of them take a long view on life and work towards increasing their wealth and power. They help those who have helped them. The worst, tend to take a more short-term view on things. They take constantly from everyone and eliminate anyone who gets in their way."

"What about our work?" Zara asked as the trio walked slowly down the hall to the dorm.

"I left a message at the central administration office while I was out. It shouldn't be a problem normally. With the headmaster and some of the others going against you... I can't say for certain what the outcome will be." Edith kindly explained without judgment.

***

Zack woke to find Zara curled up next to him. The stuffed form of Zelda had been placed between them to protect his injured side and stomach.

She had refused to leave his side after they got back from Edith's the night before. It had been a few years since she had seen him so visibly injured. The sight had awakened memories better left forgotten.

Laying still on his back, he gently poked at the skin beneath the bandage wrapping his stomach. The swelling had gone down some during the night, leaving only the tender, multi-colored skin behind. For the briefest of seconds, he was tempted to just stay in bed for the day, recovering. If he did that, then his chances of going through the portal with everyone else really would be gone.

It was a chance he was unwilling to give up.

Gingerly, and with careful movements, he slid from the bed and made his way into the bathroom. The tall mirror inside giving him his first unobstructed view on the state of his body. Everything had mottled together in different colors that drew the eye.

The scars on his stomach and upper thighs stood out in sharp relief in ugly, jagged red lines. The skin around them was particularly tender as he stood beneath a heated shower. The constant stream of hot water was a luxury both siblings enjoyed indulging in on a daily basis.

The heat helped soothe his aching muscles enough for him to carefully get dressed. He kissed Zara on the cheek and hurried out the door. She needed the extra sleep after staying up so late looking after him.

Zack ignored the looks he got in the cafeteria. The large bruise occupying the entire bottom of his face, and then again by his hairline, had them all gossiping. Each bite was a painful experience, blending in with the agony each movement caused his chest.

His body had grown soft and weak since they were rescued. It was no longer accustomed to the constant pain he had known for years before. Still, a single night of being forced to lie still on his back was enough to remind him of how he had coped before. From there, it was relatively easy to ignore the constant pain. The shooting pain that every breath or movement of his jaw caused was another matter. Those took concentration to ignore.

It was enough for now to keep him functioning and coherent enough for school. Or at least he hoped it was.

Quinn was waiting for him when he reached the otherwise empty classroom.

"I heard from Jean about what happened." He reached out and tilted Zack's head, inspecting the visible bruising. "Are you going to be okay for classes today?"

Zack kept his eyes and voice calm while giving a small shrug. "Does it matter? I still have to go to them all anyway."

"It would certainly be better if you did," Quinn agreed, pulling his hand. "Just do your best, and feel free to leave if it gets too distracting."

Nodding, Zack went to his seat and stiffly sat down. He knew he wouldn't be leaving; it wasn't an option regardless of what the teacher had said.

Tessa never showed for the morning classes, neither did Spencer, and the period passed quickly with Quinn droning on about some general knowledge of the portals. It would have been interesting if he hadn't already known all of it beforehand.

Rose and Jean were waiting for him by the training fields before the next class. Rose sucked in her breath at the sight of his face and looked sideways at her fellow teacher. "He will still be too injured to safely go through the portal next week." Her voice was as raspy and rough as ever.

"Regardless, he needs to go through either then, or before, if that is possible," Jean rebutted without hesitation.

Rose looked at her with searching eyes, and then back at the injured student in front of them. Her lips moved to the side as she bit at the front portion of her cheek in thought. "Go get changed. I can't make a decision now in any case."

Zack struggled to put on a strong face throughout the class, taking each movement slow and as precise as he could make them. He failed to fool anyone for longer than a few minutes. The amount of sweat pouring from his training uniform gave away how hard each move was for him.

Jean pulled him to the side near the end of class. "Will going through the portal really make a difference for you? Mage classes don't have healing abilities at the lower levels, those are restricted to the purely healer-based classes. I doubt I need to tell you how rare those are."

Zack gratefully took the moment to relax the stressed muscles in his core. "It's not a matter of my class." He hesitated, not sure of how much he should reveal, before deciding it didn't matter. This particular item would get revealed sooner or later regardless. "I have an ability from before. It showed up again when my status came back. It's called 'Life Burner'. It burns my life force and turns it into magic I can then use to fuel spells."

"Okay," She leaned back in amazement. "That ability sounds incredible, but what does it have to do with healing?"

Zack grimaced. She was right. It was an amazing ability... for any normal class. All aberration classes came with steep limitations, and his came with one that made it almost unusable if it wasn't for that exact ability.

"The ability comes with a passive healing effect of sorts. Whenever I am on the other side of the portals, I tend to heal faster. It helps to offset the damage the ability does to my body. I know I said it burns my life force, but that isn't quite right. It's more like it burns a portion of my soul, or some kind of ghostly, astral version of my body every time. It affects me physically in different ways depending on how much I use the ability."

She blinked in horrified understanding. "No wonder you can so easily work through the pain of your injuries."

He snorted and gave her a thin smile. "The two are less related than you would think, and now you know why I want to go through as soon as possible. The sooner I go through, the sooner I will be healed."

She looked around the training area. "We're not done with this, but if what you said is the truth, then I may be able to get you through the portal early."

Chapter 14

Zack skipped math class after lunch, instead choosing to go back to the dorm and study with Edith and Zara. He would gain nothing from attending any taught class by that pompous windbag of a math teacher from before. In his current state, he was having a hard enough time keeping his mouth in line. It would be all too easy for that teacher to get under his skin.

It was smarter to avoid that situation altogether, a decision that both Edith and Zara agreed with. He went back in time for the last class of the day with Quinn, by which point his energy was beginning to flag. It hadn't even been a full day since he was injured, and his body was protesting at the abuse it had suffered.

"Today we are going to cover the way 'Classes' work." Quinn was sitting on the edge of his desk in what they had come to understand was his preferred position to teach. "One of you get up here to write things down on the board."

He pointed to a random student in the front row, a female who was sitting next to Tessa's empty seat.

"Just write down what everyone yells out," He instructed her. "Now, who can tell me the various classes travelers can get?"

"Mage."

"Warrior, Champion, Knight."

"Archer, and Hunter."

"Rogue, and Assassin." One of Spencer's cronies spoke up with a smile, leaving no doubt in anyone's mind as to the class he wanted.

"Bloodline and Aberration," Zack spoke up, stealing the spotlight and silencing everyone.

Quinn looked up at those and nodded. "Good, now setting aside bloodline classes and the like for a later class. Can you tell us what the first recorded aberration class was and why they differ from the more regular classes?"

"There are two common differences aberration classes possess. They are typically very strong and very weak at the same time. They are built around a single goal. Take the first recorded instance of an aberration class. It was called 'Meatshield' and gave its traveler unparalleled defense and vitality. That would be its strength, its weakness, however, was that his class did not allow him to put any points to dexterity or agility. Every movement he made was slow and laborious. From what I understand, his teammates took to rolling him around like a ball because it was faster."

"Correct. Each aberration-based class is built around extremes. High power, speed, defense, etcetera, but they always have an equally prevalent weakness. You may get superior speed, but limited vitality, or super strength and no dexterity." Quinn looked at the student in front of the board and nodded.

Zack felt his mind drifting after that, and the rest of the class passed in a blur.

He had a slight fever by the time he went back to Edith's to retrieve his sister. Every thought was blurry and felt like it was being forcefully dragged out.

Zara dragged him into the dorm matron's small apartment with a worried expression. Edith was quick to check him over and discover his fever, placing a cool towel on his forehead a minute later. She left him on the couch and pulled Zara to the side to play an old board game while they waited for him to recover.

Jean knocked on the door a while later, her arms full of food. "Are they here? I tried at their dorm first, but there was no answer."

Zara peeked out from behind the older woman and motioned the soldier turned teacher inside. "He has a fever."

"I was afraid of that. He wasn't looking good earlier during training. I came to get Zack, so I could bring him to get some proper healing." She winked stealthily at Zara.

"Where are we going?" Zack muttered incoherently, the words blurring together as he was pulled to his feet.

Edith had already stacked the food on her table. "When do you expect to have him back?"

"That'll be up to how long it takes to undergo some proper healing. Do you mind watching Zara until then?" Jean knew how important his sister was to him and made sure to not forget her.

"Of course, she will always be welcome with me." During their time together, Edith had grown especially close to the young girl. It was an achievement that few could ever boast with the near infinitely distrustful Zara.

Zack's eyes were half-lidded with fever as he walked unsteadily by Jean's side. She pushed him into the backseat of her Alberitas carriage and closed the door with a shake of her head. Ignoring his grunt of pain as his ribs hit the cushioned bench. Just from her briefly touching him, she could tell how feverishly hot his skin had become.

It was becoming increasingly clear to her that all of them had severely underestimated how injured he was. It had been so easy to buy into his act that they had failed to look at him properly. How many people, let alone kids, could get up and walk around with an injured, possibly broken rib. She could only think of one or two soldiers who might be able to do that and still go to school the next day. All the while acting like nothing was wrong.

His actions had led them to believe the injuries were less severe than they truly were.

"Where are you tickling me?" Zack tried again from the back seat, his foggy mind refusing to focus on the words. "Tickling, taking, eating? One of those. I think?"

Jean bit her lips to keep from laughing and drove them away from the dorms. "I'm taking you to the portal, just like you wanted."

Zack blinked slowly, taking a long moment to understand her meaning. "Oh, that'll help. How did you get persimmons... permission?" He spoke slowly, making sure each word was the correct one, yet still managing to mess up once.

"I spoke to the Major and let him know what had happened. He said that he would be talking to the headmaster soon, but that in the meantime, he would make sure the school portal would be available for our use tonight."

That had happened faster than he thought it would. He had been expecting the mysterious Major to take a day or two to get the matter worked out, if at all. Obviously, the man had far more power over the academy and its portal than the sergeant had led him to believe.

Zack was barely coherent as they neared the complex containing the portal. Military personnel had surrounded the area and were preventing everyone from getting close.

Jean was waved through immediately, and they passed the gathering crowd of people without slowing. The building with the missing roof that contained the portal was empty, giving them a modicum of privacy. It would generate far too many questions if people realized that they had cordoned off the area for a single boy.

Unfortunately, in Zack's current state, the oddity of the situation wouldn't register until later.

"Come on, out you get." Jean carefully extracted him from the backseat and pointed him in the direction of the portal. "Are you ready for this?"

He took an unsteady step forward, his eyes shaking and refusing to focus. "This almost reminds me of the first time I went through a portal. I think I was in even worse condition then." He smiled sadly and took another step forward. "Are you going to use me like they did? I don't want to be dissected, not again!"

Jean peered at him askance, unsure of how much he was saying was the truth, and how much was fever-induced madness. "We're not going to dissect you. You have to be dead for that. I think, I hope that's right. Did they really do that to you?" She couldn't help but ask.

He nodded and stumbled a couple of steps closer to the portal. "It was either me or Zara. I knew I would heal with time. She wouldn't. I couldn't let them touch her, not that it stopped them from doing other experiments on her." He clamped his mouth shut, his mind screaming through the fog. That was a dangerous subject. He couldn't let them focus their attention on Zara. "They figured out I could heal faster after that first time."

Jean was slow to help him walk. Her mind going back to the day they had rescued the siblings. They hadn't been the only children at the facility; they had simply been the only ones that survived. There had been signs in the buildings' depths of countless children having been used as subjects over the years. They were taken in small groups and used until they died.

The research institute had not been a new one. Despite that, they had never learned who controlled it.

Shaking her head, Jean dispelled those horrible memories. It had been a horror-filled mission that had affected even the hardiest of soldiers in their squad.

Zack continued on, unaware of her dark thoughts. The glimmering surface of the portal rose up before him, and with one last surge of energy, he stumbled through it.

The surroundings changed between eye blinks. The surface under his feet switching from hardened concrete to the soft green of fresh grass and dirt.

He stumbled forward for a few more steps and then collapsed onto the soft, cool grass. The sky was dark, with the stars above lined up in impossibly straight stripes.

Jean came through the portal a beat after him and stood to the side. She would wait for the awakening process to be over before approaching him. The first time every traveler went through the portal, they would undergo their awakening. The process mapped out their full status page as well as gave them their class.

On the ground, Zack closed his eyes as he felt a rush of energy pour into his body. In front of Jean, a halo of blue and white energy surrounded his prone form. It was a familiar sight to her. It was the same visible aura that happened to every new traveler.

The energy invaded every cell of his body, inspecting them before moving on. It wasn't a painful process. Outside of an invisible pressure all over his body, there was no real feeling of what the energy was doing to him. The light grew in radiance, forcing Jean to look away when her eyelids were no longer enough to block out the light.

She had never seen the light get so bright before. To her knowledge, the process was always the same for everyone, and that included how brilliant the light would be.

Zack felt the pressure leave his body as the light faded. In front of his eyes, his status page opened automatically and showed him his updated information.

Zackary ??	Level: 1	Exp to next Level: 0/100
Class: Arcane Mystic		Race: Dimensional Child
Titles: Child of the Portals, First to Second		Elemental Affinity: Space
Strength: 07(+.3) | 10		Intelligence: 15 | 10
Dexterity: 11(+.2) | 13		Magic: 20(+1.5) | 35
Constitution: 20(+.5) | 25		Agility: 12(+.2) | 14
Abilities: Life Burner Lv. 4, Arcane Manipulation Lv. 0		SP: 0
Spells: Arcane Bolt Lv. 1		

He took a moment to take in the changes and what they meant. His class was the same as before, and oddly enough, he had even gained a new title. None of his stats, nor his level from before, remained. His magic and constitution, however, were much higher than when he was level one the first time.

New travelers generally started with stats between one and twenty. With the average being between ten and fifteen. Anything above that was regarded as being the top of normal humanity that could only be reached by the dedicated few.

From there, the class they were given took their initial stats and averaged them out. The warrior class was one with high strength and started with a base of seventeen. If the traveler only had a twelve in strength normally, then their portal stat would be set to fourteen or fifteen if they were lucky.

Zack could only sigh at his low portal intelligence stat. It was the stat responsible for the size of his mana pool. The first time around, he had dedicated the first few levels of free status points to increasing that stat. It had been a disaster and had taken him a while to figure out that was one of the downsides of his class.

As an aberration class, 'Arcane Mystic' had extreme power, but little mana. It was the very definition of a glass cannon class. Any points he put into the intelligence stat were only worth a fourth of what they would have been for any other stat.

He wasn't going to make the same mistake again. Without his ability to make up for that lack, he would have died countless times before.

"How are you feeling?" Jean asked after giving him a minute to review his information.

He closed the status page for the moment and closed his eyes. "Do you have any of those nutrition bars?" He wondered, feeling his abilities passive healing effect begin to kick in. A cooling rush filled his mind as the fog began to clear at the same time.

There was a rustling noise as she searched her pockets, handing him the two she found.

"Thanks." He bit into one of the tasteless bars and watched her. He had yet to review his new title or see if the information on his ability had changed. That could wait until later when he was alone if need be. More urgently, he needed to decide what he was going to tell her. Did he mention how some of his stats had changed from before? What kind of effect would that have?

Trying to guess what repercussions his words could have was making his head hurt again. If he said the wrong thing, would they take him and his sister back into captivity, or would they begin new experiments on someone else? He didn't want anyone else to go through what he and Zara had gone through. Though it was preferable to them being taken again.

After thinking it through, he decided he didn't owe them any detailed information.

Zack grunted, feeling his ribs shift as they began to fuse back together. His skin tingled as the bruises and damaged skin began to heal faster. It was a speed noticeable in a short amount of time. The dark bruises lightening and then disappearing over the course of the next hour. His ribs would take longer, though not as long as he had led Jean to believe.

Most of his non-life-threatening injuries could be healed with a session or two inside the portal. More serious injuries would, of course, require more time. It was something the researchers had used to their advantage after they learned of it.

"So," Jean began again after some time had passed. "Did you get the same class as before?"

He nodded. "Yup, level one mage, right back to the beginning."

"How did you learn your spells the first time around?"

Zack opened his eyes. "Do you know how mages learn their spells? Besides, why do you want to know?"

She shrugged. "I just can't see those people spending the money on a spell-book or taking the time to teach you how to form a spell the old-fashioned way."

Spellbooks were created by high-level travelers who had some kind of mage class. While inside the portal, they would copy down the runed-framework of an original spell, one they had created, as they saw it in their mind. They would then infuse the information and their understanding of the spell with a few drops of their blood and magical energy, while sealing the book. It was a time-intensive procedure, and few travelers were capable of making them, fewer still would take the time to create a book for someone they didn't know.

Learning a spell from a book was a quick way to have the spell imprinted into your mind. While the books could be taken out of the portals after they were sealed, they could only be used inside one, and were single use items. Not to mention the quality of the spell varied from traveler to traveler. Even if the one who made the book created the spell, that didn't guarantee they understood how the component of the various the runed-frameworks meshed together.

Something like that could have an effect on the performance of the spell. Luckily, such spells could be changed and improved over time, with one's own understanding and modifications.

The old-fashioned way involved meticulously studying pre-existing spell frameworks and rune-formations. The last step involved using your magic power while inside the portal to semi-permanently imprint the finished version.

It was a long and very boring process, though not particularly difficult. Enough time had passed since the portals had first appeared, that copious amounts of information had been recorded by previous travelers. As long as someone took the time to learn how it worked, they would be able to create a simple light spell within a month or two.

There was, of course, the third, and by far more common way.

"You do know that every mage gets a spell imprinted as soon as they get their class, right? It happens again at levels, five, ten, fifteen, twenty, twenty-five. You get the picture."

She shook her head. "I thought the books and learning were the main ways."

"Nope. The spells we get at those levels are our core spells. They cost less to use and are specifically tailored to our elemental affinity. Spells that are learned in other ways cost far more magical energy to cast and are generally less powerful and effective. The benefit from those other spells is variety and general usefulness. I would rather learn say a light spell from a book, than risk having it be the next one I am given normally. Not that is to say that it's actually a risk. The spells you are given tend to be more class or combat focused than that."

"Oh, so what spell did you get then?"

"It's called 'Magic Bolt'," He lied, removing the connection the name had with his special class. "I have no elemental affinity, so my given spells are different from what others would get." Another lie. His actual affinity was for 'Space'. It was a secret that only he and Zara knew.

His class held one more secret that he kept close to his chest. The ability 'Arcane Manipulation' allowed him to create spells without needing to know their runic framework. All he needed was enough magical energy and an idea of what he wanted the spell to do. The idea was easy. The energy cost, however, was not. The temporary, non-imprinted spells created in this way required a lot of energy.

With a grunt of pain, he rolled over and sat back on his knees, muffling a groan as he stood. "Do you want to just stay here, or should we explore while we wait for my ribs to heal some more?"

"It's dark," She stated the obvious and pointed across the nearby plain to the trees. "We won't be able to see much if we enter that."

Zack frowned and carefully lay back down on the soft grass. "So, how do you like being a teacher so far?"

She laughed and joined him in looking up at the sky. "Rose is nice, though she doesn't talk much for obvious reasons. It's different from what I was expecting. The military life is all I have ever known.

"My parents were military and when I awakened as a traveler, I followed their example and joined right away. I will say this, your class is by far the most well-behaved and less stuck-up of the bunch. A lot of the students have connections to or have been raised by nobility and believe the sun literally rises only because they will it."

"Like the Albrights?" He glared at a random star overhead.

"Among others," She agreed.

Chapter 15

U nder the mysterious night sky of the world inside the portal, the duo relaxed in a comfortable silence. The occasional noise from the distant trees and the wind whistling through grass were the only sounds.

Jean was used to the regimented military life, and the last few days of acting as a teacher had been stressful. She was enjoying the quiet time to settle her thoughts and nerves.

Meanwhile, Zack was using the time to check the effects of his titles and ability. Mentally, he prodded at the first of his titles, wanting to make sure that it hadn't changed. The status page that only he could see blurred and went out of focus. Stylized words superimposing themselves above the floating page.

> *Child of the Portals – A person who has taken a piece of the portal energy and made it a part of themselves. This results in a base change that makes the user more receptive to the energy of the portals. They can stay inside the portal for up to twenty-four hours at a time and are offered a choice to leave at the halfway point. It may have other undiscovered effects at this time.*

Nodding to himself, he forced it closed with a push of his mind. The details listed were indeed the same as before. The extension on the time limit was nice, but not something that he or Zara had ever been able to use. The mere thought of what would have happened to them if they had ever stayed inside the portal for extra time was enough to cause him to breakout in cold-sweats and shivers even now, years later.

Quickly, he moved onto the next title. This was a new one.

> *First to Second – You are the first person to ever awaken a second time. A portion of your major stats from the first time have been retained.*

That explained why some of his portal stats had been much higher than expected. It was a nice little bonus that would help keep him safe while inside the portals. With the titles done, he moved onto the ability had saved his life and made it a living nightmare at the same time.

> *Life Burner – Allows a person to burn their life force and turn it into magical energy at a rate of 1 to 4 at the current ability level. A passive healing effect is enabled whenever inside the portals or near a magic source. This healing prevents permanent damage from occurring due to the ability, but is not limited to only damage caused through its use.*

It was also the same as before, though Zack's older, more mature mind caught onto something that he never had before. Mana crystals were a magic source, and they were useable outside the portals. There was no reason for the information to mention the possibility unless the healing portion of the ability also worked in the normal world.

It was a thought that frankly scared him. Everything people had discovered and knew about the portals said that spells and abilities were only able to work when inside them. The 'Status Pages' were the sole exception to this rule.

If what he was thinking was true, then it would turn everything on its head. It also had darker implications for the regular non-travelers. What if someday others were able to use their abilities outside the portals?

His eyes flicked unconsciously to the first title he had ever received. It mentioned undiscovered effects. He could only hope that this was a result of the two interacting and having a synergistic effect. The other option was just too terrible to consider.

Regardless, it was something that he couldn't test for the time being. He would need to wait until he could get his hands on a mana crystal. An opportunity that would be likely to present itself when the class went through the portal for the first time in the next week.

"How's the healing?" Jean asked, after they had been laying on the ground for several hours.

He felt at his jaw before answering. "I think the bruises are mostly gone at this point. Even my jaw is feeling better now."

"And your ribs?" She prompted, sitting up.

"The healing effect isn't that good!" He protested, hiding the truth. "It's getting better, but it would take days of us being in here for it to fully heal. At this point, as long as I'm careful, I should be able to at least act normal."

The truth was that his ribs were in much better condition than before, with the fusing process having already begun.

"How much more time do you need?"

"We can head back now if you want. My fever is gone, and everything else feels much better with the bruises gone. How am I going to explain having healed overnight to everyone in the class?"

"Uh, makeup? Or I could just give you some new ones?" She sounded entirely too happy while offering up that idea.

"No!" He was quick to refuse the oh-so-generous offer. "I'll come up with something."

"Fine." She sounded disappointed. "Are you ready to head back through?"

"Sure," Zack agreed, slowly getting to his feet. The light of the portal at their backs had provided them with a constant source of light during their time inside.

"Well," Jean began, while looking him over. "You certainly look less like someone's personal punching bag than you did before."

Walking closer to the source of constantly shifting light, he studied his arms and could only agree with her. There was a noticeable lack of angry purple and blue bruising visible. The light from the portal had a washed-out coloring to it that made it impossible to see any more detail than that. He thought he could still maybe detect some yellowing leftover from the deeper bruises.

Jean brushed off the dirt from her pants and waved him over. "Stay behind me. There shouldn't be anyone inside the building, but you never know.

Prying eyes can appear anywhere and at any time. All it will take is one soldier with a loose mouth seeing you as we leave and then suddenly rumors of the military taking people through the portal early will be everywhere."

"Right." Zack stepped away from her. "That reminds me, why did the Major or sergeant agree to this? Don't get me wrong, I'm thankful for the opportunity to heal faster. My thoughts were getting strange there at the end. Why though? What does the military or you gain from doing all this? I know it is more complex than your squad just feeling guilty. Nobody would go to the lengths you all have because you simply felt guilty!"

"You're right, it would have been enough to get the two of you a placement inside the academy." She gave the area a quick scan, despite knowing everyone had been cleared out before they even arrived. "I could tell you that my placement at the school was nothing more than a useful excuse. One designed to give me closer access to the portal without raising suspicions. That is true, but not a good enough reason to do all this, and as you can clearly see, the Major doesn't mind raising suspicions."

"Why then?" Zack was growing increasingly curious. To that point, the Major, Sergeant Grieves, and even Jean had all been helpful. He knew that nothing was free, and despite what seemed like good intentions, there would be a bill for it all at some point.

"I admit I was curious myself, and I asked the sergeant earlier today, in fact. It became clear to me when they were willing to set this up simply because I mentioned your ability to heal. For some reason, they place a fair amount of importance on you and your sister." She crept closer to him, her voice dropping to a whisper that wouldn't carry. "Do you want to know what he told me?"

Zack nodded mutely, afraid that if he said anything, she would suddenly stop speaking.

"The Major believes that the two of you are some kind of key. It is why we never stopped looking for you." She pulled back abruptly and sat on the grass next to him. "What do you remember about the portal at the research facility?"

"What?" He was confused by the sudden change in direction. "Uh, it went to a jungle environment, lots of trees. There were mainly beasts and plant-type monsters inside it. I remember there being a lot of fruit hanging from the trees. There was a river running through the area, and a dark pit or cave that I never went near or entered."

She motioned him to continue when he stopped.

"What else do you want to know? You guys are the ones who took it over. I'm sure you know more about the place at this point than I do."

Jean ran her tongue across the front of her teeth and shook her head. "Not quite, and that is the point. Nobody can enter that portal anymore."

Zack blinked at her and then began to laugh. "Okay, you almost had me there. Everyone knows that as long as the person is a 'Traveler' then they can go through any portal."

"Not that portal, not anymore, in any case." Her tone changed, the seriousness of the situation leaking through. "You mentioned last night that we had sealed your status, to which I told you we didn't have that kind of technology or ability.

"Regardless of my thoughts on the matter, I mentioned the event in my nightly report along with everything else I had learned, on the off chance someone knew something. The Major himself contacted me after reading that report. And after making sure I understood how serious and dangerous the knowledge was, do you know what he wanted me to do?"

Zack shook his head and shrugged. At this point, he was having troubles following the conversation.

She gave a dry laugh. "He wanted me to ask you if you remembered when you lost access to your status page, the specific day or time period?"

He blinked and chuckled in surprise. That was not what he had been expecting.

"I don't know. We had been at the intake facility for a few days when it happened. It had been maybe four or five days by that point. I remember going to sleep one night, and then in the morning, I felt different. Less. Like I had lost something. My status page was gone, along with the few enhancements it had given me through increased stats." He was beyond confused at the constant twists and turns in the conversation.

Jean sucked in a shocked breath and softly muttered. "Wow, he really was spot on."

Zack cleared his throat. "Are you going to tell me how this all ties together now?"

"I am. Just keep in mind, this is all secondhand information that the Major told me. I don't know all the specifics." She waited for his nod of understanding and then continued.

"A few days after we rescued you and your sister. The travelers that had been sent inside the portal were forcefully ejected before their time limit was up. They couldn't remember anything that happened after they entered that day. Then the portal changed. The surface stopped moving and became hard, while all the power marking rings around the edge thickened and multiplied until it became one solid black whole."

"And the Major thinks what, that me losing access to my traveler abilities caused that?" Zack swallowed, his mind conjuring one wild theory after the other.

"Like I said, a key. He didn't tell me any more than that, but I can make a few guesses. I'm pretty sure he thinks that whatever it was the researchers did to you, the thing that allowed you to awaken early. It tied you to the portal there." Jean flopped back and looked up at the slowly brightening sky. "That's all I know or can guess for now."

Zack held his breath, resisting the urge to curse. The Major and Jean had managed to extrapolate a frankly scary amount of information from a single report. No, that wasn't right. The report had most likely simply confirmed his existing suspicions. The Major had already thought they were the key to the portal before that.

"What now?" He asked in a hoarse voice.

"I don't know. I imagine that at some point, I or someone else will be tasked with bringing you back to the facility and the portal inside. I wouldn't expect that to happen until you are strong enough to handle whatever monster is on the other side. The monster or monsters that could cause that solid black line will be stronger than anything recorded." She focused on him. "Now you know why the Major has been doing all of this. Hopefully, you can stop worrying that we want to dissect you, or use you for more experiments, or whatever it is that you keep thinking."

"Knowing the reason will definitely help, but don't expect me to suddenly start trusting any of you. That takes time, especially for me and Zara." Zack turned away from her, his throat convulsing as he fought the urge to vomit. His worst nightmare had come to pass.

The Major, and the military, as a result, knew that he, and possibly his sister, were different. The only upside to the matter was that the Major didn't seem inclined to use them for more experiments. He could take a small amount of comfort in that.

Zack swallowed and breathed in and out, working to control the overwhelming panic he was feeling. "Well, I admit the timing is certainly odd, but wouldn't it be easier to just look through the research materials and find out what they did? If you can learn what they did to me in the first place, surely that would provide the answer."

Jean snorted, her eyes carefully roving over him, taking note of his reactions. "We can't. The researchers were using magitech we had never seen before. Instead of writing everything on paper, they would somehow insert the information into a large boxy device. The military eggheads have dubbed it a 'Thinking-Box'. The rest of us just call it the 'Magic-Box'. Either way, even now, they have only managed to figure out a little about how it works. They can turn it on, but all the information it displays is encrypted, and therefore unreadable."

Zack gazed at the distant trees, the motion of the waving branches calming his frazzled nerves. "Are you going to get in trouble for telling me all of that?"

"Nope, since all of this directly concerns you, the Major had already said it was fine to tell you this much. As for the magic-box, keep that to yourself for now. The government plans to release their own version of it to the public sometime soon, so it's mostly fine for you to know about it as well."

His situation gradually came into focus as he relaxed. This was fine. They had some suspicions, and a long-term goal for him. The important thing, however, was that they weren't trying to use him right then. It would give him the time needed to decide if he could trust them. How he would act when the time came would depend on that trust.

"Come on, we really should leave before it gets too bright outside." Jean stood and raised a brow. "Your face is looking much better, and that gash below your hairline is completely gone. Not bad."

Zack wanted to curse at himself again. He had forgotten about that gash. It was a very visible representation of how fast he could actually heal. "It must not have been as bad as it looked then."

She nodded slightly. "Remember what I said before and stay close."

With a sigh of relief, he stood, making a show of keeping the pressure on his ribs to a minimum. "How close do you want me?"

"Right on my heels, and duck down a little to hide your face." She clicked her tongue in annoyance. "I should have thought to bring a mask or a pillowcase to hide your face."

Zack recoiled. "Why a pillowcase? You know what, never mind. I'll just..." He inspected his button-up uniform shirt and the bandages on his stomach. "That would probably be worse. How about I just keep my face down and between your shoulder blades?"

"That should be fine." She agreed.

Together they walked through the portal, the scenery changing in an instant. Cold concrete replaced the warm grass, and large broken walls blocked the wind.

The surroundings were still and silent. They were alone for the moment; regardless, Zack kept his face pressed against her back. The broken walls provided plenty of places for someone to peer inside. Not to mention the dark corners of the room could be hiding anything.

Quickly, they shuffled over to her fancy carriage. Jean opened the back door and pushed him inside. "Stay down and out of sight until we get back to your dorm." She commanded him in a voice that allowed for no arguments.

"How is this going to affect me going through the portal with the class next week?" He asked her once he felt they had been moving for long enough to be clear of any people.

"It is a problem. I'm sure you noticed the rather bright light you gave off earlier. That will happen with each student, and it will be rather obvious that you have already awakened if you don't sparkle like the rest." He heard fingers tapping the leather of the steering wheel. "We may have to stage an accident of some sort that ends with you being pushed through the portal first. After that, we can just tell the inspector that they missed the light show."

Zack felt his jaw slacken. Was this how the military approached things, making it up as they went along? He shook his head. No, that wasn't right. It was more likely that it was because she was the one in control this time. He didn't think that Specialist was a rank typically involved in planning missions. Then again, the squad she was a part of was different from the rest. So, what did he know?

"We're back," Jean announced, the vehicle smoothly slowing to a stop outside his dorm building. The sun was still below the horizon, if only barely. Anyone who managed to see him would only glimpse a human-shaped blob with no details.

Chapter 16

A soft hand was carefully feeling the healed skin below his hairline when Zack awoke after a meager hour and a half of sleep.

"When did you get back?" He muttered, blearily peering up at his sister, and the stuffed bear, Zelda, clutched tightly in her free arm.

"Jean stopped by Edith's after she dropped you off. I've been here ever since." Now that he was awake, Zara stopped holding back and proceeded to poke and prod everywhere that he had been injured. "The healing seems to be the same as before." She said, after satisfying her curiosity.

"Yup, my rib is almost fully healed." He stood and pulled off the bandage, binding his previously injured stomach. "And as you can see, it also healed and fixed some of the damage from the last few years."

The muscles of his stomach and arms were larger and more pronounced than they had been the day before.

"There is something else." He sat on the bed and pulled her close. "I got a new title and noticed something I had never understood in the description of my life burner ability."

Zara remained silent while he told her about both items and then moved on to everything Jean had said. "Putting aside the title, which will give you a nice head start, and the possible implications of your ability. What are we going to do about Jean and the military?" Her head was resting on Zelda's fluffy top, nibbling nervously at her lower lip.

It was a question that he himself had been thinking about near constantly since she revealed everything to him. "We are going to stay here and learn as much as we can, while eating as much as we want. For now, at least, I think we are safe enough. The military doesn't seem interested in experimenting on us. I don't think they even know you went through the portal with me."

"Can we trust them?"

He laughed. "No. I think Jean was just told enough that when she spoke with me, everything she said would appear as the whole truth. For now, we can depend on them to make sure we stay safe. If they ever learn more of our secrets, however, that could easily change."

Zara glanced down at Zelda with a hint of longing in her eyes. "Are we going to sneak me through the portal?"

"Do you think you could even go through it?" Zack returned with a frown. "Has your status returned?"

She shook her head. "No, but when we went to see the portal the other day with Jean, I had the feeling that I could go through it then, if I wanted. I've been thinking about it since, and I think our odd race or maybe our 'Child of the Portals' title may allow me to go through regardless of whether I have access to my status. It's just an idea at this point, and there is only one way to confirm it."

He thought it over before replying. "Today is Holztag, and the last day of classes for the week. If you are serious about wanting to try, then we can go tonight to watch the area and make a plan. Depending on what we learn, we can either try during the weekend or wait until next week."

"Do we go straight there after working tonight?"

"That would probably be easiest." He glanced at the clock on the wall. "I need to get ready. Are you going to come to breakfast with me?" He had partially slept, and then talked through the remainder of the time he usually used for morning exercises.

"Will you walk me back?" Zara held tightly to Zelda as she made the request.

Zack rubbed the top of her head. "If you want me to, then, of course, I will."

***

Zara got some odd looks at breakfast when they saw her carrying around George. Thankfully, no one approached them, and they were able to eat in peace.

"You are looking much better this morning," Edith told him when he dropped Zara off at her place. Jean's excuse of getting him some proper healing no longer seemed believable to her. She was a smart woman and knew enough to leave the matter alone. Some things shouldn't be pried at, especially when the military was involved.

He winced, imagining how his classmates would react. "You wouldn't happen to have some makeup or anything I could use to make it appear as though they are still there?"

"The best we could do with makeup is make it so heavy that people can see it. They will think it is covering the bruises they saw yesterday. If we do that, then I can guarantee the nobles in your class will say something mean and derogatory. Can you handle that?"

He shrugged. "No worse than usual, and it will be better than the questions I would raise otherwise." It would also have the benefit of explaining why no one had seen his bruises at breakfast.

Edith pointed to a seat at her table. "Sit, I'll go get my makeup. I just hope they are still in a condition to be used. I haven't touched the stuff in years, not since... my husband... died." Her eyes dimmed at the mention of her husband, and she quickly left the room.

"She's never mentioned that she was married before," Zara whispered to him, glancing around the room curiously, as though a picture she had never noticed before would suddenly appear.

"Well, to be fair, talking about the past around us is a fairly tricky endeavor. I'm sure it would have come up eventually once she became more familiar with us."

Edith returned a minute later with a large and rather luxurious looking container held in her arms.

"Uh, that looks expensive." Zack immediately balked at the thought of her wasting the potentially high-priced cosmetics on him. "Are you sure you want to waste them on something like this?"

She waved away his concern and set the container on the table. "I already said I don't use them anymore. They are only going to spoil and become rubbish in that state. At least this way they can be useful one last time."

He said nothing more and sat still as she and Zara proceeded to cake his face with the old makeup. The dry and clumpy mess was slowly worked into his skin by a giggling Zara. Edith would then smooth it out and make it appear as though it was hiding something and not simply caked on.

The two shared a look and stepped back at the same time.

"What do you think? Does he need more?" Edith asked her young apprentice.

Zara laughed and shook her head. It was a sound that warmed Zack's heart; it was a rare sound, or at least it had been. She had been doing it more recently.

He was handed a small mirror. "I look like one of those people walking the streets late at night!"

Edith's jaw dropped, and Zara fell to the floor in a fit of laughter.

"At least it will keep people from looking closer." He handed the mirror back with a smile and stood with a feigned grunt of pain. "I should get going."

Tessa was standing in front of the dorm when he exited. Her arms were crossed and a near-murderous look pulling her lips thin.

"You weren't in class yesterday, neither was Spencer."

She fell into step beside him and looked closely at the makeup with a critical eye. "You look ridiculous!" Her eyes tracked across the spot where his skin had been torn open by the tree, widening in surprise when there was nothing there. "Who did your healing?" Her hand shot out and grabbed hold of his upper arm, stopping him.

Tessa was momentarily distracted by the muscles under her hand, and she released him in shock. "I saw his arms just the other day. They were lean and skinny then, weren't they? I don't remember his muscles being that big before." She muttered thoughtfully to herself.

The muscles in his arms had always been defined and strong from constant use in construction and other jobs. A lack of protein in his diet, however, had kept them small and compact. Their slim size hiding the power they contained. The nutrition bars, combined with his recent healthier eating, had given his body enough material to work with during his healing.

The ability wouldn't always have such pronounced results on his body. It was mostly because of how terrible his body's state had been prior to entering the academy. Even in the normal world, his body had been in a state of healing, working to fix years of accumulated damage. The effects had combined to heal him in ways it wouldn't normally.

Zack pulled away from her, uncomfortable at the sudden contact and the look in her eyes. "We should be getting to class. Why don't you tell me what happened with Spencer and the Albrights? What did your parents have to say about his comments? I noticed you seemed to be in a bad mood earlier."

Her fiery-hazel eyes narrowed at the dodge to her own question. "Mother reacted about as well as I thought she would, in that the Albrights should be experiencing some business difficulties about now. She forced a couple of government agencies to go through their financials with a fine-tooth comb. Father, well, he just laughed and said the king would never allow them to control his work."

"What is it your mother does again?" Zack had heard Tessa mention her the night of the attack and had been wondering ever since.

"Hmm?" Her feet stuttered, and she crossed her arms. It was a classic defensive move that people used when they were insecure, among other things. "Oh, she is an advisor to the king." Tessa gleefully took in his look of disbelief, her arms dropping open.

"And Dorn thought his family could just force yours to do anything?"

"The identity of my mother is rather special, and only a few people know who she is. You should consider yourself grateful and standing among a select few."

"Why even tell me then?" He asked in exasperation, looking around for any eavesdroppers.

"I am not actually sure, but mother said that if you ever asked, I could mention it. It is odd, I admit, normally I'm barely allowed to mention her at all. My mentioning her the other night was purely an accidental slip of the tongue."

He wasn't sure he believed that. People didn't just accidentally let slip a secret they kept from everyone. It was more likely that the girl had been instructed by her mother to let it slip at some point. Why, though? What game was her mother playing?

Regardless, it was already too late for him. The lines had been clearly marked with the attack and then with Tessa's mother taking action. To everyone else, it would appear that he was firmly in their camp, whatever that meant.

His mind made those connections in an instant of clarity, destroying any shred of trust he may have formed with her.

Zack shook his head and pulled away from her. "No, I don't think it was an accident. You and your mother are playing some kind of game, I assume, against the other nobles." He scoffed and took another step away from her. "You probably even knew that sitting with me would cause a reaction from the younger idiots." He raised his hands, stalling her excuses. "Just tell me why?"

To her credit, the way Tessa looked at him didn't change at all. There was no sudden switch to an expression of revulsion because she had been forced to spend time with him. A commoner, someone beneath her vaunted station. She simply continued to stare at him, her eyes shaking for a brief moment, and then nothing.

Everyone had heard the stories, or read the books, wherein someone would get used by the nobles. It was a common enough tale, and when the noble would reveal their plan to the unwitting commoner, it always came with a look of disgusted revulsion. She didn't have that.

Tessa glanced behind him at the clock set high up on the central building. "We should get to class; I hear that Quinn will be covering our status sheets in class today." She walked up to his side and in a whisper spoke one final set of instructions. "I will be dropping by your dorm tonight before dinner. Make sure you and Zara are prepared to spend the night somewhere else. You won't be back until Sonntag night. I will make sure Edith is aware."

He didn't like being ordered around by anyone. However, he was willing to make an exception this time. The need for answers far outweighed his normal reaction to being controlled.

***

The other students had nearly all arrived by the time Zack and Tessa walked into class. Their appearance, together, set them off and everyone began talking at once.

Spencer, who had actually dared to show up for the class that day, in particular, looked livid.

Quinn let them continue talking for a minute, waiting for the few late students to arrive. He stood when it was time to start. "Everyone shut up now. Class is about to begin. That means you too, Spencer!"

The boy in question twisted his head in anger towards the teacher. "I wasn't even talking!"

"I SAID SHUT IT!" Quinn thundered, unsuccessfully hiding a smirk from the class. "You were already going to get detention for not coming to class yesterday. Now you have it twice, and both of them need to be done today, or you won't be going through the portal next week."

"But... I..." Spencer sputtered impotently.

The teacher quirked a brow, clearly daring the boy to continue. "Good," He said once it became clear he wasn't going to say anything more. "Now we have a few things to cover today. Right now, we are going to cover what the information on your status page means. Later, I will be giving you the overview of the monsters you might encounter inside the school's portal."

Quinn pointed to the board, where each of the items that appeared on a status page was written. "I'm assuming that you all know enough to understand what each of those is for. Strength is for muscles." He flexed with a self-satisfied smile. "It lets you beat things down easier."

"Dexterity is for hand-eye coordination and for precise control of your body and movements. It is useful, and for most classes, it is a secondary stat." He twirled a dagger around his fingers to demonstrate the control. Then he threw the blade over their heads to a target that had been pinned to the wall for that exact purpose.

"Constitution is directly related to how much of a beating your body can take before you die. I would suggest that all of you invest in it. If you can. We have the perfect example of what you will look like after each trip through the portal otherwise." Quinn directed the class's attention to Zack. "I would suggest using less makeup in the future, just as an FYI." He offered good-naturedly.

Zack nodded in good humor, glad that no one was looking closer than that.

"Intelligence is directly related to how much magical energy you have, and how fast you can regenerate it. Magical energy is also known as mana, the two terms can be used interchangeably for the most part. There are some subtle difference between the two, however, you don't need to worry about those yet, if ever. Also, on a separate note, if you raise this enough, then it can also make your memory better on this side.

"Magic affects the oomph, or the power of your spells. At a high enough level, some, not all mind you, but some travelers have reported that it has given them a sort of sixth sense on this side of the portals." He shrugged. "I'm not a magic-user, but it does help any attacks I make centered around my element. So keep that it mind, all your stats are important, even the ones not directly related to your class."

He groaned as he took a moment to stretch out his stiff leg.

"This is the final one, and then you can ask any questions you have about the rest of the status page. Agility affects your speed, fast-twitch muscles, and reaction time along with balance and better body control." Quinn limped over to his desk and sat on it. "Questions?"

"What are the averages for each stat?" A girl sitting near Tessa asked.

"The average for students in this academy is typically between ten and fifteen. Twenty is generally the highest you would ever see naturally. That would be the person at the top, the strongest, fastest, etcetera. If your parents have had you exercising and training since you were young, then getting stats in the fifteen range is not unreasonable."

"How rare are abilities and titles?" A quiet but dignified boy, who rarely interacted with the other students, asked.

"Abilities are common. Most, if not all, of you will get one with your class. A typical one would be 'Powerblow', a beginning attack that all warriors get. As for titles, that is hard to say." He scratched at his chin in thought. "They are rare. Unfortunately, it's hard to say just how rare they actually are.

"Off the top of my head, I can only think of maybe five travelers that I have personally met with one. That said, there are probably more who have just never reported them. Each title comes with an effect of some kind, better elemental control, a slight increase in a specific stat. The crown pays handsomely for information on titles, and yet some people prefer to keep the information to themselves."

Zack thought of his own two titles and knew which he would choose. It was for the best if no one ever knew about them, and Zara agreed.

"At what point do the effects of our portal stats influence those we have on this side?" Zack took the chance to ask something he had always wanted to know.

"The conversion rate is ten portal stats, for one normal stat. This sounds easy until you realize that all training classes only give you one stat to use at each level up. That increases to two when you reach your junior class."

Zack realized he had asked the question wrong and was in the midst of raising his hand again when Tessa asked the question he had originally intended.

"And what about for the special affects you mentioned earlier? What stat number is needed for those?"

Quinn sucked in a breath and let it out in an explosive sigh. "I was hoping none of you would ask that. I said earlier that twenty was the highest natural stat, and that is true, especially in relation to your question. For example, raising your magic to twenty-one would give you a small chance of having that sixth sense activate. It would become slightly higher at twenty-five and again at thirty or thirty-five. However, keep in mind that not everyone experiences those effects even at the higher numbers."

He looked desperately at the clock and smiled in relief. "It is something that is out of reach for most of us, and I would encourage you all to forget about it. Now it is time for training."

Chapter 17

T essa stayed by his side during training, inspecting him suspiciously every time he moved.

Zack was forced to exaggerate his movements, wincing as he played up his already healed injuries. It didn't work. By the end of class, she had already made up her mind regarding the state of his health.

Her fingers were tapping on the cafeteria table in annoyance as she watched him eat.

"How?"

"How, what?" He asked around a mouthful of meatballs and potato, careful to not spew any of it.

She leaned across the table, her fingers stretching out like claws and her red hair falling in waves around her face. "How are you no longer injured? Who did your healing? No one should have the ability those injuries would have required to heal you using mundane means so completely in such a short amount of time!"

Zack swallowed and pulled away from her. His appetite fleeing between heartbeats. He was afraid that she was about to stumble upon the answer, regardless of what he might say.

It was then that someone kicked the table and distracted them. It was a completely ineffective attack against the heavy surface that didn't even budge. To the side, Spencer could be seen hopping around on one foot while clutching the other. Two other boys stood close by with puzzled looks on their somewhat dull faces.

"What do you think you are doing?" Tessa snapped at the red, pain-filled face of the boy. "Do you think Dorn will protect you or something?"

The two thugs shared a look and stepped back. Taking the opportunity to separate themselves from whatever was to come. All they had been asked to do was stand there and look as imposing as their sixteen-year-old bodies could. The loyalty they felt towards Spencer only went as far as the business their parents did together. Once names like Dorn Albright started getting dropped, they were out.

Spencer sneered at her and turned to Zack, intent on not leaving without delivering his message. "You were warned!" He reached out, expecting one of his large companions to be there, and toppled over when they weren't.

"So, what time did you say you were picking me up tonight?" Zack asked her loud enough for the spoiled brat on the floor to hear. Despite his misgivings, he couldn't help but stir the proverbial pot with the information.

Tessa rolled her eyes and answered in an equally loud voice. "How about an hour after our last class? That should give you enough time to change and get ready."

Spencer, who was now gripping his knee as well, looked up in shock. "But... Dorn..." He sputtered, unable to understand what was going on.

"What about him?" Tessa turned to face the boy sprawled across the dirty cafeteria floor. "Dorn and his family mean nothing to me. I have no idea what made him think that he had any right to decide anything for me. He never has and never will factor into my future, regardless of what he may think!"

As if that was the cue they had been waiting for, the two thugs grabbed his shoulders and pulled him away. Dragging him across the floor, uncaring of his protestations to the rough treatment.

"Well, that was fun. Are you sure your mo-" Zack coughed, to cover the near slip of his tongue. "Your family will be able to handle everything?"

She nodded, and pulled back from him, momentarily forgetting what they had been talking about. "It'll be fine."

"Speaking of which, won't her doing all of this reveal her identity in some way?" Zack looked around and asked quietly. He remembered the thoughts he had that morning. For him to be placed firmly in her camp, the mother would need to reveal herself.

Tessa pulled away from the table. "We'll talk again later."

Zack found himself deep in thought as he carried his unfinished food to the trash and scraped the dish clean. It was an action that he would never have dreamed of doing only weeks before. Wasting food had been a sacrilegious act worthy of stoning in his mind. Now that there was plenty of food, it had taken on a slightly less status of importance in his mind.

Posters of monsters, specifically those of the beast and plant persuasions, covered the walls of the classroom when everyone returned from lunch.

"Next week, this class will be conducted in a different manner, with varying mockups in the center of the classroom. However, due to this being the first of classes, this time it will be a purely introductory and information-driven experience." Quinn barely waited for them to be seated before launching into his spiel. "Welcome to the 'Monster Biology' class. During this period and the normal closing period, we will be discussing everything about the school portal. We will begin with the monsters found inside." He tilted his head towards the posters. "And then end with the environment, and how it is different from other portals."

Zack listened with rapt attention as the muscled teacher described all the beasts he had failed to see during his trip through the portal. Some portals had a quasi-safe area around the opening, with certain monsters not liking the light and energy it put out. Those were usually found in the lower-level portals.

The locations with stronger monsters typically didn't care about the portals and ignored their existence entirely. More than one team had gone through the glowing rifts to find monsters nearly on top of them from the start. It rarely ended well for the travelers.

Finally, Quinn moved on to the subject that Zack had been looking forward to the most since lunch. The environment inside the school portal. For most of his time spent inside, it had been dark. Near the end, when it was beginning to grow brighter, he had been caught up in the conversation with Jean. He had seen very little of what was inside.

"The first thing you need to know about the space inside the school's portal is that it is a mostly closed environment. There have been a few other portals that exist on an island surrounded by water, and there are even a couple that lead to deep cave systems. What is different with ours is that it leads to a large, forested vale or hollow, if you will. There are mountains on every side, enclosing the entire area and preventing us from exploring the rest of the region. We have no idea what may or may not exist beyond their towering heights.

"Now, here is the particularly interesting and unique feature of the school's portal, and the main reason that corporations pay so much to rent time inside it. Above the mountains, floating in the sky, is an island that moves around." Quinn folded his arms and let the class absorb that information. "It is the only floating island that has ever been documented inside the portals."

"Surely there has been someone with a high level that has been able to climb the mountains and look out beyond them? Not to mention, get onto the island!" Quinn looked as though he didn't want to answer, considering that it was Spencer who had spoken.

Instead, he posed the answer as a leading question.

"Let's assume that you are a fast runner with plenty of stamina to burn. Someone with stats of around at least sixteen or seventeen in both Agility and Constitution. Realistically, that means you could cover fourteen kilometers or so an hour. Now keep in mind that you can only remain inside for twelve hours. That means you can only make it one-hundred, and sixty-eight kilometers in before being forcefully brought back. That is with you doing nothing but running the entire time, without breaks or needing to fight off monsters.

"Of course, those numbers change as you level up, grow stronger, and put more points towards agility. Here is the thing that you need to keep in mind, no one is stupid enough to only put their status points in one attribute. Those points are precious, and are limited, especially before you reach your 'Regular Class'. Putting all of that aside, let's assume someone did up their speed enough to sufficiently shorten the time. Then they still have to climb the mountain, which means they would also need strength and even more stamina."

Quinn was enjoying himself as he dually tore the boy down for his thoughtless question and taught the class at the same time. "Now, as much as I am loathed to admit it, the question actually does present some valuable points. First of all, the hollow is not over three hundred kilometers in length. It is only around a hundred kilometers total. This brings me to the second point. The portal is in the middle of the hollow and sits on a rare grassy plain inside the space."

Spencer slammed his hand on his desk in aggrieved anger. "If it is only fifty kilometers to the mountains, why did you have to go through the rest of that?"

"I was getting to that and shut up!" Quinn shot back at his least favorite pupil. "As I was saying before, the student who now has three detentions spoke up."

He ignored the loud protestations and simply spoke over them. "Things are not as simple as they appear. Getting to the mountains is relatively easy, as long as you are at a high enough level. Beast attacks, however, grow in frequency the closer you get to them. Though they do remain somewhat low level and are therefore mostly easy to kill. The real problem lies with the mountains themselves, and the beasts that inhabit them."

"There is a sudden jump in the strength of monsters between the edge of the forest and the foot of the mountain." He stopped and peered out over the class. "I think I should also take this chance to remind you of your compatibility ratings and all that they entail."

"Some of you." There was a non-subtle look towards a specific student. "Are under the impression that getting to a high-level and racking up an insane amount of stats is easy. Let me just correct that for you now. It isn't. Every level you get after reaching your regular class will be slow and only achieved through constant hard work and effort. Few of you will ever get to your 'Specialist Class'."

He let that sink in for a moment. "Let's do the math real quick. From levels two to four, you will only get one stat point at each level. Beginning with level five, you get two, then at level ten, you get three. Even if you reach level twenty-four, the level before where you would get your specialist class. You would have only gotten fifty-eight points total.

"Each of those points will get spread across your attributes with the bulk centered on your primaries. Still, remove whatever vague idea you have of flying in the sky, or jumping higher than a building. Those feats are limited to those with rare special classes, the aberrations, and the few who go past level twenty-five and above. Which means that even if you managed to get to the top of the mountain, scaling all of those odds, unless you have a specific class, you still wouldn't be able to get to the island." He coughed. "Now, going back to what I was saying before this distraction."

Zack tuned him out, lost in his own thoughts. He hadn't been aware of that before. Due to the quirks of his own aberration class and race, the number of points he got was greater than normal. It had been the same for Zara.

There was one more thing that Quinn hadn't mentioned. The restrictions on point placement during a travelers training period, which lasted until level ten. During that period, a traveler could only freely place their points on even levels. On odd levels, they were forced to only place them in the attributes their classes majored in. Sure, you could save each point and only allocate them once you reached the next level, but that is a risky move for most people. Not to mention just being plain stupid.

His mind returned to the lesson in time to hear Quinn dismissing the class. He could only hope he hadn't missed anything too important during that time.

Edith was holding a letter and sitting down when Zack arrived to pick up Zara. "What have you gotten yourself involved in now?" She asked, passing him the letter.

It was a simple hand-written note, letting her know that Zack and Zara would be gone for the next couple of days. What had her worried was the wax sigil at the bottom.

"I don't recognize the sigil." Zack passed the letter back to her.

"I'd be worried if you did. It belongs to one of the king's hidden advisors. The only information we know about the person is the sigil they use, and that supposedly, they might be a female." She was clearly worried about them.

Zack was quiet as he, and Zara walked back to their dorm. This had to be another move in whatever game Tessa and her mother were playing. It made no sense otherwise for them to use that crest instead of their family's normal one.

"Where are we going?" Zara asked him, once the door to their dorm had closed.

"Tessa is coming to pick us up. I would guess that her mother and father want to talk to us."

"But doesn't that mean that her mother is the king's hidden advisor?" Zara was quick on the uptake. "Does that mean that it is actually the king behind the meeting, then?"

"I don't think so. I'm pretty sure this is some weird game and power-play her family is doing." He shrugged. "Who can say for certain, though? Make sure you pack an overnight bag with enough clothes for two days." It was pointless to tell her to pack something nice. The nicest clothes they owned were the uniforms the school had provided.

"What about Zelda and George?" She held up George for emphasis.

He hesitated, not sure how to answer. The mere fact that Zara was willing to leave her comfort zone like this was impressive. Asking her to leave the stuffed animals that protected her emotional and mental safety was going too far.

"I'll carry George, and you can carry Zelda."

"Thanks!" She hugged him and then ran to her room to begin packing.

Zack was in awe at how much she had changed within the last couple of weeks. There had been no hesitance after she confirmed that her bears would be coming with them. He knew that a large part of that was because she would be going with him. It was a marked improvement for the scared girl, who almost always refused to even leave the apartment.

He wondered what had caused such a large change in her. Had it been Edith, the general stability their life now possessed, or was it something else? In the end, it didn't matter. The only things that mattered were that she was happy and safe. If she was indeed making progress in overcoming the trauma and mental blocks it had created, then that was even better.

He took a quick shower and changed into some of his older and more comfortable clothes. It was with some surprise that he noted that most of them no longer fit. The muscles of his lean body weren't the problem, it was the surprising realization that he had grown. The hem of his pants was now hanging nearly an inch above the top of his shoes. It was a good thing that they had made his uniform with future growth in mind.

Zack took a moment to separate the clothes that no longer fit and set them to the side. Instantly, his stock of wearable clothes shrank to a single pair of pants and three shirts. That was not counting his school uniforms, which is what he nearly always wore now.

He threw the other two shirts in his bag, along with some underclothes and a spare uniform, before zipping it shut. They would need to go shopping for clothes at some point in the near future. That thought lasted until he remembered the state of their funds. Zara had been keeping track of their money, but neither of them had gone to their part-time job for several days. They would be lucky if the job was still waiting for them when they returned from wherever Tessa was taking them.

Zara was waiting for him, with both bears at her feet, when he finished and joined her at the entryway of their dorm apartment. She was playing with her lower lip and staring at the floor. "You said this was all a game and power-play with Tessa's family. She was also the reason you got attacked and injured." She squeezed both lips together and glanced up at him. "Did they set all of that up, or expect it to happen?"

Zack picked up George and brushed off any dirt that may have gotten on him. "That is likely the case. I spoke with Tessa this morning, and the impression I was getting was that they were expecting something to happen to me. Plus, it seems her mother is the king's hidden advisor, one of them at least. There may be more. There's supposed to be this big secret about her as well, and yet if you remember, the night of the attack, she mentioned her mother readily enough. It wasn't anything concrete, but it was a comment that laid the groundwork for what she would tell me this morning."

Zara frowned, not completely understanding what he was saying. "So, she sat at the same table as you, in full view of everyone knowing what would happen?" She stamped her foot and glared at him. "Why are we going anywhere with these kinds of people? They can't be trusted, and we won't be able to protect each other if they do anything!" Her voice had risen throughout her impassioned speech until she was yelling.

Behind her, a tentative knock came from the front door.

With a growl, Zara kicked her old, shabby bag and spun to open the door. "What?" She screamed.

An embarrassed Tessa was standing there, with a stiff man wearing a dark suit standing behind her. "Are you ready?" She asked them after a moment of silence.

"How much did you hear?" Zack picked up George and then his sister's bag, tucking it alongside his own shabby bag. His arms were now full. It would be up to Zara to carry Zelda, just like they had agreed earlier.

"Just the last few words," Tessa responded uncertainly. "Um, I, uh... Ben, would you take their, um, bags?" She was flustered and stumbled over the words.

The man behind her stepped forward with a stony face and forcefully took the bags from under Zack's arm.

Chapter 18

Tessa took a deep breath, calming herself. "Ben is my family's chauffeur. Are those two bags all you will be bringing?"

"No!" Zara snapped waspishly. "We are also bringing Zelda and George!"

Behind Tessa, Ben's face darkened at the disrespectful tone.

Zack saw the change in the man and was quick to lift the stuffed bear in his arms. "This is George. Zelda is the one in her arms. I believe we should be ready to leave." He nudged his sister. "Calm down, there will be time for all of that later."

Zara glared up at him. "Don't tell me to calm down. She is the reason you got hurt again!" She spun and faced the object of her ire. "What reason could there possibly have been that needed my brother to get hurt? You saw what they did to him! It could have been so much worse! What if they had broken more of his bones, or targeted his head instead of his ribs?" She broke down into tears and held onto Zack with both arms, squishing Zelda against him.

Tessa waved away Ben. "Go put their bags in the boot of the automobile. We'll be there shortly."

He looked disgruntled, but did as she asked, without voicing any discontent.

"What is an automobile?" Zack asked her, not familiar with the word.

With a sigh, Tessa reached up and began rubbing her temples. "Is that really what you want to ask right now?"

He shrugged and then hugged Zara. "I just assumed you weren't going to explain anything important, anyway."

"Well, you are right about that." She muttered, scanning the hallway outside their dorm. "This area is not secure, and the noise we have been making will not go unnoticed for long. Let us head to the auto, err, rather, the carriage outside, and then we can talk about some of the more salient subjects."

"She's talking weird," Zara muttered into his side, as he closed and locked the dorm door.

"Yeah, she does that apparently whenever she is nervous. At least that is what she said before, no idea if it is true or just an act."

"It is the truth," Tessa said, walking beside them. "Not many people know it, however, so please keep it to yourselves."

"Now, what is an automobile? I'm guessing it is a kind of carriage, like those designed by Vortex or Alberitas?" Zack prodded for more information as they walked through the common area.

"It is." Tessa nodded. "The word actually comes from before the portals appeared. There are several variations on it that have slowly been making their way around the upper circles of society. Few nobles refer to them as carriages anymore, now they all call them 'automobiles', 'automotives', 'motor cars', or simply 'cars'. There are roots to the words in the old languages, but it was adopted more recently for a wheeled vehicle driven by a combustion engine. They existed for a short time before the portals."

Zara peeked out from her spot on Zack's side. "If they existed before, then why is the word just barely making a reappearance?" She had calmed somewhat, for the moment.

"I would guess it is because of the completely different method we now use to power them. I imagine the original designers behind the mana crystal powered motors wanted to separate their work from the earlier inferior versions."

By that point, they had reached the entrance to the dorm building. Waiting for them on the paved drive was a sleek Alberitas automotive with an extended backend and tinted windows.

"We'll be able to talk in peace once we are inside," Tessa told them, entering through the door Ben was holding open for her.

Waiting for them, or rather Zara inside the vehicle, was a large stuffed animal. It had been made to represent one of the larger bear beasts inside the portals and was bigger than both Zelda and George combined.

"I knew you would be mad at me, understandably and rightly so," Tessa began as soon as they entered. "This was prepared as a sort of peace offering for Zara, by myself and my mother. I had noticed how attached she was to the animal in her hands before."

Zara looked from the giant bear to Tessa, back to the bear, and then to Zack, who nodded. Both knew that Tessa had no idea of the full importance of what she had just done. She didn't need to, but the siblings appreciated the gesture.

"As for your concerns earlier Zara," Tessa motioned for them to sit down as Ben climbed into the front of the long car. "There was never any real danger to Zack. I was later told that Ben was watching over him from the shadows. At the first sign that they were going to do anything drastic, or too damaging, he would have stepped in and stopped them."

The younger girl seemed to calm somewhat at that news, despite it not being the crux of her concerns. "He was still injured! Don't you think we have suffered enough already?"

The red-haired girl looked away, unwilling to meet their eyes any longer. "We had no idea at the time what your history was. Mother didn't learn about it herself until after I reported your scars to her."

That answered Zack's unasked question about whether she had told them about the scars.

"Would it have changed anything if you had known?" He couldn't help but ask.

"It's possible. My mother was the one who planned it out. She probably would have requested a meeting with you two sooner, and that scene could have been avoided entirely." Tessa relaxed as they continued to talk.

"Why though? What purpose could me getting attacked by Dorn and his cronies possibly serve?"

"I had to speak with my mother after school to understand all of this myself. Very little of it had been explained to me before. You were simply the excuse, someone who showed up at the right time and nothing more.

Mother has known about the Albright family's designs on father and his research, for quite a while now. She simply needed a decent excuse to act. Despite her position, theirs is relatively impressive as well. The revelation that Dorn was eyeing me, however, was apparently unexpected and not something she was willing to consider."

"I don't know how I feel about being used as a pawn in the game of a person I have never met, let alone even seen." Zack kept an eye on Zara to see how she was reacting to the news. The subtle tightening of her hands and the creasing of her eyebrows told him this wasn't the end of the discussion for her.

"I'm not exactly a fan of it myself," Tessa replied with a strained smile. "This is the first time I have known, if only a little, the person involved in one of my mother's schemes. Unfortunately, that is the way of the nobles. It is common for us, them, to not know the people their policies and actions affect."

"Are we going to meet with your mother now?" Zara asked, not bothering to hide her displeasure with the woman.

"That is the idea," Tessa answered after a moment's hesitation. "I believe my father may be there as well, in which case I will apologize in advance for any uncomfortable questions he may ask. He had heard about the... facility before, and the work they were doing. I'm afraid he will be interested in speaking with you."

"Did your mother tell you our history?" Zack wondered at the way she had phrased it.

"I pieced bits and pieces of it from her, a little more from father, and then, of course, your scars. I won't say I know everything or even the most important aspects, but I believe I know enough."

An uncomfortable silence fell over the inside of the vehicle after that. Zara was the only one who remained indifferent to the atmosphere and was more concerned with her inspection of the new animal. Carefully she inspected the seams, the fabric each part was made of, and everything else.

Finally, she sat back with a contented smile. "I think this will do nicely at the foot of my bed. Its large size will help to discourage unwanted visitors and protect us while we sleep."

"I'm sure Zelda and George will appreciate the extra help it'll provide," Zack said in agreement.

"She, not it," Zara admonished him with a thoughtful look. "There are no bits down below."

Tessa coughed and snorted in disbelief. "They don't include those kinds of things on stuffed animals! And how do you even know what that means? You are far too young to know about those sorts of differences."

"How old do you think I am?"

The girl sitting across from them stopped and looked closely at the painfully thin girl. She had sensed a trap in the seemingly innocuous question. Zara was wearing a set of clean, yet extremely worn, clothes. The hem of her shirt was limp and frayed, with the color washed out and fading. Her pants had been inexpertly patched several times in the past, though they fit her well. They weren't hand-me-downs and instead must have been bought especially for her.

She took that information in before moving on to the girl's cute, but rather gaunt face. There were the barest hints of healthy fat appearing under the skin. Her hair had begun to regain its luster and was carefully organized into a pair of adorable buns.

It was only then that Tessa began to put everything together inside her mind. The small signs of health returning to a formerly malnourished person.

"I was thinking your age was ten, max, likely younger." She answered honestly. "Now that I look closer, though, I realize that is not the case. How old are you?"

"I'm twelve, almost thirteen."

Tessa had no response to that, and the uncomfortable silence returned.

The silence was broken by Zara for the second time, as the car slowed. "I believe she shall be known as Aisha. It fits her."

Zack covered his mouth, hiding the smirk. "Agreed. It's a good name and I think it will match her even better soon."

Tessa was confused and unable to understand the hidden meaning in their words. Luckily for her, the car had stopped without them realizing it. With a click of the door opening, they could see the chauffeur Ben patiently waiting for them to exit.

Beyond him, a large, lush garden abutted the side of an even larger mansion.

"Come, my mother is undoubtedly already waiting for us inside." Tessa gracefully accepted the waiting hand and exited the vehicle first.

"What about Aisha? I can't carry her and Zelda?"

"If you don't mind? I can bring her inside and store her in the room you will be staying in during your time here." It was the first time they had heard Ben speak, and the deep cultured voice shocked them both.

Zara slowly nodded. "I would appreciate that. Thank you." She smiled at him and hopped out with Zelda held close to her chest like armor.

A moment later, Zack followed her, George in hand. A ball of anxious uncertainty was growing rapidly in the pit of his stomach as he glanced behind them. He had no idea where they were, or even where the city was. There was nothing but trees in every direction but the one the house and garden occupied.

There was nowhere for them to escape to if this meeting went wrong. He shook his head and adjusted his thinking. Not everyone was out to hurt them. Besides, knowing Tessa's mother, a woman who had the ear of the king, was not a bad thing.

The short walk up the path to the front door passed in a flash that was both short and long at the same time. Each step had been filled with a sense of dread that warped both of the sibling's perception of time.

"Why do you both look like you are going to be ill?" Tessa asked them as they walked into the foyer of her family's mansion. An impressive set of stairs leading up to the second floor were set further in. On the main floor, he could see several closed doors and the hint of a hallway hidden behind the stairs leading further in. Above their heads was a chandelier constructed entirely of mana crystals, in an opulent display of unbridled wealth. Any doubts they had pertaining to how rich Tessa's family was fled with that single item.

Zack glanced around the open space, and after noting that Ben was the only person there, decided to tell her the truth. "How should we be feeling, then? We, as powerless orphans, have just walked into the home of people in power. People who, if they wanted to, could do anything they wanted with us without worrying about the consequences." He shook his head, and following an instinct looked up the stairs to a hanging tapestry of her family crest. "I was already used once by your schemes, and I have trust issues."

Tessa looked confused at his change in speaking at the end, and angry at what his words implied.

"Your senses are sharp," A female voice drifted out from behind the tapestry.

Tessa's head snapped up. "What are you doing up there, mother?"

An elegant woman with hair that matched her daughters, walked out from behind the hanging piece of embroidery. She was wearing a green dress, with slits down the side for ease of mobility. She was easily one of the most beautiful women that Zack had ever seen, despite the cross-shaped scar on her cheek.

"I wanted to see how they would react to our home and being here." Her eyes drifted over first Zack and then Zara, who was hiding behind him. "A simple test to see what kind of people they are. If they were arrogant wastrels with no ability, then I would have kicked them out without a second thought. If, however, they reacted like the cautious and... damaged people that they were reported to be. Then I would have at least given them a chance."

"And?" Tessa prompted her at the slightest pause.

"He noticed me. Do you even need to ask? Of course, they have passed."
Her gaze focused on Zack, then with the barest upturn of her lips, she
spoke again. "You have already gone through the portal again." It was a
statement, not a question.

Tessa whirled around. "How? Even I'm not allowed to go through early!"

"What gave it away?" He asked, deciding there was no point in maintaining
the charade any longer.

She merely smiled and didn't answer. Instead, changing the subject.
"Would you like to see your room first or talk with me?" She observed her
daughter's reaction. "Alone. I believe you and Zara have some things you
would like clarified."

Zara nodded, her expression shifting to a glare as she overcame her fear of
the woman.

"That would be for the best." Zack kept his arm around his sister, preventing her from possibly doing anything. "Clear the air, and all that."

"Indeed." She drawled. "Tessa, go get your father from his lab in the base-
ment. Let him know that we will be dining with guests in a short while."
Tessa hesitated. "Now, Testarosa dear! You can chat with them more later."

They waited for her to leave before doing anything more.

"So, how did you know that I had gone through the portal early?" The
siblings carefully made their way up the stairs, subconsciously looking for
signs of a trap.

"There is no need to be so cautious and on guard here. As you said earlier, if I wished you harm, there is hardly a need to hide it." The woman quickly grew exasperated with their slow, meticulous pace.

"Maybe, but that is also what someone who wanted us to let down our guards would say." Zack returned. Despite his words, he found himself relaxing regardless. Their cautious actions had more to do with ingrained habit than a belief she meant them any immediate harm.

Speeding up, they followed her off the second-floor landing and down a short hallway to the side. There was only one door in its short length at the very end. It was a thick, solid wood affair. The varnish on it had been worn away by countless hands over the years, creating divots along its surface in places. It was something that someone could only find in the homes of families that had existed for a very long time.

Tessa's mother pushed the door open on well-oiled and silent hinges. Her fingers making their way naturally into the deeper impressions on the wood. She held it open for them and ushered the siblings into a brightly lit study.

A desk made of the same heavy wood as the door occupied the space at one end. At the other end were a set of chairs and a single couch around a small table in front of an empty fireplace. Bookshelves, every single one full to bursting, took up the entire wall across from the door.

"This is a rather imposing room." Zack cleared his throat and spoke as the duo naturally headed for the couch.

"Good, it is meant to be. This is the office I use to meet with the occasional official, and the few other people of import who know of me." She pointed to the vague outline of a door near the desk. "My actual office is off to the side there. This one is used mostly for the impression it gives. I rarely do any actual work in this room."

Grabbing the edges of her dress, she sat down carefully across from them.

"Why did you have to hurt my brother?" Zara burst out, unable to contain the anger-filled question any longer. "Why can't you people just leave us alone? Why do you all keep targeting us? There are millions of other people out there you can use!"

The tirade continued to spew forth for a minute. It only stopped when Zara ran out of breath, her face pale, and beads of sweat spreading across her forehead. Her current weakened body wouldn't let her continue for any longer than that.

"That is true. There are millions of other people out there that I could have possibly used against the Albrights. However, none of them would have created quite as explosive a reaction from Dorn. That boy is the family's weak link and has more arrogance in his body than he does in brains. To put it simply, I used you because of the stir your acceptance into the academy and record-breaking test result caused. It made you a prime target." Mrs. Ricerca entwined her fingers and leaned forward in the chair. "I want you to know that none of this had anything to do with your background. If, and I do mean if, I had known of those events, I would have used someone else."

Chapter 19

Z ara looked as though she wanted to continue yelling, deciding instead to settle on looking away with her arms folded in defiance. Unfortunately for her, the sight had little impact on people when you were as small as her and holding a cute teddy bear.

Zack passed George to her, his knee bouncing while he thought about what to ask her first. "How much do you know of our history?" That was the singular question that would tell him how much he could safely say to her. It was also a question that he had been asking more often than he ever thought possible recently.

Their history, the things that had been done to them. That was their greatest secret, and now it seemed as though everyone knew pieces of the story. They had always known it would get out. It was inevitable when they were surrounded by people who possessed the power and influence to dig out secrets. He had just expected it to take longer than a single week to happen.

Across from them, Tessa's mother rearranged her dress, maintaining her decency and comfort. "I spoke with the Major personally, and I believe that he told me everything." She frowned. "Frankly, the way your case was handled and then lost is disturbing. I looked into it briefly, and nothing like that has happened before or since. To our knowledge, at least."

"What does that mean?" Zack implored with narrowed eyes. "Why would anyone make our information disappear in that way?"

"I relayed the information I had gathered to the Major, and it matched with everything that he had been able to learn from his sources. What really sets your situation apart from others is how everything disappeared. Cases being mishandled are unfortunately common. Those cases, however, remain in the system. Their paperwork and all the applicable information remain, which means those mistakes can be fixed. What happened with the two of you is interesting in that regard. All your information was removed, and despite that, your government housing was still secured for you."

Zara snorted at that. "Barely. That place was a piece of crap, and Zack was forced to work constantly to make sure we were fed."

"I'm not denying that. What I am trying to say is that you even having a spot in government housing should have been impossible."

"And yet we did," Zack muttered, finding himself drawn into what she was saying.

"And yet you did." She mirrored his words. "Someone wanted to make sure that you disappeared and remained out of the government's reach. While still remaining in one place. I can see two possibilities in this case, either the two of you have a guardian angel who made a late appearance. Or, and I believe this is the more likely one. The organization behind the research institute that took you played a part in ensuring you vanished."

Zara stilled in fear, her muscles instantly locking up.

Zack's condition was little better.

Tessa's mother watched over them with compassionate eyes as they battled to regain control.

"But they never came after us?" Zack managed to gasp out after a minute.

She nodded. "That is where the theory falls apart. Why would they have ensured you were out of sight, and then never come after you again? It makes no sense, and we don't have an explanation for it. Yet."

Zara had inched closer to him after that scare and was now holding both bears while pressed against his side.

Zack thought everything over before responding. "Why tell us this? What purpose does us knowing any of this serve besides scaring us?"

She appeared pleased with the question. "It serves to let you know that the mistake that left you out in the proverbial cold was not related to the Major and his efforts. It also lets you know that cooperating with me is your best chance at remaining out of that organization's clutches."

"Why would they even be interested in taking us back? They succeeded in their experiments; they no longer need me!" Exasperation and confusion laced the words as Zack spoke.

She shrugged. "Maybe they don't. They kept you hidden ostensibly for a reason, though. Whether that is for future experiments or something else, only they can say."

It was a non-answer and didn't explain anything. At that point, Zack was beginning to understand what kind of person she was, and it was annoying. In the end, she was still keeping secrets and playing her games with their lives. What was worse, is that he saw no way to get off the gameboard for the foreseeable future.

Thankfully, a knock came from the door before they could continue that frustrating conversation. The door opened a moment later without them waiting for a response.

"Tessa said the boy was here," A man in a rumpled suit burst into the room. "Hi dear," He paused when he noticed her expression. "Sorry, hello Anna. I was just excited and forgot the rules for entering your office."

Behind him, peeking through the open door, was Tessa, who had not forgotten her mother's rules.

Anna raised a hand to her brow and rubbed her temple. "It's fine, this time. If it had been anyone else... Well, you remember what happened last time."

The man shivered. "Who knew the king could be so mean?"

"Yes, well again, you did walk in on the man talking about state secrets."

"They were secrets related to my research! He didn't have to react the way that he did." An unsightly pout spread across the older man's face in an unsightly display of childishness.

From her place by the door, Tessa knocked her head against the solid wooden door in exasperation. "Mom, dad, would it kill the two of you to act normal in front of them!"

Zara giggled softly. The fear she had felt at the mention of the institute having fled with the married couple's antics.

"You can come in," Tessa's mother told her, giving up on continuing her discussion with the siblings for the moment.

Meanwhile, her father had zeroed in on Zack and was busy inspecting him with a critical eye.

"Uh, can I help you?" Zack quickly asked the man, pushing deeper into the couch cushions. The look in the older man's eye reminded him of times that were best left forgotten.

"Mathew!" Anna barked, "Now is not the time for that."

"Just one question and then I promise to behave until after dinner." Mathew, Tessa's father, crept closer to Zack until their noses were nearly touching. "Did those researchers choose you because of your compatibility with the portals, or did that happen because of what they did to you?"

Zack went cold as an uncontrollable fury rose up from within his depths. His eyes hardened and the feeling of Zara tugging at his arm was distant. How dare this man look at him with those eyes and ask him a question like that!

Abruptly, Matt was pulled back by his wife, who was looking at Zack as though he were a dangerous animal. "I know this situation is stressful," She began in a calming voice. "And he just made it worse for you, but you need to calm down. He didn't mean any harm with that thoughtless question."

Zara continued tugging on his arm until he came back to himself and regained control.

Thankfully, he hadn't done anything but sit there. Anger issues had never been a problem for Zack before, and certainly nothing like that fury he had just experienced. That was new, and not welcome in the slightest. The near loss of control it had brought on was something he could not abide.

Zack stood, pulling Zara along with him. "Sorry, but can we be excused for now? I think I need some time alone with my sister."

"Of course, Tessa will show you to the room you will be staying in. We will see you at dinner." Anna agreed with an amicable smile while motioning to her daughter.

"Thank you for understanding." Zack hurried to the door, eager to be out of that room.

Tessa didn't say anything until they had walked past the grand staircase and into a wider hallway. There were windows placed every few meters, and a door was open near the middle of the hall.

"What was that?" She stopped short of the door and turned to face them. "The air around you suddenly changed. It was like this aura of pure anger and malice."

Zack had enough and snapped at her. "What do you mean 'What was that'?" With a sneer, he continued. "What do think happens when you are interrogated by people you don't know, concerning things that you would rather forget?" Then, without waiting for a reply, he brushed past her with Zara and the two bears in tow. The door slammed shut in Tessa's stunned face.

Zara plopped herself down on the bed and played with one of Zelda's loose threads. "What happened in there? I've never seen you react like that before."

Zack paced around the room. "I don't know. I think it was caused by everyone wanting to talk about those days lately. For years, I've been able to suppress and ignore the memories from back then. Moving on without needing to face everything that was done to us. What good would that do me? We were helpless kids." He swallowed and turned to face the corner.

"When we got to the academy, everything changed. There have been constant reminders, the portal, the military, now Tessa and her family." Zack started in surprise when he felt his sister wrap him in a hug from behind. "It all came to a head in there, and I couldn't help but think that he was just like them."

Zara sniffled against his back. "I saw it too. The look in his eyes was exactly the same as theirs back then."

"How have things been for you? I know a lot of the things that have been reminding me didn't involve you directly. Outside of the incident at the portal, have you been alright at the academy?"

"I didn't want to say anything," Was the wet, muffled response, as Zara hid her face against his back. "I knew you were having it worse, whereas I was able to mostly hide away from everything."

Zack sighed and shook his head. "I was fine in all my lessons, learning about the portals, the monsters, how classes worked. Everything I never had a chance to learn before or had figured out on my own. They were usually interesting, and far enough removed from what we experienced that they weren't an issue. I guess it was all just building up, regardless."

"What are we going to do?" Zara pulled away and swiped at her eyes. "What do you want to do?"

He hesitated; the obvious answer was that they needed to learn to deal with what had happened to them. They needed to stop ignoring and running from it.

How though?

The academy had something called a psychologist on staff that was reported to help with emotional and mental trauma. That wasn't something they could risk. The secret that he had gone through the portal as a child may have gotten out already. That was fine. They had expected it to happen.

However, no one knew that Zara had also gone through. Talking to a person trained in working their way through the darkest parts of your mind seemed like the fastest way to get that exposed. Besides, who knew if they were actually even allowed to talk about the specifics with regular people in any case.

"I don't know," He finally whispered helplessly. "I just know we can't continue on like this."

"Maybe we should talk to Edith when we get back? She might have some ideas that could help." Zara offered carefully. "She has been nice to us, and already knows about your scars..." She trailed off.

Zack considered it carefully before replying. "How trustworthy do you think she is?"

"I'm not saying that we should tell her everything." The young girl flopped back onto the bed and covered her eyes with an arm. "As for how trustworthy she is. Who can say? We both know she is hiding her own secrets; we saw that this morning when she mentioned her husband. She could just find his memory painful, or there could be more to it."

"If there was more to it than that, why would she even mention him?" Zack questioned, leaning back and trapping her legs between him and the bed.

"Maybe it was a sign that she is beginning to trust us as well," Zara sighed and moved her arm to stare up at the ceiling. "Or maybe we are just overthinking something simple to a stupid degree."

"Maybe," He agreed, unwilling to move from off her legs. "We'll still talk to her when we get back and see how it goes. I'm fine with my secrets being revealed. That isn't a big deal, but I don't want anything to happen to you."

"Would it be so bad?" She wondered aloud. "In the end, I would just be lumped into the same category as you."

"That's not what I'm worried about. That part would be fine. It's the potential experiments they may run on me, and in turn you. You saw how Mathew, Tessa's dad, was looking at me. Can you honestly say he wouldn't try to experiment with us if he was given the chance?"

That was what he was trying to protect her from. People who wanted to turn her into a living lab experiment. He hadn't been able to protect her the last time; he wouldn't fail her a second time.

"I wish there was a way for them to just leave us alone," Zara muttered angrily.

Zack thought back to the change in his life burner ability. "It will happen eventually. I have no idea when, but the portals are changing things in our world as well. I'm sure the people at the top will begin to notice soon enough, if they haven't already. Little things that weren't possible before, or that act different now. The portals have been open for over a hundred years, and the mana crystals have been mined for much of that. All that mana that gets used or released as waste has to go somewhere. I doubt it simply disappears."

He wasn't sure exactly what it would mean for the world, nor did he particularly care. The people of the world had done little for him and his sister. There was even a portion of himself that was looking forward to the coming chaos. They would truly be free when that happened, if it happened. Even if it did eventually, it could be years away.

They continued to talk for a while longer, bandying about ideas that grew progressively more ridiculous and implausible. It was a nice distraction from everything, and helped to calm them both down.

When the knock came for dinner, they were ready to be around others again.

Ben, the chauffeur, was standing in front of the door when they opened it. In his arms was the large bear Zara had named Aisha.

"My apologies for bringing her over so late. Lady Testarosa believed it would be better for the two of you to have some uninterrupted time alone." He passed the bear to them and stepped back. "Now, if you care to follow me, I will lead you to the dining room."

Zara quickly placed the oversized teddy bear on the bed beside George. She grabbed Zelda and hurried back to the door.

"I thought Tessa said that you were the chauffeur?" Zack probed as they followed behind the imposing man.

"I am, but I am also one of their butlers. One rarely performs just one duty when serving in a noble household like the Ricerca's." He explained, while leading them back down to the main floor of the house.

Tessa and her mother Anna were waiting for them in the dining room. There was a long table taking up a significant portion of the room. There were only two chairs occupied at the very end, with the rest of the space being wasted.

"How are you doing?" Anna asked as they walked down the length of the room to join them.

"Better, sorry about earlier. The way he looked at me, combined with the question, was just too much." Zack pulled out a chair for Zara, across the table from their hosts, and then sat next to her.

"I thought as much," Anna nodded, her face impossible to read. "I apologize on my husband's behalf, since he will not be joining us this evening."

"Have you thought about talking to someone about everything that happened back then?" Tessa asked, watching their expressions carefully.

"We didn't have the money for anything like that before we arrived at the academy." He took a sip of water from the glass that had marked where they were to sit. "Now, well, I know there is someone who specializes in things of that nature at the academy. I don't believe it matters anyway," He shrugged, and told them the reason that had occurred to him earlier while talking it over with Zara. "Much of what happened to us involves secrets that I believe the government and military don't want to get out. I doubt someone working for an academy, even one as prestigious as the Albion Travelers academy, would have the necessary clearance."

A door to the side opened, and the first of many immaculately dressed servants entered with plates of food. The next half-hour or so was filled with mundane chit-chat about the school and their classes as they ate.

Anna found Quinn's treatment of Spencer especially amusing.

It was during the dessert of melon flavored gelato that the tone of the conversation changed. Zack had taken a few spoonful's of the cold treat for himself, enjoying the taste. Then passed the rest of the treat to Zara, who had already worked her way through the bowl she had been given.

Anna looked on, sympathy flashing briefly across her normally carefully controlled face.

Looking across the table, Zack gave them both a slight nod. "Thank you for giving us the chance to eat first. Now, why did you have us come here? The real reason if you please. I doubt you brought us here simply to 'clarify' some things is how I believe you put it earlier."

Chapter 20

"That is where you would be wrong." Anna saw they were done with the dessert and stood, where she waited for the others to follow her example. "The main purpose of inviting you here this time was to simply talk and to get your measure as a person. Anything beyond that was secondary."

She led them through the depths of the mansion and to a garden at the back.

"What about your husband?" Zack asked, stepping outside and into the verdant, lush grove of flowers and fruit-bearing trees.

"I admit that was a mistake on my part. I didn't expect either of you to respond, so..." Anna tilted her head. "Aggressively to the other's presence." She led them along a lit path, lined by flowers and apple trees with small fruits dangling from the branches that were just out of reach.

"It was his eyes," Zara informed them, speaking up for the first time since dinner. "The researchers back then would always look at us with those same eyes. As though we weren't people, but subjects to be dissected."

Tessa inhaled sharply; her gaze focused on her feet.

"I'm afraid that is a common trait among people in that line of work," Anna told them as they walked into an open space with an open-walled stone-made gazebo in the middle. "Most researchers I've met have those same eyes when they are working on a difficult problem. They tend to get absorbed in their work and forget about everything else."

There was a small tea table inside the structure, with several chairs scattered around the area. A steaming teapot was on the table alongside a bowl of berries and four small cups, all waiting for them.

Tessa sat first, throwing a few berries into her cups before pouring in the aromatic liquid. Her eyes were still fixed on anything but them. The mention of her father seemed to have really unnerved her.

Zara was more interested in eating the berries than drinking the tea.

Anna waited for them to be seated before continuing. "At some point in the future, I would like to talk to you about the research facility. However, that can wait until you are ready." She took a sip of her own and tossed the last couple of berries into her cup.

A maid appeared out of the darkness with a fresh bowl of the sweet and tart treat. The conversation paused until she had faded back into the shadows and was gone.

Zara blushed and played with her hands. "Sorry, I didn't mean to eat them all." She apologized in a soft voice.

Anna gave the young girl a rare smile, "It's fine, that's what they are there for. Whether they are used as food or as a flavor enhancer for the drink doesn't matter. Feel free to eat as many as you want."

Zack had taken the brief moment of respite to gather his thoughts on the woman's request. "It may be sometime before that is the case. I do have a question though, something that has been bugging me for a while now."

He waited for Anna to lower her cup and meet his eyes before continuing. "Was the institute a sanctioned organization at some point?"

"What would make you think it was anything of the sort?" She asked, taking a brief sip of the steaming tea.

"It's something that I have always wondered. They had access to their own personal portal. After all, that shouldn't have been possible without the government's influence. Right?"

Tessa's mother took another brief sip of her tea. "I can see why you might think that." She placed her cup back on the table and popped a berry into her mouth. "Except you are missing a couple of key pieces of information. First, whoever said that all the portals had been reported to the government?

"Second, even if they had been reported, control would not be possible for all of them. The reach of the government and that of the crown are not as great as many believe. Influence wanes over time, no matter what, or who, it belongs to. Unless the crown wanted absolute control over everything. Except, history shows what happens in those instances."

The three teens in front of her were shocked by the sudden change in her tone. Not to mention the sensitive information that had been revealed. That was a lot for them to suddenly digest, and for Zack, at least it went against everything he had been taught.

"Is it true at least that there have been no new portals created since they all appeared years ago?" Zack decided to let her non-answer pass for the moment.

There was a moment of hesitation as the mother carefully chewed and swallowed the berry. "That is a harder question than you might realize to answer." Her expression changed to a mask of cold indifference. "It should go without saying that anything I say to the three of you stays between the three of you. I won't say anything ultra-top-secret, but this is still top-secret information."

She waited for each of them to nod and verbally agree before letting the mask drop.

"Why tell us any of this then, mother?" Tessa wondered, setting her teacup down with a slight tremble.

Anna sighed and rubbed her eyes. "Things are beginning to change, and within a couple of years, or perhaps sooner, nothing I say here will matter. Consider it my way of ensuring that my daughter has the best chance possible of staying alive during what is to come." Her words were as confusing to the trio as they were ominous.

She held up a hand, forestalling their questions. "You'll learn the truth in time, possibly even parts of it tonight, I imagine."

"The researchers portal?" Zara prompted, trying to get them back on track.

"To my knowledge, which, as you can imagine, encompasses a fair bit of secret information, no new portals have appeared since that day. That said, we are consistently finding 'new ones' in remote locations where people rarely visit. To a one, each of those have possessed extremely strong monsters inside."

"How were the power lines or markers?" Zack asked, referring to the black power rings that Jean had told him about.

Anna raised a brow in surprise. "Almost always completely solid."

Zara frowned, thinking over everything she remembered seeing about the institute's portal. "The rings or lines increase over time regardless of whether people enter them. It seems that they might increase faster when no one enters them." She held Zelda close and stared at the king's advisor. "Have you discovered why? Is it merely the act of people crossing over, or is it the mining, maybe even the monster hunting?"

Zack held back a smile and stroked his sister's hair, enjoying the silky, non-straw-like texture that it now had. She may have been emotionally stunted by what had been done to them, but her mind was capable of making connections that his never could.

It was a fact that Anna was beginning to realize, and both brows this time rose in surprise. "All three seem to have differing effects on the rate they increase. What we can say for sure is that all of them are beginning to grow at a faster rate than when they first appeared."

"Which is why you said we'll learn the truth in time." Tessa frowned and folded her arms. "Something like that can't remain hidden for long."

"No, it can't." Zack agreed. "The corporations renting the school's portal have already noticed. Though I suspect they had something else in mind when they mentioned it to the authorities."

"Would you care to guess as to when they all started increasing at a more noticeable pace?" Anna had gone back to eyeing Zack with a removed, yet inquisitive stare.

It was Zara who answered, once more showing off the odd way her mind worked. "It wouldn't happen to be the same day as when the institute's portal locked itself?"

"It would indeed," Anna should her head. "Incredible. I had only drawn that connection myself after speaking extensively with the Major the last few days. The records for the operation that rescued you, and shut down that place, never crossed my desk. Possibly related to the matter of you two being lost in the system, as it were."

"Do any of the people that are working on the matter understand why they are acting that way?" Tessa asked, slowly relaxing the tight grip she had on her arms. "What will happen when the monsters inside all the portals become too strong for the other travelers to handle?"

"We aren't going to let that happen, are we, Zack?" Anna held her teacup to her lips, a hard look in her eyes.

Zack felt his back grow cold as he remembered what Jean had told him. How the Major had believed him to be some kind of key. Now the woman sitting across the small table from him had spoken with the man. It all came together, and suddenly he knew why they had been invited to the mansion.

He wasn't going to get that time to level up, as Jean believed he would before they called him. They were going to send him through the institute's portal, right away, if he had to guess.

"You intend to send me through the sealed portal. Tomorrow, I'm guessing?" Zack lifelessly took a sip of the now lukewarm tea, thinking about how they had been put in this situation.

Zara snapped a look at him, her eyes opening wide in understanding. "They can't! Jean said the power lines went completely solid black years ago. Who can say how strong the monsters inside could be?"

Anna nodded, while her daughter looked on, not understanding what they were saying. "The Major has already prepared a team of the strongest travelers in the kingdom. However, despite this being an unknown situation, or even knowing how the portal will react.

"There is no reason to expect that they will even need to fight anything on the other side. The hope at this point is that Zack will be able to force his way through the obstruction, unblocking the portal, and then come right back. Either way, as soon as the seal is removed, the rest of the team will go through after him."

The urge to lash out and let his mouth run free was nearly overwhelming. It was only Zara grabbing his hand that stopped him from doing anything. Instead, he pushed his chair back and stood, gazing at the mother and daughter with disappointed eyes.

"I had hoped the two of you were different, but in the end, you are still the same as your husband and father. Controlling the lives of people as though they belong to you, playing with their emotions all to further some ephemeral goal." He laughed hollowly. "I hope that unsealing that portal brings about consequences you could never have imagined."

"Why would you say that? The kingdom-"

"Has nothing to do with us!" Zack interrupted her, unable to contain himself any longer. "We have no friends or family here. There are no connections that would make us feel any loyalty towards this disgusting place." He stopped and turned away from the table. "Come, Zara, it seems I should go to sleep now. I imagine it will be an early morning."

She followed after him, her own eyes looking back at the seated mother and daughter with disappointed eyes. "There really is no one we can trust. Is there?"

"Don't forget, there is still Edith." He whispered in reply. Unwilling to take away the small amount of hope that she still had in people. "She at least seems to a be a good person."

"Are you-" Zara was prevented from saying more as Tessa ran up behind them.

"I'm sorry!" The girl panted out. "I had no idea what mother was planning when I invited you here."

Zack shook his head in disbelief and kept walking, relying on his memory to lead them back to their room.

"Is that how you were healed so quickly?" Tessa questioned, as they stopped outside the door of the room they were staying in. "There was a healer there when you went through the portal, wasn't there?"

Though it had been phrased as a question, it was apparent she wasn't expecting an answer. She had already made up her mind.

"I'll make sure Zara stays safe while you are gone," Tessa assured them as Zack twisted the door handle and pushed.

He snorted and shook his head in disbelief. "You'll have to forgive me for doubting anything you say. At this point, I don't even know if I would believe you if you said the sun was going to rise as normal tomorrow."

"Well, that seems a little ridiculous," She replied good-naturedly. Tessa was fully cognizant of how her actions had destroyed any trust he had in her. "I'm half-tempted to see now if I have gained some kind of world-bending powers."

Zara gave a half-giggle and then ducked behind her bear.

Tessa sighed and met Zack's eyes. "I don't agree with how my mother has gone about any of this, but I can guarantee, for whatever it might be worth, that she is doing it for the greater good."

"I'm sure she is." Zack pushed Zara into the room. "And no, it isn't worth anything."

The door shut with a firm click, and the siblings retreated farther into the room and sat on the bed. Sitting there in the middle of the bed beside George was Zara's new bear, Aisha.

Motioning for Zara to remain silent, Zack grabbed the bear and began feeling at each of the seams. He was probably just being paranoid, but he wouldn't put it past them to have put a listening device inside the stuffed animal.

Thankfully, they hadn't said anything that needed to be kept a secret earlier when they were talking in the room. It would be even easier for them to listen in on anything said inside the mansion itself.

His inspection of the seams and feeling along the inside edges led to him finding nothing. It had been a long shot regardless, hampered if nothing else by the fact that he didn't even know what he was looking for. The best he could do was find anything that seemed out of place, or had a sign pasted to the side of it saying what it was. Neither of which he found.

"Come on," He said at last. "If they expect me to go through that accursed portal tomorrow, then I am going to need all the sleep I can get."

Zara yawned, and after stepping into the attached bathroom to change, slipped under the covers of the bed. "Do they even know what to expect on the other side of that portal?"

"I don't think so," He replied while yawning, his eyes dragging down with an interminable weight. "From what I understand, everyone who went through the portal after our rescue had their memories wiped. I would assume that they wrote reports or something, for the Major's people to work off of though." He yawned again and snuggled against the fluffy pillow. "We should steal this bed and pillow for when we go back to the dorm." He mumbled, already drifting off.

Zara muttered something in agreement, already drifting off as well. The comfortable bed was even higher quality than the ones at the dorm. The beds there had been a revelation in comfort just weeks before. Now, in comparison, they seemed lumpy and unrefined.

***

It was hours later, in the darkest hours of the night, that the large mansion was attacked.

It was a cold and silent affair, with each person in mottled, dark-colored outfits that blended into the night. It was to the attacker's credit that they were using darts laced with a powerful sleeping agent instead of going for the more lethal alternatives. No matter what, they were attacking a noble's residence. If they were ever discovered and had killed anyone, nothing their leader or employer could do would save them from the king's wrath.

Not that they planned on being discovered. They had worked hard, too hard, to circumvent the family's small security force. It was what they were paid to do.

They were being paid to collect two people, and that is exactly what they were going to do. The consequences after that, lay with the employer and not them.

The servants and various butlers were all put to sleep one by one. Those that were already asleep were darted anyway, to make sure they stayed that way. Up the stairs they crept, intent on finding the two rooms they had been directed towards.

Their targets that night were a man, who was reputed to be a researcher of some renown, and his teenage daughter. They found the daughter first. She was sitting at a desk in her room, reading a book on how spells worked, ignoring the late hour. A quick dart to the back of her neck had her slumped over and asleep within moments. Carefully securing the girl, the intruders scooped her up and carried her away.

Her father was harder to find. The location of the room they had been given was empty. With the blankets smooth, and the mattress cold. No one had slept on it that night.

The contract prevented them from leaving right then, despite the misgivings the members of the team possessed. They were forced to look for the man, and to make every effort possible to bring him away. Failing that, they would need to find another way to salvage the operation.

It was an unfortunate option that would grow in importance with every minute they spent in the mansion. Outside factors were always something that needed to be considered in any operation. There was never a guarantee that they had managed to tag and dart every person on the estate.

All it would take was one person they hadn't accounted for stumbling upon something they shouldn't. Everything would fall apart from there. Their ghost-like status would be gone, and in the worst case, someone, or many someone's, would be dead.

That was not how they operated, and it was the main reason they were allowed to keep operating. This particular mission went against many of the group's rules, all because their leader had owed a favor to someone he shouldn't have.

They made their way to the opposite end of the mansion in their search for the man. It was there that they stumbled across an occupied room.

Asleep on a large bed were two kids, a teenage boy, and a younger girl. Between them were three stuffed animals, two worn with use and age, while the third was brand new.

Without hesitation, darts were shot into both kids, and then they were bundled up and taken away. The bears lay forgotten on the bed.

If they couldn't have the man, then they would simply have to settle for bringing the client more kids. They had stayed too long already.

With the two girls and boy tied up and secured in the back of a dark, silent vehicle, they retreated. Unsure as to whether the three they had taken would be enough to save their leader's proverbial hide.

Chapter 21

Z ack woke in a dark place with a trembling figure clutching tight to his side. "What? Where?" He mumbled. His mind was slow to react and understand the situation, as though a thick fog permeated everything.

"You finally awake?"

"That you Tessa?" He asked blearily, vaguely recognizing the blurry sounding voice.

"Yeah, Zara is here as well."

The fog was clearing from his mind with each passing second. Finally, he recognized the small shivering shape of his sister, clinging to him in silent fear. His eyes gradually adjusted to the dark gloom, and the general shape of a small room came into focus.

"Where are we? What happened?" He rested a hand on Zara's shaking head, giving her the small amount of comfort he could manage in the situation. A situation that was entirely too familiar for his liking.

"I am not sure; I only woke myself a few minutes ago." The dark shape of her body was pressed against the wall across from him. A hand was pressed against her neck. "I think someone used darts coated in something to put us to sleep and then we were taken."

"Did they get your mother and father?" He asked, growing worried with how Zara was acting. She hadn't said a word during the short time that he had been awake. Looking around the darkroom, his eyes struggling to pierce through the darkness, he realized why.

He muffled a curse and held her tighter. Zelda and George, her constant companions, emotional support, and protectors, were nowhere to be seen. Even in the institute, Zelda had been there with her every step of the way. The bears were quite literally the things that allowed her to function as somewhat normally as she did.

Without them... Well without them, she was left as a terrified mess of a little girl with the stunted emotional maturity of someone much younger.

"I doubt it. Father would have been in his laboratory, which no one has access to. As for mother, she should have been in her office, which she keeps locked whether she is inside or not." Tessa dropped her hand and leaned against the rock wall. The light coming in from the gaps around the door provided enough illumination to see by once their eyes had adjusted.

"You seem pretty calm, considering everything." Zack pulled his sister fully onto his lap and cradled her in his arms.

"I have no doubt that mother will organize our rescue soon enough, and even if she doesn't, they wouldn't dare to hurt us." She had begun to relax some, now that she had found her confidence.

Zack, on the other hand, understood something that she had missed. She might be safe due to her status as a noble. He and his sister, however, had no such protection.

The sound of shoes scuffing on the flooring of the hallway outside echoed in the room as someone approached. A shadow blocking the gaps around the door the light shone through. The sound of multiple latches and locks being undone echoed throughout the small room.

A moment later, the door was thrown open, and light flooded in, blinding them. An individual wearing a dark outfit and a mask stood before them. Strapped to their thigh was a small blowgun, with three lines of darts beside it in a small leather bandolier.

"Good, you're all awake." The voice was muffled and distorted in an effort designed to disguise their identity.

Tessa blinked furiously against the hot tears the sudden bright light caused. "Why were we taken? What is it your employer wants with us?"

The mask-covered head tilted to the side. "You recognize us?"

The teenage girl nodded, doing her best to look unafraid. "Partially, I've heard the stories about a team of people who will work for any noble able to throw enough coin at them. No one else would be stupid enough to attack a noble household."

"Lower-noble." The person corrected. "Even we wouldn't attack a proper household of nobles. You are correct. However, we were hired to retrieve you and your father. The other two were merely a bonus for when we couldn't find him. This brings us to the main reason I am here. Where is he?"

The focus on those specific two people, combined with the lack of knowledge about her mother and the real status of her family, told them all they needed to know. They had likely been hired by either the Albrights or

Spencer's VanCamp family. It was a clue that neither of the coherent teens missed. Zara was another matter, with her mind shutting down in order to protect her.

The question for Tessa at least was how to leverage that information without making the situation worse. For the siblings, it was a much harder and more urgent problem. If their employer learned they had captured Zack, regardless of which family was behind their capture, it would be bad.

Tessa wiped the tears from her eyes as they finished adjusting to the light. "Who was it that hired you? The Albrights, or the VanCamps?"

There was no visible reaction to the question, with any clues hidden beneath the mask.

The girl shook her head. "It doesn't matter, I suppose. Just know that this isn't a job that your group should have taken."

The person shrugged. "We had no choice in the matter, and for what it is worth, I even agree. However, that doesn't change anything. Now tell me, where can we find your father?"

"Or what?" She asked, genuinely curious as to what they would do. The group, from the little she had heard, operated within a certain boundary when it came to nobles.

"Or we start hurting your little friend over there. Make no mistake, our options when it comes to you may be limited. For him and the girl, however, that is not the case. They are not nobles or even people with any power." Again, they showed a frankly woeful lack of information in regard to the identity of their other captives.

It was Tessa's turn to tilt her head in confusion and laugh. "Are you sure about that?"

Zack watched the show with bated breath, unsure of what each side was playing towards.

"I had heard that your... group." Tessa hesitated, as though she was about to name them. "Was better than this when it comes to gathering information on your targets. I can only assume that this must have been a rush job if your information only goes this far."

The atmosphere surrounding their captor changed in the blink of an eye. Her words had managed to anger them, while also forcing a whisper of doubt into their mind. The dark-clothed figure backed away until they reached the door.

"Our organization is not so rash as to rush into injuring someone with sufficient backing." They pulled the door mostly closed before saying one last thing. "And we were indeed forced to rush into pulling off this particular job."

The door closed with a clunk, leaving only a thin strip of light around the edges once more.

Zack watched the door close in confusion. "Uh, that isn't how these things normally go in the stories. Aren't they supposed to threaten us, cut off some flesh, and just generally terrorize us into submission?"

Zara whimpered and hugged his side tighter.

"Sorry," He apologized, rubbing her back affectionately. "Don't worry, I won't let them hurt you."

Tessa relaxed back against the bare wall and breathed out explosively. "I can't believe that worked! I'd heard rumors that the way they worked was different, that they operated with a certain amount of honor. It's the only way they could have remained in business for so long otherwise."

"What are you talking about? Who are they?" Zack kept his voice low, so as to keep from scaring his sister even more.

"They're called 'Faluers' Fist', and they have been around for years now. Normally, the crown would have stamped them out without a second thought. Instead, for whatever reason, the king and queen at the time decided to make a deal with them. One that would reportedly benefit both sides." The back of her head knocked against the hard wall when leaned back. "Ever since, as long as they follow certain rules, then they will be allowed to continue operating."

"And let me guess, one of these rules involves how they treat the nobles?"

"Yup, and those under their protection."

He snorted. "The sufficient backing, they mentioned."

She made a noise of assent. "Yup, those are the only reason we are being treated differently from what you expected. If I wasn't a noble, and you and your sister weren't unknowns, then what you mentioned might indeed have been a reality. Although, I still doubt it. The rumors around Faluers' Fist have never been particularly violent."

Zack held Zara close and settled into place next to Tessa against the wall. "I would love to understand why the crown decided to let them keep operating."

"It's not that hard to understand. They were a known quantity, and above all else, they were willing to follow the rules imposed on them. At least, that is what I believe. Only the king and queen from back then could say for sure what their reasoning was. What I don't understand is their lack of decent information."

Zack nudged her in the side when she stopped speaking. "What do you mean, is that abnormal or something?"

"Well, I wasn't kidding earlier when I mentioned that I had heard their information gathering on targets was better. It needs to be for them to make sure they operate within what the crown allows."

He felt his head beginning to hurt and wondered how they had managed to find themselves in this situation. Zack had only wanted to protect his little sister while providing a decent life for them both. It was what had prompted him to take the compatibility test, despite any lingering fear of the portals. Then everything had snowballed and run out of their control.

Who would have guessed that mere weeks after taking that test, they would be caught up in the intrigue of nobles? Not him, that was for sure. Then there was the military and Tessa's mom.

It was a mess.

"So, what are the odds of this ending soon, and without-" He stopped, it was pointless to continue with that question. No matter what, he and Zara were expendable to their captors. It was just a matter of time before they learned the truth. Once they did, then he was sure the gloves would come off. "Just protect Zara, please?"

Tessa nodded as the younger girl whimpered against his side again. "I'll do my best, and I would say the odds are not in our favor. Mother may have already discovered our disappearance, and she may have even notified your military Major right away. However, putting together a rescue force of any size would take time, not a lot if they rush, but every bit adds up."

She sighed, and let her head hit the wall again. "Really, it is just a matter of who moves faster..."

"The ones who paid to have you captured or your mother." He finished for her. "I would think that the ones behind this would react faster."

"Yup, that it was I think as well. Even if mom and the military are only an hour or two away, a lot can happen in that amount of time."

Zack swallowed and glanced at the door. He knew exactly how much could happen in that time frame.

"What's wrong with her?" Tessa asked, making an effort to take their mind off the impending situation.

"Zelda and George aren't here." He answered simply. "Those two bears, especially Zelda, are a sort of safety blanket for her. Zelda was named and given to her by our parents, and has always been with her. She is her protector, and was there for her during her darkest hours. Times that I couldn't be there because I was inside a portal or being experimented on myself.

"When they are nearby, or in her arms, she can act in a mostly normal fashion. Take them away, however, and she becomes paralyzed with the memories, feelings of powerlessness, and terror of what happened in the institute." He hugged his sister close, feeling her trembles lessen ever so slightly. "That's the simple, and uncomplicated version in any case."

"What happened back then?" Tessa asked hesitantly.

The flooring outside the door squeaked as he opened his mouth to answer with the usual response. The door being thrown open kept him from saying anything. Light flooded in for the second time, their eyes watering as they were forced to adjust to the sudden brightness.

Standing in the doorway was Dorn Albright. "I thought I told you to stay away from her, peasant?" He sneered and stepped fully into the room. "They weren't able to get your father, but I consider getting this particular eyesore a decent bonus." He frowned. "Who is that in your arms?"

"My sister." Zack tightened his grip on her.

A variety of emotions flashed across the other boy's face, none of them pleasant. "I'm sure I'll find a use for her later."

"Don't get ahead of yourself, Dorn!" Tessa warned in a grave tone. "My mother will-"

"Your mother is dead!" Dorn sneered again, looking down on her.

Tessa stilled in fear, afraid that they had done something to her already.

"Everyone knows that she died years ago!" Dorn continued. "Any power and authority she may have once had disappeared with her death."

She exhaled in relief and sagged weakly against Zack's side.

"Dude," Zack shook his head, the word feeling unfamiliar on his tongue. It was a term that he had heard some of the other male students say in class. "You and your family have gone full idiot; you never go full idiot. Do you actually believe that the king, queen, and all the rest of the hoity-toity nobles will let your family go after stealing her father's research? Not to mention after you force her to what, marry you?"

Dorn glared at him. "They can't say anything after we are married. The union will be binding, and her father won't dare to go against us then! Besides," The ever-present sneer on his face grew ugly. "Only a few of them even have the power to go against my family. Once we use her father's research to gain control of the portals, that number will shrink even more!"

Zara stilled, her trembles disappearing in a second. They had been taken by people who wanted to control the portals in their own way.

"Do you know what her father is researching? I wonder if the rumors I've been hearing about you are true?" Dorn's eyes gained a sly gleam. "That you really have a perfect compatibility rating with the portals."

Zack remembered the odd look in her father's eye when he had mentioned that very thing at their first meeting. "What does that have to do with anything?"

Tessa looked away, refusing to look at him.

Meanwhile, Dorn smiled in triumph. "Oh, it has everything to do with it." He burst out laughing; his cackles echoed loudly in the small room. "I finally understand why she approached you. This is rich. I never needed to be worried in the slightest! It was her father that was interested in you, not her."

Zara pulled back from Zack, her weak arms containing a sudden steel-like strength. "Explain, NOW!" She growled, grabbing hold of Tessa's arm, and squeezing.

The red-haired girl winced and tried to pull away. "I don't know. He doesn't talk about his research with me! I have no idea what his current or even past projects are."

Zara reluctantly released her, collapsing back against her brother as the sudden burst of anger-induced strength fled as quickly as it had appeared.

Dorn watched the show in boredom. "I was about to tell you myself; you know?"

"Quit monologuing and just tell us already!" Tessa snapped, rubbing her arm and scooting away from Zack.

"Fine." He folded his arms and looked away from them petulantly. The act ruining the sense of foreboding doom he had built up to that point. The crowd of people gathered behind him in the hallway, all shook their heads in concealed disgust. "Her father, Mathew Ricerca, has been researching ways to increase a person's compatibility rating with the portals."

"Is that it?" Zack wondered in disbelief. "You are doing all of this because some crazy crackpot has been working towards increasing the experience you get on the other side?"

"Hey!" Tessa protested. "That's my father you're talking about."

Dorn ignored her outburst and replied. "No, while valuable in the long run, it wouldn't be enough for us to do any of this. That is just going to be the public reason for our actions." The sly gleam from before crept back into his eyes. "Do you understand what would go into a project like his?

What side-effects or accidental discoveries might be learned while they are pursuing their ultimate goal?"

That sense of foreboding doom came back stronger than ever, as the noble-born teen stood straight.

Zack found himself struggling to swallow around a suddenly dry mouth. "I don't know."

Tessa shrugged. "I wouldn't know either. Like I said, he doesn't discuss his projects with me."

Dorn stepped back into the hallway. "It's interesting, really. I can imagine how you must view me, Tessa, knowing that I will soon be your husband. A choice made against your will, and the wishes of your father and late mother. I've heard about how he promised her, on her deathbed no less, that the choice of your future husband would be up to you alone. And yet, the thought of how you will soon be viewing your own father as something even less than myself is…" His eyes fluttered in feigned ecstasy. "Almost enough to make up for it."

"Just say it already." Zack's voice sounded wooden and distant to his own ears.

"Fine, in order for his little team of psychopaths to have enough subjects to experiment on," Zara jerked in her brothers' arms, twisting around to fully face the much larger boy just outside the room. "They had to find a way to awaken them early, or at least create a facsimile of a proper awakening."

Zara jumped from Zack's lap with a scream and rushed to the door. Bouncing off the metal surface as it closed with a bang in front of her face.

She continued to scream and pound against the door. Paying no mind to the blood flowing from a busted lip and crooked nose.

"Shhh," Zack whispered to her, wrapping his arms around her gently from behind. "They can't hurt you, not again."

He continued to hold her as she worked out her frustration, anger, and fear against the door. Every few seconds, he would whisper something new to her that Tessa couldn't hear.

The young girl was a mess of blood, with the skin scraped from her hands, when she finally calmed a few minutes later.

Chapter 22

Tessa studied them with a look of sympathy that hadn't been there before. It was the difference between logically knowing something had been done to them. Where the knowledge was distant, with no real emotional attachment to it. And seeing firsthand how those actions had affected and shaped them. It was a shocking sight that brought the information into stark and horrifying relief.

"Could he really be doing something like that?" Zack asked in a rough voice after Zara had collapsed into his arms. Her eyes were closed, and her breathing even. The blood from her broken nose had slowed to a trickle, while the cut on her lip had already dried into a crusty mess.

"Would you even believe me if I said no?" There was a sudden weariness in her voice, as the question reminded her of what Dorn had said. "I would like to believe that my father isn't a monster." There was a soft sigh. "At the same time, I can't help but remember how he looked at you before. If he was passionate enough about a project, then maybe..." She trailed off, not knowing what more there was to say.

"How did your mom do it?" Zack didn't let the silence stick around for long. "She has an office at your house, and people must see her coming and going. Even if they don't know that she is one of the king's hidden advisors, they must know that she is at least alive."

"Mom?" Tessa shrugged. "I don't know. They had this whole affair about her being sick and dying when I was younger. Then the day after the funeral, she was back at the house, healthy as ever. Some of the servants and other staff were replaced at the same time. I guess for people she could trust. Any time she goes out, it is in a mask and outfit designed to conceal her identity. As for the office, the rumor is that since dad is always at the lab and I'm at school, part of the house was rented out to the crown for their purposes."

"And people believe that?" Zack snorted.

"It's not as far-fetched as it sounds, since they actually do exactly that. There are houses all around the country that the crown rents out a room the owners have sworn to never touch for official meetings. The locations are inspected carefully before each meeting, of course, just to make sure. It saves the crown money since they don't need to build rarely used offices everywhere. And according to mom, it gives the crown an excuse to keep an eye on some of the nobles that are farther away from the capital."

Zack shifted Zara onto her back and put her head in his lap. "And what about your mom? There have never been rumors that she is still alive and living the life of a spy? She is happy and content to only live unmasked at the mansion?"

Tessa backed away from them as his fingers gripped the young girl's crooked nose. "There are always rumors, but with the authority she wields, it is easy enough to make them go away or appear utterly ridiculous. As for the way she is forced to live. She hates it and has had enough. It is one of the many reasons that she is planning to reveal herself soon. It has been a long time coming, but she says it is finally time."

Zack pulled and straightened his sister's nose without warning. The sudden flare of pain rousing her from the emotionally exhausted slumber.

"Thanks. It was getting hard to breathe." The girl muttered, wiping a hand across the crusted blood to clear it away. Then she buried her face in his chest and closed her eyes once more.

"I guess I just don't understand how you nobles think. If Dorn is anything to go by, then institutionalized thinking is pretty prevalent among your crowd. That alone makes the deception more believable to me." He glanced at his sister's hands. Taking in their rough state and the skin that had been torn from her palms and knuckles. Gripping the hem of his old, ragged shirt, it ripped with a slight tug. Quickly, he wrapped the rags around both hands and leaned back. Wishing, as always, that there was more he could do for her.

"He'll be back soon, I'm sure. Dorn won't let the sight of him running away from her go. He's too proud for that."

"He didn't run away." Zack carefully pulled pieces of dried blood from Zara's hair. "Didn't you notice? He had already backed into the hallway before he said anything. He expected the reaction he got from one of us." He laughed hollowly. "Though, if I had to guess, he was betting on it being you or me instead."

"What?" Tessa swallowed and licked her lips, continuing the question in a soft voice as if she was afraid of the answer. "What really happened to you both when you were younger? Why did Zara react so violently to what Dorn said?"

Zack fought against the resurgence of memories, and the urge to scratch at his many scars. The thin, precise ones caused by a scalpel still ached with phantom pain. Even the few scars that had healed and disappeared ached and itched. It was enough to make him want to tear at his own skin, to get at the itch that lay just beneath the surface.

He inhaled a shuddering breath and pushed his emotions to the back of his mind. To a place where they wouldn't interfere with what he was about to tell her. The mental door holding everything at bay was thin and would crumble within minutes. Despite repeated efforts over the years, it had refused to get any stronger. In the end, it had been better to just bury everything down deep and ignore it.

He and Zara had already agreed that needed to change. Maybe, for him, this could be the first step along that path.

"We were taken shortly before I turned ten years old, and Zara was maybe seven or so. I can't quite remember our specific ages at the time. They weren't important enough to celebrate in the orphanage. One of the workers there had sold us, and probably others, to a research institute. Zara was collateral, a hostage to ensure that I did my best to help them and never rebel. In return, they promised to not experiment on her as they did me."

His finger traced the back of her neck, just below the hairline. At one time, many thin, precision scars that matched his own had been there.

"They lied, of course, though she did her best to hide it from me. I was their first, and as far as I know, one of their limited successes. It was enough to keep them from separating us, and little more." The door in his mind shook and cracked. He didn't have much time left to tell her their history.

"We were held there against our will for more than three years. Constantly being experimented on and given strange cocktails of drugs that had been mixed with items from inside the portals."

Tessa started in surprise.

"That's not possible. That's what you were going to say, right?"

She nodded.

"They're right, but also wrong. What do you think happens if you take the juice of a fruit, or pulp, a plant and mix everything together over there? Make it so everything is combined into one liquid, with the base for the mixture having come from over here?"

"Wouldn't it still disappear, like the meat in the stomach example Quinn mentioned?" Tessa had her eyes closed, and her fists were clenched tight.

"It depends. If they mix everything together properly with the right amounts of each, then it becomes something that no longer belongs to the portal. If they don't mix it properly, then parts of the mixture will disappear upon their return. In either case, the liquid would be examined, split into parts for later mixing, and then injected into a subject. Me, and sometimes her." The crack in his mental door grew wider.

"After the injection, they would cut open parts of my body to learn how it affected or changed me, if it did at all. I've heard there have been some recent innovations in medical mana-tech now that would have enabled them to see everything without cutting me." He swallowed his bitterness and sped on ahead, skipping over the truly grisly details.

"That was only at the beginning, of course. Things changed again a couple of months after we were taken." His hands clenched tight, the knuckles popping in rapid succession. "That was when they succeeded somehow, or something else happened. I don't know. But that was when my status page appeared, that was when," He shook his head and forced his hand to unclench. "A mere ten-year-old boy became a traveler. They had their own portal there. The institute had been built around the thing. Making sure knowledge of its existence was kept private and for their use alone."

Tessa's eyes flicked from him to his sister and back again in growing horror. An unladylike curse falling from her lips as everything clicked into place. "That's why she reacted that way, and my father... oh my," A second and far more profane example of impossible parentage, spewed forth.

Zack nodded and then continued with the tale. Desperate to get as much out as he could before the crumbling mental door fully collapsed. "Once I could go through the portal, they were free to change things up some. Magic works on the other side, after all. Only one researcher was also a traveler, but they only needed one to oversee everything and bring back proper notes. They could afford to be less careful by that point. Healing magic would fix most of their mistakes, and they made sure my level was always high enough to withstand anything they wanted to do to me."

The door in his mind holding everything back shattered. Tears crept down his cheeks as he forced himself to say one last thing. "I failed to protect her back then! When I was gone through the portal... the things they did to her were no less than what they did to me. I won't fail her again. I won't let some noble and his family, who are all hopped up on idiot juice, hurt her."

Zack bowed his head, resting it lightly on the top of Zara's. His throat was thick with emotion, and no matter how much he swallowed, it refused to clear. The hot tears continued to fall as a sob burst out and his entire body trembled.

It was a cathartic experience and washed away much of the frustration that had been building inside him lately.

"I won't let the Albright's hurt either of you if I can help it. After we get rescued, I'll make sure that everyone knows you both are under my family's protection." Tessa told him once he had calmed down.

"Does that protection extend to your dad?" He asked sardonically. It was a nice gesture on her part, one that would be appreciated in making certain classes more bearable. If her father was really doing what Dorn said, then he wouldn't be associating with her family for long.

"I," She hesitated and looked away. "I don't know. It would put you directly within dad's vicinity, and it would only be a matter of time before he approached you. Regardless of the true nature of his research, you would prove incredibly enticing as a source of potential information."

Zack blew his nose away from the two females, clearing away the trails of mucus clogging his nose. The room stank rancid sweat and the coppery tang of old blood, they were the first people to be held there. "Let's wait until we get out of here before deciding anything. I appreciate the offer, I truly do." He waved an arm around the dim room. "But, at the moment, nothing you say, or promise, has any real weight. Once we escape and depending on your father, if you are still willing, then I would definitely take the help and protection. There is only so much I can do for her alone."

The light coming from the door dimmed as someone approached. The heavy footfalls were easily heard inside the room. The blood-smeared door opened without any further warning, and a group of four masked individuals surrounded Zack.

Tessa was pushed to the side and Zara was roughly shoved from his protective grasp and onto the floor. His arms were held tight as they hauled him to his feet without saying a word.

"Watch out for when she wakes!" Zack told Tessa in a rush as they forcefully removed him from the room. Behind him, he spotted a set of dual locking bolts and a bar that could be placed in front of the door.

They had been without a doubt locked securely inside the room. Not that it mattered in any way when you were being held hostage by a noble and an established organization. That particular combination made even attempting to escape an exercise in futility.

The gleaming white floor of the hallway led into an intersection of equally polished flooring, with the walls of each painted a different color. They carried him down, the one with a garish shade of purple paint on the walls.

Dorn was waiting for them when they arrived. He was alone and his nice clothes were gone. They had been exchanged in favor of something that resembled the academy's training outfit. The walls of the room were padded, though the floor was bare, hard concrete.

"I've been wondering something, and it has been bugging me ever since I saw you earlier." Dorn casually walked closer to them. "What happened to all the lovely bruises I gave you before?"

A wave of too much cologne and minty breath washed over Zack as the larger boy inspected him closely.

"Let him go, I want to have some fun with him." A sadistic smile crept over the noble's face and thinned his eyes into gleeful slits. "I don't know how you managed to get healed so quickly from the last beating. That just means, however, that I can do it all over again, and really take my time to do it properly. What I have in mind, won't be so easily healed."

Zack burst into motion the second his arms were released. He had no chance of hurting the larger boy in the same manner he had been and was going to be again soon. That didn't mean he would simply pass up the chance to hit him when it was delivered on a silver platter.

With a speed faster than any of them had been expecting, Zack's fist rocketed out and crushed Dorn's nose. Smashing it flat at a severe angle and breaking the cartilage within the sensitive protrusion.

Dorn hopped back and grabbed his face, eyes watering from the pain. Drops of blood splattered down the front of his outfit and spilled to the floor. The pampered noble let loose a stream of ear-bending profanity that lasted for over a minute.

Zack smirked and ignored the pain in his fist and arms. The goons had grabbed him right after the punch landed. The grip they had on his arms was punishingly tight as they locked him in place.

"That's for making my sister break her nose earlier, you piece-" A knee to his side kept him from saying more.

"You'll pay for that! I said let him GO!" Dorn screamed, rushing at them with a loosely formed fist.

They released Zack a second late, and the weakly formed fist slammed into the boy's sternum with a crack. The blow had barely winded Zack, while several of Dorn's fingers looked crooked. It was a rookie mistake that the noble should have known better than to make. His family had made sure that he was trained in various fighting techniques in preparation for when he hopefully one day became a traveler.

None of that training mattered when he lost control.

Cradling his hand, Dorn spun and kicked out with an effective twist of his hips. The heavy boot he was wearing slammed into Zack's side with enough force to lift him onto the tips of his toes.

Zack retched and collapsed to the floor. Each breath was a struggle against the sudden pain in his side. It was a small miracle that none of his ribs had broken from the kick. It had taken less force than that to break one on the other side of his chest just days before. Going through the portal and unlocking his status was already showing some benefits it seemed.

Dorn took a moment to inspect his hand, grimacing when he saw how crooked a couple of them were.

Not paying attention to the boy, Zack put his hand on the ground and leveraged himself back into a standing position. "Is that why I was brought here? Just so you could show off and inflict some amateur grade torture?" He spit to the side, the bubble-laden liquid hot but clear. "I've been tortured before, and you can't break me with something of this level."

"We'll see about that!" Dorn snarled.

The group of four watching the show had retreated to the far wall. They were no longer involved in whatever was to come. The job they were being paid for had already been accomplished. At least, as far as they were concerned. They weren't being paid to beat and torture some kid they knew nothing about.

Zack fought back to the best of his abilities, showing a ferocity that shocked all in the room. He was a magic-user by class, but there had been a few times when he had run out of magic. Especially in the beginning. When that happened, he had needed to be able to escape or defend himself in other ways. Running away had been the preferred option when he was younger.

That had changed after their rescue. Running away from other people turned out to be more difficult than it was with monsters. They could think, work together with others, and more. He had by necessity learned to use his fists and feet to fight them off. It was all self-taught, but it was effective regardless. The small amount of training he had gotten from Rose in the training class had only enhanced that.

It wasn't enough. Not against a fully trained and much larger opponent.

Going through the portal had healed his body to a large extent, and the trip through it had been beneficial in many ways. In the end, it had simply been too short to heal years of malnourishment and injuries.

Chapter 23

Zack jumped backward, sweat dripping from his brow. Both sides of his chest ached, and his left eye was swollen shut. The lower part of his right shin ached from when he had accidentally kicked Dorn in the same place. The ill-protected bones hitting each other had left them both momentarily stunned.

Across from him, Dorn was still cradling his injured hand. There was swelling around his broken nose, and he was left to pant and breathe heavily through his mouth. He was favoring his right leg while standing in place, seemingly content to wait the other boy out.

They had been fighting if it could even be called that for only a scant few minutes. Yet, Zack was exhausted and hurting, his stamina still lacking despite his training and constant running. Injuries of any kind made you burn through your stamina reserves faster than normal.

Dorn, on the other hand, had taken a few hits, but was largely undamaged. "Is that the best you can do?" He asked in a nasally obnoxious voice, only partly because of his broken nose. It had always been annoying to listen to, not it was simply extra so. "I was expecting better from you after that sneak attack." He touched his crooked nose with a wince.

Zack backed further away from him. "I doubt you were expecting anything at all. Why else would you have told them to let me go?" He pointed at the four leaning against the wall, enjoying the show. "You realize this is the second time, right? That you have attacked me with a group on your side."

He coughed, a hint of copper touching the back of his tongue and throat. "I'm beginning to understand something about you. That underneath all the training your family put you through, the high-priced clothes and expensive haircut. You are nothing more than a coward, someone who is afraid of even facing a lowly, untrained orphan like me alone!" He wanted to groan, as he realized a second late that his mouth was running away from him again.

Dorn's face went red, his eyes flicking to their audience. He couldn't let that kind of disrespect stand! His pride alone, not to mention any other factors, wouldn't allow him to. Growling, he surged forward and swept the legs from beneath the impudent boy.

Zack toppled to the ground and rolled, desperate to get away from the stomping foot headed his way. The pinch of skin underneath a booted toe being ripped from his upper arm along with the sound of ripping fabric told everyone there he had only been mostly successful. Gritting his teeth against the flare of pain, he continued to roll away. Pain was nothing new to him, that alone would never be enough to break him.

"You honestly think I need a group of people to deal with the likes of you!" Dorn screamed, kicking a glancing blow against the ribs of the boy on the floor.

Zack felt his lungs temporarily seize up and gasped for air. "Now sure, but they had to do all of your dirty work first. They are the ones that brought me here, and then made sure I was sufficiently injured before taking up their spots on the wall."

The noble hesitated, a flicker of unrealized doubt creeping in before being ruthlessly squashed by his pride.

Not one to let the chance go to waste, Zack regained his feet and stood. One of his arms was bloody and twinging constantly from the torn skin. His ribs had progressed from simply aching to painfully inhibiting his movements. Just because he could mentally ignore the pain his body was in didn't mean anything physically. Ignoring a problem didn't make it go away.

His vision swam, and dots of bright light burst across the space. He was getting close to the end of his ability to struggle and put up a fight. He was sure they all knew it, too. Not that he was going to let that stop him. Zack had to make sure that Dorn was either too injured or tired to even think about going after Zara.

Only then could he think about stopping. Nothing else mattered.

Dorn tried to snort, only to end up coughing from the pain it caused, ending with a shake of his head. "I think I'll enjoy breaking you during our time together from now on. Only once I'm done with you will I move onto your little sister. Making you watch, in a broken state, as I torture her repeatedly."

"Why?" Zack gasped out, his blood running cold as he imagined the larger boy touching his sister. "What did we ever do to you that would make you want to do something so despicable?"

Even the four on the wall were looking on with disgusted expressions behind their faceless masks.

"You annoyed me, ignored my warning, and then dared to attack me." The boy grinned, showing off the flecks of blood on his teeth. "Besides, after that first time and now with this... I have discovered how incredibly satisfying it is to repeatedly beat down the same person."

Dorn was willing to torture another person, simply because he had found the experience intoxicating in its own way.

It was a reason that Zack couldn't abide. Such a person was worse than scum and couldn't be allowed to live. He was on the same level as those researchers that had tortured him and his sister under the guise of experiments.

For the second time that he could remember, Zack, lost control. Only this time, he wasn't sitting on a couch beside a person who he wanted to protect.

His vision narrowed until Dorn alone could be seen through his one good eye. Nothing else mattered at that moment. Not the pain in his ribs, arm, or leg. Not his inability to breathe properly. All that mattered was hurting the boy in front of him and preventing him from ever hurting another person.

Anger alone was not enough to keep his damaged body going for long. The lights in the room flickered as Zack struggled with all he had. Unconsciously reaching for the magic that had kept him alive in the past.

His legs gave out first from a lack of oxygen, the weak, limp noodles refusing to support his weight any longer. Despite that, he struggled on with a single-minded focus that scared everyone in the room.

Nothing Dorn tried kept the boy down for long. Until finally the toe of his boot hit him in the temple, knocking him out.

"What was that?" He wheezed, backing away from the unconscious figure. The fingers on his injured hand were bent in ghastly directions. A lucky swipe from Zack had broken them even more than before. The crazed boy had even gotten a few hits with a surprising amount of power on his stomach and kidneys.

"If I had to guess, I would say that you finally made him angry enough to forget about everything else. All that mattered to him after that was hurting you as much as possible."

Another of the four-spoke up then. "You shouldn't have made this boy your enemy. People like him who are unstable are the worst opponents you could have."

"Should I just kill him then?" Dorn asked, the adrenaline high beginning to fade.

"That is not up for us to decide. All we can say is that you will not be doing it here. We are thieves and kidnappers, occasionally even killers, when a job goes wrong. However, we are not murderers. If you intend to kill him, you will be doing it on your own and outside of our facilities." The speaker was someone new to the scene who had just limped into the room. It was a distinguished, older-looking gentleman in a fine suit and a walking cane in one hand.

"Sir!" The four along the wall snapped to attention.

"Bring him back to the room with the others."

"Wait," Dorn protested.

"No, the contract our leader foolishly agreed to has been completed." The man looked disappointedly at the four. "Nowhere did we agree to feed your sick and degenerate tendencies. That is not how we do business. Is that clear?"

The four nodded, hanging their heads.

Dorn flushed in anger. "I'll make sure my father hears about this."

"Please do. He and your grandfather know how we operate. I'll be interested in learning what they have to say concerning your proclivities." He stepped to the side of the door, clearing the way for Zack to be carried through. "I must say, I am rather disappointed in not only my people, but also in you."

"Who are you?" Dorn watched Zack's unconscious body be carried away before looking at the unmasked man. "I don't recognize you."

"Nor would you. I run in circles far more exclusive than you will even glimpse for years to come." The bottom of the cane clunked with every heavy step he took. It was clear the item was more than just an accessory as he leaned on the extra support. "All you need to know is that I am not someone you can easily afford to offend. Something that you have already done with this little display of uncultured brutality."

Dorn swallowed and shook his head. "Don't get in my way, old man. This is between me and that boy."

The tip of a cane poked at a drying puddle of blood. "And now you have disappointed and offended me for a second time. I look forward to what is coming. Your family poked a hornet's nest they should have stayed clear of." He wiped the cane on Dorn's leg with a gentle smirk. "Something that, from what I understand, they have done before. I'm afraid a bill your family won't be able to afford is about to come due."

***

Zack barely held back a groan as he came back from oblivion to find himself being carried. His eye from before had swollen completely shut, and he was having trouble breathing, among other things. Several of his teeth were loose, and the taste of blood clung heavily to his tongue.

"What happened?" He asked after swallowing the taste down. There was fog covering his thoughts, slowing everything down. It was also preventing him from following the mental trail back to whatever had happened to him.

"What happened is you just got your bacon saved." Despite the muffling effect the masks they wore caused, Zack could tell that the speaker was a woman this time. "That noble brat was thinking of finishing the job this time."

Zack tried to focus and push past the fog. His brain felt as though it was rocking on the deck of an ocean-born ship, as everything slipped and flip-flopped away from him.

He swallowed and licked his cracked and bloody lips. "Why? I didn't think he was that far gone in the head."

"You pushed him too far, or rather, I guess it was the reverse. He pushed you too far, and what he saw scared him." One of the others answered from near his feet.

"Enough, we're here. One of you hurry up and open the door. And then let's leave. I don't want to be hanging around if the Second comes looking for him."

Zack blearily saw a familiar door opening before he was carried inside and deposited carefully on the floor. The click of the door, and the subtle sound of deadbolts sliding into place, all that marked the four's departure.

Looking around the room, he spotted Tessa first. One of her cheeks was swelling and her gaze was fixed pityingly on the corner opposite her. There Zara had her head buried against her knees and was rocking slowly back and forth. Quietly, he heard her saying his name, over and over again.

Clenching his teeth, he rolled towards his little sister. "It's alright. I'm back. I'm right here." Gently, being careful of his injured side, he pulled her over and held her against his chest. "What happened?" He asked, directing the question to Tessa.

Zara remained unresponsive to his words and continued to mumble his name while trembling. It took a few more seconds before she began to relax into his familiar embrace and touch.

"She woke and then freaked out when she saw that you were no longer in here with us."

He nodded. "I figured something like that might happen. It's why I told you to watch out for when she did wake up." A finger traced his cheek. So she would know specifically what he was referring to.

"What about you? What happened?"

"Dorn happened," Zara gradually began to relax and unclench against his side. "They brought me to the same room as him, and then we fought, I think. Honestly, most of what happened is all blurry at the moment." Just speaking that much had made his head begin to pound anew. The cool floor against the back of his sweat-soaked body was helping keep the headache mostly at bay.

From outside the room came the knocking sound of a cane hitting the flooring as someone walked towards their room. There was the whisper of metal being moved as the door was unlocked and then swung open.

Standing in the opening was an older man leaning heavily against his walking cane. Beads of sweat ringed the space beneath his snowy white hair. Behind him were two people, a large man, and an equally muscular woman. They were wearing the same dark outfits as the rest; except they had forgone the masks.

"Help them up," The older man ordered the two. "My apologies for the way you three have been treated."

Zara whimpered and clung even tighter to him. With an enduring smile, he wrapped his arms around her as the large man worked around the extra body to lift him up.

Tessa hesitantly took the woman's hand. "Who are you?"

"My name is unimportant for the moment. What is important, however, is that I am the second-in-command of Faluers' Fist. Our leader found himself in debt to the Albright's and was forced to make this rather costly mistake." He leaned against the doorframe, the beaded sweat beginning to roll down the side of his head. "My apologies, but would it be possible for us to continue this conversation somewhere with chairs? My leg is about to give out."

The two teens nodded after a moment and followed him from the room.

Zack held his sister as they walked down the hall. His sides and chest hurt, not to mention the aching fog inside his head. With every breath pushing against his injured ribs, still, he refused to let her go and carried her without a complaint.

They reached the same intersection he had seen before. This time, instead of turning down the purple-painted corridor, they continued straight with the walls transitioning into a light blue. It led to a more central part of wherever they were being held. Soon enough, they began to see people, both masked and unmasked, going about their work.

Zack was sweating and struggling to get enough air when they arrived. The old man had been leaning progressively harder on his cane. His limp growing worse over the short few minutes the walk took.

They were taken to an office with comfortable chairs and a couch in front of a desk piled high with papers.

Zack made a beeline for the couch while the old man sank into the first chair he came across.

"Send in Beth, would you?" The second-in-command asked the two who had accompanied them.

They nodded and left the room, leaving the four alone.

Tessa was the only one who remained standing, unsure of where to sit. Did she want to crowd onto the couch with the siblings, or sit across from the man in control of the situation? One was a show of solidarity, while the other could be seen in a variety of different ways. Not all of them, good.

She knew which one her mother would tell her to take. Despite that, she found herself moving towards the couch, under the approving gaze of their host.

The door opened and a woman approaching middle age, with dyed forest-green hair, poked her head inside. "Snacks, drinks, and first-aid items?" She asked after quickly taking everything in.

"And a heat pack for my leg, if you would?" The man asked, shifting uncomfortably on the chair.

"I told you to stop walking on it so much!" She gently told him off before withdrawing her head and closing the door.

"Now then, where were we?" He thought for a moment. "For now, I suppose you can just call me Second. It is what I am referred to inside the Fist. That will serve to give you something to call me by." He gazed at the three under the bright light of his office and sighed. "I apologize again for the way you have been treated by this organization."

Beth bustled back in, her arms laden with different items. A platter with a steaming pot of fragrant liquid, with four cups and some small sandwiches, was set down first. After that, she passed a magi-crystal powered heat pad to Second, before turning to the three on the couch.

She clicked her tongue and scowled. "Who did this to you two?" Referring to the very visible injuries Zack and Zara had.

Zack gratefully accepted the first-aid bag from her and used the alcohol pads inside to clean Zara's hands and face. "It wasn't anyone that works here, or is a part of the organization?" He shook his head, unsure of how to refer to the people. "They were caused by Dorn Albright."

She straightened, her gaze going blank. "The Albright's?"

"Don't worry, Beth," Second consoled her, the pad strapped securely to his injured leg. "It is already being taken care of by someone else. Their family is about to lose much, if not all, of the influence they hold within the country."

Beth relaxed and nodded. "Good. Do you need anything else, or shall I continue with what we discussed earlier?"

"Continue. I am expecting our guests to arrive soon." Second informed, with a ghost of a smile.

Zara finally opened her eyes as Zack used the alcohol pad to clean the blood from her face. "You left." Her voice was a sad whisper. The stinging smell of the alcohol finishing the process of bringing her back from the fugue-induced state her mind had entered to protect her.

"I didn't have a choice," He whispered back.

Chapter 24

Z ara reached up, and ignoring the state of her own hands gently traced the swelling around Zack's eye. "Who did this?"

"It was Dorn again." He used the moment to finish cleaning the blood from her face and then move on to smearing some cream onto her hands. He would only start looking after his own injuries once he was done with her.

While he was busy taking care of his sister, Tessa was more focused on the man self-identified as Second. "You seem to know something that even your leader doesn't."

Second leaned forward and poured himself a cup of tea. A couple of dark red and blue berries following the liquid out of the spout. "I do. It is my job to know everything possible. If he had bothered to ask me before accepting the Albright's conditions on either his initial request or this job? I would have cautioned him against getting into bed with that family."

She grabbed a small sandwich and proceeded to nibble on it while thinking. "Who is it you are expecting to arrive soon?"

"We're having a nice talk here, little lady. Don't make that change." His kind disposition vanished in a second. "I just said that it is my job to know everything, that includes who the king and queen's hidden advisors are, as well as everything involving those people."

Tessa frowned and tilted her head in thought. The rest of the sandwich disappearing into her mouth before speaking again. "You are the other hidden advisor." It was a statement, not a question.

"That is an interesting leap to make." He took a sip of his tea, a berry floating to the surface and bouncing off his lip.

"That isn't a denial."

He tipped the cup to her and changed the direction of the conversation. "Do you know why I am going through all this trouble?"

"I would assume, because of some privileged information, you know, instead of it simply being the right thing to do!" Zack interjected, letting them know that he was still following their conversation.

"Careful boy, I have the means to learn things you might want to know in the future." Second swirled the dregs left in his cup.

Zack jerked and looked away from the bandage he was wrapping around Zara's hand. "There are only a few things I think we would care to know."

The old man carefully put his cup back on the platter. "I admit, there are many things about you both that I do not yet know. It has only been a short amount of time since I learned of your existence, after all. Don't let that fool you, however, given enough time I can, and will, know everything there is to know about you both."

Zack finished wrapping her hands and focused on him. "If that is truly the case, then I would like to talk more with you at a later time." He swallowed before continuing. "I have some information that I am sure even you don't know, I can give in payment." He was referring to his ability to use mana crystals outside the portal. If anyone would know the true worth of that information, it would be this man. He would know what it represented and its possible implications.

Second nodded. "That is how I prefer to conduct information based business between friends. The quality of information will decide how much information I give you at that time or is banked for later purposes."

Tessa coughed. "You were saying about why you are going through the trouble of rescuing us from the cell your own people put us in?"

Zack turned back to his sister, and then to his own wounds after seeing that he had taken care of everything visible on her already. "Let go, please." He whispered to her, pulling off his shirt when she hesitantly complied. A mass of angry red lines that would later turn into bruises greeted the eyes of all present.

"Where is Dorn?" Zara questioned with a dark look.

"I already sent him away," Second said with a frown. "I had been debating on whether I needed to have a conversation with his grandfather before the crown's ire comes down on them. After seeing this, however, I believe the family is no longer redeemable. Something like this, that boy's attitude, is rarely developed within one generation. Unless Dorn is completely insane in some way. Which I do not believe him to be. At least not in a predisposed manner. He has the qualities of someone who was raised to think a particular way."

Zara was returning the favor and cleaning each of his cuts and injuries. "It doesn't matter. He'll get his at some point."

Tessa nodded, "He will, you can count on it." She faced away from the scarred body at her side. "Let's try this again. Why did you bother to help us?"

"You should probably take these and drink some liquid," Second passed a couple of pills to Zack. "These should help with that headache and nausea that I'm sure you are feeling right now. You should be more careful when it comes to head injuries and possible concussions. They can have lingering effects if you don't take care of them properly."

Tessa's face was as red as her hair by that point, as the old man ignored her once again.

Second shook his head mirthfully and smiled at her. "You really should calm down, dear. The question is not important enough to cause you such distress." He coughed and looked away, hiding a smirk. "Besides, I may have been exaggerating the importance and complexity of the answer."

Zack winced as his sister wrapped his ribs for the second time that week and swallowed down the pills without complaint. Carrying his sister through the corridors had made the pain in his head pound with each beat of his heart. "I knew it. My answer was right. Wasn't it?"

"In a fashion," Second agreed. "You already know I do indeed have access to privileged information. That is part of my job. That, however, is not the main reason for bringing you here now. I could have simply left you all in the cell until you are rescued." He looked at an old mechanical pocket watch he pulled from a pocket. "Which should be occurring any minute now."

"Why then?" Tessa asked, gradually calming as he began to talk.

"Consider it a power play, as well as a show of respect for your mother."

"A power play?" Zara tucked the tail of the wrap into place and began cleaning the blood from Zack's arm. "That would mean that the crown wants control of this place?" She glanced at Tessa. "Assuming, of course, that you really are who she thinks."

"I don't think it'll work out quite that cleanly," Zack winced as the alcohol ravaged the torn flesh on his upper arm. "If the only group that shows up is from Tessa's family, then it would be possible. Unfortunately, it is more likely a few people from the military will come as well. I would assume that their presence would throw your plan off." He faltered and looked down at his lap. "Then again, since supposedly the Fist is authorized by the crown. It may not be a problem for you."

Second played with the watch, his gaze changing the longer he looked at them. "You both show a level of awareness and reasoning that I wouldn't expect in people so young or uneducated." He slipped the watch back into his pocket and reached for his cane. "Being uneducated can be a boon at times. It allows the person to come up with ideas that someone who has been schooled might not. You don't know the intricacies of what is and isn't possible."

Second, tightened the straps on the heat pad around his leg, and with the assistance of his cane, stood. "You only have your own observations to work off of, and the bits of knowledge you acquired along the way."

Zara was confused. "I don't understand what you mean. Are we right or wrong?"

"You're both right, but the way you came about your respective conclusions, I believe is wrong." He hobbled over to the door and winked back at them. "Make sure to keep this conversation to yourselves, and Anna, of course. I will also be recommending that little Zara be admitted into the academy under the crown's special scholarship."

He stopped with his hand on the door and turned to look directly at the siblings. "With the protection of the crown, nothing will happen to her." The door opened and revealed a squad of armed men with sergeant Grieves in the lead. Beth was standing to the side, unharmed, with her hands up. "Oh, good. I did hear people outside."

Grieves scowled at the old man and walked into the room. "You're already injured again?" He remarked, spotting Zack's obvious wounds. "Put on a shirt!" He commanded, not letting anyone else into the room for the moment.

Zack complied as quickly as he could. His stiff movements dragged the ragged remains of his shirt back into place, working to hide the obvious scars. "Who all came to rescue us?"

"I brought a small team and miss Ricerca's family, sent several teams of their own. It is my understanding that there is also one other team that was deployed. It is being led by the Major, and one of the king's advisors. They are moving against the family that was behind this." His eyes flicked to Tessa as he said that.

A couple of medics came in once the sergeant moved to the side and began inspecting and treating the girls. He reserved inspecting Zack for himself. The existence of the boy's scars was still a sensitive subject and would remain that way for a little longer.

In turn, Second waited patiently to the side, where he could watch everything that was happening in both rooms. The medics quickly finished with the more visible issues and stepped back. Tessa had only suffered a bruised and swollen cheek from Zara's flailing earlier. While the younger girl had swelling around her nose and lips along with the damage to her hands.

The one who had suffered and taken the most damage was clearly Zack.

"Can you walk out of here?" Grieves asked Zack.

"My brain, mind... it feels weird, but I should be able to," Zack responded slowly, with a growing frown. "Everything feels... distant." He slumped onto the couch with his eyes closed and breathing steadily.

"There is nothing to worry about." Second, told the gathered people quickly. "I gave him some meds that will help with the pain, nausea, and the likely concussion he has as well."

"He even has a concussion, again? Are you people trying to permanently damage the boy?" Grieves growled, turning on Second.

"It wasn't us who did this to him." He grimaced. "The people assigned to them did nothing to stop it from happening, but they aren't responsible for the attack on him. The blame for that lays directly with Dorn Albright."

"He was here?"

"I sent him back earlier." Second, informed him with a nod.

"How long ago was that?" Grieves was building a timeline in his head.

The old man groaned and hung his head. "It was a little over half an hour ago. I was expecting you to arrive here when you did, but I'm guessing the other team you mentioned reached the Albright's faster."

The sergeant nodded and growled out some orders to his subordinates in the other room. "Dorn Albright is on the loose, and either on his way home or on the run. Notify the Major and any teams we have on the road! He is to be brought back to base and put into secure holding once found!"

Zara remained glued to her brother's side through all of this. She had even refused to move for the medics earlier, making their job harder than it needed to be.

Tessa was more willing to comply with their requests and be patient initially. Now that patience had run its course, she wanted to leave. They had been taken from her home late in the night and been up ever since they woke up in that room. Her frayed nerves combined with the irritation that came with a lack of decent non-drugged sleep meant she was ready to go back home.

Now that she knew they were safe, the fear and apprehension that had been keeping her awake and aware was wearing off. The medics noticed her condition and slipped close to the sergeant's side.

He listened to their whispered words and gave a short nod. "Let's wrap this up, grab the kids, the old man, and his secretary. Knock out the rest and leave them where they fall. I want to be back in our vehicles and on the road within twenty minutes!"

"I do have a name you know!" Second, remarked sharply, while leaning on his cane.

"The fate of this place is in our hands; I don't care if you have a name." Grieves spun around and left the room first.

Zack was shaken awake, and then he, along with Zara, were marched from the room first. Tessa and the others were right behind them.

Bodies littered the floors; with the bulk being unconscious. Others were being held down with their hands and legs tied together. Only a couple were lying still in pools of blood.

Second shook his head sadly and leaned against Beth. It would be hard for the organization to visibly come back from this. That was fine with him. It had been growing too fast in recent years, taking in too many undisciplined prospects.

With him as the new head, things would be different. Visibility was not a good thing in the first place. This would give them the chance to fade back from the public's perception and put them back in the shadows where they belonged.

Sprawled face-down in the atrium with his legs tied together was the current leader of Faluers' Fist. He was being held in place by a group of people that Tessa recognized as working for her family. The security detachment at their mansion had to be kept small as a result of her mother's work. They were well trained, but had still been taken unawares this time.

"Bring him as well," Grieves growled, passing through the open space without stopping.

Tessa nodded when the group working for her family looked to her for guidance. "It's fine. The military will control him from here on."

"Yes, ma'am." They quickly tied his hands together and then connected the rope to his feet before passing the hobbled man off to the military personnel.

***

Zack yawned and slumped against the uncomfortable bench wearily. The meds Second had given him were still coursing through his system. Beside him, Zara and Tessa yawned as well, giving in to the act's contagious nature.

Across from them, Second had his bad leg out straight and to the side. Sprawled across the middle section of the carriage flooring, lying facedown, was the current leader of Faluers' Fist. His hand and legs were still tied together, and a rag had been shoved into his mouth.

"Where are you taking us?" Tessa asked when Grieves climbed in behind Beth and locked the door.

He thumped the roof three times before answering. "You three are going back to your house and get some sleep." The tinted windows lit up with sunlight as they left the underground area the vehicle had been parked in. "The rest of us will be going to a separate location. I will have specialist McCleary waiting nearby to bring you two to the institute later as well."

"The two of us?" Zara huddled closer to Zack. The mere thought of going back to that place was beyond terrifying to her.

Grieves nodded. "Well Zack for sure, but you don't seem eager to be apart from him."

"They're still moving forward with the plan, then?" Zack asked groggily.

"Last I heard they were, who can say if that will change after their meeting with the Albright's." He stretched out and placed the heels of his boots squarely in the small of the leaders' back from his spot on the floor.

Zack felt as though he was forgetting something, but couldn't be bothered to pursue that thought as his eyes drifted closed once more. Zara snuggled closer to him, the slightest of tremors running through her chest. She was indeed doing better emotionally than earlier. However, the long-term pre-existing mental and emotional trauma was not an easy fix that would simply vanish.

The trip back to the Ricerca mansion was relatively quick, as the hideout was still within the city's boundaries.

The three teens were let out with the briefest of stops before the black vehicle sped back down the driveway. All of them were tired, and Zack, in particular, was having a hard time walking in a straight line. It was up to his little sister to guide him up the stairs and to their room.

Meanwhile, Tessa was debating whether she wanted to head to bed right away or find her father first. The accusations Dorn had levied against the man had her tired mind on edge. She knew she should let him know they were safe. The problem was, in her current state, there was no guarantee she wouldn't try to pursue the subject.

"Can you grab or pull the mana crystal from that light?" Zack asked his sister once they were safely back in their room. The door locked tight behind them. He was pointing to a lamp beside the bed. There was a small dim crystal slotted into its base. It was rare to see appliances that still used them in that fashion. Most had switched over to the cheaper magi-crystals as they were easier to mass produce.

She nodded and pushed him onto the bed. After grabbing Zelda, George, and Aisha, she worked the mana crystal loose and passed it to him.

Right away, he could feel the healing from his ability begin to kick in. With such a small crystal, the healing was slow, but effective enough to make his damaged skin and muscles tingle pleasantly.

"Thanks," He muttered groggily, feeling her climb onto the bed and tuck herself in beside him.

"Can we go back to just living at the apartment again?" Zara wondered, feeling her eyes struggling to stay open now that they were safe, and she had her bears around her again. "You got hurt a lot less there, and we didn't have to worry about the nobles involving us in their petty squabbles."

"I don't think that is an option anymore. They know we exist now and that is enough." Was all he managed to squeeze out before sleep claimed him.

Chapter 25

The mana crystal in his hand was dark and lifeless when Zack finally stirred with a groan. Everything ached and felt tender. His head, however, felt much better with the listless fog and pressure from before gone.

Zara was sitting on the bed watching him, Zelda grasped tightly to her chest with George draped across her legs. The swelling around her nose had gone down some, and the skin was beginning to change colors with the first hints of bruising.

"How long have you been awake?" He smacked his lips together, feeling them crack in protest. His mouth was as dry as a desert. "Is there any water in here?"

She climbed off the bed and scurried over to the desk. "Just a little while. I was watching the crystal in your hand change colors as it drained."

Mana crystals possessed a sort of vibrancy to them. It wasn't a glow, there was no source of inner light. What they did have was a milky white coloring that would turn dark when it was drained.

She returned a moment later with a glass of water in hand. "How are you feeling?" She touched the area around his eye as he drank the glass down.

The severe swelling that had been there previously was almost completely gone. The skin had progressed to a deep, purple-colored bruising that hurt when she touched it, no matter how light it was. However, he could see through that eye again.

"Better, not perfect, but much better." He sat up and placed the empty glass on a nearby nightstand. "The fog in my mind is gone, at least." He swallowed and stared at her. "It's a good thing I can heal like this, otherwise the repeated concussions could have made that thought slowing fog permanent."

"I would have taken care of you." She hugged Zelda tighter. "I'm glad that you are alright though. We need to get our hands on some more crystals."

"Not from here," He was quick to say, guessing where her thoughts were going. "I don't want to steal more from Tessa's family than we already have with this one." He flicked the dead crystal into the air and caught it. "They may not have been upfront with their intentions, but to this point, they haven't hurt us."

He was ignoring the part they had played in his initial confrontation with Dorn. Honestly, if he was a petty person, then he could lay everything that had happened at their feet. That wasn't his style. People were responsible for their own actions, with a few exceptions, of course. There were no absolutes in life. He understood that better than anyone, but perhaps his sister.

"Fine. How are we going to get them then? We can't afford to buy them? The money we've earned working at the school isn't enough for even a low quality one."

"We'll just have to retrieve them ourselves. As soon as possible, I'll sneak you into the school portal. While we are inside, we'll grab as many as we can from either mining or the monsters." Zack slid to the edge of the bed and stood. He needed a moment to steady himself as the room appeared to tilt.

"Come on, let's go find Tessa." He said after everything stopped spinning.

Zara handed him George and placed Aisha in the middle of the bed. Zelda was kept in her arms, a place he doubted the bear had left since they returned hours earlier. It just made him want to get her through the portal as soon as possible.

Tucking the bear under his arm, he unlocked the door and stopped, resting his head against the wood. "Do you want to talk about what happened now or later, when we are back at the dorm?"

"I," She came up behind him and grabbed his shirt. "I can't right now. It's all I can do to just ignore it all." Her soft voice wavered and quaked with every word she uttered. "It brought back so many memories, and then you were gone, and Zelda and George weren't there to protect me." She shivered and shook her head. "I can't, just, please, not right now."

"That's fine." He reached back and smoothed her hair comfortingly. "I get it, you know I do. I just wanted to check. We talked last night about getting therapy, to help us deal with everything. It doesn't matter if the person you talk to is me or someone else. I just want you to be ready whenever the time for that comes."

"It will depend on Edith, as long as we aren't wrong about her, and she is willing to listen to everything that happened." Zara glanced up at her brother with sad eyes. "It isn't a fun tale for us to relive. I can only imagine it wouldn't be pleasant for the listener either."

"No, you're probably right." He held her close, taking a moment to comfort them both before unlocking and opening the bedroom door.

Jean was waiting in the foyer area when they walked down the stairs. She was slowly tapping a foot and looking at a painting on the wall. "I must admit, she comes from a line of good-looking people." She said in a way of greeting.

The siblings took in the painting and frowned. "How can you tell? I wouldn't even know that was supposed to be a person if you hadn't said anything."

Jean laughed and rolled her eyes. "I'm not talking about the painting; I have no idea what this is supposed to be. I just came from a meeting with Anna, the girl's mother. She is impressive, to say the least."

Zack grunted, unwilling to go down that particular rabbit hole despite agreeing. Anna was a very good-looking woman, and the fierce scar on her cheek did nothing to diminish that either. You wouldn't hear him saying that out loud though.

"What's the plan?" Zara asked, gathering up her courage. "Are you taking us to the institute now?"

"No, that was put on hold after they were informed of how severe Zack's injuries were, among other factors." She studied him with a raised brow. "I was honestly expecting you to be in worse condition with how they were describing you." She shrugged and moved on. "Instead, I've been assigned with bringing you both back to the dorm and then with taking

Zack into the school portal for a quick round of healing. The Major is even dispatching a healer to meet us there, so it will actually just be a quick visit this time."

The sudden angry sound of Tessa shouting distracted them from saying any more. The three shared a quick glance and crept quietly past the staircase to a room near the back of the house. It was an area none of them had been in before, but the raised voices kept them from getting lost.

Peeking through the open door, they witnessed Tessa confronting her father. He was sitting next to a window with a book in one hand and a cup of steaming tea in the other.

"Have you been doing experiments with awakening a traveler's potential in people early or not?" She sucked in a deep breath. "And more than anything else, I want to know why that idiot Dorn knows more about your work than I do?"

Zara grabbed Zack's arm; her eyes were hard and shaking with a mix of fear and anger.

"I don't know why the Albright's have access to my work, but it would certainly explain their sudden interest in us." Mathew set the book and cup of tea to the side and stood. "Fortunately... or unfortunately, depending on how you look at it, I suppose they don't know as much as they think they do."

Tessa stepped back, maintaining a cautious distance from her father.

The man winced at her action. "I'm guessing this has something to do with that boy and his sister upstairs? I spoke with your mother in length after seeing how he reacted to me, and I think I know why you are acting this way. I can't deny that those researcher's methods were effective. I mean, they got the boy through the portal, after all." He coughed and reached for the tea. "But my research and methods are nothing like theirs."

"What they did to them is terrible! Have you seen his scars?" Tessa shook her head and took another step back. "No, of course you haven't."

"I said their methods were effective, not that I condoned them. Given the opportunity, I would not refuse to use the knowledge they gleamed just because of that. It would make everything those kids went through pointless if we ignored everything they had learned. I repeat, however, that the research my team is doing, and our methods have little in common with what that place did."

Tessa played with a woven strand of her hair, taking a hesitant step forward. "Fine, tell me what you are doing and why the Albright's thought your methods were so terrible."

"I can't say as to why they would ever think our methods were unsavory or cruel in nature. If I had to make a guess, then I would say it has more to do with them and things they have done in the past or are still doing." The last few wisps of steam from his cup drifted away as the tea finally cooled. "Before you began yelling, you mentioned my research into increasing someone's compatibility rating. That is true and has proven somewhat effective. It might even be worth it for you to undergo the process before you go through the portal."

Tessa winced and took several steps back.

"Okay, that was too far, I understand. Sorry, it was just a suggestion." Matt sighed, realizing his own blunder.

"You would do that to me? Your own daughter?" She gasped out, horrified.

"You have the wrong idea, again." Her father ran a hand through his hair and slumped back on to the chair. "Honey, please just listen. I promise, my research, my methods are nothing like what happened at that institute. Please, just, please quit comparing my work to theirs."

Tessa stilled at the defeat in his voice. "Sorry, you're right. I have no idea how normal researchers conduct their experiments. You've always refused to discuss your work with me, and while I know that has to do with secrets and sensitive information, it has still always made everything you do somewhat mysterious."

He nodded. "I can't change that, sorry, but maybe we can talk to your mother, and she can ask the crown for permission. This, however, is my own personal project and I can talk about it with whoever I want."

Matt straightened a tad, knowing that she was at least willing to listen. "The experiment itself is relatively harmless and involves concentrated and then liquefied mana crystals. I won't go into the specifics, but know that there is no cutting or dissecting of anyone involved. There are some injections into the person." He wavered. "Or subject, however you want to refer to them, but that is all."

"And that works? I mean, everyone is close to mana crystals in some form all the time now." Tessa interjected doubtfully.

"Like I said, no specifics, and there is far more that we do with the mixture, or formula if you will, that gets injected. There are other items related to this all as well. Point being, very little of it is invasive or painful in any way." He scratched the tip of his nose and smiled. "The little discoveries along the way are what make researching these subjects so interesting and fun.

Take the one you mentioned before, about awakening a traveler's potential early."

"That happened somewhat by accident. We were looking for a way to accurately measure a person's compatibility before they awaken. As you know, the test can be done at any time, but the result is more a gauge of potential than an accurate reading."

Tessa nodded, not daring to interrupt him, not now that he was finally talking about his work.

"I do need to correct your information here, however. What we have accomplished is not any sort of early awakening. These people can't go through the portals. That was one of the first things we investigated. All it does is make the status page appear for them. That alone creates a more solid link to the portals that allows us to more accurately test their compatibility rating."

Zara loosened her grip on Zack, relieved to hear that they weren't abusing people. "How do you select them in the first place if they haven't awakened yet?" She asked, stepping into the room and announcing their presence.

"The initial compatibility rating," Mathew explained without missing a beat. "It isn't a guarantee, mind you, but those with higher ratings are more likely to awaken than those with a lower score. From there we just play the odds. Most of the subjects have indeed awakened to at least their status information. The few, I think we only have two at this point, though keep in mind our pool of, uh, people, is rather small, to begin with, get moved to other experiments. In this case, one related to why they didn't awaken to even that point. It's all about gathering more information and then piecing it together in a cohesive and legible manner."

Zara walked closer to the man, her grip on Zelda tightening with every step. She stopped in front of him and peered into his eyes, as though she could see the depths of his soul. "Fine, we'll believe you. It seems you really are just a slightly crazy, research-obsessed person, and not like those who held us captive. They always had a look in their eyes as though part of themselves was missing. You still have what they didn't."

"Come, we should be getting the two of you back to the dorm. The healer won't wait all day." Jean clapped her hands and shuffled them both out.

"Wait!" Tessa shouted, momentarily stopping them at the door of the room. "What were they missing?"

Zara smiled sadly and reached for Zack's hand. She kept her mouth closed and didn't answer as they walked out and continued towards the front door of the mansion.

Waiting for them outside was Ben, who had already gathered their bags and belongings. The large bear Zara had named Aisha was also waiting for them to the side, propped upright on the stone railing. Wordlessly, he carried everything to Jean's waiting vehicle and loaded it all up for them. It was only as he finished that he said anything to them.

"Lady Ricerca directed me to apologize to you both on her behalf. You were pulled into a situation beyond your control during a visit wherein your safety should have been guaranteed. She also said that you needn't worry about it happening a second time. Once she reveals herself, no one will dare even look at her family with ill-intentions."

"When is she planning on revealing herself?" Zack asked, pausing with one hand on the door handle.

"Tomorrow, I believe," Ben answered readily. "The crown hosts an open forum every Sonntag for the people to air any complaints they may have. It is a dangerous prospect to do so, despite the king and queen's best efforts to keep the people safe. Despite that, it is always well attended by those looking for entertainment, if nothing else. She is intent on using the occasion for maximum effect and word of mouth."

"I'll be looking forward to class on Montag then," Zack replied with a grin, and closed the door.

Jean nodded to the man, and then they drove away. "Zara, do you mind coming with us to the portal and just waiting there while we go inside? The healer has already been waiting for a while, I'm sure, and I'd rather not keep them away from their other duties." She glanced up at the rear-view mirror to the side and saw Zack trying to get comfortable. "How injured are you, really?"

He hesitated, thinking of the best way to answer.

"It's probably just the meds that old man gave him. Grieves also mentioned that he probably has a concussion from Dorn's repeated attacks to his head." Zara supplied, playing with a loose thread around Zelda's ear. She had been quick to notice his struggle.

The Specialist turned back to the road. "Do you know what he gave him?"

"It was just a few pills. His secretary Beth brought them at his request," Zack told her while looking out the tinted window.

"It was probably medicine geared more towards numbing your body then, than fixing you. He would have been interested in making sure you could walk out under your own power, especially with the Sergeant there." Jean made a guess and pushed the matter from her mind. It wasn't something that concerned her in any case. "What about you Zara? You didn't answer the question from before. Are you willing to wait outside the portal? I remember how you reacted to it before."

"I'll be fine this time." She tugged harder on the thread in Zelda's ear and showed it to Zack.

He ruffled her hair and gently took the cherished bear from her. "Don't worry, I'll check her over when we get back to the dorm and sew everything back together. It's been a while since I checked all her seams, anyway." He played with the ear for a moment and then passed it back to her.

"Do we need to duck down out of sight?" Zack questioned as they neared the complex around the portal. He remembered how Jean had him laying down as they left the last time.

"It's fine. The windows are tinted now. No one will be able to see inside unless they are standing right beside the carriage." She drove them in without slowing at the guard station.

Inside the crumbling remains of the warehouse that contained the portal was a sole person leaning against a vehicle impatiently.

"Where is everyone? Do they take Erdetag off or something?" Zack found that option hard to believe with how desperate corporations always were for money. There was no way they would let something like a weekend keep them away from the bounty inside the portals.

Jean laughed and stopped beside the waiting woman. "Yeah, right, that will never happen. No, the Major just told them to get out for a while again. It's another reason we need to hurry this up. We have a lot more freedom to do things like that because this one belongs to the school and not a corporation."

"What about the portals owned by the government or military?"

Zara's eyes were glued to the portal as they exited the vehicle.

"Those are too far away to use, and this one is within an hour's distance of the castle. It just makes more sense to inconvenience others sometimes." Jean explained, closing her door.

The rapid tapping of an impatient foot reached their ears. "Finally! Let's hurry this up. I have to be at a different portal soon, and it's a long drive."

Chapter 26

The three slipped through the portal while Zara stayed back. The scene that greeted them was the same as before, with the only difference being that it was now lit by an unseen sun.

The healer reached out and grabbed hold of Zack. Her hands glowed with an inner light that highlighted the veins beneath the skin as a muttered spell fell from her pale lips.

She frowned and shook her head. "It looks like some of the damage, especially around the inside of your head, has already been healed by something or someone. The swelling inside your brain is almost completely gone, everything else though..." She cast a second spell, the glow extending up her arms till it stretched past her elbows. The light seeping through the loose sleeves of her blouse.

Her eyes flicked towards Jean, a hint of pity flashing through them. "There are a lot of micro-fractures in your ribs, legs, and arms. There are also signs of previously healed damage to your spine, neck, and skull. It looks as though some of the healing was interrupted and then started again at a later time, creating differences in the strength of the healed areas."

She bit her lips and cast a third spell. This time, the glow went all the way up to her shoulders.

"You shouldn't have done that," Jean told the woman with a sigh as the glow faded. "The Major will need to talk to you after this now."

The healer nodded mutely with a horrified expression. "What happened to you? Who did all this? It's as though you were dissected, piece by piece, and then put back together again. There is scar tissue everywhere inside your body from the remains of countless improper healing spells. It's as though you were literally cut into pieces and then put back together again, time after time."

It was the extreme abuse that had resulted in him having the 'Life Burner' ability and the healing effect that came with it. The constant experiments they put him through inside the portal, where they could heal him. The pain they caused, the damage, and the experiences, it all came together to form an ability. One, they had then used to their advantage by making the experiments even more extreme.

"Thanks for reminding me," Zack muttered in a hoarse voice at the sudden surge of memories. There were parts of that time that he didn't talk about with anyone, even Zara. This healer was treading directly into one of those.

"Just heal him already!" Jean snapped at the woman. "As for you," She glared at Zack. "I think the Major is going to have some questions when he hears about this."

He shrugged. "Fine, he knows where to find me, but that doesn't mean I'll answer his questions." Zack flinched as the healer dug her fingers into his flesh, the torn remains of his shirt offering no resistance. "Some things should remain private."

"Sorry," The woman muttered, her fingers digging in until her nails drew blood. "If I'm going to fix some of this older, scarred inner tissue, I'll need a better connection to your body. How have you been living with all of this? Just walking around or moving your arms must be excruciating."

"Not that I've noticed," Zack denied her claim.

"Then that is even worse!" She retorted, her former annoyance fading away as she began to work on someone who truly needed her help.

He looked away from them and began studying the horizon and the forest in the distance. The mana crystals inside this portal were his best chance of getting any without drawing extra attention. It wasn't a perfect plan, but it was what they had to work with.

It also gave him something to concentrate on besides what was happening to his body. The remaining injuries to his head were healed first. Removing the last traces of concussion and damage to his skull before she moved on to the next item that had caught her attention. The headaches and other pains he had stopped registering years ago flared anew and then dulled as she worked to fix the residual damage.

Sweat quickly formed on her brow as she pushed her healing spells and control to their limits. It was simple for her to fix what Dorn had broken hours before. Just healing those weren't enough for her. The desire to fix everything she could pervaded her every thought.

It was a herculean task that would have broken any other healer. As it was, in that single session, it was all she could do to minimize the tears and excess scar tissue in the cartilage and ligaments around his joints. There was enough existing damage even after she exhausted all her mana, that several more sessions at a bare-minimum would be required.

"That's as much as I can do for now." Her blouse had rings of sweat around her neck and armpits as she sagged tiredly.

Jean helped to support the healer, while Zack moved his arms and legs in concerned surprise. Each movement felt strange, foreign, as though the appendages no longer belonged to him. There was something missing, and the sudden lack of whatever it was worried him.

"It's alright, you already did far more than I was expecting." Jean was comforting the woman while they walked slowly towards the nearby portal. They had already been inside the portal for far longer than she had originally planned. "Come on Zack, Zara is waiting."

He nodded dumbly and followed them on shaky legs. It wasn't difficult for him to understand what was different. It was the size of the change that startled him and kept his limbs from feeling like they belonged. Pain that he had long since stopped mentally registering was missing, and it left each movement feeling easier and freer.

Zara was sitting with her legs swinging against the side of the vehicle with the door open when they returned. Her favorite bear, Zelda, was sitting facing her, while George was squished into the space between her hip and the front seat. She was talking quietly to the bears.

"Anything happen here?" Jean asked her, helping the healer to her own vehicle. "Sorry, it took us longer than expected."

"No, it was quiet. A couple of people peeked their heads through the entryway a few minutes ago, but that was all." Zara made no mention of where she had been at the time. "What took so long? Were his injuries that severe?"

Zack shook his head, despite understanding that it wasn't a serious question. Zara knew about his healing ability and had seen its effects firsthand earlier.

"I was," The healer cut off when Zack looked at her sharply. "Taking in the view." She finished in a lame, poor attempt to hide that she had been about to say something else.

"Hmm," She looked at the woman suspiciously. Her view was cut off suddenly as Jean shoved the healer into her vehicle.

Zack was trailing behind them on shaky, halting legs that he had to keep looking down at. The feeling that they didn't belong to him was slowly fading with each step. It was a process that was as welcome as it was unsettling.

The healer left without Zack ever having heard her name. She was no longer heading to another portal as originally planned, now she was going to meet with the Major.

Jean pulled him to the side away from where Zara was sitting and spoke to him in a quiet voice. "I have no idea what just happened in there, and to be honest, I don't think I want to. The parts that I do understand already turn my stomach and make me sick. I had thought you were joking before when you mentioned them dissecting you. The truth is even worse than I thought."

He glared at her. "That's fine. There is little I would say on the matter, in any case. Like I said before, some things should remain private. No one needs to know everything that they did to me, especially not Zara."

Jean hesitated and then nodded at the unspoken demand. None of what she did know would make its way to the young girl's ears. "Anyway, none of this has anything to do with why I actually pulled you over here. I simply wanted to tell you that you didn't need to worry about others learning of the damage done to your body in the same way Leigha did."

"Was that the healer woman's name? She was never introduced." He interrupted, looking for clarification.

"Yes, her name is Leigha, and she is the best healer we have, period, full-stop. The strength of her examination spells and the control she has over directing her healing spells are leagues ahead of anyone else. Most healers aren't capable of the control needed to direct a healing spell to heal scar tissue in the manner she did. If it got out... I like Quinn and Rose. I would love to be able to help them. But the matter isn't up to me. Leigha is a member of the military and they decide who she heals for the most part."

She sighed and looked away. "So, please keep her abilities to yourself. What you saw with her examination spell is, as I'm sure you know from experience, abnormal. Most spells of that nature simply tell the healer where the damage is most severe with no or little specifics. Hers, tell her everything."

Zack stared at her in puzzlement. "I won't say anything about her I shouldn't. Don't worry. And I am indeed aware of how different her examination spell was from normal. However, since I already know that; was there really a need to pull me over here just to tell me to be quiet about her?"

"I couldn't be sure without talking to you, but remember this conversation. We good?" Jean spun around without waiting for his response and calmly walked back to the vehicle.

"Wait, what? That doesn't answer anything!" He sputtered, in confusion.

Zara handed him George, as he slid into the back beside her.

"What did you find out?" Zack whispered, leaning close to her.

"I'll tell you later," She whispered back, her gaze flicking to Jean. "So, why did it take so long?"

"She was healing some of the damage from before. Apparently, there was plenty of scar tissue that had formed from all of their experiments. It would be a good idea to get her to look at you as well at some point."

"Did she fix it all?" Zara was pinching Zelda's lips and playing with the thin piece of red material that marked her tongue.

"No, there was too much for her to do in one session. She did her best though, and I can already feel the difference." He kept his answers vague but truthful, hiding the worst aspects, as he always did.

Jean drove them back to the dorm and then left without saying anything more to either of them. They had no idea if she would be back later to take them to the institute or if they had gotten another week's reprieve.

The brief hold she had mentioned before at the Ricerca house had been because of his injuries, which were no longer a factor. If they were lucky though, then the Major would be stuck talking to Leigha for a while. Even if it was just one more day, they would take it gladly.

"Come on, let's go inside our dorm to talk first, and then we can chat with Edith about getting some therapy." Zack picked up their bags and Aisha in one hand and George in the other. The hesitancy from before had already left his steps, and his legs moved with an ease he hadn't known since he was a small child.

He had heard of people who suffered from phantom limb syndrome. It was something that affected someone when they had lost a limb, and they could still feel sensations from it. That was not what he was experiencing, though there were some similarities, only in reverse. He hadn't lost his limbs, but still felt as though they weren't really his in the beginning. And that was just for the small amount that she had been able to heal.

What would he feel if she was ever able to heal everything?

It was close to dinnertime, and people were roving around the inside of the dorm building. Everyone they came across stopped and stared at the siblings. Zara's existence had already become an open secret in the building. However, this was the first time many of them had seen her.

If the old man Second, did what he said, then that situation would soon change.

Zara shrank back and blocked everyone from view, using Zelda's fluffy body. She led the charge to their dorm and had it unlocked and was hidden inside within seconds.

Zack closed and locked the door with a sigh. They had been gone for just over the length of a day, but it felt so much longer than that. He dropped the bags by the couch and flopped down onto the cushions beside his sister, using George as a pillow.

"What did you see or hear while we were inside the portal?" He asked after they had both taken a minute to relax.

"Guess whose company is one of the biggest renters of the school's portal?" She sat up and moved Zelda to the side, tugging George out from beneath his head. "Albright Industries apparently has had all of their contracts put on hold for the moment. It was an order that came down from the king and queen sometime this morning."

Zack sat up with a thoughtful expression. "Did you happen to hear when their rented times were, and if anybody else had taken them over yet?"

She grinned and nodded. "I did indeed. They owned the block of time for this entire weekend, and since the contracts are only on hold and not canceled, no one else can take over those slots."

"Good. I managed to get a better look at the inside of the portal earlier. If we are lucky, then we should be able to get some mana crystals with only a few hours of effort." He returned her grin and poked at George and Zelda's respective heads. "It looks like we'll be sneaking you into the portal tonight. We should get some food in us before talking to Edith."

"No, I..." Zara trailed off. "Let's talk to her tomorrow. I think it would be better if I went through the portal first."

"That's fine. I don't mind waiting another day before talking to her. I know we need to, but frankly, we've been talking about or dealing with what happened back then so much already. I'll take any break I can get at this point, even if it is only for a few hours." He pushed off the couch with a gasp as the joints in his arms and legs cracked and popped into new positions. "I'll see if we have anything to eat in the kitchen, otherwise we are either heading to the cafeteria or eating nutrition bars."

"Ugh, those things taste like chalk." She complained, but knew she would eat them. Properly nutritious food was precious, besides both of them had eaten far worse tasting... things. The word food didn't quite fit some of them either.

"Eh, they're not that bad." Zack opened the door of the coldbox. "What are you going to do with her?" He pointed to Aisha, who had been left on the floor just inside the door.

"Are we sure she isn't bugged?" Zara hopped off the couch and approached the much larger bear.

"I looked back at Tessa's house, but I have no idea what something like that would even look like. All I can say is there was nothing obviously wrong or different with her." He pulled out a container and sniffed the contents. "We have some leftovers from a couple of days ago. They still smell good."

"That'll be fine, I'm not super hungry right now anyway," Zara said as she lugged the new bear to the couch. "Should we bring her with us, you think?"

Zack put the food on plates and then stuck them in the oven before replying. "We might as well. Her size might lead to some interesting effects."

"I don't care about that; I just want to be able to talk to Zelda again."

"I've always been jealous of your ability and class." He leaned against the counter while waiting for the food to get hot. The magi-crystal powered oven was extremely efficient, and it would only take a minute or two to work. "Having someone I could talk to over there when I was alone, or worse, when I was with the researchers..." Zack scuffed the toe of his boot against the floor. "It would have been nice"

She gave a laugh and switched it around on him. "I freaked out so bad the first time it happened."

"I remember," He echoed her laugh. "You could not stop screaming about the voice in your head."

"And now I'm ready to have it back." Zara hugged Zelda and moved over to the table as he pulled out a pair of steaming plates.

"Don't worry, she'll be back and talking your ear off over there in no time."

They ate in contented silence, both thinking about their trip through the portal that night. Zara was thinking about what would happen once they were inside. While Zack was thinking about how to sneak past the guards and anyone else around with the least amount of trouble.

The food disappeared into their bellies as they ate quickly and separated towards their respective rooms.

Zack pulled out his pack and threw a couple of metal water bottles inside, alongside some nutrition bars. There was no telling how long they would be inside the portal, assuming, of course, that they made it inside. He would rather be prepared, or at least as prepared as was currently possible.

They were woefully under-geared in all regards, without any secondary weapons, armor, or other needed items. He could only hope that they weren't attacked by anything too strong when they were inside. His magic should be able to handle anything weak while keeping them safe.

If there was one thing he had learned over the years, it was that the unexpected always happened when you were least prepared. That, and to expect the unexpected. It had been a hard-won lesson, and one he hoped they wouldn't need to learn this time.

Zara came to his door a little later, with her own bag already on her back. Zelda was strapped to the bag, and George was in her arms. Aisha was sitting on the floor once more. He would have to be responsible for carrying her.

"This had better work." He muttered, picking up the large bear. "Is the front door locked?"

She nodded. "I even made sure most of the lights were turned off as well."

"Alright then, get in here. We'll leave through the window." A perk that came with the larger dorm room, or more likely a modification from a previous tenant, was the lack of bars on the window. Even the window in Zara's room had them. The one in Zack's room, however, was hidden from view behind a mix of shrubs and the trunk of a nearby tree.

He had wondered if Edith knew, but stopped short of mentioning it. Why would he alert her to something that might, and in this case, was useful? That would just be stupid.

It was full-dark by that point, and the sounds of students moving around outside had thinned.

Zack grabbed Aisha and lifted the window all the way up. "Let's go and don't forget to remain in the shadows of the dorm."

Chapter 27

A voiding the few people that were still roving around was a simple task for the siblings. All they had to do was avoid the paths. The students rarely left the lit paths at night, not daring to venture into the beckoning darkness beyond.

The siblings kept to the darker portions of the academy grounds until they were well away from the dorms and other buildings. Minutes later, they were on the path that would lead them to the portal complex.

Thankfully, due to them working at the school, there had been a copious number of chances for them to explore the area. Naturally, that also included the areas around the guardhouse outside the complex. The entrance from the academy side had laxer security guards than those on the road.

The students knew they couldn't sneak into the portal when it was being used, and few had the confidence to go inside without a group anyway. There was safety in numbers, which the training classes guaranteed.

The security could afford to be somewhat lazy.

Zack led the way, keeping one eye on the guard station, and his ears focused for the sound of any approaching footsteps. Taking it slowly, he inched underneath the viewing window and avoided the odd-looking tube with glass inset at the end. He had no idea what it was, but a sixth sense told him it would be trouble if he didn't.

Zara followed close behind him, making sure to pay attention to the same things he did. This was their chance, and she wasn't going to waste it by not being careful.

The inside of the complex was quiet, without the usual number of people moving about coordinating everything. The only people moving around at all were the small and infrequent groups of guards. They had been hurriedly pressed into doing the extra work of walking around the compound. Normally it was a job that whichever corporation was there that day handled.

It was easy to avoid the unwilling and inattentive guards. The siblings were careful, and soon enough, they were crouched in the bushes, feet away from the main building.

Zack and Zara monitored the area before making another move. There was no telling how much trouble they might be in if they were caught so close to the portal. Carrying around and keeping the bears hidden also made everything more difficult than it otherwise would have been.

The door opened on silent hinges, revealing the empty interior to their eyes. To the side, the large warehouse doors were closed. The only light illuminating the interior came from the stars shining through the ruined ceiling and the glimmering portal.

Zara stepped forward first, her grip on George loosening. The bear sagged to the ground as she walked closer to the portal. A quick shake of her head later, she looked back at Zack. "Do you want to go through together?"

He hefted up Aisha. "I'm fine with that. Do you need more time, or are you ready to go through now?"

"Now, definitely now. I'm still mostly numb to it from spending so much time near the portal earlier, but the sooner we go through, the better." While he had gone through earlier with Jean and the healer, she had been doing more than simply eavesdropping on the soldiers.

Just being near it was a mentally and emotionally taxing experience. One that she had used to push herself past her emotional trauma's associated with them. It was a short-term fix that would not get her inside, that hadn't been her goal earlier. It had merely been meant as the first step of something more.

They linked their free hands and walked into the portal. The surface resisted Zara's entrance for a moment, the rippling membrane peeling away as Zack pulled her all the way through. Exactly as they had known, or at least believed it would. She had suspected and felt that even without access to her status page, she would be able to go through the portal.

It was one of the many methods that had been tried unsuccessfully in the past with other travelers. This time, however, it had worked.

Zack kept his eyes peeled towards the distant forest and their surroundings as Zara collapsed with a gasp and began to glow. She closed her eyes and curled into a ball, as the familiar rush of energy came pouring into her body. A halo of blue and white energy grew in radiance, the light surrounding her prone form.

The energy sank into her skin and began the process of inspecting and changing every cell.

Around them, the bright glow revealed everything in stark relief. The mix of harsh bright blue and white light bleeding everything of their color.

What Zack saw; he didn't like. Near the edge of the forest, monsters that had initially begun to retreat from the bright eye-searing light began to turn around as it faded. Within seconds, they started to run towards Zack and Zara in rapid fashion. He dropped Aisha beside where George had fallen to the ground and prepared to meet them.

He was merely a level one with some outside ordinary base stats from his aberration class and 'First to Second' title. The class gave his magical attacks plenty of extra power, but that didn't mean it was enough to jump more than a few levels. Not against monsters, in any case. His homeroom teacher, Quinn, had never mentioned the level of the monsters in the portal. Now he was about to find out the hard way what they were.

Zara groaned and stirred as the last of the glow from her awakening faded and disappeared. "That was much more intense than it was the first time."

"I'm not surprised, considering we had to force you through the portal." Zack helped her to her feet and quickly brushed the loose grass from her side. "Please tell me you got the same class, spell, and ability as before! We have incoming!"

Zara took a moment to gaze at her newly revealed status page and smiled. "I'm an 'Arcane Puppeteer' again with the same abilities and spells. I even got a title similar to yours, plus I might be able to use the mana crystals as well."

He hugged her, happy that she would soon have her little friend back in her life. "How much time do you need for the spell and ability to take effect?"

She pulled away and bit her lower lip. "The spell used to only take a minute or so, but the ability takes like thirty minutes the first time." She peered around, trying to pierce the darkness and spot the coming monsters. "Do we have that kind of time?"

"No, no, we don't!" Zack unstrapped Zelda from her bag and pushed her towards the other bears on the ground. "I'll hold them off, but I'll need all the help I can get from you as well."

By that point, the sound of monsters thumping over the grassland could be heard and felt.

"I'll start with Aisha then; hopefully extra power comes with her bigger size." Zara grabbed the large bear and began tracing invisible patterns into its fur. A purple glow reminiscent of Zack's own magic began to seep into the over-sized teddy bear.

Zack took a deep breath and focused on the approaching monsters. He needed to make each shot of his magic count. The number of spells he would get without his ability coming into play was limited. Regardless, he knew he would be depending on it, as he always did.

The first of the beast-classified monsters stepped into the light provided by the portal.

Unexpectedly, the sight calmed Zack. This was something he knew how to deal with. He may have been weaker than before, but the situation itself was almost eerily familiar. Only the presence of his little sister made it different from the other times he had faced off alone against hordes of monsters.

The large panther-like beast was joined by an ape and then a snake, and more. Soon they were surrounded by the monsters, all just barely inside the visible area and no closer.

He had no idea why they weren't attacking. However, every second they delayed was another moment closer to Zara completing her puppet spell. The bear, Aisha, stirred and stood. The action prompting the gathering beasts to attack.

Zack concentrated on the spell and pointed at the group in front of them. His aberration class did not require him to utter a keyword to trigger his spells. He only needed to envision the spell and will it to activate. Pointing was simply a helpful visual guide.

A bolt of magic shot across the intervening distance and hit the ape in the chest. His elemental affinity for 'Space' came into play as pieces of the beast disappeared and reappeared elsewhere. The magical attack continued into the monster behind it without pausing. It was an instant death for the hulking ape.

He hadn't been expecting his affinity for space to affect his very first attack, but he was glad it had. Pieces of ape rained downed from the sky as the location of their reappearance was revealed. The affinity led to some rather messy battles whenever it decided to activate. His control of it had never been great.

Zara flicked off a piece of hairy chest meat without a word and began her second spell. She had seen far worse things than pieces of a beast falling from the sky. It would take something far worse than that to even make her blink.

Aisha shook her body and mindlessly charged forward. Puppets under the control of her basic spell could only obey simple orders, such as to attack. Thankfully, the spell modified how the targets were held together, hardening them, and making what were normally soft, fluffy paws into semi-deadly weapons.

Zack spotted his next target and activated the spell. He felt the magical energy drain from his body as the bolt appeared and sped across the clearing to its target. It was a feeling that was as familiar as it was aggravating. There was no way to track how much energy he had left for spells, outside of his own feelings.

For most people it wasn't an issue, their spells used far less mana than his did. The sheer amount his magic required made it hard to track if he had enough to fuel more than three shots.

Aisha lumbered over the grass; her blunt paws extended in mindless rage. She jumped onto the back of the snake and began pounding on the scales. The blows were relatively soft but very distracting to the beast, causing it to whip around and trip the other monsters.

Zack took aim at a rapidly approaching bird and fired off his third arcane bolt. It took the last of his natural magical energy with it. The bird desperately flapped to the side in a bid to avoid the attack. The bolt pierced through its wing and sent the beast plummeting to the ground beside the snake.

George was the next bear to stand and charge towards the momentarily distracted horde of monsters.

"It feels wrong to awaken her as nothing more than a simple puppet," Zara muttered, stroking Zelda's worn fur. The bear was special to her and had been with her the longest.

"I know." Zack spared her an understanding glance as she began the third spell. Her class gave her far more mana than his, but she also had nothing in the way of offensive spells. Everything she could do really depended on her puppets in one way or another.

Zack clenched his hand tight and prepared for what was about to come next. Once upon a time, he had almost been numb to the soul-searing pain of his ability. He feared those days were long enough past that he would need to deal with the full brunt of what it brought to bear.

There was one plus side of sorts to using his ability. The rate it gathered mana for spells was far faster than normal. The normal cooldown for magic that existed as a mage gathered their magical energy and cast the spell was nearly non-existent. It was a benefit that even his sister didn't have with her class.

Of course, the benefit was offset by him needing to withstand the sometimes very distracting pain that came with it.

In front of them, George was in the process of ripping a scale free from the snake to use as a weapon. Aisha had moved on from attacking its back to directly above its far more sensitive and less protected head.

That left the rest of the panthers, apes, snakes, and other jungle and forest creatures that somehow all lived together for Zack to deal with. At least he would get plenty of experience out of the deal. Both of them would.

Pointing at the closest monster not occupied by the puppet bears, he fired off a bolt, followed by another, and then another. His foot felt as though it was on fire, his toes dipped in acid, while the skin on the underside was being flayed. His left butt cheek was next, as he continued to use his magic as fast as he could. The cheek went ice cold, and each nerve ending began to ache and then scream as they were individually torn open.

Zack stumbled and fell to his knees, Zara catching him at the last moment. She had finished turning Zelda into a puppet, and her part in the fight was over for now. Until one of the bears got injured and needed her help again, at least.

The twentieth arcane bolt shot out as she helped to support his weight. The number of beasts dwindled rapidly as the bolts would randomly send pieces of them flying away. It wasn't always a one-hit kill, but it was almost always enough damage to take them out of the fight for the moment. The bears would come in and finish them off after that. Each of the gore-covered fluff machines had equipped themselves with pieces of their fallen foes to use as weapons.

Zara wasn't only supporting him; her magic was also supporting the bears. Invisible strings of mana connected them to her, and then to the pieces that were torn from them. Fluffy ears, paws, and more were all ripped off and reattached by magic as the stronger monsters retaliated. The pieces moved across the ground and swam through the air to stitch themselves back on.

A ring of death and bodies missing pieces surrounded them. The chunks had either disappeared with Zack's spells or had been taken by the bears for their own use. Regardless, within minutes, the horde had been thinned considerably, and the rest had started to flee.

Zara was leaning heavily against Zack, her skin clammy and beaded with a cold sweat. The amount of mana she had been forced to pour out to keep the three bears functioning had pushed her to her limits. She had actually been forced to stop healing them as her pool of mana ran dry for the moment.

Zack was in even worse condition. Physically, he was fine. The damage his ability caused mostly affected the soul or astral version of his body, unless he pushed it too far. The pain, however, was real, as the two were intrinsically linked at a core level. In some ways, that made it worse. It forced his body and brain to both send differing signals that created a confusing and chaotic anguish.

Zack sucked in a deep breath and groaned. His eyes burned from an excess of built-up salt, and the once green grass had turned into a sticky red quagmire. The mess had solidified around the edges into a pasty glue that was holding his old pants to the ground.

Zelda walked through the mixture, her fake fur paws slurping with every step. Behind her, George was in the midst of retrieving an arm that had been torn from his body, along with all the missing fluffing. Aisha was lying on top of a spiny lizard, who had its claws stuck all the way through her chest. She was no longer moving and was missing her legs along with a paw.

He hoped the puppet spell was still working on her. If it had failed completely, then he would need to sew her limbs back on later. Which would mean that carrying her would be even more awkward on the way back than it had the first time.

He had been hoping to use the room in his pack for mana crystals, not carting around nasty, gore encrusted pieces of a teddy bear. Zack pushed that thought from his mind. It was mean to Aisha and Zara. He would do what needed to be done and not complain about it, regardless of the outcome.

Zelda stopped in front of them and gently picked Zara up first and carried her away from the mess to rest on the clean grass. Then she came back, and in the same gentle manner, pried him free and then carried him over to Zara's side.

"Thanks," He whimpered, as despite the bear's gentle efforts, it had still hurt to be moved.

Zara nodded and sent Zelda off to begin the grisly work of dissecting the beasts. It didn't happen often this near the portal, but occasionally one would have a mana crystal inside them.

"How many levels did you get out of that?" She asked, while reaching into his bag and retrieving some water.

"I haven't checked yet. You?" He accepted the second bottle of water from her and drank it down greedily.

She laughed and started to cry; her tears a complex mixture of emotions. "There were nearly thirty monsters that attacked us, and I only got to level three!"

"Don't forget that we were sharing the experience." He stared up at the dark sky, and let the empty metal bottle fall to his side. "How close are you to level four?" He was desperately trying to keep from moving and aggravating the damage that had started to bleed through from his astral form.

"Not very close," She pouted and drained the last of the water from her bottle. "I still need over two hundred more experience." Zara rolled over and looked at him. "Do you think Second will have me do the compatibility test?"

"Probably, why? Interested in finally learning what your actual score is?" Zack was grateful for the small distraction the conversation was providing.

She nodded. "It would be nice to know how much of the experience from the fight just now I lost out on." Her brow furrowed in thought. "Then again, knowing that I'm missing out on experience due to having a bad compatibility will bug me endlessly. The same could be said for me not knowing though as well!" She rolled over and kicked the ground in frustration.

Zack rolled his eyes, secretly relieved that she was handling everything so well. He wasn't sure how he had expected her to react to being in the portal again... No, that wasn't true, he did know. He had expected her to awaken, and then use her ability to animate Zelda right away. Or to lose it completely. This had been a nice, happy medium.

Instead, they had been attacked, and that particular reunion had been forced to be delayed.

George walked towards them, his loose fluff and missing arm clutched in the armpit of his good arm. He dropped it all by Zara's side and went to help Zelda in dismantling the monsters.

"Is Aisha still a puppet?"

"Just barely," Zara struggled into a sitting position and looked at the sorry state of her newest bear. "It'll be a bit before I have enough mana to fix her

up, and even longer before I can do anything more complicated with her."
In other words, properly animating all three of her bears would take some
time.

Chapter 28

The monsters were nearly all dismantled, and Aisha was back up and helping by the time Zack felt even remotely well enough to move. The bears were using sharpened scales as knives to cut everything apart. Unfortunately, despite the beasts originating from slightly farther inside the portal region, no mana crystals had been found inside them.

Sitting up, Zack glanced from his sister to the bear she was watching closely. "Do you have enough mana to fully animate her now?" He asked gently.

Zara started in surprise and nodded. "Would it be alright if I went ahead and did it now?" She asked, with an untold amount of longing.

He nodded and gingerly climbed to his sore feet. The damage bleeding through from his astral form had stopped and even begun reversing to a degree as it slowly healed. It would be awhile yet, though, before he was anywhere close to being in decent condition.

"I'll give you some privacy and go closer to the trees." Zack ruffled her hair and shuffled off with a muffled, pained grunt. He had been putting off looking at his status page since the battle ended, and it was time to see what had changed.

Zara may have been disappointed by not getting more levels, but she had been pleased with the number of status points she had gotten. Aberration classes typically got more points per level. In their case, they both received a single additional point. However, they also got another point with every level because of their race. Additionally, their title 'Child of the Portals' gave them two points on the landmark levels.

All of that meant that while they may have their weaknesses, they would also have their strengths.

Looking back, Zack saw a blood-encrusted Zelda tottering over to a teary-eyed Zara. He and his sister had a special connection formed through their shared experience. Zelda, however, was her first real friend. The bear had been given to her by their parents, and she had latched onto it with a vengeance. Then, she had been forced through the portal with him and figured out how to animate the bear.

Everything had changed for her after that.

He turned away from the private moment and edged closer to the trees. He wasn't looking for a fight, only some privacy of his own so he could review his status page. Zack moved away from a suspicious-looking vine and sat down, with his back against a tree closest to the clearing.

Relaxing against the smooth bark, he pulled up his status page and stared at it in surprise.

Zackary ??	Level: 4	Exp to next Level: 5/982
Class: Arcane Mystic		Race: Dimensional Child
Titles: Child of the Portals, First to Second		Elemental Affinity: Space
Strength: 07.3 | 10		Intelligence: 15(+.1) | 11(+1)
Dexterity: 11.2 | 13		Magic: 21.5(+.4) | 39(+4)
Constitution: 20.5 | 25		Agility: 12.2 | 14
Abilities: Life Burner Lv. 4, Arcane Manipulation Lv. 0		SP: 9
Spells: Arcane Bolt Lv. 1		

Getting to level four was only somewhat unexpected to him, after hearing that Zara had gotten to level three. If she hadn't said anything, then he wouldn't have expected it. Instead, it simply highlighted how much stronger the monsters had been than them and how screwed they nearly were.

That leveling speed would slow quite a bit after level five, even with his compatibility rating. The amount required for each level after that grew exponentially with each landmark level.

Zack glared at his level and then at his nine available points in regret. He desperately wanted to place them in 'Constitution'. Unfortunately, as an even level of four, he could only place his points in one of his class's major stats. Which as a magic class, even if he was an aberration, those were still 'Intelligence' and 'Magic'.

Both were stats that his class modulated on its own, and they would increase with a set pattern. Intelligence increased by one point at every odd level. He had gotten a point in it already from reaching level three. While magic increased by two on every even level. The plus four symbol next to it denoted the increase from levels two and four.

Any other points he put towards them counted for very little. It was a system that kept him powerful, but with little mana to spare for anything else.

He would simply have to wait until level five before placing any of the available status points.

Closing his page, he batted the vine crawling across the ground to the side and stood. Back near the portal, Zara looked to be nearing completion with her animation spell on Zelda. The first of the three bears she would be doing it on, and the one he expected to include a long and tear-filled reunion.

None of the others had ever been animated before. He had given George to her shortly after their rescue, and as such, the bear had never been through the portal before now.

Speaking of the other bears, he drifted over to where they were separating the scales, tendons, and other useable pieces. The items couldn't be brought outside the portal, but they could be used as armor while they were still inside. Or, in the case of the bears, as everything, weapons and armor.

The bear's pace was slow as they were forced to work in an injured and incomplete state. George was still missing an arm and some of his inner fluff. Aisha, meanwhile, was missing her entire lower half and was scooting around on a snake scale she was fused to with some dried blood.

Glancing at his sister, Zack looked back at the tree line and frowned. He didn't want to just sit around and wait until she was ready. At the same time, however, he was still injured. His magical energy levels were back to normal, and he could fire off another two or three shots without injuring himself. Unfortunately, it would take longer for his astral form to finish healing.

The problem was, there were almost never just two or three monsters when it came to beasts in a forest. They lived close together and were easily alerted by noises, or bright lights, as had happened earlier.

Going in alone would be beyond stupid in his current condition.

Putting his back to the portal, he stared out into the darkness and carefully remembered everything he had seen earlier that day. A hazy overlay of the forest appeared in his mind's eye. It was enough to remind him of a couple locations he had marked as points of interest. Places where he thought they might be mining the mana crystals at.

If nothing else, it gave them a possible direction to head towards when Zara was done animating each of the bears.

Something that she was close to being done with on Zelda. If the intricate and nonsensical collection of runes and glyphs appearing in magical script meant what he thought they did. Unlike when she used her puppet spell, the latter half of her 'Puppet Master' ability was always visible.

Zara hated the abilities name and preferred to just call it her animation ability most of the time, since that's what it did. It had always bugged her and felt off for some reason.

The sight drew his attention despite his best efforts to give her some privacy. He found himself drawn to the light and the bear that it all sank into. It was a magical sight that he had rarely seen the like before.

The process took only a few moments to finish from the time he noticed.

George and Aisha stilled, unconsciously stopping as their controller held her breath.

Zelda rolled over on the grass and shook her head. The movements of her arms and legs momentarily uncoordinated as they flayed about in the air. Zara didn't dare to breathe as the bear tried to climb to her feet twice, falling on her rump each time, and succeeding on the third try. She tottered over to the girl and lifted a grime encrusted teddy bear-sized paw to her cheek.

Zara sniffled and wrapped her friend in her arms, paying no mind to how dirty she was.

Zack was sure Zelda was already talking to her, but he would never be able to hear her. Only Zara was capable of that. Feeling curiously sad, he turned away and waited for them to finish with their reunion.

Sometime later, Zack felt a soft tap on his shoulder. Standing behind him, coming up to just around the height of his shoulder while he was sitting, was Zelda.

"Hi," He coughed, his voice rough and dry. He pulled out a bottle of water from his bag and looked towards the portal, and took a quick sip of tepid water. "She going to wake up the other two already?"

Zelda nodded.

"Will you be able to talk to them?" He asked, suddenly curious about what relationship the bears would have, if any, with each other.

Zelda tilted her head and shrugged. Apparently, she didn't know the answer either. It wasn't surprising, this would be the first time that Zara would be fully animating more than just her after all.

"What do you want to do while we wait? Stand guard, explore the tree line, maybe go farther in?" He glanced at the pile of materials that was beginning to stink. "Or construct some armor and weapons for you and the other two first? What do you think?"

She brought a filthy paw to beneath her chin and pretended to gag, waving the offending limb away from her face.

"Sorry, I can't do anything about that for you. The river is farther in, and I don't know where the nearest stream is. And we're not wasting a water bottle on cleaning any of you." He quickly stored the aforementioned item before she got any ideas.

Zelda stamped her foot and glared at him for a second, picking up a nearby stick when it did no good. "Armor and weapons." She scrawled the words across the ground several times, each time crossing it out and trying again when she inevitably misspelled a word.

"You want to make weapons and armor for the three of you first?" He clarified.

She nodded.

"Okay, let's get to work then."

The pair worked in companionable silence for several minutes before Zelda picked up her stick once more.

"Thank you for taking care of me all these years," The bear had obviously been thinking about the message for a while as she misspelled fewer words.

"What do mean?" He wondered.

Zelda dragged a paw along one of the many seams he had sewn together over the years. The color of the threads, not quite matching the rest. Pieces of grime and dried blood flaked off and fell with the movement.

Zack frowned and knelt before her. "You remember all of that? How?"

Zelda began to nod and then stopped. The stick in her hand tapping thoughtfully against the ground. "Pieces here and there, not everything. Connection to her grew... dim, strained, almost gone at times, but I held on, I refused to let her go-" The writing grew increasingly messy, and hard to read.

He pushed the stick from her paws and pulled her close, looking into her marble eyes. "So, you know everything that would happen to her even after she left the portals? All the experiments they did to her, how we had to live after we were rescued?" It was hard to keep the bitterness from his voice.

She nodded, with a slight tilt of her filthy head, unsure of where he was going with that train of thought. He suddenly engulfed her in a hug, holding his breath so he wouldn't accidentally breathe in her smell.

"Thank you," He whispered, as he held her. He tightened the hug and then released the bear.

Zack stood and ineffectually tried to brush the grass and other debris from the knees of his pants. Pants that, if he was being honest with himself, were officially on their last leg. They were old, worn, and patched before this little trip. Now they were being held together more by the dried pieces of blood and various beasts that had gathered on the thin material than any remaining cloth.

He ignored the stiff snap and crackle as his clothes tore and shed a layer of dried filth. Instead, he picked up a tendon and a smaller scale. Behind him, Zelda stamped her foot as he ignored her. Tying the tendon to the claw of a dead lizard, he used the scale to scrape the excess material from it. Honestly, he had no idea how the bears had managed to get the tendons out as quickly as they had. Normally, they were a rather time-intensive endeavor to retrieve, not that he was going to complain.

The tendons, or sinew as it was actually called now that it was outside of a living body, were incredibly strong once they were dried. It was the perfect material for constructing some quick but relatively durable weapons or armor. Exactly what the three bears needed at the moment.

He would try to think of a more permanent solution later.

Zack would clean, and Zelda would then use the claws to slowly drill holes into the many scales. It was a long and boring process. One that grew faster when they were joined by a newly animated George a while later.

He and Zelda did indeed seem to be able to converse as they worked together in an increasingly efficient manner. It was something that he had been somewhat expecting and made sense if George also could talk to his sister.

"Zack!" Zara screamed when she finished animating Aisha. The large new bear had doubled over and was ripping a hole open in its throat.

"What's going on?" He asked, running over to her.

Zara was sweating from her constant efforts in animating the bears and was standing on one knee. "I'm not sure! She just keeps saying that it hurts."

"What hurts?"

She shrugged. "I don't know. Can you help her?"

"How am I supposed to help her when you don't even know what's wrong with her?" Zack protested, stepping closer to the bear regardless. He slapped her large paws away and reached for the hole she had started to tear in her throat. "I have no idea if this will hurt, but sorry." He gripped the edges and pulled, ripping it open. Thrusting his hand into the opening, he began to root around in her fluffing, to her obvious discomfort.

It only took a few seconds for that to be too much, and Aisha retreated from him. She shoved her own paw into the now larger hole. Then, carefully pushing it against the inside of her chest, she pulled out a small object and handed it to Zack.

"Does she know what it is?" He asked with a sinking feeling. There were no markings on what he now saw was a rather intricate device with a tiny mana crystal the size of a grain of sand powering it.

Zara shook her head. "She wasn't awake yet when they put it in. What do you think it is?" She proceeded to fix the hole in Aisha's throat while they talked.

He plucked the tiny, processed magi-crystal from the device and stored it in an empty water bottle. "I can't say for sure, but considering who she came from, and what we thought she might have before. I would say it's likely that it's a listening device of some kind."

Zara bit the corner of her lip. "So, they know we are in here, then?"

He nodded. "Probably. I would expect to see Anna and Second waiting for us when we leave as well." His hand tightened around the listening device, breaking it.

Her brows drew close together in thought. "What does that mean for any mana crystals we bring back tonight, then? Will they try to confiscate them?"

Zack shoved the remains into his pocket and thought over her question. "I'm not sure. On one hand, they are used by corporations for everything, but on the other, they are also readily available to the public. It wouldn't make a lot of sense for them to confiscate them, but it is certainly a possibility."

"We should hide some of them just in case, then." Zara decided, finishing her work on Aisha.

"We only have so many water bottles," Zack said, mentioning the obvious location, before glancing at the next obvious one.

Aisha covered her throat and hid behind the much smaller Zelda.

Zara shook her head emphatically. "No! That would hurt them!"

"Fi-" He stopped and looked from her to George. "How's George doing then?" They had put a secret pouch in the bear years before. Now that he was animated, Zack was wondering if the addition was hurting or bothering him.

Zara looked startled, apparently having forgotten about the spot where she hid all their extra money. "George, are you doing alright?"

The bear nodded and reached behind to touch the spot where the zipper was hidden. He was aware it was there, but didn't seem to be bothered by it for some reason.

They stood around thinking for a minute longer before Zack ushered them towards the materials.

"Come on, we can decide when we actually have the crystals to worry about. There is no point in thinking about it too much before then."

"Where are we heading towards?" Zara asked him, as the bears tied pieces of other beasts to themselves as armor and weapons.

Zack pointed out three separate directions to her. "There are three locations that I was able to somewhat identify as being likely locations when I was inside earlier. The first is closer to the mountains, a typical location for a mine. The second is in the middle of the forest. Maybe in an open mine of sorts, or with stronger monsters, both common options. The third is the river, with loose crystals just gathering along the bottom in certain areas."

Zara rolled her eyes. "Those are kind of obvious."

He shrugged. "What can I say? There was no one inside, and there hadn't been anyone for a few hours. You know how fast portals tend to fix the damage humans do to them, especially when they are empty."

"The mountains are too far," She said, moving on with the conversation. "The depths of the forest are probably too dangerous for us. There are too many places where we could be surrounded and cut off from the bears. You could easily handle a few monsters, but in the forest, it would be too easy for there to be a near-endless wave of them."

"The river it is, then."

On the far side of the clearing behind the portal was an area a lot of travelers ignored, simply because they never thought to look. It was more of the green clearing and forest, but there was also a river that came down from the mountains that were part of the hollow. There was something about coming out of the portal, looking in a certain direction that kept most travelers from ever thinking to look the other way.

They waited for the bears to finish arming themselves and then walked around the portal.

The river was only maybe a hundred meters into the depths of the forest. They were able to hear rushing water as soon as they reached the edge of the trees. Along with that came the sound of beasts and other kinds of monsters occupying the forest.

Zara swallowed. "I didn't realize the river was so far inside the forest. It almost makes no difference what choice I made, does it?"

Zack snorted. "The trees will be much thinner as we get closer to the river, so it'll be a lot easier. Trust me, the trees will be dense for maybe fifteen meters or so and then they should begin to thin. This is still the better route."

Chapter 29

Zara glowered worriedly at the trees, inching closer to her brother. "Fifteen, maybe sixteen meters of dense trees where they have all the advantages, and then another thirty meters or so, if we are lucky, where they thin out." She frowned and shook her head. "I don't like it. We got lucky earlier because they charged us, and you still nearly killed yourself!" Her shout echoed through a suddenly silent forest.

"What other choice do we have?" He ignored the accusation. There was nothing he could do about it now. Zack knew she was likely right about the fight earlier; they had gotten incredibly lucky. The different monsters and beasts hadn't worked together. Some had even gotten in each other's way. It had been a massive mess, one that was to their advantage.

The forest in front of them would be nothing like that. No matter how short of a time they planned on being inside it.

They hesitated, waiting for the normal noises of the forest to return.

Zelda swaggered forward and began to shadowbox with the needle-like scales tied to her arms. Aisha and George joined her a moment later, and Zara watched in amusement as they attempted to clumsily copy her movements.

He sighed. "Okay, fine, you win. We won't go inside the trees."

Zelda snapped around and kicked George and Aisha, sending them both flying.

"Uh, she was actually trying to prove the opposite," Zara muttered, barely holding back a laugh.

"How was I supposed to know that?" He protested. "All that demonstration proved is that Zelda is the only one that can take care of herself. Which makes sense, considering she has been around the longest. The others don't know anything. You would be constantly expending mana to reinforce and heal them. Which I guess is normal for the way you usually fight."

Zack was taking his sister's worries and her words seriously. She had a knack for piecing things together on clues he would normally ignore as background information. If she said that they got lucky earlier, then it was likely the entire fight was closer than he had realized.

Looking back at his condition, in the end, he could only agree with her. When the damage started to bleed through from his astral form, as it had at the very end, it was a bad sign. The pain bleeding through was normal. The damage bleeding through, however, meant he had already pushed it too far. Any farther, and he would have entered potentially dangerous, uncharted waters with the ability.

That fight could have easily ended differently if they had been anywhere else, say, for instance, inside a forest. Actually, inside the wooded area, it would have been far, far worse. The beasts there would have worked together and not gotten in each other's way. They would have been able to use the environment to their natural advantage and more that he couldn't think of off the top of his head.

It would have been a nightmare.

"I'm not at a hundred percent yet," Zack whispered. "My regular mana levels are back to normal, but my astral form is still recovering from before. I can fight, just no prolonged battles." He snorted, "Can you imagine a regular person with a training class being able to do what we just did?"

Zara simply shook her head and backed farther away from trees and sat down to think. "If the entire class had gotten involved, they might have been able to do something. Assuming that there was no teacher there to help, I'd give them slim odds of even surviving at best. I just don't know. I assume some of them have been training for years. It isn't the same or as good as the advantages we have... but maybe a few would get lucky."

"Yeah, if Jean or Rose was there, that horde probably wouldn't have survived more than a minute or so." Zack settled down next to his sister, and together they watched Zelda teaching the other bears how to fight. "Don't forget, Jean is in the military, under the ever secretive Major. So, I would assume that she is a high regular class, maybe even a low specialist."

Zara shook her head. "There is no way she's a low specialist, not with that rank. I'm thinking she's mid to high regular class at best. Not that it really matters. Everything we know about the man indicates he surrounds himself with people who are both loyal and incredibly competent. We already know she is competent in the regular world, but she was chosen as a training teacher of sorts for a prestigious academy. The position isn't a guarantee, but her real background and reason behind the position pretty much are. She needs to be strong enough to handle anything that might happen inside the portal."

"What are your thoughts on Rose, then?"

She shrugged. "No idea. I haven't met her. From what you have said about her and Quinn being ex-travelers, though, I can make some guesses. They are probably mid-to-high range regular classes at most as well. Anything too low and they would never have gotten teaching positions at the academy as they wouldn't have been qualified. Anything too high and they wouldn't have needed to teach as they would have been set for life and simply retired."

Zack thought over her different conclusions, along with the ways she had come to them. It was always useful to decide on his own if she was correct, or if she had missed something. It had yet to happen, but he held a certain amount of elderly brother hope in his heart that he would someday be able to tease her about it.

He shook his head and slapped his cheeks. "How did we even get on that topic? I thought we were talking about whether or not we were going to enter the forest."

Zara scratched lightly at her cheek and looked away. "Uh, you got distracted?"

"Sure, I got distracted." Zack glanced up at the night sky that had begun to shift from starry black to the silvery light of a full moon, only without the moon. "Not sure that would help much inside the forest anyway." Referencing the sudden increase in light.

"The mana crystals would be nice. Being able to heal you if anything happens again, frankly, would ease my mind a great deal. Having them in reserve for emergencies would be great," She sighed and leaned back a little. "But maybe we are going about this the wrong way. You are already going to sell the information about your ability and its implications to Second.

He would obviously then know you need mana crystals. I'm sure either he or Anna would be willing to get some for us. They could even be included as part of the initial deal for the information."

Zelda stopped mid-punch, George getting a lucky kick to her side in while she was distracted. The older bear smacked him away and angrily stomped her way over to Zara and Zack.

"No, you can keep training them if that is what you want. We haven't decided yet. I was just saying that this wasn't the best plan to get mana crystals is all. I still needed to come through to wake you all up, though."

Zack sat to the side, listening to a thoroughly one-sided conversation between his sister and a bear. It was a sight he had seen before, but not in a long time, and the memories it brought back were one of the few good ones he had of back then.

Zelda kicked his foot, bringing him rudely back to the present. It would seem that the argument had concluded while he was thinking about the past. She pointed her scale needle first at him and then at the forest.

"Hey, what was that for?" He pulled the needle-free from her arm and acted like he threw it into the forest, the low light fooling them. "There, now go fetch. I thought you were supposed to be a bear all this time, not a dog, but what do I know?"

Zelda's head swiveled from him to the forest and back several times before she tackled him. To the side, Zara had fallen over laughing and was unable to provide any further translating services.

"Alright, I give, I give. Here!" He was quick to offer up the needle to the strong and scrappy bear, who specialized in making fleshy things like him hurt, a lot. Not that she would do that to him, but why run the risk?

He could have sworn he heard the bear snort as she picked up the needle and playfully poked him with it.

Zara rolled over a moment later and wiped the tears from her eyes. "Go get it Zido!" She broke down giggling again.

Zelda held her dirty paw up to her eyes and then pointed it at Zack's in a familiar gesture. Then, with that completed, she walked over to the hysterical girl and sat on her. A moment later, she was joined by George and Aisha; the latter taking up her place on the girl's legs.

"She wanted to go inside," Zara gasped out, still regaining her breath. She was holding the three bears and sitting next to her brother with a contented smile on her face. "After so long of not being able to do anything, she wants to, uh, exercise some more before we go back through the portal."

"If she wants to take the three of them a few meters into the trees to train them, I don't mind. It's up to you and what you can handle for the most part. Zelda just needs to make sure that they remain within an area where I can provide help if it is needed." He stared at the trees and the eerily silent forest behind them.

The wind rustled their hair and stirred the leaves on their branches, sending a few spinning away. That is when it struck him, as he listened to the noise of the leaves abruptly fade away. It wasn't that the forest had gone silent; it was that something had muffled everything inside.

"Zara, Zelda, change of plans. We're leaving now!" He was glad that they had stopped before entering the forest. Who knew what was buried somewhere in those trees? It was powerful, too powerful for them to handle, is all he knew, and that was enough. "The training session will have to wait for another time."

It had clearly been a stupid and ill-thought-out idea for them to come inside the portal for anything more than awakening Zara. Who was it that said the school portal was weaker than other portals? Zack wanted to smack whoever it was, along with himself.

He had been too confident for absolutely no reason! He knew next to nothing about this portal and the dangers that it contained. The lessons that would cover those topics had only just begun, and they would be running through the information for months at least.

He could excuse putting himself in danger needlessly, less so when it came to his little sister. There would always be dangers in her life, but they shouldn't come from him. He should be working to mitigate them and make her safer, not put her in harm's way needlessly.

Zara backed away from the forest without question. The bears surrounded her instantly and moved in unison with the girl as they acted as her guards.

Zack followed a moment later after he judged she was far enough away. He maintained eye contact with the forest, his feet stuttering to a stop as the pressure of a powerful being made itself known. The pressure didn't come from the hidden creature possessing a high level, though that was likely the case. No, this came from the ability that only ruler class beasts and monsters had.

He closed his eyes and bowed to the tree line. "Thank you for showing us mercy and allowing our retreat." It was a gamble as to whether the unseen being would understand the gesture or his words. People were constantly moving around the portals, talking, attacking, destroying, even animals could be taught to understand limited communication.

Not enough was known about ruler class existences. By nature, they were rarely seen. The number of times they had even been heard about living in a specific portal could be counted on one hand. Zack had no idea if that was because they killed everyone they encountered, or because they typically lived in the depths travelers rarely ventured in. Or some other more esoteric reason.

All he knew was that they were in a sort of trouble that no one would have ever guessed they would find.

Zack felt his feet lift from the ground as he was pulled closer to the trees. Behind him, his sister screamed.

Struggling to look up, he found the area enshrouded in a darkness, magic in origin. It was designed to hide the caster's identity, and it performed its job well. Except for one possibly unimportant detail. The only thing he could see were two glowing yellow eyes, with elongated slit-shaped irises typical of nocturnal predators. Like a cat, or snake.

Zack was slowly spun around in the air, affording him the view of Zelda and the others holding a struggling Zara back.

"You are different from the others." An oddly accented voice belonging to the owner of the eyes spoke as he finished a revolution. "You do not fully belong to the world from which that portal comes, but you do not fully belong to this one either. Do you belong to the others?"

Zack swallowed and licked his lips. "You know about where the portals go?"

"Of course, but we do not go through them. There is no reason to, not for those like myself, anyway." Zack drifted closer to the eyes, and he heard a sniff. "What are you? It is as though you belong to everywhere, and not just one world. Is your sister the same?"

"Probably?" Zack prayed that it was the right answer.

The being gently let him float to the ground, its eyes never leaving him.

"This leaves me in a difficult position. The people who come through that portal have taken that which is not theirs to take and have done so for many cycles. The Great Change is nearly upon us. No one knows what form it will take. However, as the name implies, it will change things according to the whims of some unknown God, Maker, or Divine Being. Regardless, I wish to see them pay for what they have taken, but you do not belong to that world."

Zack felt the words like a punch to his gut and had no way of refuting them. The words were true in several variations of the meaning. The only tie he had to Albion, to Aperra, was his sister, who stood a good thirty meters behind him. Both their races read as something other than human, and they had titles confirming that. He wanted to say that their parents had been born on Aperra, in the country of Albion, but who could say for sure?

In one short exchange, a simple fact had managed to be driven home for Zack. He and his sister, they had nothing truly linking them to Albion, or to Aperra, and without that, could they even say they belonged to that world?

Zack shook his head, dispelling the odd train of thoughts, and met its gaze head-on. "They know something is coming. The portals have been changing, getting stronger, stranger. I'm sure there are other things that I'm not privy to."

"There are, and they will only grow worse until it all boils over." The eyes shifted position, as though it had tilted its head in amusement. "For some reason though, I think you might be able to change that, make it easier on them, and maybe even give back some of what they stole from us. I wonder what the other rulers would say if they knew I had seen you?"

"How much time do we have?" He asked quickly, feeling the ruler beginning to pull back its darkness.

"It's hard to say. It is called the Great Change for a reason. No one can accurately predict something that is constantly changing. Without your intervention, between," It stopped to do some mental math. "Five and ten of that world's cycles. With your help, if you figure out how, who knows? It could happen tomorrow. You should leave now. I look forward to seeing how things change."

Zack waited a moment longer and then turned, hurrying back to his sister. His mind was a jumble of information and half-remembered conversations and snippets with Jean and sergeant Grieves.

Zara tackled him as he ran up to them, the bears not daring to let go of her before then. It was impossible to understand what she was trying to say through the sobs, so he simply held her for the moment. Zelda tugged on the destroyed hem of his shirt and pointed up at the silver sky.

Hovering over a hundred meters above them was a dark blob with two yellow orbs glowing in the middle, not doing anything. The being hidden inside was simply watching and listening. A moment later, a deep purple mana crystal was tossed at their feet. A breath after that, the blob rose high into the sky and soared towards the floating island in the distance.

Zelda carefully handed him the crystal, while Zara took deep breaths and regained control of herself.

"Stupid bears, I could have taken the yellow-eyed blob... thing." She finished lamely, pulling George into her lap and Aisha to her side. The action taking the sting from her words. "What was that anyway?"

"It was a ruler class being."

Zara paled and patted the two bears nearby. "Such good bears, so smart and obedient."

Zelda kicked the obviously two-faced girl's foot and went to sit by Zack.

"Why is there a ruler class being in the school portal?" The girl hissed, a moment later wiping the tears from her eyes.

Zack flipped the fist-sized mana crystal over in his hands. He had never seen or even heard of a purple one before. Of course, he had also never heard of the dark stones they use for complex engravings. The world was a large and complicated place, and the amount of knowledge he had was pitifully small.

Still, it was better to be safe than sorry. You never knew what you didn't know until you knew it or needed to know it.

Holding a crystal so different from anything else he had ever seen really drove that home. He could feel how dense the mana inside it was, and there was something else. This crystal was different from the others' travelers found. He wasn't sure how, but the way mana moved inside it was different. It bugged him and unfortunately, it would have to wait for another time.

Chapter 30

Z ara threw George at him. "I said, why is there a ruler class being inside the school portal?"

Zack set a disgruntled George to the side of Zelda. "I would guess that this is their territory. The more important question is why we were lucky or unlucky enough for it to appear here now? To which, I have no idea." He hesitated and then motioned her closer. "That's not all though." He relayed everything that had been said, looking for any insights she might have.

"Well, first off, I doubt mom and dad came from another world. They just weren't that cool. Not to mention if they crossed worlds only to die here, it would be way too sad and lame."

"What about our status pages never listing our last names? Could that have any relation to them not belonging as well, or just us not belonging?" Zack didn't like pushing her on any subject about their parents. However, if they needed to mention them, it was better to get it done in one fell swoop instead of dragging it out.

The young girl sighed and pulled the closest willing bear onto her lap, which turned out to be Aisha. At the same time, Zelda stood and hurried over to help comfort her. "Is there any point in speculating? We are never going to know in either case. No one knows how the system works at its core, and as for our parents, well, they are even worse!"

The venomous vitriol in her voice shouldn't have shocked him, and yet it still managed to.

"They left no records, and we don't know who we are. It doesn't matter if mom and dad were regular travelers or people from another world that somehow found themselves displaced onto Aperra. The fact of the matter is, they didn't tell us anything, and then they left. Leaving us alone. That is all that matters. Now, let's move on. Please?" She finished softly.

Zack coughed awkwardly and looked away sadly. He knew mentioning them had been a bad idea, and she wasn't wrong for the most part. Unlike her, however, he had known them, no matter fuzzy and indistinct the memories of back then were. The warmth and love they had felt for their children had been real. He was sure of that.

"Okay, so we are back to it being whatever was done to us, and the portal all combined somehow changing us? If that is the case, then doesn't it mean that it could be replicated?" Zack had kind of liked the feeling he felt when even the ruler class being had considered him something special.

Zara frowned, thinking the question over seriously before answering. "There were a lot of random variables involved in what they did to us, as well as that specific event. So, I'm going to say that the chances of it happening again are unlikely. Then again, who knows what the actual requirements are? We could have just barely met them, or been considered super-overachievers, you know?" She sighed and leaned against the large bear on her lap. "Sorry, I know that isn't what you want to hear."

"No, it isn't, but it's better to hear the truth, or at least your thoughts, than not."

"Besides all that, though, this Great Change business is interesting." George, who had been a little slow on the uptake, finally stood and trundled over to join the bear pile developing on her lap. "I have some thoughts on that, and I'm sure you do as well. Particularly related to the power markers on the portals beginning to change at a faster pace than before. Along with a certain portal at that research building." She welcomed the new bear with an understanding and grateful smile.

Zelda was the exception, not the standard. She had been developing for years even before they were rescued. After the rescue, and unknowingly to them, even though her body had been dormant, her mind had not.

The other two bears were like toddlers mentally in comparison. Their initial growth would be fast, with them quickly passing into a more adolescence equivalent stage. It would take longer for them to reach nearly the same mental age as either Zelda or Zara.

"That is indeed where my thoughts went when this Change business was mentioned. Us being considered as keys by the Major is also rather serendipitous."

"That's one word for it. Suspicious is another somewhat more magical term." Zelda nodded her head emphatically, before pushing George from the pile and proceeded to stand on him. The extra height elevating her enough to where she could pat Zara on the head.

Zack tapped the side of his nose in agreement and stood. "Come on, we should keep moving back towards the portal while we talk."

Zara hugged Zelda and kissed the one clean spot on her face. Standing, she held Aisha and George's paws and fell in beside her brother.

"That is actually what I was getting at before, and I know we've had this conversation before on other things. Most recently, when we learned about the power markers, how some portals moved, and more. The government is hiding information from us, from the travelers, probably from everyone except a privileged few."

"Hold on, I think I know where you are going with this, and I just want to clarify something first." Zara interrupted him, while Zelda clambered up his back, using the straps of the pack, and perched herself on his shoulders. "Earlier, when you were telling me everything that had happened, I couldn't help but wonder about how intelligent the ruler sounded in the story. Tell me, was it really that intelligent, or did you smarten it up some to humanize what was an otherwise faceless blob, or something when you told it?"

"That's my little sister, smart girl." Zack smiled and passed the purple crystal to Zelda's questing paws. It was great to see the smart girl he knew she was slowly beginning to come into her own. Living in that piece of crap, unsafe government-owned apartment had been doing them more harm than he realized. Not that there had been another choice, regardless. "And no, I wasn't. That's really the way it was and talked."

"But how? There is no way they could keep something that big a secret for over a hundred years?" She retorted in disbelief.

"I'm pretty sure the time limit, and how things are designed on our end, can be thanked for that one. Think about it, and I know you weren't there for this, but Quinn somewhat talked about this issue in class the other day. What it boils down to is time equals money, travelers get paid by their corporation or government. That means they need to stay near the miners instead of exploring. The crystals come back after a bit, so there is no need for them to search for replacement sites. Then, of course, there are also the monsters they would need to contend with that get stronger the farther in you go."

"That would mean the entire system would have to have been created and rigged from the very beginning to keep people from finding out."

"No, I would say more that one was designed to keep people from venturing into places they shouldn't. Something that doesn't appear to apply to us, I might add. The other, the system designed by the governments of Aperra. That one is the issue here."

"Still, it means that someone in the beginning knew a lot of powerful people, considering you rightly mentioned the different governments working together. It again begs the question about how word of intelligent beasts or monsters never made their way out?"

Zack wiped some of the dried grime from his face and gave the same answer he always did. "How do we know it didn't? Face it, sis, we don't know anything. Where would we have heard a rumor like that in the first place? School? I rarely went, and you never did. The Institute? The researchers were busy pretending our bodies were their playthings, and they were gods."

Zelda smacked him on the head with the mana crystal.

"Ow!" He grabbed it from her and turned to face his sister. "Sorry, that came out harsher than I meant it to. What I'm trying to say is we live in a box. Rumors pertaining to the portals or travelers aren't the kind of things you would hear on the streets where we lived before. We are still finding our feet in the academy, and for all we know, though I doubt it, their existence could be common knowledge to everyone but us."

"You deserved that." She high-fived the bear on his shoulders, releasing her grip on both George and Aisha. "But, no, you're right, despite the way you said it. Our common knowledge is sadly lacking in a lot of ways. Unfortunately, by its very nature, it isn't something we can easily fix right now. I'm sure Edith and even Tessa would be willing to help, but if they don't think of something..." She sighed.

"Yeah, it does mean that we need to be more careful around Jean and the military though."

"If only-"

"There are a lot of 'if only's' in life," Zack cautioned her. "Don't get caught up in wishing for something we can't have."

"What are we going to do with that?" She asked, pointing to the purple crystal, and changing the subject.

"We can't let Anna and whoever is waiting with her have it, that's for sure." They skirted around something slithering in the dark grass. Neither was sure if they would offend the ruler if they fought anything on the way to the portal.

"It won't fit in the bottles, or in George's pouch." Zara decided after mentally measuring it.

"The bottles will probably be the first place they look when we show up without anything else." He mentioned further.

Zelda bopped him on the head to get his attention and then climbed down from his shoulders.

"She says she'll do it," Zara said softly a moment later. "She was super chatty for the first little bit, but after not being able to talk to anyone for so many years, she's quieter than before. It's like she keeps forgetting that I can hear her again." Her cheeks twitched as tears glistened and slid wetly down them, while a soft sniffle came from her. "Poor little Zelda, she must have been so scared and lonely."

Zelda ran to her and hugged the girl's legs while shaking her head.

Zack wrapped them both in hugs, feeling his legs engulfed by the other two somewhat clueless bears. They held that position for a while before separating and continuing towards the portal.

"Is she sure she wants to carry the mana crystal inside her somewhere? She doesn't have a pouch-like George does. If Aisha's reaction is anything to go by, then having this thing inside her will be extremely uncomfortable. Not to mention we have to make the initial cut to shove it through and then find some way to secure it inside her so it doesn't move."

"Wow, way to talk her out of it." She squatted in front of the bear she loved with all her heart. "He's right, Zelda, this is not going to be pleasant for you in the slightest. Are you sure?"

Zack could have sworn he saw the bear's chin quiver, except that was impossible. Her face was all sewn on, and not mobile in the slightest.

Zelda nodded.

"Fine, let's get to the portal and use its light to see everything better by before making any cuts in her. Even if Zara can heal her up good as new,

I'd rather get it right in as few tries as possible." He grumbled, hurrying them along.

Zack had to admit to a certain fondness towards the currently disgusting furball. She had been with them for a long time, and she had protected Zara and kept her sane when he couldn't. He didn't want to hurt her, even if she had volunteered for it, and that was exactly what he was about to do.

The clearing around the portal had been dragged clean of remains during their time away. Heavy paw prints and drag marks crisscrossed the area, destroying what little grass had been left. All that was left now was a soupy quagmire of bloody mud.

Where the snake had lain only talon marks, digging deep into the ground remained. They hadn't been expecting flying beasts or monsters and were glad that it had arrived late to the party. Especially since it had been strong enough to carry the rather large snake away on its own. At least, that is what they guessed, since there were no other talon marks in the area.

They huddled close to the portal, where there was the most light to see by. Aisha and George were facing out, to watch for any approaching monsters. Zara insisted on holding Zelda's paw while Zack operated on her.

"Can you put her to sleep or something?" He asked, scraping the edge of the scale needle the bear had claimed as hers on a rock, hoping to sharpen the edge even a little more before doing this.

"That isn't how my ability works. My control over each of them is limited." Zara picked some hardened flakes of blood from the paw she was holding. "At least I think aberration classes and abilities like ours don't come with manuals. Last I checked, anyway. Well, we at least are limited to what is listed on the status page and what we can figure out."

He grunted and threw the rock to the side, giving up. "Can you imagine if we didn't have to figure out everything on our own? If we knew what the requirements were to get the abilities or spells we wanted?"

They shared a laugh at the preposterous idea, and then Zack was ready.

Zelda climbed into his lap and laid on her stomach. A long line of multi-colored stitches ran down her back. This would not be the first time he had worked on her, not even close. It was simply the first wherein she would be actively more than the teddy bear she appeared to be.

"Alright, let's do this." He plucked the first thread, making his way down the line, doing his best to ignore her tremors.

When Zack had cut enough of the threads, he braced himself for the next part and pulled her back wide open.

Zara made a distressed sound, and he felt the ends wanting to close. "Not yet," He snapped. "We have to secure the mana crystal inside, so it doesn't move around, no matter what. I'm sorry Zelda and Zara, both of you just hold on a little longer."

Working with an idea he had earlier on how to secure it inside her. Zack used some leftover sinew to tie the crystal to the scale needle and placed it inside her. The sinew and scale would both vanish once they left the portal, but this next part would remain.

The scale would keep the crystal in place while he moved and packed her inner fluffing around it. Sure, he could do the job without it, but this would be faster, and without everything moving around and loosening constantly.

"Take a deep breath. This next part is going to hurt, a lot, but then I'll be done, and we can go back home." Zack rested for a moment, his hands trembling slightly as they pushed a clump of dead grass to the side.

Zara glared at him and moved to hold Zelda's entire head. "Get on with it! Why are you making this longer than it needs to be?" She hissed angrily.

He was hesitating because it didn't feel good hurting the stupid little bear! Still, he put his hands back in her and began packing the fluffing around the crystal and needle. Her legs and arms deformed some as he pulled the needed extra to surround it. Now, even if someone were to poke and feel her chest, it should hopefully escape their notice.

"Do it." He said, pulling his hands free.

Excess pieces of fluff were pulled inside as her back pieces were pulled down and back into place. The only thing different from before was that her multi-colored stitches had now been replaced with ones that matched her coloring. It was an odd thing to fix; he thought.

"How does it feel?" Zack asked gently.

Zara's eyes widened, and then she snorted. "Where did you learn to talk like that? What do you mean, Zack brought you along on to some construction sites?"

"It was only a couple of times, and just in the beginning," He scratched the tip of his nose, refusing to look at her. "Anyway, what did she say?"

"She said that it feels like something is shoved up her uh..." Zara stuttered and looked away. "Stupid bear, talking like that." She muttered. "In any case, she doesn't like it. Let's hurry on through so she doesn't have to feel it any longer. We can worry about removing it and hiding it later."

They had the distinctly unhappy and unmoving bear strapped to Zara's bag a few moments later. Her arms and legs looked a little thin, and her belly bigger than before, but they were always around her. Few others should notice the difference, or if they did assume that she needed anything more than a good shake to redistribute her insides.

Zack picked up Aisha, ignoring the scales-turned-armor she had continued to accumulate during their time inside. He had a feeling the big bear did not like pain.

Zara picked up George, and the siblings nodded; their time inside had come to an end. It was pure luck that they had even managed to accomplish both of their objectives. The first was easy and accomplished as soon as he pulled his sister through the film covering the portal entrance. The second had been harder to get and only achieved when it was tossed from the sky by a being he wasn't sure he wanted to meet again.

Zack stopped; his foot poised in the air before the portal. Something the ruler being had said, or in this case not said, finally clicking into place. "This isn't their world either." His foot fell, and he spun around. "When it mentioned people coming through the portals and taking what wasn't theirs, we assumed that meant it had claimed them, and maybe it has. Now. It never called this place is its world either. Don't you see, there might not actually be a conspiracy by the government. The ruler could be leading a bunch of refugees that are a more recent addition. It did mention other worlds."

"It's thin," Zara hesitated, "No less insane than the other ideas we've tossed around, and certainly less paranoia-inducing."

He nodded and shrugged. "It has no more proof than any of the others either, for or against. I just... I don't want to go back through and start second-guessing everything Anna, Second, Jean, and the others tell us. We've lived that way before, Zara, and it's no way to continue living. This theory, at least, gives us an alternative, however slim."

Chapter 31

The siblings walked free of the portal and stopped, calmly taking in the crowd of people and vehicles in front of them. They had been expecting some of them; if not quite so many.

"We figured you'd be here." Zack reached into his pocket and tossed the mangled device that had been inside Aisha, minus the small, processed magi-crystal, to Anna's feet. It skittered across the hard concrete floor and came to a stop several feet behind her. He shrugged. "I don't think it works anymore, in any case, not after going through the portal."

Zara moved closer to her brother, ignoring the soldiers as they shuffled about at the sudden movement.

"We were, however, expecting less of a crowd, just you, Second, and maybe a few others. It looks like you brought an entire platoon's worth of soldiers and then some."

Anna shook her head, her eyes seething as she coldly replied. "That was my original intent yes, someone else had other ideas on the matter."

Specialist Jean McCleary stepped out from behind a vehicle at the back, her face set into a steely mask that revealed nothing. A man Zack recognized vaguely as the Major was at her side.

"Are you good?" She asked, clipping the word, her eyes flicking from him to the man at her side. It was a hint that only he would understand. A clue she had laid the groundwork for on a whim, hoping she would never need to use it. Now she had, and she still wasn't sure why. She was loyal to the Major, not this kid. She just did not want him to go through anymore. Both he and his constantly terrified and timid little sister had gone through enough.

Zack remembered the last time she had said that word to him in this place. His mind raced, putting the different clues from their conversation together.

He remembered what the ruler had just told him as well and paled. He did not belong here. Was that something that the Healer woman had been able to see with her examination spell? Was there something different about him and his sister on the inside that affected their status pages?

No, they were not good. They were as far from it as was possible at that moment.

He swallowed and gave them a tight smile, flicking a piece of dried blood from his clothes. "I believe so. There were more beasts than I was expecting after our earlier visits. Nothing we couldn't handle though."

Second, raised a brow at his cavalier attitude and answer. No other two travelers at level one could hope to handle a group of beasts and walk away without visible injuries.

"You can thank me for that, I'm afraid," Anna glided forward on silent steps. "The actions we took against the Albrights earlier had a rather, shall we say, disruptive effect on their corporation and its current operations. Their teams own the current time slot for the portal and without them actively working to keep the number of beasts down. Well, you saw the effect."

Second frowned from behind her and spoke up. "I'm surprised you were able to handle them all. How many did you say you ran into exactly?"

"I didn't," Zack replied, thinking the same thing. Was it possible the Ruler had been protecting them as they walked towards it, or had they gotten unbelievably lucky, again? What had they done to draw its interest in the first place? Could it smell that they were different from so far away?

Zara gripped his shirt from behind, as the Major walked towards them. He was a man just on the upper scale of average height, thin old scars, lightened by time, lined his cheeks. The worn uniform marked him as a man who was rarely behind the desk. The gleam of his bald head was a new sight to them and matched his gleaming eyes.

"It's been a while," The imposing man said, his voice surprisingly smooth and comforting.

"It has. We thought you had forgotten about us for a while there."

"Not forgotten, just lost, and then when we found you, I was busy." He didn't apologize. They were an obligation. There were no personal feelings involved to be sorry about.

"And you are no longer busy?" He probed. Zara pressed closer behind him, pushing the stiffened material of his shirt against his back.

"No, I am still very busy. I simply received a piece of information this afternoon?" He stopped and pulled out a beat-up old crystal pocket watch. The processed magi-crystal inside was dim and due for replacement soon. "Yesterday evening rather, that I found rather disturbing in nature. I felt it was time to put my work aside for the moment and come meet with the two of you. Little did I know that you had plans of your own. Anna and Second," He sneered the name. "Are the ones who convinced me it would be better to not cross over with my soldiers and haul you back safely... That we should wait."

"That was probably wise..." Zack began hesitantly, unsure of how much to say. Much of what had gone on in there was personal to the two of them and would remain private. Just mentioning the existence of the Ruler, however, might be fine?

"Just mention it as the blob in the sky," Zara whispered to him, pressing her head against his back.

Everyone leaned forward, waiting for him to finish the sentence.

"A, uh," Zack scratched the back of his head, sending a wave of flakes down on Zara's equally nasty head. "I'm not sure how to say this, but we know what's on the island. Now at least, can't say for sure how long it has been there." He dithered uncomfortably, playing it up while smirking inside.

Everyone had been dying to know what was on the floating island since the portal first appeared.

"Well?" Anna snapped in exasperation.

Zack brightened as an idea came to him. "Hey Second, I know I'm telling everyone here, but this info should count for something, right?"

The older man wheezed in surprise and leaned on his ever-present cane. "Sure, if it's good, then I'll give you something for it when we talk later, in addition to our other deal." He smiled good-naturedly and waited with the rest.

Zack wiped the smile from his face and prepared to tell them a bald-faced lie of a story. "It's a ruler class being."

Anna was the first to recover. "All soldiers out now!" Her voice roared through the space, near-deafening each of them.

"Now!" The Major shouted a beat later, backing up her order. His lack of protest at her commanding his soldiers to do anything revealing the true order of power for the siblings. He held Jean back while the rest shuffled out.

"How do you know about the ruler class existences?" Second asked carefully once they were alone.

"What do you mean?" Zack was genuinely confused by the question. "Everyone knows about them. We all know they exist, and that's about it, since they rarely appear."

Second sighed in relief. "I understand, my apologies. Please continue."

He studied the older gentleman for a second before turning away. "When we went through the portal, Zara went through the awakening process. Lots of light, sparkles, fireworks, music, applause, you know how it works." Zara jabbed him in the back as his tongue began to run away from him.

He coughed and continued. "Anyway, the light drew a decent-sized horde of monsters. Luckily for us, none of them were interested in working together. I was able to hold them off until she could help, and then, working together, we finished them off. It was a rather bloody affair, but we managed."

He waved at the blood that had dried, cracked, and flaked off from all over their bodies. "I admit, some of this came from my scavenging efforts. I'm somewhat out of practice in that regard. Anyway, when we tried to leave the area around the portal, this dark blob with two glowing yellow eyes appeared in the sky above us. What is the one thing that has always been documented in regards to ruler class beings?"

It was Jean who answered. "Their ability to suppress others? It comes out as a kind of pressure, I believe."

"Yup, and every time we tried to cross some invisible line, bam, we'd get hit with it. Eventually, we gave up, and just waited for me to heal up some more before coming back through." He hoped that would be enough to throw them off the scent. As a bonus, it would also explain why they hadn't been able to go far enough inside to get any mana crystals.

"Did it-" Second shook his head. "No, never mind."

Zack was beginning to think the white-haired man might know something more about the ruler class than he was saying. His reaction, well, all of their reactions had been odd, but his especially so.

"Why did it appear now?" Anna asked the others, looking for their opinions. "What has changed within the last while that would have encouraged something like that to make an appearance?"

"The Albrights?" Second guessed with a smile.

"No, and don't even go there. This is so far beyond them, it's not even funny. Now be serious."

"Another three portals went solid black on their power markers yesterday. It's part of what I was taking care of before I came here. Whatever is changing them is becoming faster, and a more serious problem. Already the country is down to only a mere handful of portals that the corporations and travelers are willing to enter."

Second scowled, "Why didn't I hear about any of this?"

"Probably because we were busy with other things," Anna sighed. "First with the Albrights, and then coming here and waiting. We could have brought some paperwork or something to do if we had known it would be so long."

Zack shrugged. "No one asked you to bug the teddy bear you gave my sister. That's kind of low, by the way."

"Why did you bring the bears?" Jean wondered aloud.

"They're comforting and I like them!" Zara poked her head out from behind her brother to answer the question somewhat timidly.

They couldn't exactly tell them the real reason; the puppeteer class was an aberration one. It was one more piece of information they could use to barter with in the future. Nothing remained secret forever. At least with them at the helm, they could decide when it came out.

"In any case, I think this is sufficient evidence that the girl needs to be protected." Anna stood straight and pulled a heavily decorated medallion Zack didn't recognize from her waistcoat pocket. "As one of my last acts as the King's hidden advisor." Jean inhaled sharply. "Close your mouth dear, I'll be announcing my retirement from the position as soon as this business with the Albrights is taken care of. That is personal."

She flipped the medallion into the air, where it hung, spinning with a hum. "As has previously been discussed, Zara, younger sister of Zack, has been granted the crown's special scholarship and early admittance to the Albion Travelers Academy, effective immediately. All rights and protections afforded a member of the crown have been bestowed upon her, until such time as the scholarship is either removed, or she has graduated." Anna snapped her fingers, and the medallion stopped spinning. A deep bass note burst forth from it before dropping into her hand.

Second smirked at them. This is what he had mentioned before, back at the base of Faluers' Fist.

Zara was shivering against his back at the implications the scholarship represented.

"You can't do that! You can't force her to attend classes with those people!" Zack shouted forcefully, stepping back from them. "Do you have any idea how hard of a time she has just talking to people? You didn't see her at the Fist's base yesterday, or whenever it was. How do you think she..." He squeezed his eyes shut; his fists clenched tight.

"What do you think I will do to any student or teacher who causes her further pain?" He knew this was a good thing. It was a step that would help her in the long run. If they had told him at the same time he was accepted, he probably would have jumped for joy. Now, the memory of her shivering and talking incoherently to herself in a panic was burned fresh in his mind.

Anna held up a placating hand. "Don't worry, we'll figure something out. She'll have the use of tutors to help her, and we'll work with you both. This is mainly to keep her safe, and to keep others from getting any ideas. As a plus, it will also allow her to enter the portal with you during the academy training sessions."

Jean sensed the woman was done talking and clapped her hands. "It's already done, and it's for the best. Now, let's get you and the bears cleaned up some, and then get you back to the dorms." She hurried out to fetch the rest of the soldiers that had been ordered away.

Zara gathered up her courage and stepped out from behind her brother to look at Anna. "Thank you for this opportunity. I appreciate it and promise to make the most of it that I can within my limitations." She finished speaking and bit her lip, meeting the eyes of the monster only she could see.

She did her best to ignore the blood dripping from its talon-like nails, or the fangs poking through its lips. A moment later, the nails retracted, and fingers with too many joints grew to take their place as misshapen affairs. She knew the monsters she saw weren't real. The real ones didn't change their form or shift like those she saw. This was a result of what had been done to her, and what she believed all or nearly all humans to be now.

It was something she needed to face every day, and with everyone but her brother and those she was close to.

Jean walked back in with some soldiers at her back lugging a thick water hose.

"Your lives are about to change," Anna told them kindly, an odd expression flickering across her eyes. "Come on, you old goat. I have some paperwork to fill out. You can keep me company and tell me about the days before the portals arrived."

They walked over to an elegant vehicle the likes of which the siblings had never seen before.

"You like that?" Jean whispered, seeing them eye the sleek machine. They nodded. "It's apparently a limited run, collaboration piece between Vortex and Alberitas. Only a hundred of them were made. Isn't it gorgeous?"

Zack was the only one to nod this time, while Zara merely shrugged. It was nice looking, but she was more interested in what it would feel like to sit inside it than the outside. Surely, with an exterior like that, the interior could only be decadently comfortable.

"Now come over here, and let's get the two of you and those bears not washed up, but at least sprayed down with water." The Specialist ordered them about, moving them away from the portal they had remained near the entire time.

"What was the information you received that you found so disturbing in nature?" Zack asked the Major who was standing to the side as they were quickly sprayed down. His shirt and pants almost disintegrating completely under the spray.

Jean tossed him a spare uniform she had someone hurriedly grab from a vehicle to wear. While Zara looked away, pointing a sopping and much cleaner, Zelda directly at him as a result.

"A certain healer birdy whispered in my ear, the full extent of your injuries." Zack felt like releasing a breath he hadn't even known he was holding when the man told him that.

"We had always known they did experiments on the both of you. We even knew they had succeeded with you. Congratulations on hiding the secret about your sister, by the way. You did well with that one. Too many people would have been tempted if they heard about her, or you."

The Major felt at his pockets and cursed when he couldn't find whatever it was he was looking for. "I had to submit a special report to the king and queen's eyes only regarding you. The rest of the information went into the normal report without an issue. Your existence was problematic in a lot of ways. You don't have to worry from what I know about that scholarship, which isn't a lot as it is rarely used. She will be protected. This is the best outcome for her, for both of you, really."

Zack nodded mutely and used the remains of his shirt to scrub his hair and body down before dressing.

"When Leigha came to visit me and rather tearfully relayed what she had learned about you..." The Major paused and studied him, taking in the scars before they vanished under the ill-fitting uniform. A trace of emotion entered his voice as he continued. "Healers don't cry boy, they forget how after a while. Eventually, they've just seen too much, that nothing shocks them anymore. What she saw inside you, it shocked her, it almost broke her. It was all she could do to get away from you without showing it. It's a bigger taboo than most realize, to ever let the patient realize you care."

Zack wasn't sure, as the noise from Zara getting sprayed down was rather loud, but he was positive the Major had thrown in a few expletives he was going to have to look up later. Construction workers could apparently learn something from the military in that regard.

"She was sobbing the entire time she was in my office, and still going strong when she left. I admit, even I got chills when she described some of the procedures they would have had to do to you to get those scar patterns."

The Major stilled Zack's hands on the buttons of the shirt and looked him square in the eye. "I don't apologize for much; I don't often feel the need to.

The truth is, when I listened to her, I felt the need to apologize to you and your sister. That we didn't make those researchers, guards, and everyone else involved in that facility suffer more before their deaths. The truth is, they were all to a one, executed rather cleanly and painlessly, and for that, I am sorry."

"But-" Zack croaked and swallowed before trying again. "But they were all executed, right? None of them got away, or were rescued by whichever organization ran the place? They are actually gone?" He was staring past the man towards his sister as he asked. "She used to be so afraid that one of them would randomly stumble across us on the street and follow us home."

"She doesn't need to be afraid of that, not for a while now, and especially not once her protections come into place."

Chapter 32

The Major waved away the nearby soldier, who seemed intent on spraying down Aisha with everything the hose had and then some. The spray sent flecks of grime and blood into the air, where parts of it would disappear a moment later. The poor bear was a soggy mess and would need a good deep cleaning back at the dorm or she would stain.

"I won't talk about some of the other things Leigha mentioned to me, not yet, at least. Just let it be known that the two of you have my attention, even more so than before. We should sit down together and talk at some point in the near future, clear the air, if nothing else. Decide how far we can trust each other, and what else you might know about that portal at the institute." The Major gave him a small thin smile along with a wink and then turned away. "Specialist McCleary, take a fire team and see these two home to their dorm, then come and report back to me."

The soldiers all snapped to attention as the superior officer on-site left, taking the bulk of his own men with him. The few that were left were ones that had been brought along or had already been there. There was more than enough for Specialist McCleary to do as had been ordered of her. A fire team typically consisted of four members, the leader, in this case, Jean, and then three others.

Zack picked up a sopping Aisha and proceeded to ring the water from her the best he could. "I really hope you can't feel any of this." He muttered to the bear, knowing from Zelda that she had been aware when she was on this side of the portal. It was another example of magic working here, if only in a limited fashion.

It shouldn't be possible, and yet it was. At least for him and Zara. That was dangerous information to have. It was even more dangerous to have it leak out at the wrong time.

Zara had been given a uniform shirt to wear over her clothes, and it hung over her small frame like a dress. He exchanged Aisha for George and proceeded to wring out that bear as well, with another muttered apology.

Jean had finished putting together her team before he could decide if he dared to try wringing out Zelda. They left her strapped to Zara's pack and moved to join them near the vehicle.

"Sorry Specialist McCleary, but please STAND DOWN!" A soldier near one of the other vehicles knelt and held up a weapon most travelers disdained. It was called a 'Mana-tech Pneumatic Powered Rifle' or just a 'Majair' for short. They didn't work for long inside the portals like any other tech, so they were useless. Which meant that they were only useful on this side, and against people.

Similar to how electricity had faded away and been replaced, black powder and its resulting variants had been done away with as well. Mana crystals and the magi-crystals that were eventually created as a processed form for smaller items were just more reliable.

Jean moved to cover the kids. "Why are you doing this? The Major won't let you go. You have to know that?" She was careful to not make any more movements until she fully understood the situation. There were still other soldiers in the warehouse with them, yet they weren't making a move to help.

"We don't work for the Major. We aren't part of the precious group that he brought with him." The man's barrel wavered slightly. "As for why I'm doing this, it's simple, money. The price of everything is beginning to go up. Corporations have started to charge through the nose for mana crystals. Without them or the processed versions, I can't light my house, heat it, or cook the food that is more expensive because shipping costs went up as well."

A few of the other soldiers stepped forward and reached into the vehicle at the man's back. They came out with Majair rifles of their own. His words had apparently stirred them from off the proverbial fence. Each of the rifles began to whine softly as they charged.

"I don't want to do this ma'am, I have nothing against you or those kids, but the Albright brat is paying us a lot. Enough that we won't have to worry about money even if they keep raising prices on everything. Now, please, all we want is the kids. That is all he asked for, especially the girl." The man had the decency to look disgusted as he spoke. "Someone here apparently already reported to him that she came out of the portal. He was... rather interested in that."

"Get on with it," A man growled, ripping off his uniform top and revealing an Albright corporation shirt and logo beneath. "You aren't the only one getting a massive payday, and I, for one, can't wait to spend the next few days just counting it all in another country."

A couple more of them ripped off their tops to reveal similar shirts, and Jean's expression grew grimmer with each one. Soldiers could be reasoned with. Even those in desperate need of money usually didn't want to betray their comrades. She was even willing to bet that if the man had approached the Major with this information that he would have made off rather handsomely.

Travelers, however, for the most part, were more mercenary in nature. They worked for the highest bidder if they had the skills, and whoever would take them if they didn't. Even among them, most had a sense of moral decency. Of course, as with all humans, there was trash.

The travelers in Albright garb in front of them naturally fell under that distinction.

The three soldiers around the siblings pressed in closer while waiting for orders from Specialist McCleary.

"Give me Zelda, and then duck down, but be ready to run just in case," Zack whispered to Zara, passing Aisha to her, and taking George. He would strap the bear to her pack in place of Zelda if there was time.

Jean hesitated, unsure of what to do. Both sides were armed, but one was at a clear and definite advantage. Her side still had their weapons holstered and uncharged for one, and they had to worry about protecting the kids for another. Giving them up was not an option.

"This is taking too long," An Albright goon growled, his rifle bucked, and the air cracked. Blood and chunks of grey matter splashed down on the newly cleaned pair and the stuffed bears. The soldier to their right collapsed to the ground. Part of his face now missing.

"What are you doing?" The soldier who had started the entire mess screeched, unable to take his eyes off the dead man.

Zara wiped the warm blood from her face without reacting and then reached over to do the same for Zack and Zelda.

"I told you, this is taking too long. We need to get a move on before someone comes back to take a look or something. Let's kill the other two and then take the Specialist as insurance. The Major kept her in here earlier after all. That must mean something."

A dawning horror was growing in the soldier's eyes as he realized what he had done. He had deluded himself into thinking that this would be a bloodless affair, with none of his family-in-arms getting hurt. Now they had. One of them was dead. His blood already congealing as it spread slowly across the night chilled floor.

He had a choice to make. Was he going to stand by these people, or by the family he had known for years? His rifle twitched to the side, and his head instantly gained two new holes with another resounding crack. He had been too slow.

"You honestly thought we were going to let you live and take a portion of our money?" The man snorted and kicked the body to the side, the lifeless legs flopping underneath the closest vehicle. "Not likely."

The rest of the Albright goons chuckled and kept their Majair rifles trained on their targets.

"Now choose your targets," The soldiers and Jean reacted, pulling out their military-grade weapons. The smaller hand model, pistol Majair's had the option of partial charges and that is what they went with. The shots would be weaker, but speed was more important at the moment than power.

Those shots cost both men their lives, but combined with the shot from Jean, they managed to also take out three of the opposing forces. It was too little in the end. However, the men had not gone down without a fight.

"Sorry, Zack, Zara," Jean ground out in defeat, dropping her weapon. Sure, she might get off one, maybe even two more shots if she was lucky. If she did that, however, then no one would be able to watch out for the two of them. She had gotten her blood and could be satisfied with that for the moment. The shot she had fired had taken the talkative idiot squarely in the chest, where it was nearly impossible to miss at this range. Even a low-powered charge had enough force to drill through a person's chest with energy to spare.

None of his supposed comrades seemed interested in helping to save his life, despite him still gasping away. It was the same for the other two that had been shot. These people were here for the paycheck and nothing more. The fewer of them there were at the end, the bigger that paycheck for them would be. That was the kind of math anyone could do.

The three were quickly surrounded and tossed into a vehicle. Zack and Zara refused to let go of the bears and kicked the men away when they tried to pry them from their fingers. It only took one well-placed kick for each of them to decide they didn't care if the siblings held onto the harmless stuffed animals.

Instead, they chose to focus their attention on tying Jean's hands and feet. All the while keeping their weapons trained on her should she choose to kick them.

They had been ordered to deliver the kids alive. Her, they were merely keeping as insurance, nothing more. Shooting her meant little to them if the trouble she caused outweighed the potential benefits she brought in their minds.

Any chance she had of protecting them meant she needed to stay alive. She was lucky they hadn't just killed her for shooting one of their own a minute earlier. So, she complied and let them tie her hands and feet before getting roughly tossed into the back of the vehicle.

"We should hurry. I want to be well away from this place when the Major and whoever those other two are find out about this." A twitchy man sitting next to Zack told the two sitting upfront.

"Don't worry, we will be," The driver said, backing the vehicle up. The front wheels bounced up into the air as they ran over the man's legs from before. The three laughed and made a couple of crude jokes as they heard bones break and crunch from outside.

There was a muttered, "Disgusting," from Jean in the back.

Zack did his best to ignore them all and cleaned the remaining blood Zara had missed from her face. Aisha and Zelda, however, were lost causes. He had planned on giving all three bears a nice thorough, deep cleaning once they got back to the dorm. Hopefully, before they were permanently stained. There was little chance of that happening now.

"She is not going to be happy if all that blood stains," Zara whispered to him, apparently thinking the same thing.

"No, she won't," Zack agreed.

The idiot at his side elbowed him and told them both to shut up. There was nothing more for them to do but look out the windows and listen to the rather crude topics that were bandied back and forth between the three men.

The dark, starry night sky had barely begun to lighten on the distant horizon, turning everything into shadows and depriving the two of any interesting scenery. The driver kept the vehicle to roads that were seemingly less traveled. Avoiding the nearby capital city entirely and heading out towards the farming region that surrounded every city. Distant lights from a few early risers or those late to bed could be seen as they neared a farming settlement.

Occasionally they would hear Jean shifting around in the back, and would take turns looking back to make sure she was alright.

"Where are you taking us?" Zack finally asked after they had been sitting and listening to them for some time.

"I told you, we're taking you to see that Dorn brat." The driver answered impatiently.

"Yes, I understand that." Zack drawled. "I was speaking more location and time or distance-wise. Information that would be valuable if, say, I wanted to perhaps pee. Would it be faster to just water this fellow next to me like a tree, or hold it because we are almost there?"

Zara lightly jabbed him in the side, but still giggled. It would be a miracle if his mouth didn't get him killed one of these days. He really needed to work harder at controlling it. Still, feeling the goon squirm away from him at the childish threat was entertaining in its own right.

"Don't you dare. We'll be there in just a minute." The driver looked back in disgust, causing the vehicle to swerve all over the road.

Zack shrugged and winked at Zara.

True to his word, the driver pulled off the main road a minute later and took them down a long, dark driveway. At the end of it was a single, extensive building with an attached warehouse. He drove the vehicle through the open doors of the warehouse and stopped at the very back. A set of closed, wide double doors were illuminated by the headlights.

"Alright, now get out and find a corner to water, and don't think of running. We still have your sister!" The driver turned around and said with a growl.

Zack did his best to keep a smirk from his face as he replied. "I'm good. I don't actually need to go. I just wanted to let her know how much longer she has to prepare, is all." He tilted his head towards the open back.

Jean popped into view behind the man sitting next to him and plunged her knife into the man's back from behind. The sharp blade slid through the thin padding of the military seat and skewered his heart. Killing him instantly.

Working free of the ropes had taken some time, which they had generously given her with the long trip. Then she simply had to wait for the right time and use the knife she always had hidden in the small of her back. The one in her boot had been taken earlier.

Just like that, their captors were down to two.

Which they didn't like, naturally.

The goon sitting upfront with the driver pulled out one of the confiscated military model Majair pistols and pointed it at her. "If it wasn't for our shares of the money, just having jumped in size a rather sizeable amount, I'd be thinking you're far more trouble than you're worth right about now. Like I said, though, what you just did is worth a whole lot. So, I'm going to let you live, retie your hands and legs, and instead let that walking piggy bank named Dorn decide what to do with you. Now everybody out."

He kept the weapon trained on her the entire time, not giving her another chance to act up.

Jean carefully raised her hands and waited for the driver to get out and run around to the back. Her hands were tied even more securely this time, while her legs were merely hobbled so she couldn't run or kick.

Zara yawned as she opened the door and climbed out, Aisha hanging limply in her arms. She couldn't remember when she had last slept, and it was getting to her. The thinly padded seats had been uncomfortable, and a light doze was the best she had managed.

Zack shuffled out behind her, Zelda clutched tightly in his arms. Something the two goons made sure to mock them about.

"What is with you two and teddy bears? Aren't you too old to be carrying around things like that?"

Zack moved Zara behind before answering in a tired tone. "You're just the Albright corporation's goons and our captors. What does it even matter to you? Let's just get this taken care of."

"You're that eager to die and have your sister taken from you?" The driver, who now had his own weapon out and trained on Jean, asked in surprise.

"No, I am just curious as to which of you will be the next to die, is all." He debated with a smirk.

The two-armed men shared a look, knowing the truth behind his words. There was too much money on the line for them to not at least try and take it all. It was their way as greedy travelers who worked for the highest bidder. Money topped all allegiances.

"Whatever, go through the doors. We have a little surprise waiting for you on the other side." The one who had been driving told them with a malicious smirk of his own.

Zara moved around to his side as the second kidnapper opened the door for them. He ushered them in with a wave of the sleek Majair.

"Who was it that told me before about nobles and corporations hiding the existence of more portals from the crown?" Zack asked Jean somewhat rhetorically as they walked through the doors.

Hovering ever so slightly above the floor was a portal the Albrights had never reported the existence of. Zara nudged him softly and pointed at the markings around its edge. The power marking bands were almost completely black, with only the thinnest of light areas separating them. The inside of this portal would contain very strong monsters, as well as some dense mana crystals.

"Not me, but they were definitely right. They do, do that." Jean was looking at the portal in growing horror and resignation. She had also noticed the strength indicators of the portal.

"Now let's get you three to go through first. The bank, I mean Dorn, is waiting on the other side. It was stupid of him if you ask me to enter before we got here, but what do I know?"

"Not much apparently." Jean pointed to the glowing remains of some pipe ash and pushed the children forward. "They just barely entered as well. I wonder why they didn't wait?" She looked down at her uniform and then smirked. "Maybe they got the wrong idea about you two."

Zack rolled his eyes, but played along. "True, I wonder if I was wrong. Maybe neither of you will be getting away with the money."

The two Majair pistols began to whine as they charged. "We'll see about that!"

Chapter 33

Zara took Zack's hand and together they stepped through the portal, with Jean a few steps behind them. A world brightened by dawn across a cold, desolate landscape appeared before their eyes. Puffs of frozen air were whisked away as soon as they formed by the brisk and chilling wind. A thick crust of hardened snow crunched underfoot as they walked away from the portal.

Twenty feet in front of them stood a coat-wearing and fully prepared Dorn. By his side and held by the quickly bluing skin of her arm was a captive and thoroughly unprepared Edith. There were marks of a struggle all over her face. Her lips were split and covered in blood, and a gash ran across her cheek.

Standing behind them were five travelers with swords, spears, and whatever other weapon they favored. Each of them had on masks and full-body suits that would help to regulate their temperature. It might not be traditional monster armor, but in this frigid place, it was probably even better. It gave them mobility, warmth, and some protection as well.

Something that Zack and Zara certainly didn't have.

"Why did you have us come inside a portal?" Zack shouted across the distance.

Jean walked through the portal a second later and joined them.

Dorn smirked and shoved Edith behind him to the travelers. "A few different reasons. I wanted to make sure that neither of you had trackers on you." He glared at Jean. "The military seemed inordinately obsessed with protecting you. And now I know why. It all has to do with your little sister there. She was always the prize they were trying to protect; you were just the excuse!"

The siblings shared a look with Jean and began laughing at him.

Behind them, the two goons walked through the portal with coats on. Obviously having taken the chance after pushing Jean through to grab them. The Majair's were still gripped tight in their hands while they waited for someone to make a move.

"We want our money!" The driver shouted to Dorn, taking his eyes off the other goon for just a second.

It was enough. He raised the Majair and pulled the trigger, and his former comrade's head disintegrated into a pink mist. Without delaying, he quickly tossed the weapon away as it began to spark and self-destruct. Pieces started to fall off in blackened and smoking chunks until only the various core components remained. There were several of the dark crystals that were used for controlling things that they had seen before. Along the bottom of the barrel there was also a magi-crystal that had been processed into a cylinder to run along it.

The crystals each sputtered, darkened, and then cracked, breaking into pieces as they watched.

He had been lucky to get the shot off in the first place, as weapons and technology, in general, didn't like being in the portals.

Zack pushed Zara to Jean, momentarily dropped Zelda in the snow, and began removing the dead man's coat under everyone's astonished expression.

He shook off the bloodied ice crystals and handed it to Zara. "Here, it's big enough that it should fit over the pack as well."

Dorn and the rest had yet to move from their place, while the goon who had killed the man looked shaken.

"What?" He asked Jean, who was looking at him oddly.

"You just handed your sister a bloody coat that you pulled off a dead body without even blinking. I'm trying to decide whether I'm impressed, horrified, or sad about what happened to make you two this way?"

"It's partly what the portals do to us mentally," Zara told her softly, pulling on the warm coat over her small shivering frame. At the same time, exchanging Aisha for Zelda. The larger bear would hopefully help keep him warm. "And partly that, yeah, we've just seen too much blood at this point. Mostly Zack's, but also monsters, and occasionally other peoples when they decided we should watch some of the experiments for educational purposes." The young girl shrugged. "Blood just doesn't bother us anymore."

Zack straightened with Aisha in his arms, the cold wind biting through the uniform he had been given. Across from them, Edith was in an even worse state and wouldn't last for much longer if she didn't get warm soon. He was confident that he could take out Dorn. That wasn't an issue. The idiot behind them could be handled by either Jean or Zara.

The problem was the five travelers holding Edith hostage. He had no idea how strong or weak they might be, or how much damage his spells would do to them.

He motioned for them to continue, and then whispered to Zara from the corner of his mouth. "How much time do you need to wake them up again, and will it be visible?"

She smiled up at him, a hint of anger in her eyes. "I need twenty to thirty seconds for each of them. I can hide the effect for Zelda by standing behind you, but she is not going to be happy. She still has the thing in her from before. As for George, if Jean stands behind me and retrieves him, then I might be able to wake him up as well. I won't be able to do Aisha until everything has already started though."

"Good, we'll need to be quick, otherwise Edith is going to freeze over there."

Jean shot them questioning looks but didn't say anything.

Dorn came back with a pack full of money, mana crystals and some processed magi-crystals. "Here you go, your payment as promised. I guess you get to keep it all to yourself now. Smart man."

Zara swallowed her sudden buildup of saliva, her eyes wide at the sight of all the money. It was more than she had ever seen before, and a fraction of it would have allowed them to eat well for years.

The goon stepped forward, uncertainly. "And you're alright with what just happened. Me shooting him in the head and the boy grabbing the coat like that?"

Dorn shrugged and backed away. "It doesn't matter to me if you don't feel like sharing. You have your money though. Now get out of here."

Across from them, one of the travelers reached for their belt and pulled out a throwing knife.

The goon was busy looking down at the large pack of money, and not his surroundings. The blade whistled through the air, the harsh wind shifting it off-course ever so slightly. Before the Albright mercenary could react, the blade plunged into his chest and out the back. The wind affecting your aim didn't matter as much when you had enough strength to throw the knife through someone.

The fact that he didn't die right away but instead held on for several seconds was because of his own level and stats. Still, it was hard to fight against the hole in his chest and the blood loss. A healer could have saved him. Without one, he was just a dead man breathing.

Dorn kicked him in the face and retrieved the pack. "This is my money. You look like you have a decent level. What are you doing playing these games anyway?" He carried the pack back to the others and faced the three again. "Now where were we?"

Zack stared at the gore encrusted coat, with a hole through it, and looked at Jean. "You want a coat?"

"No!" She denied the offer emphatically.

"Alright, just thought I'd offer." He turned away from the body, deciding he wasn't quite that desperate yet either. His own skin was tingling as his ability healed the damage that had already begun to set in. They needed to hurry this up for Edith and Jean's sake, if nothing else.

"Zelda is ready. I'm going to have her pull out George so I can start on him now," Zara whispered.

"I believe you were telling us that you brought us inside the portal because you were worried about trackers and that you were an idiot," Zack called to him. "Jean, how many of those five do you think you can handle?" He asked while barely moving his lips.

"I can't say for sure. I'm a general weapons specialist, good with all, but great with none. It's why I was the one always teaching the students how to use the weapons, and Rose oversaw everything else. Without a weapon, I'm fast and agile. I can be a distraction, but I wouldn't count on much more." She lifted her tied hands. "Besides, in case you've forgotten, my hands are currently tied together, and my legs are hobbled. I can't even knee someone like this, let alone run."

"I did not say that I was an IDIOT!" Dorn exploded, unable to contain himself against the other boy's total lack of respect.

Zara peeked out from behind Zack. "I don't know. That was kind of a delayed reaction."

It took him another second to respond. "It's the wind!"

"So, what you're saying is that you brought us in here, separated us by like ten meters in a windy area, and then wanted to have a conversation?" Zack yelled across, looking worriedly at how blue Edith's lips had become.

"We need to get Edith away from them soon, or she'll freeze to death." He told them, glancing back at how Jean was doing. Her shivering was becoming more pronounced, and her lips had a tinge of darker coloring to them.

Dorn had his group move closer to them, and Zack began to realize that something was off.

"Jean, we are hostages, right?" She nodded slowly, understanding where he was going with the question. "Then why does he seem so afraid to approach us? I mean, if he didn't have Edith, we could have easily just gone back through the portal by now."

The five mysterious travelers helping Dorn hadn't surrounded them. In fact, outside of throwing a knife and holding Edith, they hadn't done anything. There was no one holding Zack or the others in place. Just the possible threat of a knife in the back and Edith's fate hanging in the balance.

"You know, my parents told me never to use this portal. It's a tightly guarded family secret, and only a few people outside the family even know it exists. Those few all work for my family's corporation in select positions. Of course, some people like those I hired to fetch the two of you were told, but they were going to die anyway. Besides, they were too stupid to know that this portal isn't recorded anywhere. To them, it was just like any other."

Zack felt his eyes glazing over at the pointless monologue. "Oh, come on!" He let loose his inner construction worker and began cursing the boy, his parentage, and everything else he could think of.

Jean laughed softly when he finished. "You need some lessons from the Major, but I give that a barely passing grade." Her chattering teeth made it hard to understand the words.

"George is ready," Zara whispered.

"Good," Zack straightened and looked at Dorn. "Now, if you are done with the pointless family idolizing, bragging, and whatever else you had planned, can we get a move on with this? Not all of us are dressed for the weather."

Dorn chuckled, and a malicious smile spread across his face. "I know. Why do you think I brought you here? It was to break you and your precious little sister. We'll start off by making you watch as the dorm matron freezes to death. From what I understand, the three of you have gotten somewhat close, so it'll work as an appetizer. Then we'll move onto little miss fake teacher over there." His ugly smile morphed and twisted until it resembled something demonic-looking, and a scared Zara hid behind Zack's back.

"Why?" Zack couldn't understand the noble-born boy's thinking. "Why would you do any of this? What did we ever do to you that would require you to go to such lengths?"

"You took Tessa from me!" Dorn roared.

"No, I didn't. She was never yours to begin with! She's her own person, and she only sat at my table to talk!" Zack shot back, feeling a headache coming on.

"Then you destroyed my family! We have nothing left except what we hid over the years. Which I admit is a rather sizeable amount. Still, our title, our lands, our authority, everything is gone!"

"That would have happened regardless," Jean clarified. "Tessa's mother has been gathering evidence against your family for years. She was just waiting for the right time to use it all and destroy any remnants of your nobility and standing before the crown. You kidnapping Tessa, along with Zack and Zara, gave her that opportunity. She would have found another if this one hadn't presented itself." She forced her teeth to stop chattering while she spoke.

It was Dorn's turn to be shocked into momentary near silence. "Why? What did we do to her? Wait, her mother? She died years ago. What are you talking about?"

Jean gave a shivering shrug. "I have no idea what your family did to her, but it was bad enough for her to do something like this. She became a hidden advisor to the king and faked her death all to accomplish the destruction of your family." Zack quietly passed her Aisha; he could take the full effects of the cold better than she could.

"So, let me ask again," Zack began wearily, in a tone that belied his age. "What did we do to you? Why couldn't you have just let us live in peace and attend the academy like we wanted? Why was it so important to you to flex the fact that you're a noble in an academy full of them?"

For a second, the three held their collective breaths, wondering if something so simple could work.

Dorn looked at them and then shook his head. "I don't need to answer the questions of commoners, especially those from someone without even a last name."

The answer was no, it couldn't. Dorn had invested too much into it already to turn around, regardless of the truth of the matter.

"Kill everyone but the little girl. She'll be useful in the future. Make sure she watches each of them die. I still want her mind broken, like a puppet." Dorn commanded the five behind him, no longer interested in dragging things out.

Zack glanced back at Jean with a sad, tired smile and imparted some truth. "See, this is why we don't trust anyone, especially the nobles."

"I've got Dorn. You handle the others," Zara told him quickly, from behind.

"Just make sure Zelda stays close to me, in case I need the crystal."

"Can you use it in here?"

"I guess we'll find out."

Their rapid-fire conversation took seconds to complete.

"Jean, you remember when I told you I had no elemental affinity?" He asked, raising his hand to point at the traveler who had thrown the knife before, his hand already reaching for another blade.

She nodded.

"I lied." A deep purple bolt with hints of black shot from his finger before anyone could react and hit the traveler in the face mask. The bolt disintegrating the mask almost instantly. It was apparently more for warmth than protection.

Unlike against the monsters before, the single shot wasn't enough to kill the traveler, but it was more than enough to remove them from the fight. Pieces of their face and eyes vanished and reappeared on the ground or in the sky. They were still alive for the moment. However, without a high-level healing spell soon, who could say how long they could survive with their skull exposed to the freezing elements?

"Zelda, George, bring that meanie down!" Zara ordered the bears, before beginning to awaken Aisha.

"There's a knife somewhere behind us you could use to cut the ropes." Zack reminded Jean, before running forward. The shorter the distance, the less time they would have to avoid his magic.

They threw Edith to the side, not worried about her causing them any trouble. She may have been a traveler in the past, but that was years ago. Now she was nothing more than an out of practice in whatever class she was, dead-weight.

Zack didn't have the time to worry about the older woman and could only hope she was alright as he jumped into the fray. There were still four of the mysterious and undoubtedly much higher-leveled travelers to deal with. He had gotten lucky with that first shot and by avoiding their suits. It wouldn't happen again, he was sure.

Preparing himself for what he was about to do, Zack firmly visualized a spell in his head. He was using the "Arcane Manipulation" ability that came with his class. It allowed him to use nearly any spell he could clearly imagine, but it also took more time to prepare than his regular magic. Not to mention the cost. The relatively simple spell he was about to do took three times the energy that one of his arcane bolts did, emptying him dry in an instant.

It was just in time. A staff whistled through the air and cracked into his arm, breaking it instantly. Zack shoved the pain to the side and used that momentary contact as a conduit for the lightning spell. The electricity poured down the wooden staff. The heat and arcs charring the polished finished and scaring the holder into releasing it, not realizing that wood was a poor conductor of electricity.

Their society had moved away from the old power source and had largely forgotten its complexities.

The result was not what Zack had been hoping to accomplish, but he was committed. An arcane bolt flew from his finger and nicked the quick traveler in the leg. The suits they were wearing showed their effectiveness as the elementless bolt failed to dig through the strange material. That didn't mean the attack failed to injure the traveler. With a snapping noise and a scream of pain, the leg collapsed beneath them, unable to hold any weight.

That was two, kind of down, or at least slowed and separated from the other, faster three. He could live with those odds.

Hopefully.

From the side, he heard Dorn yell as Zelda, and George began pummeling him into the snow. It was a good sound and more than enough to give him a little boost of extra energy.

Chapter 34

Zack ducked and threw himself to the side, his sixth sense twinging like mad. The blade of a sword skimming silently past where his head had just been. The action jostled his newly broken arm, forcing the pain he had shoved aside to the forefront of his mind. A gasp of pain escaped his mouth, his feet pausing for a half-second while he got his bearings.

He saw the incoming spear too late, accepting the rushed attack as it plunged into his belly and out his back. An arcane bolt took the face-off of another of the attacking travelers, leaving them with only two mobile and actively attacking.

Zack coughed, thick bloody saliva drooling down from his lips, and looked down at the shaft protruding from his chest. All he could think was that he was glad it had missed his spine, even if it was getting harder to breathe. If the attack had been any less rushed, or just a little bit more strength had been used. It missing his spine wouldn't matter, because that section of spine would be gone regardless. There would be a fist-sized hole in his chest, instead of a shaft.

"Is that the best you got?" He asked the last two who had stopped in front of him, their weapons at the ready. The pain pulled at his attention, wanting to distract him with the delicious intricacies of his body's current agony. He'd experienced far worse and was able to shove the mental effects aside without skipping a beat.

They tilted their masked heads in unison and then dared to look at their two fallen comrades and the one injured and currently crawling towards them. They turned back to him and pulled off their masks, revealing a pair of women. Neither was what he would call beautiful, but their eyes revealed a depth of strength that made such things unimportant.

"Impressive boy, if you were a little older, and hadn't just killed my husband, I think we might have gotten along." The one on the left said before ripping the spear back through his chest. The hole widened and pieces of severed intestine poked through like bloody worms.

Zack gasped and collapsed to his knees, trying to draw in a breath. All the while desperately remembering everything he could about the healing session with Leigha. The knowledge would help to reinforce the intent behind his spell, making it more effective. He would need it for this to work properly.

He rarely messed with healing spells, preferring to let his ability work its proverbial magic. It was slower, sure, but it got everything. Healing spells were typically location-focused, and they didn't work well on the damage that bled through from his astral body. He was fine with localized in this instance. It was plain to see where the damage was, after all.

He just hoped the energy cost would be bearable. There were still three more enemies they needed to eliminate.

"You shouldn't have done that," He ground out with all the air he could spare before beginning the spell. A deep purple glow surrounded the hole in his chest, causing them both to step back in surprise.

He had been able to shoot somewhere between twenty and thirty arcane bolts as a level one before the damage became too great. Granted, he was mostly a level four in name only, however, his class still added points to his magic power and intelligence. His mana pool had to at least be of a size where he could use one spell minimum. While it wasn't that bad now, it was only a matter of time.

It was time to see what kind of difference that made to a spell he rarely tried to use. For that matter, it made him wonder how high their levels were to be able to shake off his magic attacks. Quinn had made it sound like anything above twenty in a stat was superhuman. Well, his magic was almost double that. So, it begged the question. What was going on?

He groaned as a solid quarter of his astral health was converted to energy for the healing spell. Hopefully, that was because of the severity of the wound and not the spell itself. Otherwise, healing would be off the table for a long time to come. His constitution would need to be improved a lot before this would be a viable spell in an emergency.

His Life Burner ability may be level four, but with his current magic stat being so high, it was struggling to keep up. The Arcane Mystic class truly would have been a useless piece of trash without that ability to back him.

The tips of his toes began to tingle and grow cold, the astral-borne pain quickly spreading up his legs. The appendages felt heavy and weak, as though the life had been sucked out of them. The tingle spread to engulf both legs, a feeling similar to sleeping limb syndrome on steroids.

"What are your levels?" Zack gasped out. He bit his lower lip and took a moment to force his legs to obey his commands. Coming to a stand as his stomach knitted itself back together.

They gaped at the rapid pace of the healing magic.

"That isn't the color of healing magic." One of them said.

"No, it isn't. Now answer my question." Zack demanded, wiping the blood from his lips, already feeling better. "And for that matter, where are you even from? I've never heard of anyone having suits like yours." His legs shook slightly from the strain of holding him upright. He wouldn't be running anywhere for the moment.

Material from Aperra would never have stood up to his magic attack like that. The problem was, they couldn't have made something like that on this side of the portal, either. The lines were too sleek, and the quality looked to be top-notch. It had to have been made by a professional, not a typical traveler constructing their armor on the go, as was normal.

The two women shared a look and then glanced again as his skin finished growing back together. Inside his chest, the magic was still working at a rapid pace to heal the damaged organs and tissues. As a side effect, it also fixed any scar tissue it found in the immediate area.

"What kind of a mage are you?" The one who had tried to cut his head off earlier asked.

Zack growled and raised both hands, his broken arm trembling at the abuse, pointing them at the chests of the two travelers. Where he couldn't miss. "I won't ask again, and trust me, these will hurt you more than they did your friend crawling on the ground." Both hands began to glow with a dark purple light, as he began gathering the ethereal energy known as mana.

"We're faster-"

Zack blasted the one on the left, who happened to be holding a spear dripping with his blood. His high elemental affinity came through once more, and the purple bolt was laced with black for the split second it was visible. The arcane bolt ate through the suit and her chest, leaving her with a gaping wound even worse than his had been.

"You were saying?" He asked, raising his glowing hand to point at the last one's forehead. The inside of his chest cramped under an astral vise as more energy was pulled to fuel the spell. Thankfully, it wasn't much.

Her dark eyes flickered with fear and anger as the realization that she was unlikely to leave the portal alive settled in. "We were all low-rank regular classes, between level fifteen and seventeen. None of us had any hope of ever getting to our specialist class. It's why we were sent on this mission. Our slow leveling speed made us more expendable than the others, and we're from the country of Shouvain." She spilled everything in a rush.

"Never heard of it."

"It doesn't share a border with Albion."

"Why come here then?" Zack raised his other hand again and shot the figure crawling towards them. He had begun gathering energy for the next bolt as soon as he had fired the last one, just in case. The bolt hit the previously injured traveler in the face, killing them instantly and sending pieces of their skull wherever the spell pleased. He would show no mercy to those who attacked him or his little sister. His broken arm went blessedly numb as its astral form fueled the spell.

The woman swallowed at the casual display of power and hurried to continue. "The portals in our kingdom have become unstable, as of late. We were chosen to spy on the surrounding countries and discover if any of them were the cause or experiencing the same issue."

"And what did you learn?"

"Each of the three countries we visited before here was also experiencing problems with their portals." She explained quietly.

"What about those suits then, and how did you get involved with Dorn?"

"I'm not sure about the suits either. They were a surprise given to us before we left, some sort of new magitech melding process they invented, I think. The most we were told about them is that they can only go through the portals a limited number of times.

"As for Dorn... he seemed like a good mark to get information from. His family was influential and obviously crooked. He himself had an undeserved ego larger than most and rarely thought his actions through. Normally, he would have been the perfect target." She dropped her sword and slowly knelt before Zack. "Please, just make it quick." She pleaded with him in a defeated tone.

Jean crunched her way through the snow and listened to the woman plead for her life. It was no wonder after seeing how Zack had mowed through her companions. She wouldn't say it had been easy for him. He had been hit and injured severely during the process, after all. From a performance standpoint, however, seeing him impossibly heal the damage, and then fire off his weird magic... It gave her chills, and she was sure it was worse for the woman.

"Wait," She started shivering again as soon as she stopped moving. "If we let you live, will you swear to not seek vengeance for your comrades, and come back to tell us all the information you know about the portals being unstable?"

"I," She stopped and hung her head even lower. "I cannot swear that, my lover was also among this group. My pride would not let me go without attacking the boy and either killing him or dying in the process."

"Thank you for being honest. I thought that might be the case, but needed to ask just in case. Do you have any last words?" Jean picked up the fallen sword, gasping as the ice-cold leather grip bit at her freezing fingers. It was a good thing that she had put a few points towards her constitution over the years. It was helping her to withstand the effects of the bitterly cold environment.

"No, now let me join-"

The sword whistled through the air and bit deeply into the woman's neck, cutting her off mid-sentence.

Jean pulled the sword free and laid her body carefully face up on the snow where she could look up at the sky during her last moments.

"Thank you," She managed to gasp out before the light left her eyes.

"Kids should never have to perform an execution," Jean told Zack. "Killing is a fact of life, unfortunately." She waved a hand at the various bodies around them. "But an execution like this holds a different place in your mind and on your soul. Those are done in the heat of the moment when they are attacking. Something like this is," She sighed. "Is just cold."

Zack glanced at the traveler who had been crawling through the snow and mentally shrugged. They were enemies who were attacking him and Zara, which was good enough for him. The rest didn't matter. Maybe someday it would, but for now, it was simple, and that worked best.

"You help Edith. I'll go take care of Dorn with Zara." He ordered the professional soldier before turning around and wobbling off on unsteady legs. There were more important things to do than debate how much sleep he wouldn't lose over taking out someone who threatened them. He had the power now to keep them safe, and he would use it.

Dorn was a bloody mess when he managed to make his way over. His nose was clearly broken from Zara's boot, if he had to guess. Zelda had found an icicle somewhere and was using it to poke holes down the boy's leg, his other already a bloody ruined mess. George, meanwhile, had packed the hardened snow around his paws and had gone to town on the noble's arms. Aisha was simply sitting on his chest, watching the other two.

Zara was glaring coldly down at the whimpering boy. "You wanted to break my mind! I'll break yours, you piece of human filth. You're no better than the others!"

Zack came up beside her and joined her in looking down at the boy, who had overturned their lives. "Does this feel good, being on the other end of the power-divide?"

"Please," Dorn blubbered.

"We gave you a chance to answer our questions, to call things off, and leave us alone. Instead, you kept talking about killing us, and worse, breaking my sister's mind." Zack stared at him in disgust. "What kind of person would ever think that it's okay to break a little girl's mind?"

Zara kicked him at that. His legs, which were still recovering from earlier, barely felt the blow. "I'm not little. I'm twelve, almost thirteen." She protested.

"Zara, you're tiny, we both are." Zack sighed gratefully as the tense atmosphere that had been building began to fade.

"It's my right as a noble!" He protested weakly.

Zara rolled her eyes and kicked him in the face, knocking out a few more of his teeth. "That's not what being a noble means. Even I know that!"

Dorn screamed as Zelda poked him especially hard with her icicle, digging it in deep into the meat of his calf.

"What is with you and sharp, pointy objects?" Zack couldn't help asking the bear. "First it was that scale needle, and now it's an icicle. Is it because that's all that's around or because you just like stabbing things?"

Zelda turned away and innocently hid the icicle behind her back while tilting her head upwards as though whistling a phantom tune.

"Yeah, that's what I thought." He turned back to a panting Dorn and raised his hand, a purple glow suffusing it a moment later. There would be no mercy for the boy, not after all he had done, and especially not after everything he had threatened to do to Zara.

Aisha hopped off and pulled George away with her.

"Be less of a psychopath in your next life." The arcane bolt went straight through his head and deep into the snow without stopping. The boy had been so low-leveled, this may have even been his first time inside a portal.

No wonder he wanted to come through first. He hadn't wanted them to see him awakening.

"Let's gather up the bodies and collect the suits those travelers were wearing," Zack told Zara, who was already heading towards the pack of money.

"We'll never go hungry again with this, no matter what happens after this." She said with a smile.

Together they headed over to where Jean was leaning over a still Edith, the smiles dropping from their faces as they saw.

"Edith?" Zara yelled.

"How is she?"

Jean frowned as shook her head. "I don't know. She's breathing, but it's so cold I can't say if she is just unconscious or in a coma. This isn't my field of expertise. What is though, are portals, and we have been in this one for too long already. Let's grab those suits, any weapons we can carry, and get out of here now."

The bears had already begun shifting the bodies closer to the portal. A feat made easier due to Aisha's size, which allowed her to move a body by herself. Whereas George and Zelda had to work together on each one. Something that rankled the smaller bears.

Jean picked up the still, ice-cold woman while reversing her grip on the sword, laying it flat against her arm. "I've got her. You get those bodies. We need to get her out first."

They nodded in agreement, and she took off at a run for the portal.

"She'll be alright, right?" Zara wondered softly.

"They have Leigha, and Edith was a traveler at some point in the past. She's stronger than she looks." If he knew what was wrong with her, then he could have attempted to heal her with his magic. Casting the examination spell and being able to properly understand it were two completely different things. That came from practice, books, experience, things he didn't have.

The ground bucked, sending them to their knees as a deep bass tone shook the air and set off an avalanche in the distance.

Jean stumbled and screamed as she bounced off the surface of the portal, Edith flying from her arms.

Messages, similar to their status pages, appeared in front of each of their eyes.

Sufficient Dimensional Fragment power levels reached.
Presence of Dimensional Children detected; special class prerequisites for activation completed.
Access to world parallel fragment code-named -Aperra- locked.
Beginning countdown to Dimensional Fragment Change:
Precursor Number Unknown to the Great Change.
All living beings please evacuate through the nearest available active portal. All Ruler Class existences are to assist in the evacuation.

Jean scrambled to pick up Edith and then felt at the surface of the portal. Her hand skittering pointlessly off the slowly darkening surface.

Zack felt the bottom of his stomach drop from his chest as the full meaning of the message trickled through his mind. One, they were stuck inside the portal. Two, it was somehow related to them. Three, Jean now knew they were Dimensional Children, if not what exactly that meant. And four, they needed to find another active portal somehow soon, and he really doubted there was any close by.

He took a moment to panic internally and then opened his eyes. "Start taking the suits off the bodies. Put on whichever one fits the best. Take their clothes and shoes as well if they are better. We are going to need every advantage we can get." He looked up. "Aisha, bring the bodies over here. Things have changed. Jean, come on, we don't have much time!"

His firm tone shook the more experienced woman free, and she nodded. "Good, make sure to also grab anything else useful from them as well. Packs, food, water, weapons. If access to our world is locked, then that hopefully means the time limit is also momentarily gone." She looked out over the cold, desolate wasteland around them.

"We could be in here for a while before a ruler notices us or we get lucky. I hope the two of you got a few levels from that fight just now because you're going to need them. And don't think I've forgotten about the other things; we just have more items to focus on right now."

Zack and Zara shared a knowing smirk. "I think we'll be fine on levels. Now, let's get Edith wrapped up before she gets worse. We have a long hike ahead of us."

Epilogue

Second leaned his cane against the edge of the chair and sat down with a relieved groan.

"You're getting old." His companion said, closing the door to the hidden room.

"I don't want to hear that from you," Second playfully snapped back, stretching out his bad leg. It had been giving him more problems as of late.

"It's a good thing no one is around to hear you talk to me like that." The king chuckled and sat across from him, a small table filled with official documents separating them.

Second grunted and filled a couple of tumblers with an amber liquor. "How's Caroline been doing lately?"

The king accepted the glass gratefully and swirled it around before answering. "She's worried, and you know how she tends to obsess over the details. She keeps reading the reports and trying to understand them. Nothing makes sense anymore, and it's been difficult for her." He took a sip, rolling the liquid around on his tongue before swallowing. "Tell me about the boy and his sister."

"What specifically would you like to know about them?"

The king picked up a handwritten report and shook it at him. "A ruler approached them! Did it say anything? What do they know?" He took a much larger swallow from the glass.

"He didn't say, and I couldn't ask without giving too much away to the others." Second answered readily, staring down at the amber depths of his glass. "Anna knows the truth, of course. The Major probably does as well. The issue was with specialist McCleary and the siblings. I don't know. I had to make a call in the moment."

The king stood and began pacing around the small room, rubbing furiously at his glabella the entire time. "No, you did the right thing."

"Orlo, sit down and quit doing that!" Second, reprimanded the man he had watched over for going on forty years. "Caroline hates it when you do that, and I had to listen to her nag at me for an hour the last time you rubbed it raw. So, stop it."

He sat down and began looking through the papers. Anything to keep his hands busy. "We won't be able to hide the truth from people for much longer, in any case. It's practically a miracle that we've managed it for as long as we have already. It's been getting harder to hide it anyway." He sighed and leaned back, looking up at the ceiling, suddenly more tired than he could remember being.

"Maybe it's time people knew the truth about what's coming, what's going to happen, or at least as much as we know." Orlo continued with a chuckle, mostly speaking to himself. "And maybe it's time we stopped hiding the existence of intelligent beings, beasts, and monsters living inside the portals and other worlds. It would free up nearly a tenth of the country's defense budget alone if we did that."

Second waited silently for his king to finish his musings. He may be close to the man, but it was not his place to offer unsolicited advice on topics he knew little about. Information was his specialty, not running a country.

Orlo shook his head and looked back at the papers, rearranging them carefully. "Where are the kids now? Since the girl is a special scholarship holder, that practically makes her family, for now at least. It makes sense that I should meet them both at least once, preferably before the announcement."

Second, laughed. "You'll be able to ask them some rather pointed questions in private that way. Good. I was going to pick up the boy for a meeting later today, anyway. The Major arranged to have them escorted back to their dorm."

The king frowned, his hand unconsciously reaching for the spot between his eyes. "How exactly is the Major involved with?" He lifted a report and read off the names. "Zack and Zara? Why don't they have a last name listed? Whatever, it doesn't matter. Tell me, why is the military involved with these two kids?"

Second, raised his tumbler and swallowed the contents in a single go, pausing to refill the glass before answering. "Well, that's quite the story, and it took me a bit of digging myself to find what I have. It all began when-"

End Book 1

Acknowledgements

I would like to thank my alpha readers, and my family, who spend endless hours reading and re-reading everything I write, as well as seeking out any plot holes and typos. It has taken me a long time to get to the point in my life where I can actually sit down and write like I have wanted to for so very long, to all the people that have encouraged me over the years and helped make this possible, I thank you!

About the Author

Joshua Kern was born in a little town situated somewhere in Ohio and raised in an even smaller town someplace in Colorado. He attended University for a time, where he discovered that while he enjoyed Electrical Engineering and Computer Science his true passion lay in writing. He lives primarily in Colorado but has been known to move around as the need arises. When not writing, Joshua enjoys riding motorcycles, reading anything he can get his hands on, and anime.

Other Books by Joshua Kern

Refton & Thomas

Forgotten Spies

Forgotten Child

The Game of Gods

Arc 1 – Human

The Beginning

The Death of Champions

Arc 2 – Demi-God

Fragments

A Tower Novella

Pieces of Divinity

Arc 3 – God

Everything Ends

The Dungeon Alaria

Arc 1 – Integration

The Dungeon Alaria

The Creator's Daughter

Arc 2 – ??

The Nameless Chronicles

Portals of Albion

Portals of Change

Realms & Runes

Runic Cultivator

The Well Within

The Well Within

Stand Alone

The Ridden

Duologies & Box Sets

The Game of Gods: Arc 1 Duology Box Set

The Dungeon Alaria: The World of Alaria Arc 1 Duology Box Set